ALLISON LEIGH

started early by writing a Halloween play that her grade school class performed. Since then, though her tastes have changed, her love for reading has not. And her writing appetite simply grows more voracious by the day.

She has been a finalist for a RITA® Award and a Holt Medallion. But her best rewards as a writer come when she receives word from a reader that they laughed, cried or lost a night of sleep while reading one of her books.

Born in Southern California, Allison has lived in several different cities in four different states. She has been, at one time or another, a cosmetologist, a computer programmer and a secretary. She has recently begun writing full-time after spending nearly a decade as an administrative assistant for a busy neighborhood church. She currently makes her home in Arizona with her family and loves to hear from her readers, who can write to her at P.O. Box 40772, Mesa, AZ 85274–0772.

USA TODAY Bestselling Author

Allison Leigh

Mother in a Moment

Millionaire's Instant Baby

HARLEQUIN®

TORONTO • NEW YORK • LONDON
AMSTERDAM • PARIS • SYDNEY • HAMBURG
STOCKHOLM • ATHENS • TOKYO • MILAN • MADRID
PRAGUE • WARSAW • BUDAPEST • AUCKLAND

ISBN-13: 978-0-373-68819-7

MOTHER IN A MOMENT & MILLIONAIRE'S INSTANT BABY

Copyright © 2011 by Harlequin Books S.A.

The publisher acknowledges the copyright holders of the individual works as follows:

MOTHER IN A MOMENT
Copyright © 2000 by Allison Lee Kinnaird

MILLIONAIRE'S INSTANT BABY
Copyright © 2000 by Harlequin Books S.A.

This edition published by arrangement with Harlequin Books S.A.

For questions and comments about the quality of this book please contact us at Customer_eCare@Harlequin.ca.

® and TM are trademarks of the publisher. Trademarks indicated with ® are registered in the United States Patent and Trademark Office, the Canadian Trade Marks Office and in other countries.

www.eHarlequin.com

Printed in U.S.A.

CONTENTS

To my editor, Ann Leslie Tuttle,
who always manages to make me dig deeper,
and never, ever loses her patience.

MOTHER IN A MOMENT

Chapter One

"You want me to...*what?*"

Darby White chewed on the inside of her lip, involuntarily taking a step back from the appalled reaction of the tall man standing in front of her. She couldn't blame him, under the circumstances.

Circumstances. She swallowed the knot that had been in her throat for the past few hours and looked away while the social worker again explained to Garrett Cullum what they were doing on his doorstep on what should have been a lovely Minnesota summer evening.

"Accident...fatal...children...Social Services."

Darby looked down the quiet street as the social worker spoke. Most of the houses had two stories and were on modestly sized grassy lots. A few of the yards had picket fences, a few were brightened with flowerbeds.

But no matter how hard she tried focusing on this normal, average neighborhood, attempting to block out the news they'd come to deliver, there was no blocking out the memory of the car accident. She'd heard it and had run out onto the street and seen the mangled vehicles.

Her eyes burned and she turned back to the man in

the doorway, who looked shell-shocked. And his gaze, as if he sensed her eyes on him, turned toward her even though Laura Malone was still explaining the course of events that had brought them to his door.

Dark green, they were. Surrounded by smoky, smudgy lashes, which on a face less masculine would have seemed feminine. And Darby felt a twinge of guilt for noticing such a thing at a time like this—he'd just learned that his sister and brother-in-law had been killed in an automobile accident earlier that day, and she was cataloging his features.

"You were there?" His voice, husky and low-pitched, rolled from where he stood in his open doorway, down the three steps to where Darby stood with the social worker. "At the accident?"

She nodded, but it was her companion who spoke. "Ms. White was first on the scene, Mr. Cullum. Are you sure you wouldn't like to discuss this inside?"

He shook his head, just as he'd done when they'd arrived. He still watched Darby, and her throat went even tighter. "And Elise...my sister spoke to you. Said she wanted *me* to take care of her kids. She said that. Before she—"

Again, Darby nodded. She felt chilled, even though the night was warm. She cleared her throat. "Her only thoughts were of her children."

"Who were safely inside the child-care center where you work."

"Yes. Marc and Elise were—" She hesitated, scrambling for composure. "Were on their way to pick them up. And the accident happened, um, on the corner...

outside our building. I'm so sorry," she whispered. "The children—"

"An associate from my office is with the children right now," Laura cut in. "We thought it best until we'd had a chance to speak with you." She had at least twenty years on Darby's twenty-six, but even she looked a little red-eyed. "If you're unable to take your nieces and nephews, they'll be placed in a temporary foster home until we're able to reach their grandfather. We understand he left on a business trip earlier today. His plane is probably just now arriving in Florida, and we've got someone waiting at the airport there to tell him what has happened. We have very good foster homes in Fisher Falls, but it is something that we would all like to avoid, if possible. Family members are almost always preferred."

His square jaw tightened. "How did you know I was here? I've only been in Fisher Falls for two weeks."

"Your business card was in Elise's purse," Darby said. "Your address here was written on the back of it."

"I'm surprised she kept it," he murmured. Then blinked and raked one long-fingered hand through his thick black hair, leaving it standing in rumpled spikes. His shoulders rose and fell heavily as he looked back, into the modest-size house. "I'm not exactly set up for kids here. This place is just a rental."

Darby wasn't sure if he was speaking to them or to himself. He turned around again and focused those mossy-green eyes on her. "The kids you want me to take in. How old are they?"

Darby blinked, and abruptly gathered herself. Just because he was their uncle didn't mean he had to know their exact ages, she reasoned. He was new to town, as he'd admitted. Perhaps he hadn't seen them in a while.

"Regan is four, Reid is three. The triplets are nine months." She thought she heard him mutter an oath, but decided she'd imagined it. "They're wonderful children, really." Oh, why was she telling this man that? She cared for the Northrop children periodically at the Smiling Faces Child-Care Center; he was their blood. The children had been entrusted to him by their mother's last words; surely he knew how sweet his own nieces and nephews were.

"Mr. Cullum, I know this is a difficult situation. I'm sure we can arrange for any items you may need," Laura inserted calmly. "That is, if you do agree to your sister's wishes. We're not trying to force you to do so. I'm certain your father, once he returns from Florida will be anxious to—"

Darby barely heard the rest of the other woman's words as she watched Garrett Cullum's green eyes harden. No longer soft and mossy-green, they held all the warmth of ice chips. And Darby was glad that he wasn't looking at her just then.

"Where do I pick them up?" he asked abruptly.

The cell phone attached to Laura Malone's hip suddenly chirped to life, and she excused herself. "I'm sorry," she said. "I have to take this. I'm the senior social—"

Garrett waved away Laura's apology and looked at Darby, clearly expecting her to answer him. "They're still at the center," she told him. "We've got car seats and other things that you can use until…well, until." Darby felt sure that Molly Myers, the center's administrator, wouldn't protest her lending out their precious equipment. And in a few days, when Molly returned from her conference down in Minneapolis, she'd confirm it. Darby figured this infraction of the center's rules was understandable. Considering the circumstances.

Her throat tightened up again and her head ached deep behind her eyes. She drew in a short breath and focused hard on the pickup truck parked in the driveway. "Is that yours?" There was no way he'd be able to cart five children around in it. "We'll use my car," she suggested.

"Why?"

She jumped a little. He'd stepped down the porch and stood next to her. Towering over her. "Car seats." Four of them. Regan was old enough to use a seat belt. It would be a close fit, particularly since Garrett Cullum was broad in the shoulder and long in the leg. He was easily as tall as her brother, and Dane cleared six feet by a good two inches.

There was nothing brotherly about Garrett Cullum, though.

"Mr. Cullum." Laura Malone had finished her call and was holding out a business card. "Darby can take you back to the center. I'm sure she'll help as much as possible in seeing the children settled with you. She's been very helpful today, even fending off some reporters. If we weren't shorthanded already, I'd accompany you myself. I'll contact you when we've got a date to meet with the judge who will finalize the matter of the children."

Garrett slowly took the card.

"It probably won't be for a week or so," Laura warned. "We're just backed up all over the place with people going away for summer vacations. You'll be assigned a permanent caseworker, too. But if you need anything in the meantime, my number is on the card, plus on the back you'll note the name and numbers of the psychologists working with our department on cases such as this. You'll probably want to talk to—"

He pocketed the card, but his expression was closed. "Thanks."

The social worker nodded, then paused before walking toward her car parked at the curb. Her stoic expression softened for a moment. "Mr. Cullum, Garrett, I know you don't remember me, but I knew your mother. We went to high school together. And I knew Elise and Marc. Not well, but…well, I *am* very sorry for your loss."

Then Darby and Garrett Cullum were alone.

She looked down at her hands, twisted together, as the evening silence seemed to thicken. No amount of training, of schooling, of experience had equipped her for a moment like this. "Perhaps we should go," she finally suggested. Then frowned at the desperation she heard in her own voice. That wouldn't do. Not at all.

Her keys jangled when she pulled them from the pocket of her pleated shorts and she started toward her car. The green paint was beginning to peel and the engine occasionally backfired, but the tires were sound and it held more passengers than the cab of his pickup truck.

to know her. But she had, and she'd acted as if she was delighted to see him. When he had cynically asked what she wanted, she'd laughed gaily and waved her hand, as if to dismiss his question. But when she'd asked why *he* was in town, he'd told her. Her smile hadn't wavered at all at his clear statement that he was establishing a new branch of his construction company in Fisher Falls, even though she had to know that he would be in direct competition with their father.

And for reasons that still confounded him, he'd ended up giving her his address and phone number here in town when she'd handed over to him a linen business card imprinted with her name and number in gold script.

As if they were likely to call each other up for a chat or something, for Christ's sake.

He pinched the bridge of his nose, remembering that his half sister wouldn't be calling anyone ever again.

"Are you all right?"

He dropped his hand and looked at Darby. "No, I'm not all right." He saw her bite her lip as she focused again on the road ahead.

But he wasn't feeling impatient with her—only with himself. He stifled an oath and tore at his collar again, finally yanking his tie free and pulling it off. He balled it in his fist and looked at her.

The light was gradually fading, but it had been light enough to see her when he'd opened the door to find her and the social worker standing outside. Unlike Laura Malone, who'd been wearing a navy blue suit, Darby White wore tan shorts and shirt. The shorts were neither too long nor too short, and the legs they revealed were shapely and firm and way too long for someone whose head barely reached his shoulder. Her blue eyes had been moist, and she had a short mop of reddish hair that stuck out at all sorts of angles around her head.

Neither carrot-red nor auburn nor blond, but somewhere in between, the choppy, wavy feathers had captured the setting sun, causing each strand to gleam with fiery light, and she'd looked oddly appealing. Now, in the car's interior, her hair looked like licks of flame against her pale face, and he added *vulnerable* to the mix.

"The kids. What have they been told?" He watched her slender hands tighten even more around the steering wheel, and felt his stomach tighten, too.

"Um, nothing," she said huskily. "We kept them from seeing the cars through the front windows at the center. Laura thought the news might be better coming from you or Mr. Carson."

He exhaled roughly. Great.

She pulled into a well-lit parking lot beside the cheery-looking building, and Garrett couldn't help himself—he looked toward the corner. There was nothing remaining to indicate that a tragedy had occurred there earlier that day. The traffic signal still turned yellow, then red, even though there were no cars there to stop.

He closed his eyes for a moment, thinking of all that hadn't been. And all that wouldn't be.

When he opened them, Darby with her rusty hair and brimming eyes filled his vision. She touched his hand. "It'll be all right."

He doubted it. But still he found his hand turning

over, closing around hers. For a lingering moment it helped.

Then she drew away. She ducked her head, but he still saw her swipe her fingers over her cheeks. They went inside through a door that jingled merrily, where the lights were bright and cheerful. Where five little kids waited.

Slept, actually.

The girl with blond curls streaming over her shoulders lay facedown on a blue mat and was obviously the oldest. That would be Regan. And sleeping on a mat beside her, equally blond, but with hair cut short must be Reid.

Garrett shoved his hands in his pockets and stood at a distance as he watched Darby greet the matronly woman who'd been sitting in a rocking chair with a magazine on her lap. The other woman was from Social Services, he assumed, when she shut her magazine with a snap and gathered up a bulging briefcase.

He was glad when Darby quickly and quietly went about gathering up two car seats and pushed them into his arms. Action had always been his preference to inaction.

But when they'd fastened three seats into the backseat and one into the center of the front bench seat, Darby stood back from the car and frowned. "I'm sorry. I should have had you follow in your truck. We're going to be more crowded than I'd thought."

"I'll drive," he said and smoothly plucked the keys she was worrying between her fingers away from her. "You and Regan can fit in one seat belt."

"But—"

"It'll have to do," he said shortly. "The streets of Fisher Falls are all rolled up now. Traffic is nil."

Still, she shook her head. "I think we should split up. Some in my car, some in her—" She turned her head just in time to see the Social Services woman drive away, taking with her any chance of creative carpooling. "Well, fudge."

Garrett felt pretty much the same, though he wouldn't have couched it in such genteel terms. Obviously the Social Services people hadn't felt any qualms about leaving five kids with him. As if the fact that he was their mother's half brother was enough evidence of suitability.

It angered him, suddenly. For all any of them knew, he could be a monster. A hideous parental figure. And this Darby was a child-care worker. Not even an official representative of Social Services. "This is crazy," he muttered, staring at the keys in his hand.

"I know it's little comfort at a time like this, but you will adjust to your loss," Darby said. Her voice was still husky, and Garrett realized that it wasn't just tears that put that velvety-soft rasp in it. "You and Elise must have been very close."

"Close?" He snorted softly. "No, I wouldn't say that." He couldn't begin to figure why he'd even responded to that statement. He'd never been one to speak freely. Not with the few people he considered his friends, and sure as hell not with strangers, even when they came equipped with sympathetic blue eyes and mile-long legs.

Dammit. His sister was dead, he'd actually agreed to take responsibility for five kids who didn't know him from Adam and he was leering at Darby White.

She wasn't even his type. He preferred tall blondes with some curve around their bones. This pint-size woman looked as if she'd poke him with the sharp angles of her shoulders if he got too close.

He realized he was still watching her. Saw the way her eyes widened a bit, the way her lips parted for breath, as if she'd caught his thoughts. She looked shocked.

And why wouldn't she be?

He turned his back on her and went inside the building, where he picked up a padded bag patterned with little blue and yellow ducks. It was stuffed with disposable diapers and brightly colored plastic toys and God knew what else. He carried it to the car and stuck it on the floor in the backseat.

Darby was still standing in the same spot on the other side of the car from him. Now she just looked puzzled. "Then why?"

"Why what?" But he knew.

She moistened her lips and shook her head, looking away. "It's really none of my business."

Since he agreed with her there, he left it at that.

Only she didn't.

She followed him into the center and stood beside him, looking down at the children sleeping on their mats. Across the spacious room, three well-padded little bottoms stuck up in the air from three cribs where they, too, slept.

"If you weren't close," Darby asked in a soft voice, "why would your sister want you to raise her children?"

Chapter Two

Why, indeed?

Garrett had no idea. Elise couldn't possibly have known what she'd been saying. Or, in the chaos of the moment, Darby had somehow misunderstood. All he knew was that he was going to take full advantage of the situation.

"Well," she finally said, when it became clear that he wasn't going to answer, "I'm sure that it will all work out. When your dad returns, you can—"

"I don't have a dad."

"Oh. But, I thought—Laura indicated that you—"

"Caldwell Carson was Elise's dad. To me he was just the married guy who knocked up my mother. Everybody in this town knew he was responsible, but he's the only one to pretend it never happened. And the only thing I need to work out is loading these guys into the car and getting them back to my place. So are you going to help or not?"

Her soft lips closed. Without looking at him, she knelt down beside Reid and gently gathered up the boy into her arms and carried him out into the night.

Garrett blew out a breath and crouched next to Regan. She jerked and blinked and stared at him through eyes that were as brown as her mother's had been.

He felt a swift and unexpected knot form inside him. Grief. Where the hell did it come from? He didn't like it. So he shoved it back into oblivion and warily eyed the little girl. As warily as she regarded him, he noticed.

"Who're you?" Suspicion vibrated from her small person.

"I'm your uncle Garrett."

Her face became fearful, and she pushed away from him, yelling, "Stranger!" over and over again. She ran to Darby, who'd reentered the building, and practically jumped into her arms. She twined her legs around Darby's waist and buried her blond head against Darby's shoulder.

"Maybe you could get the triplets," she suggested calmly. "I'll wait in the car with Regan and Reid."

Sure. Get the triplets. No sweat.

Right.

There was nothing for him to do but agree, so he turned toward the cribs lining the wall. Cheerful balloons and kites had been painted above the cribs, and he focused on them as he walked closer.

If he was a drinker, he'd be thinking about now that this was all some alcohol-induced hallucination. Some nightmarish fog that he would wake up from, sooner or later. But when he stood next to the cribs and looked down at two scrunched-up butts and one wide-eyed baby, who was now chewing on the corner of a blanket, Garrett knew there was no waking from this nightmare.

He was thirty-five years old, for God's sake. Why did looking into the round little face of a nine-month-old tot with a head nearly as bald as the cue ball on his pool table back home in Albuquerque make him want to head in the opposite direction? Fast.

The baby's mouth parted in a grin, baring several stubby little teeth. He...*she?*...stood up and wrapped little starfish hands around the edge of the crib and bounced its little knees. Garrett's unease wasn't going anywhere, he knew, so he just reached out and picked up the kid, holding it at arm's length as he strode outside to the car. The kid didn't seem to mind. It grinned, drooled and wriggled its legs as if Garrett was some longtime friend.

Darby was standing by the car, and he pushed the baby at her. She had little choice but to accept, and Garrett went back inside, leaving her to fasten the child into one of the safety seats crammed into the backseat.

The other two babies were still sound asleep. Garrett scooped them both up, hoped they wouldn't wake and start screaming at him, too, and took them outside.

By the time he pulled into his driveway next to his pickup, all of them having been packed into Darby's car so snugly that he felt some real sympathy for sardines, his head was pounding with the force of jackhammers.

And the fun was just beginning.

"Mr. Cullum?" Darby was looking at him over Regan's sleeping form. "I think we should get the children inside."

He shoved open the car door and unfolded himself. "I'm gonna need a van," he muttered, and nearly cringed at the notion.

Getting the children inside the house proved to be nearly as much work as getting them settled inside the car. But finally the job was done. The triplets were situated in the center of his wide bed—the only piece of furniture he'd acquired new when he'd moved into the rental. It was king-size, extra-long and fit him to a *T*. Right now his long, fat pillows were lined around the edges like some puffy corral, to keep the sleeping triplets in the center, and the likelihood of him getting a decent night's sleep grew even dimmer.

Tad, Keely and Bridget. One boy and two girls.

"They look like three peas in a pod," he muttered, staring at the sight from the doorway. Darby had put Regan and Reid in the second bedroom. Fortunately, it had come furnished with twin beds.

"You'll get used to them," Darby assured. "And you don't have to dress them alike that way just because their—" Her voice broke off awkwardly.

"Because their mother did," Garrett finished flatly. Trust Elise—pretty, proper, pampered—to dress her triplets alike. "You don't have to avoid her name."

"I wasn't." But her distressed expression told a different story. "You'll be able to tell the triplets apart before long," she reassured.

"Sure," Garrett agreed abruptly. "When it's time to change a diaper, I'll know whether I've got Tad in hand or not."

Her lips twitched the moment before she turned away. "If it helps, Keely is the only one with eight teeth already."

"Great. Another clue." Garrett followed Darby down the narrow stairs, back into the living room, where they'd already dumped the diaper bag and the assortment of other items she'd filched from the child-care center.

She glanced around. "I must go. Did you put my car keys somewhere?"

He slowly drew them out of his pocket and held them up in the air. "You're responsible for this situation, Darby White. You don't think I'm gonna let you go all that easily, do you?"

Responsible.

Darby felt the blood drain from her head, and her knees wobbled. She stared at Garrett. How could he know? How could anyone know?

He was swearing under his breath and pushing her into a chair, nudging her head down between her knees. She pushed at his hands, but he held her firm. She squirmed. "What are you doing?"

"You looked like you were gonna pass out."

He bent his knees and crouched in front of her, finally allowing Darby to lift her head. But he was so close she could see the flecks of brown in his green eyes, and she wanted to lower her head once more. Her throat tightened again. "Mr. Cullum, I don't know how you—"

"Garrett."

"I...what?"

"Call me Garrett. Seems stupid to be so formal under the circumstances."

Not even Dane had lashes as long as this man's, and Dane was so handsome Darby used to tease him about being pretty. She swallowed nervously. "I'm terribly sorry about—"

"Dumping five kids on me? Don't feel sorry for me,"

he murmured. "Feel sorry for *them*. And if it weren't for you speaking up about what Elise told you, they wouldn't be saddled with an uncle who doesn't have a clue what to do with 'em." He straightened. "You can't just abandon us now."

The room swam again and Darby pressed her fingertips to her closed eyes. From blind panic to pitiful relief in the span of a heartbeat was almost more than she could take.

She moistened her lips and dropped her hands, looking up at him. He'd removed his jacket some time ago, and the sleeves of his white linen shirt were folded up his forearms. He looked grim, tired and appealing. And she was appalled at herself for even noticing that at a time like this. For all she knew, he had a wife tucked away somewhere. Or a fiancée. Or a harem.

He also looked something else, she realized with a start. Beneath his steady, green gaze he was just as panicked as she'd felt. And why not? His life had changed today.

She sat up. "Mr. Cull—Garrett, you do have a choice regarding the children. Laura did say that your brother-in-law had no family on his side, but obviously you're not the only remaining relative of the children. Your... Mr. Carson is probably on his way back from his business trip, if he hasn't arrived already. I'm sure between the two of you, you'll manage to—"

"Have you met him?"

"Well, no, actually. I know of him, of course. You can't live in Fisher Falls and not know who Caldwell Carson is. He *is* the mayor, after all. And if not for that,

I've heard his company built more than half the homes in the state."

"Yeah, he's a busy boy, Caldwell is." He ran his hand around the back of his neck. "And between the two of us, we'll be working out exactly nothing. The kids are with me. They'll stay with me." His lips thinned. "It's what Elise wanted, right?"

Darby nodded. It was the one thing she could confirm with complete honesty. And now that job done, it was time for her to go. To remove herself from the situation before she brought more harm to innocent people.

Harm. Such an inadequate word for what she'd caused.

"I need to go." She stood and held out her hand for her keys, but he didn't drop them into her palm, and unease rippled through her. "My keys?"

They jingled, sounding loud in the silence of the house, when he finally released them into her hand. She pushed them into her pocket and headed for the door. "Good luck with the children."

"Meaning you think I'll need it."

"If one of the triplets wakens during the night, I suggest giving a bottle. I saw some cans of formula in the diaper bag as well as clean bottles. It's premixed. Just pour it in the bottle. The children will probably take a while to settle into a new—" her throat clamped tight "—a new routine. Just give yourselves plenty of time to, ah, to adjust," she finished huskily. She didn't dare look at Garrett. If she did she would start crying.

And if she started crying, she wasn't sure if she could stop.

The past few months had been so calm. So quiet. She'd started to breathe again. And now this. Elise and Marc had been young, in their prime, with five innocent children completing their home. They hadn't deserved this.

And she felt guilty for even fearing that her brief period of peace might be threatened as a result.

"You know the kids pretty well." Garrett's voice stopped her as she pushed open the screen door. "And they know you."

Darby nodded. It seemed ridiculous to tell him goodnight. There was nothing good about this day. "The children usually spend two or three half-days a week at the center. You'll probably want to sign them up fulltime. But I should warn you that there is a waiting list. You might have better luck looking at some of the other places in town if that's the route you want to go."

His expression didn't change, but she knew without a single doubt that he was cursing inside his head. Her brother, Dane, got that same look when he was inordinately frustrated.

He'd worn that look a lot around Darby before she'd finally found some backbone and left home three months ago.

Her gaze focused on Garrett, and her shoulders sagged. If she had found her backbone and stayed at home, where everyone had insisted she'd belonged—save her great-aunt Georgie, that is—then today's events would never have occurred. The children sleeping in the bedrooms of this simple, boxy house would be tucked in under the watchful eye of their mother and father—instead of the grimly determined one of their uncle.

"I wouldn't have to worry about waiting lists if you'd come here to watch the kids."

She was more tired than she thought, because he made no sense whatsoever. "I already have a job. I work at Smiling Faces, Mr. Cullum."

"Garrett. You could work here instead. I'll match your salary."

"I...*no.* No, I'm sorry. That's simply not possible." She stepped out onto the porch and quickly shut the screen door.

It was insane. She couldn't even contemplate it. Working at the center was one thing. Being this man's... nanny, was entirely another.

He followed her. Right over to her car. "Why not? Do you have kids of your own?"

Her stomach tightened. "No."

"A husband who'd object? A lover?"

"I'm not married."

His lids lowered. "And...?"

Her cheeks burned. She sidled around him and yanked open the car door. It squealed. "Don't you have a wife or...someone who can watch the children for you?"

"If I had a wife, I wouldn't need a nanny."

"Perhaps she has a demanding career."

"There is no career. No wife. I'm a harmless, single male. I pay my taxes on time, haven't broken any laws lately and shower at least once a month whether I need it or not."

She fumbled her keys from her pocket and sank into the seat, frowning harder.

"Don't you care about the children?"

"Of course I do!" She drew in a sharp breath. "Which is not the point." She tried to pull the door closed, but he folded one hand over the top and held it fast. She looked from his hand to his face. But that made her breathless in a way she didn't dare examine, and she looked back at his hand. "I'd like to leave, Mr. Cullum."

His fingers slowly straightened, though he didn't remove his hand completely. "Double your salary."

She yanked the door closed. The window was still lowered. "Don't be ridiculous. This isn't about money."

"No, it's about five kids who don't deserve to wake up tomorrow with no parents."

His words hit her like a blow to her midsection. Her hand trembled so badly it took her two tries to fit the key in the ignition. The engine sputtered, died.

"Darby, you obviously cared enough about them to see that Elise's wishes were followed. Just consider the idea, would you?"

Even if she did consider it, what good would it do? The children would become attached to her and she to them. When she had to leave—and she *would*—it would be just one more loss in their young lives that they neither deserved nor expected.

She'd done what she could when she'd run out onto the street that afternoon. She'd given CPR. She'd applied tourniquets that had done no good. She'd avoided one reporter, sicced a police officer on another and tried not to completely lose her wits when she'd recognized poor Phil as the driver of the other car. She'd known he must have died instantly.

She'd cradled Elise's head in her arms as the injured woman had urgently whispered about her children. She'd told the police, then Social Services, about Elise's last words.

There wasn't anything more that Darby could do.

Nothing that she could undo.

So the best thing for her to do was go. This man, Elise's brother, would rise to the task of caring for his new charges. She could see it in his face. And just because she was still shaking and distressed over the day's events didn't give her any excuse to sugar-coat her own involvement.

She turned the ignition again, holding her breath until the engine caught. She looked up at Garrett as she put the car into Reverse.

And felt herself waver yet again.

The children would be confused and desperately missing their mommy and daddy. Their lives had been torn to pieces through no fault of their own.

Her hands tightened around the steering wheel and she moistened her lips. If she was careful, if she remembered her...her place, maybe she could—

A movement behind them had her automatically glancing in the rearview mirror. The sight of a white van pulling up at the curb was like a dousing with icy water. The side of the van was painted with the colorful logo of the local television station.

"I can't help you, Garrett. I'm sorry."

She didn't look at him as she pulled out of the driveway and drove away. In her mirror, she saw someone step from the van and approach Garrett.

Naturally. The mayor's long-absent son had returned to town just in time to become the unexpected guardian of his nieces and nephews. In a small place like Fisher Falls, that was big news.

If she didn't stay away from the scene, the news would grow even bigger. And Darby couldn't face that.

Not even for those sweet kids.

Not even for a man like Garrett Cullum.

Chapter Three

"I'm going to go over and see Darby White. She won't refuse in person." Garrett looked across the metal desk to his assistant as he hung up the phone. He'd just been refused child care from the last center in Fisher Falls. And this one had been run by a church. "No room" seemed to be the stock answer in this town. But Garrett knew better. "We can't help out the black-sheep son of our beloved mayor" was what they really meant.

Carmel Delgado rolled her eyes and huffed. "She's already refused you."

Didn't he know it. His temporary office was housed in a trailer on the building site of what would soon be G&G Construction's seventh office, and rather than being filled with desks and filing cabinets for his staff, one end was filled with a playpen, rocking horse and an enormous cardboard box of toys. A box that, he noted absently, the triplets were more interested in chewing on than anything. For now, thankfully, the kids seemed quiet and content enough with their lunch.

"I suppose this means I get to watch 'em for you while you're gone."

"Consider it practice for when you and Enrico finally get hitched and have babies." He yanked open one drawer. Then another, looking for his keys.

Carmel snorted delicately. "Nobody's gonna rope me into marriage. Not even hunky Enrico." She held out one finger. The set of keys hung from her long orange-painted nail. "And back to the point—babysitting isn't in my job description."

He grabbed the keys. "You're my assistant. So assist."

"I want a raise," she called after him as he left the office, and the fearsome five, behind.

Garrett ignored her as he headed for the new Suburban he'd luckily found at one of the car lots in town. It held the fearsome five and it wasn't a van, so he was satisfied.

The truth was, no matter how much Carmel complained, he'd have been sunk without her the past few days. If anyone deserved a raise, it was his flamboyant assistant. But he needed her doing what she was paid to do, not playing nanny to the fearsome five, nor fending off the good town mayor.

Bringing the kids to the office was not a workable solution. They were a distraction to all of his staff, not just Carmel. They had bids to get out, a subcontractor to fire and fifty other things that had slid because he'd been too busy shoveling mashed peas into ravenous little mouths, and changing diapers.

Well, Carmel had changed most of the diapers, he acknowledged as he wheeled the Suburban over the ruts in the dirt road leading to and from the building site. *Definitely* not in her job description.

He had to find an alternative, and Darby White was it. He'd exhausted every other avenue.

Everyone had their price. He would just have to find out what hers was.

Ten minutes later he was walking through the front door of Smiling Faces Child-Care Center. The noise hit him first. A baby crying. A lot of childish, squealing laughter. Someone singing.

Holy God. Give him the chorus of hammer and nails over this racket.

"Can I help you?" A young woman standing behind the long counter separating the entry from the rest of the center widened her eyes and smiled hopefully. She was tall, and had thick blond hair streaming down around her shoulders.

He felt not one speck of interest. He had more important things to take care of. "I'm here to see Darby White."

Her smile dimmed a fraction. She looked over her shoulder, scanning the room. But Garrett had already spotted Darby's distinctive hair, and he rounded the waist-high gate.

"Wait. You can't just go back— Okaaay, I guess you can."

Garrett stepped through the chaos and stopped behind Darby. She was standing in a circle, holding hands with a half dozen kids who looked no older than Reid. They were singing as their circle revolved.

When she was opposite him, her feet stopped. Surprise widened her eyes. Stiffened her shoulders. The children giggled and let go, forming their own wobbly circle without her.

"Garrett. Did you bring the children in today, after all?"

"No. I spoke with your administrator. Molly? Yesterday. The waiting list for full-time care is six months long." In six months, he and the kids would be back in New Mexico where child-care would be more easily solved since Caldwell's damned influence didn't stretch quite that far. Since Garrett had his own share of influence there. "The best I can get is the two hours a day three times a week that Elise had already set up. But you knew that."

She didn't deny it. "How are they?"

"Reid won't sleep at night, and Regan hates me." Yet they'd both screamed bloody murder when he'd tried to get them ready to bring them to Smiling Faces for their regular time. They didn't seem to want to let him out of their sight. Call him a coward, but he'd backed down and instead carted them all to the trailer-office.

Darby pressed her lips together. "Of course Regan doesn't hate you."

"My assistant is about ready to quit unless I arrange something more suitable than bringing the fearsome five to work with me."

Her chin tilted. "There's nothing fearsome about your nieces and nephews. You've told them...I assume."

"Regan is the only one old enough to have some concept of what it means." He hadn't realized Darby's eyes were quite so blue. "That's what the psychologist said. I think that all the kids really understand is that their mom and dad left and didn't come back."

"It's a lot of changes for them."

"Which you could make easier if you'd help me."

Darby looked around. She wasn't surprised in the least that they were the focus of numerous interested stares. Anyone who looked as good as this man did, guaranteed plenty of interest.

It didn't bear thinking about that she was interested enough to take a good, long look at him herself. It had been two years since she'd stood next to a man and felt even the slightest flicker. This was beyond a recipe for disaster, though.

She moistened her lips and angled her back against Beth's avid stare. It didn't take a genius to know what the pretty blonde receptionist would be gossiping about next. The woman's mouth was constantly running, and Darby gave her as wide a berth as humanly possible considering they worked at the same place. "Garrett, I can't discuss this with you here. Everyone is watching us."

"Then where? I'm not leaving you alone until I get the answer I need."

"Find someone else!" She lowered her voice and drew him to the rear of the room where the cribs were pushed against the wall. "There are other child-care centers in Fisher Falls. Smiling Faces isn't the only one. There are referral services. Family child-care in private homes. I'm not the only person in town capable of solving your problem. Find another nanny." She lifted her shoulder. "Beth, the blonde over there? She'd take you up in a heartbeat if you asked her."

"She'd be too busy figuring out how to get in my bed to watch the kids."

Darby flushed. It was probably true. And he obviously didn't think he needed to worry about Darby on that score. Big surprise. On her own, she'd never managed to attract much male interest.

"You're the only one in town who didn't think twice about carrying out Elise's wishes," he said.

"So?"

His slashing eyebrows pulled together. "You really don't know, do you?"

She dashed her hair off her forehead. "Know what?"

"Caldwell owns this town and nearly everyone in it."

"He is our mayor. People are naturally loyal to him."

"He wants custody of the children. He filed a suit for them even before they put my sister and her husband in the ground yesterday," Garrett said flatly.

She sighed. Custody battles were never pretty.

"I haven't lived here since I was fifteen," he continued, "and those people who *do* remember me, don't do it with fondness. So let's just say that I'm not exactly overrun with friends I can count on to help me out."

"Well, maybe the best answer is for their grandfather to have them," Darby reasoned. "I'm sure your sister had her reasons for saying what she did, but if Mayor Carson wants them and you're not equipped for caring for them— It's nothing to be ashamed of, Garrett. The important thing here is the children's welfare. Right?"

"She had good reasons." A muscle ticked in his jaw. "Just because he's mayor doesn't mean he is a decent parent. Elise probably knew he'd ruin them just like he ruined us. There's a custody hearing scheduled for next Wednesday to rule on the temporary order put in place when Elise died. At least help me out until then. It's not even a week away."

A week, she thought. What would one week mean?

A lot, her saner self argued. A person's entire life could change in an instant. Compared to that, a week— six days, actually—could be an eternity.

"You don't even know me," she argued. "How do you know I won't steal the silver or something while you're at work?"

"It's not my silver. House is rented, remember?"

She frowned.

"Molly Myers has already vouched for you. So has Laura Malone and everyone else I've spoken with. You may have only been in town a short while, but you've managed to make an impression."

She stilled. "You've been checking on me."

He didn't deny it. "You're living with Georgina Vansant. If that's not a character reference, I don't know what is. I've heard that she's having some health problems right now, but I doubt if she's suddenly begun suffering fools."

"I don't live with Georgie. She lets me stay in her gatehouse." Insisted on it, in fact. Georgie thought that Darby needed the independence after all that had happened. Darby had offered to stay with her dear old aunt in Georgie's beautiful main house, but she knew it made Georgie happier to think that she was getting her feet under her.

"Close enough. Six days, Darby. I'll settle for that if it's all I can get. Don't do it for me, even. Do it for the kids."

She pushed her tongue against her teeth. As a child she'd understood what it felt like to be a pawn in someone else's chess game, and as far as she could tell, it seemed that Garrett and Caldwell were gearing up for a whale of a game. And the children, as always happened, would be the ones to suffer.

But their suffering would never be an issue if the accident hadn't happened in the first place.

She sighed and looked up at him. Trouble, she reminded herself. Nothing but trouble. This man, no matter how fascinating his mossy-green eyes were, was undoubtedly one attractive bundle of trouble. Which is something she needed to avoid.

But she'd told him to put the children's welfare first. Could she do less after what she'd caused?

She could handle a week, couldn't she? She wouldn't be foolish enough to lose her heart again to children that would never be hers. She certainly wouldn't lose her heart to this man she wasn't sure she even liked.

"Would you need someone from say, nine to five?" she asked rather desperately. "Or earlier? Children can wake very early and perhaps you'd need someone—"

"Around the clock," he said smoothly. "That wouldn't be a problem, would it? You said you're not encumbered with a relationship."

She frowned. "That isn't the point, Garrett. I can't… live with you." Not even for six days.

"Why not? My business keeps me busy enough that I'm hardly around anyway."

"You've taken on responsibility for five children," she countered warily. "Surely you plan to be around some?"

"The children will be provided for. I can afford it."

"But will they be loved?" She closed her hand over his arm. "Garrett, if you don't plan to love those kids, why on earth are you rearranging everyone's lives so you can keep them, when your father is obviously willing to do so himself?"

He looked at her hand on his arm, and she followed his gaze. His arm was roped with muscle and tendon and was as warm as the sunshine. She dropped her hand, curling her fingers against the tingle that lingered.

He was silent for a moment. "Because I stood over my sister's fresh grave yesterday and promised her that I would not fail her."

Suddenly her heart ached. Simply ached. "She knew that. Before she—" She swallowed. "Elise said you always kept your promises."

A shadow came and went in his eyes. "Then help me not fail her kids," he said simply.

Her resolve swayed. Maybe she did like him. A little. "All right," she gave in. "But only until next Wednesday."

His smile wasn't wide. It wasn't gloating or triumphant or anything else she might have expected in the face of her agreement. What it was, she decided, was a crinkle beside his eyes. A look that said *thanks*.

A look that would disappear should he ever learn that three people had died—including his own sister—because of Darby's presence in Fisher Falls.

Chapter Four

By the time Darby pulled her car to a stop at the curb in front of Garrett's house later that evening, she had convinced herself that she'd made a monumental error in judgment.

She hadn't even been able to talk it over with Georgie. When she'd gone up to the house to see her, Georgie had been sleeping, thanks to the latest round of meds she was receiving for her condition. So she'd had to content herself with leaving a note for Georgie with her homecare nurse.

For now Darby was on her own with this decision.

She looked at Garrett's house and feared she'd decided badly.

Why on earth had she agreed to this? Six days, six hours, six minutes. It was all too much for her to contemplate. To stay in that house there, with the golden light spilling from the front picture window, for even the shortest period of time was only asking for trouble.

Her boss, Molly, hadn't exactly been delighted, either, when Darby had requested the necessary days off from work. Smiling Faces was at its capacity, and extra staff simply wasn't available. But Molly had softened when Darby had admitted that she was trying to help out the Northrop children. She'd even looked at Darby with a speculative look that Darby had had no trouble deciphering.

She'd seen that look often enough in Georgie's eyes, too. Whenever she started thinking of suitable male companions for Darby, her eyes turned sparkly and sly. If Darby *had* been able to talk the situation over with her elderly aunt, Georgie would have probably been delighted.

Frankly, she didn't need Molly or Georgie conjuring notions of Darby and Garrett. It would be ridiculous. Even if the situation weren't what it was, Darby was not in the market for a man. She had enough on her plate just keeping herself focused, thank you very much. She had no desire to offer her heart up on a chopping block again. The last time she'd done so, two years earlier, had been her final graduate course in that foolishness. She'd finally learned her lesson.

She looked at Garrett's house again. She blew out a noisy breath and pushed open her car door, reaching in the backseat for the overnight bag she'd packed. She slung the strap over her shoulder. The bag didn't weigh a lot. She didn't need much, after all. Six days spent taking care of children didn't require much fanciness in the fashion arena.

She had barely started up the sidewalk leading to the house when she heard a baby's infuriated yowl. She hurried her pace, bounding up the steps to the screen door. She lifted her hand to knock, then jumped back when the door flew open.

Darby looked down to see Regan a moment before the little girl pounced on her legs, nearly taking them both right back down the porch steps. Darby hastily grabbed the rail for balance and realized that another person had appeared in the doorway, too.

She patted Regan's back and tried to mentally force blood to circulate through the girl's strangling grip on her legs. "Hello. I'm—"

"Hallelujah, extra hands have arrived. You must be Darby. I'm Carmel."

Before Darby could blink, the other woman—shorter than Darby, and that was saying something—wrapped her hand around Darby's arm and dragged her and Regan through the door. "Garrett," she called over her shoulder as she pulled the door shut and fastened the latch. "The savior has arrived." Liquid brown-black eyes turned back to Darby. "Thank God you're here. We're drowning."

Darby flushed. Regan finally let go of Darby's leg and lifted her arms. She picked up the child and tried not to wonder too hard over *who* Carmel was.

"We don't got a pool anymore to get drownded in," Regan whispered worriedly in Darby's ear. "Are we gonna go 'way like Mommy and Daddy?"

Darby hugged the girl and set her on her feet, keeping hold of her little hand. It didn't matter who Carmel was. Darby's purpose here was clear in her mind. "No," she told Regan calmly. "Where's your uncle Garrett?"

"In the kitchen," Carmel answered. She straightened her shiny red shirt and patted down her equally flaming shoulder-length curls before turning on her spiked heel and clattering down the tiled hallway toward, Darby presumed, the kitchen.

Feeling like a faded dishrag in the wake of Carmel's, well, *color,* Darby followed. She noticed the playpen in the living room, the toys littering the floor, the full laundry basket sitting on the couch. The kitchen was no better. The bottom cupboard doors were all opened, and pots and pans and plastic bowls and lids spilled out onto the linoleum.

It looked as if an earthquake had hit.

And smack in the middle of it sat the triplets, lined up in their trio of high chairs. Keely was the one caterwauling, but Garrett, who sat in front of the high chairs on a straight-back kitchen chair with green goop dripping down the front of his white shirt, appeared to be the one in true pain.

He looked over at Darby, and his face was so grim and determined that she had to fight a smile. Then he raked his hand through his hair, leaving a streak of green lumps behind, and Regan made a little gasping sound. As if she wanted to laugh but couldn't quite get the sound out.

"Nice look for you there, boss," Carmel said smoothly. She was gathering up an enormous neon-yellow purse, clearly planning her escape route. "Too bad the folks from *GQ* aren't here with their cameras."

"Darby, this pain in the rear is my assistant, Carmel Delgado. Carmel, Darby White."

"Nice to meet you," Carmel said cheerfully. "I'm outta here to my nice motel room that has a *working* air conditioner and room service for dinner. Unlike this place."

"Carmel—"

"See you tomorrow!" She clattered back out of the room. In seconds they heard the slam of the screen door followed by the roar of a car engine.

Darby realized she was staring at Garrett and quickly looked down at Regan. It was well after eight o'clock. And the house was definitely warm, still retaining the heat of the day even though it was very pleasant outside now. "Have any of you eaten dinner?"

Regan shook her head.

"Where's Reid?"

"Digging up the backyard, most likely. It seems to be something that he really excels at," Garrett answered. He'd turned back to the babies. Keely's yelling had, thankfully, subsided.

"Go get Reid," Darby instructed Regan. "And wash your hands, then come and sit at the table."

The little girl didn't look thrilled, but she went. Darby set her overnighter on the floor by the wall and looked at Garrett.

"Don't say it," he said flatly. "They should have been in bed an hour ago. And I have been trying to give them dinner for two hours now. I was gonna order pizza or something, but Regan vetoed everything I suggested. Whatever she says, Reid pipes right along with her."

"Actually, I was going to say that you might have better luck with the triplets if you gave them some finger food. They're at the age where they want to feed themselves. Or try, anyway."

"Which would explain why they've been throwing their food back at me," he muttered. He scooted back the chair and rose, seeming to realize what a mess his shirt was. Dusky color rose in his throat, and Darby told herself she was *not* charmed. This was just a job.

She walked purposefully to the refrigerator and opened the door. The offerings were slim, but he did have eggs and milk. She pulled out both and set them on the counter, then began opening cupboards—the ones up top that hadn't already been divested of their contents. "Why don't you get cleaned up, too," she suggested without looking his way.

He went.

And Darby breathed easier. She found a clean dishcloth and wiped up the mess the triplets had already made, then gave them each a handful of dry cereal. Regan trooped in with a disheveled Reid, and they disappeared in a room off the kitchen. She heard water running, then giggles.

Darby figured she'd go into the bathroom later and find bubbles and water flooding half the room, but she didn't care. The children were giggling and the happy sound warmed her. Then, overhead, she heard a hideous, groaning rattle of pipes.

A shower, she realized. And a prompt vision of Garrett pulling off his food-decorated shirt popped into her mind.

She shook her head sharply and reached for the waffle iron that sat on the floor under the table. Waffles and scrambled eggs for dinner wasn't exactly imaginative. But it would have to do for now. Until she could get to the grocery store and stock up on—

"Whoa, Nellie," she muttered out loud. All she needed to worry about was the next few days. After that, Mr. Garrett Cullum and his crew would have to depend on other arrangements. Darby was only here as a stopgap.

Garrett paused in the doorway to the kitchen. It looked almost like the kitchen that had come with the house when he'd first rented it a few weeks ago. Except for the row of high chairs and the kids, that was.

And except for a rusty-haired sprite who'd worked wonders in a bare half hour. Then, as if he'd cleared his throat or stomped his foot to announce his presence, Darby turned around and looked at him.

His chest locked up for a second. She'd rolled up the short sleeves of her tan T-shirt, displaying the sleek, perfect curve of her shoulders. He managed to smile crookedly and drag his eyes from the T-shirt that clung damply to her chest. So she wasn't quite as bony as he'd thought. "Looks like you were target practice for someone yourself," he said.

Darby's eyes flicked to Regan, and she smiled gently. "Just a little accident with our water glasses," she said as she moved toward the table.

Garrett realized she was setting a loaded plate onto the table, and he looked away from Regan's ducked head. Regan had probably had the same "accident" as she'd had when she'd dumped her milk on Garrett the day before.

"It's not much," Darby murmured, gesturing a little so he knew the plate was for him.

Salivating over the nanny was *not* an option. So he focused on the food, instead. "Are you kidding? I didn't have to fix it, and I didn't have to order it at a restaurant. Looks great." He sat down at the table and reached for the syrup. It was in a tidy little pitcher, not the entire bottle stuck in the center of the table the way his mother's cousin would have done it. He dumped the warm syrup on his waffle and watched Darby wipe sticky hands and faces. "But you don't need to cook for me."

Her eyebrows rose as she glanced at him. Then she turned her pretty eyes away again. "I have to feed them and myself. You're just one more," she said evenly.

Which put him nicely in his place. *Just one more.* Nobody special. No surprise there.

Over his fork he watched Darby pluck Keely from the high chair and settle her on the floor. He thought it was Keely, anyway. She didn't do anything but crawl speedily out of the kitchen.

"I think I should get a big old black marker and write their names on their shirts," he said. "Easier than counting teeth or checking under the diaper."

Darby smiled faintly as she wiped up another sticky little face.

Regan and Reid were watching him from their seats across the table. Finding him wanting, no doubt. He smiled at them and received the glorious response of Regan, immediately followed by Reid, scrambling out of their chairs and racing from the room. He gave up the smile and found Darby looking at him.

"They need time."

"They need their parents," he countered grimly. "Unfortunately, that isn't gonna happen."

Darby's eyes looked wet. She blinked and turned

away, then with the other two babies propped on both hips she followed the children who'd already escaped.

He thought about following, too. But the restored-to-order kitchen seemed to mock him. In just a short time Darby had cooked, fed and cleaned up. Even the living room had been restored to some semblance of order. She was utterly competent, just as he'd known she would be. And the kids hadn't looked at her with anything but trust despite the spilled water across her shirt.

He might be the uncle, but just as Regan had said, he *was* the stranger here.

Appetite gone, he finished eating, anyway, then rinsed his dishes and added them to the dishwasher that Darby had left all ready to go. He flipped the switch, and it groaned to life.

Upstairs, thanks to walls he considered miserably thin, he could hear the children talking and the lower murmur of Darby's husky voice. He stood at the base of the staircase and listened for a moment. He wrapped his hand around the plain wood banister. Put his foot on the first step.

But he went no farther.

Then the telephone rang and he went to answer it, using the phone in the downstairs den that also served as an office. It was one of his subcontractors calling from Dallas, wanting to go over some details of a shopping center project there. By the time he finished with the call, it was nearly ten and he'd managed to put away whatever it was that had stopped him from going up the stairs earlier.

The sight of Darby sitting on the lumpy couch in the

living room reminded him, though. What had she said at Smiling Faces?

I can't live with you.

He'd glossed over it at the time. But now, it was all he could think about. Six days or not, she was staying under his roof.

She saw him, and if anything, seemed to draw even more tightly into the corner of the couch. She'd replaced her tan T-shirt with a white one. Big and baggy and eclipsing.

"I'm not the bad guy, you know," he said. He sat down on the fake-leather recliner with a rip in the arm.

Surprise widened her eyes. "Did I say you were?"

"It's not exactly cold here in the house, and you're huddling there like you expect to be devoured by the wolf."

She immediately straightened out her legs from beneath her. "Wolves have never been interested in me," she demurred.

Sleek thighs, curving calves, narrow ankles hidden beneath little, white folded-down socks. He was better off with her legs hidden beneath the folds of that gigantic T-shirt.

He looked at the empty fireplace, thinking she'd met some mighty stupid wolves. "The kids asleep?"

"Yes. Where did you get the cribs for the triplets?"

"From Elise's house. Laura managed to arrange it. Yesterday after the funeral."

She fell silent. Her fingers pleated the hem of her shirt. "The, uh, the master bedroom is pretty full, up there. What with the cribs. And the...bed."

"Wall to wall," he agreed absently. She really did have pretty knees. And in the light from the lamp behind the couch her skin looked like cream.

"And the other room with the twin beds. Regan and Reid seem very comfortable there."

"Except Reid doesn't seem to sleep through the night any better than the triplets do."

She chewed her lip and looked away. "Well."

Then it dawned on him, and amusement unexpectedly hit him. "You can use the master," he said. "I'll use the pullout in the den."

"Oh. I don't want to put you out of your bed."

"You just don't want to sleep in the same room as Bridget, Tad and Keely."

Her cheeks colored. "No, of course I don't mind that. I mean, I'm here to take care of them, after all."

"But?"

"Perhaps we could put the triplets in the, uh, the den. And I'll sleep there with them."

"The den is smaller than the second bedroom upstairs. The simplest solution is for you to take my bed." He watched her closely. "Unless sleeping in my bed is a problem?" He knew exactly how that sounded. And damned if he didn't care. No, that wasn't right. He *did* care. And he wanted to hear her answer.

"It's not as if you will be there with me."

He smiled faintly. Her cheeks were fiery-red, but her husky voice was as tart as vinegar. "Then we have no problem. You take the bed. I'll make do. Elsewhere."

She blinked. "You were teasing me."

"Maybe a little," he allowed. Better that she think

that. "My intentions are honorable." Sort of. "I've already moved some of my stuff out. Put on clean sheets. There's an attached bathroom with a shower that almost works. Clean towels and all."

Her cheeks reddened all over again. Charming him. Making him feel a hair guilty for involving her in his plan. Just because every time Darby looked at him with that energy that seemed to crackle about her, and every time she opened her mouth to speak in that husky, rich voice, making his brain short-circuit and turn from the business at hand to hot afternoons, tangled sheets and throaty moans didn't mean he couldn't control himself. He'd hired Darby to do a job. She would be well compensated. Double her normal pay.

Speaking of which—

"I'll also give you a check up front for your time," he said. He'd bet his antique tool collection that Darby's conscience would never let her run out on a job that she'd already been paid for.

"Actually, I'd prefer cash. If that's all right." She stood and brushed her hands down her shirt, then moved to the fireplace, studying the framed photos that sat on the plain mantel. "I'm not trying to avoid taxes or anything," she assured. "I just don't have a bank account."

"Don't trust bankers?"

She plucked one photo off the mantel. Her shoulder lifted casually. "What can I say? I'm strictly a money-in-the-mattress kind of girl."

Right. It was no skin off his nose how she preferred to be paid. "Cash it is, then. I'll have Carmel take care of it in the morning. I'll be gone all day tomorrow, so if you need anything you can call her at the office. She can track me down, though I doubt there's anything you'll need me for, anyway. I'll make sure to leave the numbers for you."

She smiled at him, but it was quick and nervous. Then she changed the subject. "This is a nice photograph of the falls."

Apparently, she still wasn't too anxious to take over his bed. He looked at the framed photo in her hand. "Is it? They all came with the place." He certainly made no claim to the pictures. Not the ones on the mantel or those hanging on the walls. The house had come furnished, right down to the ugly pink vases with the faded silk flower bouquets that bracketed the mantel.

"Georgie once mentioned that there is a legend surrounding the waterfall, but she didn't tell me what it was. Do you know?"

He knew. He just didn't believe. "That when two people discover love while looking at the falls, they'll have that love for a lifetime and beyond. Bull, if you ask me."

She nibbled her lip and set down the photo. "Did you, um, get all this stuff from your sister's house, too? Along with the cribs?" She touched her hand to a wind-up swing and set it in motion. "It's amazing how much stuff you need for children."

He nodded. The room was littered with enough baby equipment and toys to stock a children's boutique. "It would have been easier to move into Elise's place, but apparently Caldwell owns it. He's already put it on the market. Carmel managed to get this stuff out of the house before he sold all of *it,* too." Or moved it to his stone mansion on the hill in preparation for the grand-children he was probably certain he'd be able to take away from Garrett.

Darby latched on to yet another topic. Almost des-perately. "Your secretary seems very nice."

"Assistant. And she is nice. Worth twice her pay, but don't tell her I said that."

"Does she have children?"

"No."

"Mmm." Finally Darby seemed to run out of ques-tions to ask, inane topics to broach. "Well. I guess I'll go to…go on up. Stairs. Now."

He stood and pretended that he didn't see her nearly jump out of her cute white tennis shoes. "I'll take your bag up for you." It was still where she'd left it in the kitchen.

"No!" She darted in front of him and snatched up the long strap, practically yanking it out of his hand. "Don't be silly. It's not heavy."

He looked down at her. "You're an intriguing mix-ture, Darby White," he murmured. A natural with the children. A woman with a voluptuous voice that sent shivers down his back.

"There's nothing intriguing about me." She slid past him. "I'm just a…regular woman. Nothing special." Her voice whispered down the stairs as she lightly ran up. "Good night."

Garrett slowly reached out and turned off the lamp, plunging the room into darkness. He heard the soft thump of a door closing. Even though the house was silent, he knew it wasn't empty. It was an odd feeling.

Whether it was the presence of children he'd chosen to take responsibility for, or the presence of a woman who seemed panicked at the idea of spending the night under the same roof as a man, Garrett couldn't say.

The longer he thought about it, the more he was certain he was better off not knowing the answer.

Finally he went into the den. But instead of pulling out the sofa bed, he sat down at the desk and the pile of work waiting for him. He'd returned to Fisher Falls for one specific purpose.

Taking in his sister's children hadn't changed that in the least.

Chapter Five

Intriguing. The word kept hovering in Darby's mind. Annoying her.

She shook out a miniature-size T-shirt, folded it in two and added it to the growing stack on the kitchen table. Between three nine-month-olds and Reid and Regan, Darby had lost count of how many loads of wash she'd done in the past few days.

She didn't mind, though. Doing laundry was something that an "ordinary" woman would take care of. Cutting peanut butter and jelly sandwiches into cute triangles and strips was something an "ordinary" woman would do. An "intriguing" woman would not do those things.

Darby certainly hadn't done any of those things. Not even the last time she'd gotten entangled with a man and his winsome children. Bryan had had a host of servants and—

She pushed away the thought as she heard the distinctive jingle of keys in the front door. She finished folding the last shirt and stowed the laundry basket in the small laundry room and came out just as Garrett walked into the kitchen.

He dropped several long, cardboard tubes on the table. "Thought you'd be in bed by now."

She picked up the stack of laundry, catching one of the tubes as it began rolling off the table. *Good evening to you, too,* she thought. "I need to talk to you. You haven't been around much." Talk about an understatement. The man had practically vanished after the first evening Darby had arrived. He obviously worked killing hours, whether it was the weekend or not.

"I'm here now."

Even though she'd spent hours, days, building up a nicely steaming need to resolve a few things with this man, the words she'd thought, rehearsed, planned, stuck in her throat. It was the jeans he was wearing, she decided. Jeans and a gray T-shirt that clung to his chest and shoulders in an unsettling way. Up to now she'd only seen him wearing dress shirts, loosened ties and well-cut dark suits.

"You want me to guess what's on your mind?" Garrett asked after a moment. "Kids doing okay?"

She nodded. He hadn't shaved, either, she noticed. And he had a dingy piece of gauze bandage wrapped around one of his fingers.

"Nobody sick?"

"No." Her hands curled at her side. So what if he looked big and tough and tired and had a bandage that was positively raggedy? She'd never seen the appeal in whisker-bristled men, and he was certainly big enough to get himself a clean bandage for his banged finger.

"Well, actually, Tad's been running a bit of a temp," she admitted. "He's cutting another tooth. They're all asleep, now. I hope you don't mind, but I took them with me earlier today to visit Georgie."

"How's she doing?"

"She has good days and bad. She definitely enjoyed seeing the children. They had fun exploring the house. She has a ballroom. It's fairly empty, and we just let the triplets loose in there. Bridget's crawling more. And Keely's standing all on her own."

Garrett looked completely uninterested.

"Well, anyway. They've been asleep for hours now."

"That's good. Isn't it?" He looked at the kitchen window. The dark kitchen window. "It *is* late," he offered.

She ignored the way his eyes crinkled at the corners. His amusement wasn't appealing. "Exactly. It is late. Tomorrow is Sunday."

"Okay."

Her fingernails were poking into her palms. She unclenched her hands. "What arrangements have you made?"

Since the night of her arrival, Darby had talked more with Garrett's assistant than she had with him. But if Carmel knew anything about Garrett's long-range plans beyond the hearing—looming ever closer as Wednesday approached—she wasn't admitting it.

"Getting anxious to leave?"

"I'm concerned about the children," she said carefully.

"Aren't we all," he muttered. "The custody hearing will be here soon enough. If Caldwell has his way, I won't need a nanny at all."

"So you *haven't* made other arrangements, yet."

He looked at her. "Have you eaten? Of course you have," he answered himself. He walked around Darby and pulled open the refrigerator door.

She knew what he saw. She'd finally made arrangements with the nearby grocer to make a delivery that morning when it was obvious that Garrett wasn't going to do so himself. The refrigerator and cupboards were now well stocked. With the tip she'd added on, the arrangement had only gouged into half of the cash Carmel had delivered to Darby just as Garrett had promised.

Hiring someone to fix the air-conditioning had taken the other half of her pay. But her pay, or lack of it, wasn't really an issue she cared to get into. Garrett was obviously not made of money—as evidenced by his modest living conditions—even though he'd been generous about her pay.

He pulled out a can of cola and turned to face her as he popped the top and lifted it to his mouth. She looked away as he drank, his long, strong throat working.

Then he finally lowered the can and sighed. "No. I haven't made other arrangements."

"But we agreed that I would help you out for only this week."

"I didn't say I haven't *tried* to make other arrangements." He finished off the soda and crumpled the can with one hand. "The same problems still exist that existed last week, Darby. You're my only option. And even if you weren't," he added firmly, "you're my best option. The children adore you. How can you walk away from them?"

"How can *you* ignore them the way you have been?"

The words escaped without thought and she pressed her lips together. She was only the hired help, she reminded herself. *Temporary* hired help. She'd grown up with "help" all around her, and she knew that there were times when her father considered their input acceptable and times when he hadn't. "I'm sorry. I shouldn't have said that."

He pulled out a chair and sat down, legs stretching halfway across the cozy kitchen. "Don't stand there like that," he said. "You remind me of the nuns from my elementary school. Except you're missing the ruler to rap over my knuckles."

She reluctantly pulled out the chair opposite him and sat. With one hand, he rolled one of the long tubes a few inches back and forth across the table. That dirty bandage of his was going to drive her nuts. "I don't believe you ever went to parochial school," she finally said stiffly.

He shrugged. "You'll hear the rumors sooner or later. I wasn't exactly a teacher's pet. I told you before, Darby. People aren't jumping out of the woodwork to help me out. They're too afraid of upsetting The Mighty Caldwell."

"Laura isn't afraid," Darby countered. "If she had been, she wouldn't have listened to anything I had to say about Elise's wishes. I think you may be exaggerating your—" she hesitated when his eyebrow peaked, then plunged on "—your difficulties somewhat. I've found this town very welcoming. And if you just give people a chance, instead of assuming the worst, you'll be surprised. Nobody here is going to want you to fail with the children."

He watched her from beneath lazy lids. Then he sat up straighter in his chair and propped his arms on the table, cocking his head to the side. "Are you for real?"

Darby swallowed and leaned back an inch—all that the ladder-back chair allowed. "I just think—"

"You'll see Wednesday at the hearing what kind of assumptions I've been making or not making," he said blandly. "In fact, once Caldwell finds out that you've been helping me these last few days, you're not going to be on his Christmas list anymore, either."

"I'm not afraid of your father." What she *did* fear was walking into that courtroom on Wednesday. She just hadn't figured a way of getting out of it.

He lifted one hand. "Call him Mayor or Caldwell or Sir Snake," he suggested. "But don't call him my father." His eyes narrowed. "He hasn't called here, or been by, has he?"

"No." Which, when she thought about it, surprised her a little. The children *were* his grandchildren.

"Good. You don't need to be afraid of him, even if he does. I'll protect you from him. Just continue taking care of the kids. I'll make it worthwhile. Despite the looks of this place, I can afford whatever you ask."

She shook her head, wondering where the conversation had gone amiss. "You're as bad as Dane," she murmured wonderingly.

"Who's Dane?"

Her lips parted. "I...nobody." How could she be so careless? She brushed back her bangs and stood. "I can heat up some supper for you," she offered. "We had fried chicken. There's still some left."

Garrett caught her hand as she moved past him, nervous energy seeming to pour from her pores. He ran his thumb over the back of her smooth hand. It was slender and long-fingered. Elegant, he thought. "Nobody?"

"Garrett, please." She tugged at her hand, but he didn't let go.

"I know why I'm edgy," he said. "And I can understand why you might be annoyed with me about not making other arrangements for the fearsome five, but you're about ready to jump out of your skin. Who is Dane?"

He didn't know why he was making a big deal about it. If she had a secret or two, who was he to begrudge her of them? He had a whopper of one, himself. And because he did, his conscience needed to know that he was at least giving the kids a caretaker whom they actually liked. One who would stick around awhile. Not be lured off by some guy named *Dane*.

Darby's face was pale. "My brother," she finally said stiffly.

Surprised, Garrett let her go. She wrapped the hand he'd held in her other, rubbing it. He frowned. He hadn't held her that tightly. "Why didn't you just say so?"

"I...we don't get along," Darby said, turning away. "Do you want that chicken or not?" She took a plate out of the cupboard, and Garrett saw that her hand was trembling.

Hell.

He rose and put his hands around her shoulders,

gently turning her to face him. The sight of her glistening eyes grabbed his gut and twisted hard. He took the plate from her and set it aside. "Hey. I'm sorry. Don't do that."

She blinked and averted her face.

He caught her chin and gently lifted. "I know all about family feuds," he murmured. She looked up at him with those sky-blue eyes, and he clamped down on the heat that suddenly churned inside him. *That* was the last damned thing they needed.

Then she moistened her lips. Just a nervous, barely noticeable movement, and her soft lower lip glistened.

Ah, hell.

He drew his thumb over her chin. The hint of stubbornness in it saved her face from being perfectly oval. He could feel her pulse beating in her throat; rippling little beats that teased the heavy chug of his own pulse.

"Garrett." She pressed her palms flat against his shirt, and he could have sworn that he felt the distinct shape of each one of those long, elegant fingers.

"Shh." His thumb drifted over her lips and her eyes fluttered closed.

Beneath his thumb he felt her lips move. "I don't know which is worse," she whispered. "When you're all cold and distant or when you're…not."

"I told you to shush," he muttered. "Your voice. It's—"

"Rough," she finished.

"Husky," he corrected. Like a brush of velvet over his nerve endings.

She suddenly stepped back, looking anywhere but at him. Her fingertips touched her throat for a moment before she picked up the plate and held it in front of her like a shield. "My vocal chords were, um, injured when I was a kid. I know. I sound like a habitual smoker or something."

It was good she'd backed away. She had more sense than he did. "You sound like you," he said. But listening to her talk was an exercise in erotic torture. She said his name, and he nearly lost the ability to reason. And the kitchen still seemed filled with tension.

Tension that he'd caused because he'd let himself forget, for just a minute, that he needed more from this woman than the taste of her lips. He needed Darby for the kids. Without her in his corner, he knew his chances in court against Caldwell were slim. It was only her word, after all, that Elise had wanted him to take her and Marc's children. His attorney, Hayden Southerland, who had finally arrived from New Mexico, had confirmed it.

Actually what Hayden had said was that the only thing better than an unimpeachable nanny would be an unimpeachable wife. Since Garrett had no prospects on that score, he'd better remember to keep his hands off the one nanny he had in the offing here in Fisher Falls.

Once he got back home to Albuquerque, he'd see about hiring one of Carmel's aunts; she seemed to have about twenty of 'em. They were all devoted to their grandbabies but Garrett figured once he was back home, he could convince at least one of them that it would be worth their while to watch a few more.

He gathered up the tubes of blueprints from the table. "Don't worry about the chicken," he told Darby. "I've got work to do, anyway." Carrying the plans, he headed out of the kitchen for the den.

Just exactly like Dane, Darby thought, watching him go. Her brother would work 24/7 if he could, and it seemed that Garrett would, too.

She quietly prepared a plate, heating the chicken in the microwave before adding a gelatin salad and a buttered roll. Garrett didn't particularly look the type to eat orange gelatin with bananas inside it, but Regan had helped Darby make it that afternoon, so that's what he would get. She poured a glass of milk, prepared everything on a tray and carried it, along with the small first aid kit from beneath the kitchen sink, to Garrett's den, turning off lights as she went.

He hadn't exaggerated about the work, she realized when she stepped inside the small room. He'd unrolled some blueprints across his desk and was thoroughly focused on them. She set the tray on the small table next to the couch that he was supposedly unfolding into a bed each night. Frankly, she didn't see how he could. The room was simply too cramped.

"Let me see that bandage." She flipped open the first aid kit on his desk and held out her hand.

He looked at his hand, as if surprised to see the sloppy bandage still circling his finger. "It's nothing."

"The bandage is dirty. Whatever you've done, you

wouldn't want it to get infected, would you?" She wriggled her fingers, demanding.

His expression unreadable, he held up his hand and she unwrapped the tape and gauze, making a face at the cut beneath. "I thought you told people what to do at that construction company you run, not that you were out pounding nails with your own bare hands."

"Wasn't a nail." He didn't flinch as she cleansed the cut. "I was helping to install a window. It dropped. Made a helluva mess."

"Made a pretty good cut, too," she murmured. "You know you probably should have had a stitch or two." She closed the edges with a butterfly bandage, then topped it with a cushy sterile pad.

"I was too busy getting on the horn to order another window. It was a custom job. It'll take weeks to get another."

"Figures you'd be more concerned with some window than your own health."

"It's just a cut, Darby."

"Cuts can get infected," she said smoothly. "Keep it covered." She pressed the last bit of tape into place and gathered up the old bandage and the wrappings from the new one and left the room.

She put the first aid kit back in the kitchen, then went upstairs. In the second bedroom, she picked up Regan's stuffed bear and tucked it back in bed with her. Reid had kicked off his blanket and Darby's hand hovered over the edge of it, but she didn't move it for fear that he'd wake. He slept so uneasily, poor sweetheart.

Finally Darby let him be. It wasn't cold in the house,

after all. She went into the master bedroom and checked the triplets. Tad's face still felt a little warm to her, but he slept as soundly as Bridget and Keely.

She gathered up her nightshirt and her little bag of toiletries and went to use the bathroom downstairs. She didn't want to wake up the children by using the en suite. As she crept down the dark stairs, she could see the light shining in Garrett's den, could hear the low murmur of his voice. He was talking on the phone.

Good, she thought as she closed herself in the bathroom and turned on the light. That meant he'd be busy long enough for her to get ready for bed, then scoot back upstairs through the dark, with him none the wiser. This was the first evening he was home early enough for her to even *feel* awkward about showering downstairs. She flipped on the shower, letting it warm while she cleaned her face and brushed her teeth. Then she showered and dried off in record time, gathered up her stuff and opened the door.

"The air conditioner is working again."

Darby gasped and jumped back, hitting the wall behind her. The bundle of clothes, towel and toiletries tumbled out of her grasp, and she glared at Garrett's shape in the dark hallway. "I had it fixed. And you scared me to death!" She went down on her knees, hands searching in the dark for her things. She found her clothes, at least.

Light suddenly flooded the narrow hallway and she looked up to see him standing over her, his long fingers and pristine bandage still resting against the wall switch. "Need help?" he asked smoothly.

She flushed and looked back down, snatching up the bits of ivory silk that passed for bra and panties and burying them along with her shirt and shorts inside her damp bath towel. She reached forward and plucked the toiletry bag from where it rested against the toe of his scuffed work boot. "No, I don't need help." She stood and wished the light wasn't quite so bright there in the hall. Her oatmeal-colored nightshirt hung to her knees, but she still felt exposed.

Definitely not a good thing after that crazy episode in the kitchen. He wasn't her type, and she wasn't his. And even if they were, it was still out of the question. She was only here to help with the children. She owed them that, at least.

"Why aren't you using one of the baths upstairs?"

"I didn't want to wake the children." She began inching her way along the hall. "The pipes for both showers up there rattle really badly, and the water pressure is terrible. I'm sorry if I disturbed you." The stairs were nearly behind her now.

His lips twisted. "Too late for that. Who fixed the AC?"

"The guy Georgie uses." The toiletry bag fell off the stack in her arms again as she started up the stairs.

Before she could reach it, Garrett bent and picked it up. "Did he leave a bill?"

"I paid him when he came." She reached out for the bag. Standing on the second riser, they were nearly eye to eye. "Could I have that back, please?"

"I was planning to fix it myself."

"Well, now you don't have to. My bag?"

"How much was it?"

"Five ninety-five."

His eyebrows rose. "To fix the thermostat? Darby, he's a crook. Give me his name and I'll straighten him out."

"For the bag," Darby said sweetly. "Five dollars and ninety-five cents. On sale at the discount store as I recall. And I'd like it back. Unless you're wanting to borrow my razor because your own is dull?"

That stubble-shadowed jaw cocked. "How much was the repair bill, Darby?" She told him and still he didn't hand back her little bag. "I'll reimburse you," he said.

She wasn't going to argue about it. Despite her suspicion that he really wasn't as flush financially as he assured her, it wasn't as if she, herself, still had unlimited resources at her fingertips. "Fine."

He looked over her head. "I'm sorry the pipes are so bad. When it was just me here, it was no big deal. I'll see what I can do about fixing it."

She lifted her shoulder, feeling uncomfortable. "After Wednesday, it won't make any difference to me," she reminded and promptly felt like a shrew for doing so. "I'm sorry. That sounded harsh."

"It sounded honest," he said evenly. "Good night, Darby."

She watched him walk back into the den where he closed the door. She blew out a breath and trudged up the stairs to the room she shared with the triplets. *Brilliantly handled, Darby.*

She hung the towel in the bathroom and checked Tad's forehead once more before sitting on the far side of the enormous bed. She pulled a clean outfit from the small chest situated beside the bed and the wall and set it out for the morning, but didn't close the drawer. Under the neatly rolled socks and undies, she could see the edge of the magazine she'd brought.

It was stupid to carry it with her, of course. There was no need. Every word was etched in her memory.

Yet she took it with her wherever she went. A talisman? A warning reminder?

Still, Darby pulled the slick, colorful periodical from beneath her clothing. It was two years old and easily fell open to the article. On one page was a collage of photographs. Some were old black-and-whites. Most were more recent. Fuzzy distance shots, painfully clear close-ups.

Sighing a little, Darby sat back against the pillows. There was Dane when he'd finally been promoted to president of the company. She ran her fingertip along the image of his face. Seven years her senior, he was impossible and overbearing. And she didn't like admitting that she missed him even the slightest little bit.

But she did.

For a long time they'd been a team. Until he took his place alongside their father, and Darby had once again been alone.

She turned the page to another set of photos. Her graduation. The front of the Schute Clinic in Kentucky where she'd had her first nursing job. The formal engagement photograph. The caption—Intriguing Debra White Rutherford To Wed Media Mogul Heir Bryan Augustine. Only there had been no marriage. No happily ever after. Only a yearlong engagement that ended in humiliation.

One of the triplets snuffled, and Darby looked over at the cribs. She knew why she was looking at the magazine. Looking at the chronicle of her family's life; each memory a stabbing little wound.

In the kitchen with Garrett, breathing in his warm scent, feeling his heartbeat beneath his gray shirt, she'd forgotten. For a moment. And she couldn't afford to ever forget. Now, since the accident with Garrett's sister, she didn't deserve to forget.

She climbed off the bed, shoving the magazine back in its hiding place beneath her socks and went over to the cribs. She looked down at the sweetly scented babies. "I'm sorry," she whispered. "If I could undo it all, I would."

They slept on.

And Darby snapped off the small table lamp and forced herself to climb into the bed that belonged to the man downstairs. She only wished she could close off thoughts of that man as easily as she'd closed the drawer on the magazine.

Instead, she lay there, wakeful for a long while. Staring into the dark, trying to convince herself that the pillow beneath her head didn't smell wonderfully of Garrett.

Chapter Six

"I'm hungry."

Garrett lowered the newspaper he was reading to the kitchen table and looked at his niece. Her hair stuck out in tangles and the pink-striped sundress she wore looked as if it was on backward. It was only seven in the morning. "Do you want a bagel?" He held up his own.

She shook her head and he set the bagel half back on his plate. "What *do* you want, Regan?" He wasn't going to play guessing games when it came to food with her. He'd done that too many times before Darby had come to stay, and he wasn't falling for it again.

"Waffles."

"Then you'll have to wait for Darby to get up so she can fix them for you," he told her. "I don't do waffles."

She sniffed, and she was so much like Elise had been—all snooty and regal—that he felt irritation rise. He jabbed his fingers through his hair and focused on his niece, reminding himself to be patient. She was only four, and her world had violently changed only a week ago. "I can heat up a frozen waffle," he offered.

"Frozen waffles aren't *real* waffles," she said.

He shrugged. He wasn't going to take offense at a comment from a four-year-old waffle connoisseur.

"Then you'll have to wait for Darby. Where is Reid?"
He leaned over to the counter and snagged the coffeepot
to refill his mug.

Regan scooted out a chair and climbed up on it, sitting high on her knees and leaning over the edge of
the table, anchoring his newspaper with her elbows. "I
dunno. I don't like you."

"Why?"

Her eyebrows drew together. She poked at the edge
of the newspaper with her fingertip, deliberately tearing
it. "'Cause you're mean."

Garrett looked at her over his coffee. "And you're
rude," he returned smoothly.

"No, I'm not. I'm a princess. My mommy told me
so."

"I'm sure she did. But even princesses have good
manners."

"They certainly do," Darby commented from the
doorway. She held out her hand for Regan. "Apologize
to your uncle Garrett for what you said."

"She doesn't have to apologize for telling me what
she thinks," Garrett said. He held up the page of the
newspaper that was ripped crookedly through the article
he'd been reading. "You can apologize for doing this,"
he told Regan.

She pouted. "It was a accident."

"You can still be sorry for an accident," Darby said.
"Excuse us." She didn't look at Garrett as she led the
girl out of the room.

He could hear them talking, then the temper-filled
stomp of small feet going upstairs. Darby returned and

headed for the coffee. She poured a cup and held it to her face, inhaling deeply. "Nectar of the gods," she murmured.

He dragged his attention from her legs. But it wasn't easy. Not with the thigh-length white sundress she wore. "Is Regan upstairs making a voodoo doll of me to stick pins into?"

"No. She's just testing you, Garrett. To see where the boundaries are."

"I'm not a complete idiot."

Her lips parted. "I...know that." She set aside her coffee cup and pulled a carton of eggs out of the fridge. "I expected you to be at work by now."

"Disappointed?"

She whirled around, and he smiled faintly. Rolling her eyes, she turned back to what she was doing.

"I thought I'd take a crack at the plumbing," he admitted. "The office won't fall apart without me for a few hours."

She was cracking eggs into a pan. "Why don't you just hire someone? The owner should take care of it, anyway, just like all the other things wrong around here."

"They should, but they haven't. And I'm a hands-on guy, what can I say? Do you always wear white or tan-colored clothes?"

Her movements slowed for only a moment. "Yes. I'm a bland kind of girl. What can I say?"

"Hardly bland. More like a refreshing vanilla ice cream on a hot summer day."

Her eyes were amused. "My, my. Poetry. What are

you angling for now? Another 'barely a week' of child care?"

He shook out his paper and started reading again. There was another article about the accident. This time, instead of the usual focus about Elise's family connections, the subject of the article was the other driver, who'd apparently had some pretty serious connections himself. To the kind of wealth and power that Caldwell could only dream.

"Just saying what I think. Like Regan does. Did you see this article? That Phil Candela guy was apparently some mucky-muck with Rutherford Transportation outta Kentucky. Wonder what he was doing in Fisher Falls."

"Maybe he was on his way through to somewhere else," she said abruptly. "What are you really doing here? Why aren't you out conquering the world of construction?"

"Fixing the plumbing," he assured. His coffee mug was empty again and he stood, reaching for the pot. What he was really doing was trying to follow Hayden's suggestion that, if he wanted to win in court against Caldwell, he needed to show at least some makings of a family man.

"Want more?" He held up the pot. She shook her head, and he realized her cup was still brimming full. "Still too hot to drink?"

"Oh, I don't drink the stuff. Tastes horrid. I just like the smell."

"Sacrilege," he grumbled, pouring the rest of the pot into his cup. "Heresy."

"Good taste." She slid two fried eggs onto a plate and

handed them to him, shutting off the stove in the same motion. "Eat your eggs. I'm going to get the kids now, so if you don't want to get in the way of flying food, you'll eat them quickly and escape."

He took the plate. "Darby." She paused in the doorway, looking back at him. "About last night. In here."

Her skin turned pink. "It was late," she dismissed.

He hadn't quite known what he'd been going to say. But he knew it wasn't that. "Yeah, right," he said blandly. "Late."

Four hours later he was cursing the idiot who'd installed the pipes, the idiot inspector who'd approved them and the idiot corporation that owned the house and probably a dozen others just like it. He'd hunched into crawlspaces, climbed through the sloppily insulated attic, torn out a good piece of wall and dug a ditch near the foundation deep enough to swim in.

"Having fun?"

He looked up at Darby from hosing off his muddy hands. She'd brought the kids out to the backyard and they'd all been chasing a bright beach ball around the grass. In fact, Darby had several grass stains on her sundress, which wasn't a dress at all, he'd realized. The skirt of her dress was actually shorts, as he'd seen when she'd been trying to teach Regan how to turn cartwheels.

She seemed almost driven to show the kids a fun time.

"There's a leak that could sink a ship," he muttered.

"No ship could sink in this much mud." She gestured

toward his jeans. Mud caked them up to the knees. "The children have been begging to play in it like their uncle Garrett has been."

"Hell, yeah. It'll be one big game to replace the entire section of pipe from the main to the house."

The ball bounced their way, and Darby caught it, laughing when her bare foot slipped in the mud. She barely caught herself from falling on her rear. "You said you were a hands-on guy. If you don't want to fix it yourself, hire someone. You run a construction company, for heaven's sake!" She tossed the ball at him and it bounced off his chin before he dropped the hose and caught it in his muddy hands.

Actually, he owned the construction company, but he didn't correct her. He tossed the ball back at her, and it left a muddy mark against her white outfit, right over the enticing thrust of her breasts. She stared down at herself, her expression surprised. Then her lashes lowered.

His eyes narrowed at the sly look she cast him. Suddenly she struck, reaching the hose just before he did, and turning it full on in his face.

Ignoring the streaming water, he hooked his arm around her waist and tipped her off her feet, holding her easily over the mud bath below them.

"No, no, wait," she gasped, giggling so hard her face was red. "I'm sorry. Really. That was…was completely inappropriate of me."

He squinted through the water she was still squirting in his face. "Inappropriate?" He finally managed to redirect the hose. Right at her. "I'll show you inappropriate."

She shrieked and wriggled, her hands pushing at him.

Garrett laughed. And it struck him then that it had been a long time since he'd done so. Water soaked his shirt, soaked her clothes. The children were watching them, agog. He laughed so hard his chest hurt.

He laughed so hard, his hold on Darby loosened. She twisted free, her feet tangling with his legs, and down they went.

Mud splattered.

Water gushed.

"I can't believe you did this!" Darby tried to sit up and ended up only spreading more mud. She planted her hands on Garrett's chest for traction.

"Me? I didn't trip us," he pointed out. He was sprawled on his back, half in the muddy trench, half on the grass. There were streaks of mud on his cheek. "Besides, you started it all with the bouncing ball."

He lifted his head to look at her. "You know, I don't think I've laughed in this town since I was five years old."

Darby's throat tightened. She realized her hands were still pressed against his chest. It might as well have been bare for all the protection his soaking-wet T-shirt provided. "I didn't laugh a whole lot in my childhood, either," she admitted.

"You need a bath." Regan stood beside them, her nose wrinkled.

Darby chuckled. "You've certainly got that right, peaches."

"I'm not a peach. I'm a princess."

Garrett reached out and dashed his fingertip across her nose, leaving a streak of mud. "A princess with mud on her nose."

Reid ran up beside his sister, sticking out his face. "Do me. Do me."

Darby watched Regan's expression. The little girl didn't know whether to laugh or be insulted. But when Reid giggled wildly at the dollop of mud Garrett deposited on his button nose, she finally grinned. She crouched down and gathered up a handful of the slick stuff and turned on her heel, running toward the triplets who were corralled in the playpen.

Darby groaned. "Too much of a good thing," she decided quickly and scrambled to her feet. She caught up to Regan and redirected the girl. In minutes Regan and Reid were making mud pies, and the toddlers had escaped their own "anointing."

She had muddy handprints all over her dress, and her legs and feet were coated. Garrett was hosing himself off again. She started across the yard toward him, stopping short when he suddenly yanked off his shirt and dropped it on the ground beside him before turning the hose over his head like a shower.

Regan tugged on her shorts, and Darby dragged her gaze from the sight of water streaming off Garrett's broad shoulders.

"Uncle Garrett's getting naked."

"No, sweetheart." Her voice felt strangled. "He just took off his shirt because he's all muddy from working on the plumbing. See? He's just cleaning up a little."

She couldn't keep from looking back at him and felt her stomach jolt at the sight.

She brushed her wet hair back from her face and focused on the much safer sight of her miniature charges. "While you guys are making mud desserts there, I'm going to make our main course. We'll eat out here. Have a picnic. Sound good?"

Enthusiastic cheers followed her as she walked toward Garrett. He'd turned the hose on an assortment of tools. "Mind if I use the hose there for a little rinsing myself?"

He pointed the hose at her legs, and she shivered a little as the cold water washed away the mud. But it was a good shiver because the day was almost unbearably hot. "So, are you going to be able to fix the leak you found?"

He didn't look at her as he nodded, and Darby stifled a sigh. For a while there he'd laughed. The sound had delighted her just as much as when she'd heard Regan and Reid giggling in the bathroom that first night.

Now, however, he'd apparently put his sense of humor back on ice.

"I'm going to fix some lunch. Would you like some?"

"No. I'm gonna pick up some materials to get this mess taken care of." He bent over, hooking his fingers through the handle of his red toolbox.

Darby folded her arms, looking anywhere but at the play of muscles across his smooth, hard back. You'd think she'd never seen a male torso before.

You haven't. Not one like this.

She ignored the voice. "You've got to eat," she said to him.

"I'll grab something while I'm gone." He straightened, hefting the heavy box with ease.

"But—"

"Darby." His jaw looked tight. "Let me take care of the plumbing and my stomach, and you take care of the five minis. Deal?"

She frowned, glancing at the children. They were perfectly occupied in the yard. Safely fenced in. The only dangers were squishy, messy mud and grass stains. She followed Garrett around the side of the house, latching the gate behind her. "Have I upset you? I know I'm just the nanny and you're the boss, but it was just so funny. I couldn't resist."

"Some things I can't resist, either," he said roughly. "And dammit, Darby, you're soaking wet."

She ran her hands through her wet hair. "So are you."

"I'm not wearing white." He ran his finger along the narrow strap over her shoulder. "You are."

She flushed, hastily crossing her arms over her chest. "I didn't realize."

"I did."

"I'm sorry."

Garrett exhaled in a thin stream and stepped in her path when she turned to go. "I'm not. But that's a problem I'm just gonna have to deal with."

Her chin angled. "There's no problem. I wasn't throwing myself at you."

"No, you were throwing mud and—"

"I said I was sorry."

"You were throwing smiles and laughter, too. And the kids loved it. So stop apologizing."

Her mouth closed. But only for a moment. "Is the water turned back on inside the house, then?"

"Yeah."

"Good. Well. Okay, then. Be sure you put a fresh bandage on your finger."

He'd told himself he wouldn't. "I loved it, too," he admitted. And sliding his hand around her neck, he pulled her to him and pressed his mouth to hers.

He heard her squeak. Felt her gasp. Tasted her shock. Her surprise.

Her hands touched his arms. Rose to his shoulders. Destroyed his intentions. His toolbox hit the ground with a heavy thud.

He slid one arm around her narrow waist. It was like holding a fluttering wild thing against him. Like tasting an exotic, heady spice. He kissed her jaw. The pulse thundering frantically beneath her ear. "Open your mouth," he muttered.

She inhaled and he felt the thrust of her breasts against him. The heat that had been simmering inside him bubbled. He covered her mouth again, tasting. Going deeper, needing—"Well, this is about what I expected of you."

The intrusive voice barely penetrated Garrett's brain. But Darby sprang back from him as if she'd been shot.

He shifted, shielding her behind him, and stared at the one man he could truly say he hated.

Caldwell Carson.

"I've never much been interested in what you expect," Garrett said evenly.

"Carrying on in plain sight of my grandchildren with one of your—"

"Don't say it," Garrett warned. "And they're *my* nieces and nephews. In case you've forgotten."

"I've forgotten nothing," Caldwell snapped. "Particularly the fact that Elise never had anything to do with you. This story you've managed to concoct may have convinced a few people for now, but it won't last."

Darby slid past Garrett's restraining arm, dismay darkening her bright eyes. "Mayor Carson, I know your loss has been terrible. But Elise did say—"

"Who are you?"

Garrett silenced her with a look. "Take the kids inside," he ordered flatly. "And keep them there until he's gone."

She bit her lip, clearly reluctant. But finally she went, leaving Garrett alone with his father. "What are you doing here, Caldwell? Slumming?"

"I came to see my grandchildren. That secretary of yours has put me off long enough. You wouldn't take my calls, so here I am. I want to see them."

"Not today, Gramps."

"You can't keep them from me."

"I can as long as I'm their guardian."

"That'll end on Wednesday."

"So you keep threatening. Frankly, I'm pretty bored with it all."

"Do you have *no* respect for your sister at all?"

Cold anger settled inside him. "Have you? You slapped a For Sale sign on her house before anyone could blink. You were huddling with your lawyers before my *sister* was even buried." His lips twisted. "You never did have any respect for the dead."

"Your mother would be ashamed of you."

Garrett's hand curled. It took everything he possessed not to raise it. "The only shame in my mother's life was her involvement with you."

"I loved Bonnie."

"I'm sure your wife found that as comforting as the rest of us. You loved *women*," Garrett corrected flatly. "My mother was just one more to you." He stared at Caldwell, seeing the physical resemblance between himself and the older man and hating it. "No comment?"

"You can't keep those children from me," Caldwell finally said. His voice was harsh. "For God's sake, son. They're all I have left."

Garrett knew that. How well he knew that, and how well he knew just how much like this cold old man he really was. "Don't call me son."

Then he picked up his tool chest and walked away.

He stopped short at the sight of Darby standing inside the fence. The children were nowhere in sight.

"Garrett, I—" she hesitated "—are you all right?"

His jaw tightened until it ached. He wanted, needed, her on his side to win his case against Caldwell. But right now, the soft look in her eyes was more than he could take.

"I told you to go inside," he said flatly. But instead

of having the desired effect, the look in her eyes softened even more before she turned and headed into the house.

Leaving him. Alone.

Chapter Seven

Thunder crashed overhead, sounding as if mountains were caving in on the house. Darby pressed her hands to her ears, wishing she could blot out the violent sounds of the electrical storm raging outside.

Another rumble. Starting far off in the distance, rolling closer and closer, building strength, plowing over Garrett's two-story rented house. Windows rattled. Glasses inside the cupboard rattled. The entire house seemed to rattle.

Darby shuddered and decided that sitting in the kitchen wasn't the place to be, after all.

She gathered up the newspapers that had been piling up on the counter and carried them, along with her iced tea, into the living room. It was odd, she thought, listening to the storm brewing while it was swelteringly hot outside. There just seemed to be something wrong with that picture.

Georgie had told her about the storms that seemed to shake the world with fury. All noise and no show, she'd said.

Frankly, Darby figured the noise was bad enough to give the unwary a heart attack.

She set the newspapers on the couch, peered into the playpen where Keely and Bridget were sleeping, sound as could be. She didn't know how it was possible to sleep while thunder shook the house, but she wasn't going to argue with it. Tad was gnawing halfheartedly on his frozen teething ring. Hopefully, he'd fall asleep, too.

Regan and Reid weren't seemingly bothered by the racket, either. The two blond heads barely looked up from the video they were watching over the coloring books Georgie had given them.

She sat down on the couch and flipped through the newspapers, hoping that she wouldn't see another article about Phil Candela's connection to Rutherford Transportation. So far, the newspaper had run several little blurbs about the man, including details of his funeral in Kentucky. Darby had sent flowers, but she'd been too cowardly to sign her name to them.

She bypassed articles about the increase of housing starts in Fisher Falls and the appointment of a new police chief, skimmed one about an upcoming carnival and lingered over a half-page advertisement of G&G Construction and Development, which was currently hiring in the area.

She flipped to the comic-strip section, which was more her usual focus and had been for years and years.

It was an old habit learned when she'd been only fifteen and the front pages were always containing some piece of news about her family. Her father was squiring around another starlet or heiress even as he inked the deal to acquire another small, struggling company. Her brother had won another race, received another award.

Every time there had been an article, Darby had found herself being approached by yet another person claiming to be her friend. A friend who wanted an introduction to her sexy older brother. A friend who wanted an invitation to their estate, just coincidentally when the governor and his wife were visiting for the weekend.

It had taken Darby a while to understand that *she* wasn't the appeal for these people, but when she'd finally learned, she'd learned it well.

Too bad she hadn't learned it before it was time to walk down the aisle with a groom who'd decided she wasn't worth her father's bribe after all.

Disgusted with the depressing thoughts, Darby pushed aside the papers and leaned into the playpen to pick up Tad. "You don't need a bribe to like me, do you, Tad?"

But instead of spitting out his teething ring and grinning at her the way he always did, he just looked at her with his brown eyes fever bright.

Darby's adrenaline kicked in. She propped him on her hip and carried him upstairs to take his temp. Something that he did not like at all.

And she didn't like at all the fact that it was so high. He was teething, but that didn't account for a temp this high.

She didn't even know any of the pediatricians in town. The only doctor with whom she'd had any dealings had been Georgie's physician.

Smiling into Tad's unhappy face, she maneuvered him into shorts and a clean shirt and carried him back downstairs. He rested his hot face against her neck, his fingers tangling in her shirt.

"Regan, sweetie." She sat down on the coffee table where Regan and Reid were drawing. "Do you remember ever going to the doctor?"

Regan nodded. "For a shot." Her eyes slid to Reid. "He cried. But I didn't."

Reid pushed her arm. "Uh-huh," he argued. "You did too cry."

"Do you remember his name?"

"Who?"

"The doctor, Regan. What did you call the doctor when he gave you the shot?"

Her lips pursed. Then she shrugged and picked up another crayon. "I dunno."

Darby gave up on that tack. Another boom of thunder rocketed the windows, and Tad started to cry. She hugged him gently and searched out a phone book. There were three pediatricians in town, but when she called them, none had any of the Northrop children listed in their records.

She called Garrett, but reached only Carmel, who said she was on her way out the door to a meeting and Garrett was at one of their building sites. Growing more frustrated by the minute, Darby called Smiling Faces. The only medical information in the children's files was their parents' insurance policy number and a notarized form that said Smiling Faces could obtain medical care for the children in an emergency—two things that didn't help Darby in the least. Molly finally offered to send

Beth over to watch the children while Darby took Tad to the hospital for a quick check.

It was about the least appealing solution Darby could have imagined, but at least she wouldn't have to cart all five of them around in the brewing storm. When Beth finally arrived, Darby wanted to drag the young woman into the house and throttle her for taking so long. Instead, she gathered up Tad and hurried out to her car, fastening him into the car seat as she kept one eye on the angry-looking sky overhead. So far, Georgie's words had proved true. All noise.

Tad started crying again when her car backfired, and she tried singing to distract him. It didn't work and by the time she carried him into the emergency room at the hospital, she felt like crying herself.

Particularly when the admitting nurse refused to admit him without the guardian's approval. Darby leaned over the desk and stared the prune-faced woman in the face. Calmly explaining the situation had gotten her nowhere. "I want this child examined. Right now." There wasn't one other single person in the waiting room.

"Then find the child's guardian," the other woman retorted.

"I've told you. He's not available right now. For heaven's sake! This is the mayor's grandson," Darby gritted.

"I don't care if he's the president's grandson."

Darby hissed with annoyance. Carrying Tad on her hip, she walked right past the admitting desk, through the double doors, to the first exam room, ignoring the voluble protests following her. "You can't just go back there!"

"Watch me," Darby muttered. She pressed her lips to Tad's hot forehead, looking around until she found an otoscope. He'd been tugging at his ears, and she wasn't surprised to find them both red. Inflamed. She carried him back out to the admitting desk where a security officer had been summoned. "He needs an antibiotic," Darby said.

"Miss White, I don't know *who* you think you are, but—"

"What's going on here?"

Darby whirled on her heel, gaping at Garrett who was standing behind her. When he'd left the house, he'd been wearing a black suit. But now he was in worn-white jeans and a black T-shirt that hugged his chest and arms. She swallowed, determined not to think about how it had felt to be held against that wide, warm chest, and cuddled Tad. "You look as if you've been installing windows yourself again. When did you get here?"

"Just now. Carmel told me you were looking for me and when I called the house, someone named Beth told me you'd brought Tad here." His gaze flicked over the infuriated admitting nurse and the bored security guard. "So what's the deal?"

"Otitis—" she broke off at the sharpened look he gave her. "Ear infection," she finished. "I suspect. But they won't examine him without your permission."

"So I'm giving my permission now." Garrett raised his eyebrow at the nurse. "Well? Some reason why you're still sitting on your thumbs?"

The nurse rose, shoving a blank form toward them. "Give him to me."

Darby shook her head. Tad was clinging to her with a grip that was nearly painful, but even if he hadn't been, she wouldn't have surrendered the precious boy to this cranky woman. "I'll come with you."

They went into the same examining room. Two minutes later, the doctor arrived and confirmed what Darby already knew. He wrote out a prescription and disappeared with a flap of his lab coat. Darby and Tad rejoined Garrett before he'd even finished completing the lengthy medical form.

"Ear infection," she said, handing the square of white paper to Garrett. "We need that filled right away." She carried Tad over to a molded plastic chair in the waiting room and sat down, holding him in her lap.

After several minutes Garrett walked their way, folding a pink sheet of paper and tucking it in the pocket of his jeans. "That nurse isn't real happy with you," he murmured as they left.

Darby sniffed. "That woman shouldn't even call herself a nurse. She didn't have one iota of compassion for Tad here. I'd be ashamed if I were her."

Thunder banged overhead, seeming to agree with her. Tad cringed. Darby shuddered. And Garrett grinned. "Don't like the percussion?"

"Not much." She tried to reach her purse, but couldn't. Not with the way Tad had his arms and legs wrapped around her. She gently detached him and handed him toward Garrett.

His grin faltered, then he took the tot, holding him awkwardly.

Tad howled.

Darby frowned at them both. "For heaven's sake, Garrett. Hold him next to you. He's probably afraid you're going to drop him like that." She rooted through her purse, found her keys, then dropped them again when another clap of thunder exploded around them.

"I think I'll drive to the pharmacy," Garrett suggested. He pushed Tad back into her arms and tugged her over to his truck. "We'll get your rust bucket later."

She knew she should be insulted, but she was too glad to climb into the safety of his big truck where the thunder overhead didn't seem to be quite so near. She fastened Tad into one of the built-in car seats the shiny new vehicle possessed, then Garrett drove out of the hospital's parking lot, heading to the drugstore that was just down the block.

He went inside and came out a short time later with a small white sack that he tossed into her lap. Darby didn't waste any time. She climbed into the backseat and gave Tad a dose of the sticky pink liquid right then and there.

Garrett watched her in the rearview mirror. Saw the way she tenderly smoothed Tad's wispy blond hair and tucked his soft little blanket against his cheek, murmuring sweet nothings under her breath as she tended to him.

Then she climbed back into the front seat and sighed deeply. Her fingertips drummed against her thigh, just below the hem of her toast-colored shorts. "I should've known he was getting sick. Garrett, I didn't even know who their pediatrician is. It wasn't even on record at Smiling Faces. You've got to get that information so this doesn't happen again."

He nodded. "I'll get whatever you need."

Her blue gaze settled on him. "It's not what *I* need. It's stuff that *you* need. As their guardian."

"Fine. I'll make sure I get it." He glanced in the mirror again at his nephew. "Is he going to be okay?"

"Sure. He'll be fine, as long as the antibiotic does its work. He'll probably be feeling better within a few hours, actually."

"That fast?"

"Children are pretty resilient." She looked out the window.

"Good. I wouldn't want Caldwell to go around saying tomorrow at the hearing that they were receiving inadequate care. He doesn't need any additional ammunition against me."

"Not even the mayor could prevent ear infections," she murmured. "Children just get them. Some more often than others."

"You're good with them." He forced his attention away from the vulnerable curve of her neck, exposed by the scoop-necked shirt she wore and her feathery hair, and concentrated on negotiating the surprisingly busy rush-hour traffic. "It's a wonder you don't have a passel of kids yourself already. You'll be a good mother."

"No husband," she reminded him.

"Lack of a husband didn't stop my mother." He

wished he'd kept his mouth shut as soon as the words were out.

"Yes, well, having parents who are married isn't always what it's cracked up to be, either."

She looked as enthusiastic about her statement as he felt about his. Then another explosion of thunder rocked through the air and she leaned forward, looking up through the windshield at the sky. "I can't believe it's not raining. Does it do this a lot?"

"Every year. You haven't been here that long?"

"Just a few months," she admitted.

"Where from?"

Her shoulder lifted. "Everywhere. Nowhere."

"And Georgina Vansant took you in."

"She's my...friend. I've known her a long time."

Garrett was certain that wasn't what Darby had been going to say. "She's a good woman. Fair. She offered me a job once. Way back when."

Her lips curved. "Really. Doing what?"

"Yard work." He smiled faintly, remembering. "She probably thought if I was busy enough trimming the hedges around her property I couldn't get into trouble elsewhere."

"Did you work for her, then?"

He shook his head, his smile dying. "Nope. Never even saw her house up close. My mother sent me to New Mexico to live with her cousin, instead."

"How did you like it there?"

He pulled into the driveway and parked. "I lived. Obviously. He was an ex-cop turned finish carpenter.

He put me to work with him, mostly because he didn't trust me out of his sight at first."

"So that's how you got into construction?"

"Yeah."

"Well, it seems that has worked out fairly well for you."

He nodded and watched as she climbed into the back to release Tad's restraints, then carry him into the house. Garrett pocketed his keys and followed.

As soon as he entered the living room, Regan popped up and ran headlong into him, wrapping her arms around his leg as if he were her absolute favorite treat. He was so surprised he nearly jerked back. She smiled up at him, her brown eyes twinkling and her blond curls bouncing. "I drew you a picture," she announced.

Garrett gingerly unlatched her hands. "Uh, that's nice."

She skipped back to the coffee table and waved a piece of paper in the air. "See?"

Darby came down the steps just then. "That's beautiful, Regan. Why don't we put it on the refrigerator door so we can look at it every day."

Regan nodded and disappeared into the kitchen with Reid right on her heels.

Beth—Garrett remembered her now from the day he'd gone to Smiling Faces—was smiling at him. Her teeth were white and even and her white-blond hair flowed over shapely shoulders, curling just beneath a pair of breasts that gave new meaning to the short-sleeved pink sweater she wore.

She swayed over to Garrett, her long lashes fluttering.

"You poor man," she pouted. "You must be just over-whelmed with everything that has happened."

"No."

His short answer didn't deter her. "I can't imagine how you're getting by." Flutter-flutter. "I was so glad that I could help you out today when you needed me."

"Darby needed you."

"That's right," Darby said from the kitchen doorway. "So thanks a lot, Beth." She crossed the carpet, holding out a folded bill. "That ought to cover your time, I think."

Beth's expression tightened a hair. "Don't be silly, Darby. I wouldn't dream of taking money for helping you out."

Darby's eyebrows rose. "Oh. I guess I misunderstood you then when you said it'd be ten dollars an hour."

Garrett swallowed a chuckle at the consternation on Beth's face. "I'll be in the den," he said, and escaped while the escaping was good.

Darby continued holding out the cash. Beth snatched it out of her hand, her lips tight. "You didn't have to do this in front of *him*," she hissed.

Darby shrugged. "Thanks for coming over. I do appreciate it." That was sincere, at least.

"When are you coming back to Smiling Faces?" Beth's eyes were fastened hungrily on the closed door to Garrett's den.

"If Garrett has his way, no time soon." She ought to feel ashamed for baiting Beth, but then Beth should be ashamed for the way she was practically throwing herself at Garrett.

And she didn't exactly appreciate the disbelieving look the other woman cast her way.

"Molly's not going to like that," Beth predicted. "You know, the only reason she hired you in the first place is because she's friends with Mrs. Vansant."

Since it was true, Darby couldn't very well argue the point. She started herding Beth to the door. "Whatever I end up doing, I'll work it out with Molly." She smiled. "Unless you've been promoted and are handling more than the check-in desk?"

Beth's lips tightened. She gathered up her purse and flounced out of the house.

"Thank you and goodbye," Darby murmured after the door slammed shut.

Thunder pounded overhead, making the windows shake again.

"Now there goes a woman who is not the least bit intriguing."

Darby turned to see Garrett standing in the doorway of his den. "Who? Beth?" The windows rattled again, and Darby quickly moved deeper into the living room. Away from the windows. "She's all right. She's just—"

"On the prowl for a man."

She picked up several crayons that had rolled from the coffee table to the floor. "I bet you say that about all women."

"I wouldn't say that about you."

She pushed the crayons into the box. "Am I supposed to be flattered by that or insulted?"

He crouched down beside her, reaching for the red

crayon that she'd missed under the table. "Neither. It's just another intriguing thing about you."

Darby snatched the crayon out of his hand and jammed it into the box with the others. "Stop calling me intriguing. I'm nothing of the sort."

"Did you ever go to college?"

She stood up so fast that she felt light-headed. "What? Yes."

"What did you study?"

"Is this your version of Twenty Questions?" He kept watching her, and her lips tightened. "Nursing," she said shortly. "Now, I've got to get dinner started."

He followed her into the kitchen. "That explains this, then." He held up his hand. His cut had healed enough that it was covered only with an adhesive bandage. "So why are you playing nursery worker instead of nurse?"

"I didn't say I *was* one." Darby grabbed a deep pot and filled it with water. She wasn't one anymore, that's for sure. Nurses were licensed and licenses could be traced. "We're having spaghetti. But we don't have any garlic bread. Would you mind running to the store to get some?" Anything, anything to get him to move away. To get him out of her personal space so she could think of something more than the way he smelled so warm and male and— "In other words you don't want to discuss your nursing aspirations."

She turned the water up higher.

"Garlic bread," he murmured. "I'll see what I can do." He smiled faintly and left.

Darby drew in a deep breath and let it out in a rush.

What a mess she'd gotten herself into.

She turned off the water and set the pot on the stove, glancing out the window at Regan and Reid who were chasing each other around in the backyard, perfectly oblivious to the crackling thunder.

A mess she was beginning to feel awfully comfortable in.

Chapter Eight

"Relax, would you?" Hayden spoke softly as he leaned a few inches toward Garrett. "I've heard Judge March is a pretty straight shooter, but if he sees you looking as if the top of your head is going to explode, he might think you're a risky choice for guardian."

Garrett forced his hands to relax. Hayden was right, he knew. "Courtrooms," he said grimly. "Haven't ever liked 'em much."

"Probably because you were on the receiving end of justice," Hayden murmured. "It was a long time ago. Forget it. You are a nationwide developer. You can hold your own against anyone now, including the mayor."

Garrett sure as hell hoped so.

The judge, beanpole tall and white-haired, entered the courtroom and everyone present rose, sitting again only after the judge impatiently waved at them.

Garrett glanced back over the small crowd that had been gathering. Darby sat in the back row. A wide-brimmed straw hat sat on her head, preventing him from seeing her expression. He doubted that it had changed much, though, since earlier that morning when Carmel had arrived at the house. His assistant had agreed to watch the children during the hearing, and Garrett suspected that it was only Carmel's presence that had kept Darby from backing out entirely.

Since he'd brought up that nursing thing the evening before, she'd barely spoken to him.

Judge March was eyeing the courtroom. "Seems we've got a lot of spectators," he commented. "This isn't a hockey match so I'm gonna ask the sheriff here to clear the courtroom."

Voices murmured, and feet shuffled reluctantly from the courtroom. Garrett looked back again. Darby had left, too. Without her, his case was toast.

"Morning, Mayor," the judge was saying. "I'm real sorry about your daughter. I'm real sorry about us being here today at all. Seems like situations like this always get worse before they get better." He shook his head and slid a pair of eyeglasses on his beaked nose. "Let's try to keep this as uncomplicated as we can. I'd like to get out of here before lunch. Any arguments?" He eyed the occupants of both tables and with none forthcoming, nodded with satisfaction. "All right, then."

Darby felt as if a dozen curious eyes were watching her and, wanting only to escape, she walked down the wide marble-floored hallway toward the drinking fountain. She slipped her hat off long enough to bend over the bubbler and take a quick drink.

But the cool, refreshing water did little to alleviate the tension that clawed at her. Until the accident had occurred on the corner outside of Smiling Faces, she'd almost managed to forget the fear of being recognized.

Going to the market had become something to enjoy rather than something to dread. Walking in the park was no longer an exercise in furtiveness, but something to cherish. Now it was all back. In spades.

From beneath the brim of her summer hat, she eyed the crowd that was still hovering outside of the court-room doors. At least four of them were reporters. She would have recognized the look of them even without the steno pads or the microcassette recorders.

The exit was right behind her. So close she could feel it reaching out to her. Beckoning. Inviting her to slip out the doors. To start running. To keep going, not stopping until she'd found a new place…another haven where she could start anew. Where she was still just a normal woman.

Just thinking it made her breathless. She actually pressed her hand against the heavy wooden panel. One push and she'd be through. She'd go and keep going.

She stared at her splayed fingers. Garrett had to regret what had happened between them when his father had come by the house the day he'd been working on the plumbing. Other than his unexpected appearance at the hospital, he'd been back to his usual self. He hadn't even eaten dinner with her and the children after he'd returned with the garlic bread. He'd just left the foil-covered loaf on the counter, asked her to leave out her car keys so he could arrange to have her car returned from the hospital, reminded her about the hearing and shut himself in the den.

No more spontaneous laughter. No more projects around the house. No more kisses…

Not that she wanted any, of course.

It was just as well that he'd gone back to being Mr. Business.

The only thing Garrett wanted from her was help with the children and to give her account of the accident at this hearing. He didn't understand her reluctance, and she couldn't give him the reason for it. She'd seen custody hearings up close and personal. She'd have to lift her hand and swear truthfulness. Could she do that, without telling her true name?

Could she protect herself at the expense of Elise's dying words?

She inhaled shakily and dropped her hand, turning once more to face the closed courtroom doors. Her legs felt like wet noodles, and she sat down on one of the cold stone benches bracketing the double doors leading into the courtroom. She folded her hands in her lap.

And waited.

Ballet lessons. Riding lessons. Lessons of every kind and size and shape. Followed by an Ivy League education.

Garrett returned Hayden's look. Caldwell had been waxing eloquent for so long about the childhood he'd given his precious Elise that it was enough to make Garrett gag.

Instead, he watched the judge's expression as Caldwell went on and on. Almost rambling. But if the judge had feelings one way or another what he was hearing, there was no hint of it in his expression. Any more than there'd been an indication of what he'd thought of

Garrett's qualifications to care for the children when he'd been on the stand himself.

"This claim of Garrett's that Elise wanted her children to live with him can be nothing but a fabrication, and for him to drag us through this farce of—"

Hayden objected and the judge wearily rubbed his eyes. "That's enough, Mayor. We all know your feelings on this. You've made them plain enough. Why don't you return to your seat. Mr. Southerland, if you'd call in your witness, I'd like to hear what she has to say."

Garrett didn't bat an eye when Caldwell stepped down from the witness box, his brows pulled fiercely together as he looked Garrett's way. Caldwell's animosity didn't faze him any more than it ever did.

But he waited, still, when Hayden stepped out of the courtroom for a moment. The second he was gone stretched Garrett's nerves to screaming. But there she was. Walking back into the courtroom with Hayden. Looking cool and delicate in her filmy white ankle-length dress and straw hat.

Her eyes looked his way as she passed between the two tables where the opponents sat. Her husky voice trembled as she was sworn in, and when she stepped up into the witness box and sat down, he could see she was pale.

A pulse visibly beat in her throat. She rested her arms over the wooden chair arms casually enough, but Garrett could see the white knuckles from fingers curled too tightly over the ends.

"Now, Ms. White, why don't you tell us how you came to be involved in this set-to."

"Your Honor." Hayden rose. "If you'd permit me to—"

The judge waved his hand impatiently. "Sit down, Counselor. I'm getting a headache from the lot of you. I've a good mind to ban attorneys from my courtroom. Ms. White?"

Darby turned her blue gaze toward Garrett. She gave him a look he couldn't interpret, then slowly unfastened her fingers from the chair and folded them in her lap. She cleared her throat. Then, with spare words that Garrett could only admire after Caldwell's verbosity, described her actions when the terrible collision had occurred outside of her workplace. She concluded with Elise's last words.

Caldwell immediately pushed to his feet, making his chair screech against the floor. "Obviously, Elise was *not* in a stable frame of mind. And this woman's word can't be trusted, anyway! She's involved with Garrett, for God's sake."

Caldwell's attorney practically dragged his client back down onto his chair, his words fast and low. Finally Caldwell subsided and the judge turned to Darby, waiting.

"Mrs. Northrop was quite lucid, considering," Darby answered Caldwell's first point. "She knew her husband was…gone. She knew she wasn't going to make it to the hospital. She'd been carrying Mr. Cullum's business card in her purse. It was right where she said it would be."

"Did she speak of anyone else other than Mr. Cullum?"

Garrett saw the telltale glisten in her eyes as she looked at Caldwell. "No," she admitted quietly. "I'm sorry."

"Any other people around who heard what she said?"

Darby shook her head. "The EMTs hadn't yet arrived." She swallowed, staring at her hands. "I kept administering CPR until they took over, but it was too late."

"Then it's just her word that Garrett didn't make this up," Caldwell burst out again. "They're in this together! All to keep me from my own flesh and blood—"

"Enough, Mayor." The judge's command rang out. "I said we were keeping this informal, because I happen to like things that way. But one more outburst and I'll hold you in contempt. Understand?"

"I...hadn't met Mr. Cullum before the accident," Darby said shakily. "But I know the children because of Smiling Faces. Garrett...Mr. Cullum, needed someone to help care for them, and I agreed."

"Which is just what the report from Laura Malone said," the judge commented. "How do you think the children are doing?"

Her lips parted, her surprise at the question evident to Garrett even if it wasn't obvious to everyone else. "Quite well," she said after a moment. "Considering. Their appetites are healthy, their sleep habits seem relatively normal. They're active, curious children. Tad does have an ear infection right now, but he's on medication for it and is improving."

"Ear infections. My grandson is plagued with them."

The judge smiled slightly. "Thank you, Ms. White. You're excused."

Relief that the ordeal was over flooded through Darby. It was all she could do not to leap from the witness box. She rose and walked to the rear of the courtroom.

She didn't know if she was expected to leave or not. But she didn't want to go out into the corridor and face the curiosity of the reporters, if they were still hanging around. And her experience of reporters led her to believe that they would be.

So she quietly slipped into a seat in the back row.

"This is a difficult situation," Judge March was saying. "Elise and Marc left no will, no provisions financial or otherwise for their children. The Northrops were, in fact, experiencing some financial difficulty as I understand it. But, as I said when we sat down here this morning, the welfare of the children is the only concern of this court."

Ten minutes later it was over. Just like that. Garrett got to keep the children.

For a while, at least.

Caldwell stormed out of the courtroom, his attorney trotting unhappily after him. When the doors swished open, she heard the rapid-fire questions begin. In a smooth motion, the door whooshed closed, blotting out the voices.

She stood and waited while Garrett spoke with his attorney. Then the other man turned to Darby and shook her hand. "You did very well on the stand."

She shifted nervously, feeling like a complete fraud,

even though she had been strictly truthful about her account of the accident.

He smiled. "Not everyone does," he assured her. Then his eyes narrowed for a moment. "I keep thinking we've met."

Darby's face felt stiff. She raised her eyebrows, lifting her shoulder casually. "Don't think so." It was all she could do to push out the words.

"Well. Anyway. Thanks. Garrett, I'll see you tomorrow. We've got that meeting with Zoning tomorrow."

"Make sure Carmel's got it on my schedule."

Hayden nodded, then he left. Leaving Darby alone with Garrett.

She looked anywhere but at him. "Mr. Carson is pretty upset."

"So it seems." He paused for a moment. "I wasn't sure you'd hang around after the judge kicked everyone out of the place," he finally said. "I'm glad I was wrong."

"Courtrooms," she excused weakly. "Not my favorite place."

"Nor mine. Spent too much time in 'em when I was the reigning delinquent of Fisher Falls."

"You?" Her gaze drifted over him. In a charcoal-colored suit fitted across his wide shoulders, his lean face once again clean shaven, his springy black hair brushed back from his face, he looked the very picture of uprightness and responsibility.

"I had a liking for hotwiring cars," he admitted.

Her jaw loosened. "You stole cars?"

"I…liberated them from a certain owner with frequent regularity."

"Mr. Carson's cars?"

His grin was slow and utterly wicked. "Pretty and smart," he said. "Come on. Let's get outta here."

She kept her smile in place with an effort. *Please, let the reporters be gone.* "Carmel is probably tearing her hair out by now."

"She'd be saying that no matter how well things went. Figures it'll keep me feeling guilty. But I'm not ready to go home. I thought we'd go somewhere for lunch. You know. Somewhere that doesn't involve finger foods and sipper cups. You game?"

She moistened her lips. "I'm not sure that's a good idea."

"We need to talk about the kids."

"We don't have to go to a restaurant to do that."

"Humor me."

It was a mistake. She knew it. But looking at him, all she could think about at that moment was the way he'd tipped back his head into the mud the other day and laughed. "Garrett—"

He nudged back the brim of her hat. "The Overlook," he murmured. "They have a dessert menu there that'll make you cry. And if not that, at least lick your lips."

She felt her ears heat, realizing she had pretty well done just that as she'd watched his mouth form his words. "I don't know. I hear it's a pricey place."

"I think I can swing it," he said dryly.

She pressed her lips together, looking away. "I...all right. But we really shouldn't be out long. It wouldn't be fair to Carmel."

He nodded once, satisfied, and pushed open the door

for her to pass through. She was so distracted by the hand he tucked against the small of her back that she barely remembered to adjust her hat as she walked out into the corridor.

But she needn't have worried, because the wide hallway was empty. The spectators, reporters included, had gone and for a moment she felt weak with relief.

Garrett jabbed the elevator button and looked at her. "You all right? You look a little shaky."

She managed a smile. "I must be hungrier than I thought. Didn't smell my coffee this morning."

He didn't look convinced, but the elevator doors slid open and Darby stepped into the nearly full car before he could comment. Lunch hour was obviously calling to the government workers who populated the top floors of the pillared building.

The occupants shifted, making room for Garrett's tall body, and Darby found herself wedged into the corner. She swallowed and looked up at the lit display above the door.

They had only three floors to descend, but it might as well have been twelve for the way the elevator seemed to grind along. She could feel her chest tightening, her lungs struggling for breath. Knowing what was happening didn't help her to prevent it. A screaming knot rose in her throat, welling, swelling upward—

The doors slid open, passengers erupting around her into the lobby.

"Come on." Garrett's arm closed around her shoulders. "Outside."

Suddenly she was outside. Fresh air filled her lungs.

She felt sunlight on her arms, heard laughter from a passing group of office workers heading down the steps to the street.

She was pressed against Garrett's side, her nose buried in his shoulder. "Oh, God." She pushed away, as far as his arms allowed. Embarrassment burned inside her. "I'm sorry."

"Don't be sorry. Let's just get to the truck." He guided her down the shallow steps. "Or maybe you'd rather walk. The Overlook isn't that far from here."

"Really? You wouldn't mind walking?"

In answer, he shrugged off his suit jacket and slung it over his shoulder. "I've been known to put one foot in front of the other now and then." He smiled faintly and took her arm, walking leisurely along the tree-lined sidewalk. "But don't tell Carmel, or she'll start refusing to fetch and carry for me."

"I can't imagine there is anything that Carmel would refuse you."

"You haven't seen our Monday-morning battles over who's supposed to make the coffee."

Darby managed a smile. He was deliberately trying to put her at ease. It was so utterly backward, and he didn't even know it.

They walked on in silence. In and out of the shadows of the lacy leaves overhead. They crossed streets, left behind the business of the courthouse district, walking along a winding street that led gently upward. Past the park at the base of the waterfalls, past long, private drives that led to gracious older estates.

Estates like her aunt's.

Like Caldwell Carson's.

The road narrowed and Garrett moved to Darby's left side, between her and the sporadic traffic. On the other side of her, a waist-high stone wall guarded the edge of the increasingly deep drop-off. Below, Fisher Falls lay like a sparkling jewel. Several yards ahead, she could see the discreet sign of The Overlook.

She ran her hand along the aging stone. "It is so beautiful here."

"You make that sound like a bad thing."

"Not bad," she demurred. "Just hard to leave."

"You're planning on going somewhere?"

"Not if I can avoid it," she admitted truthfully. "Didn't you miss it when you left?" She lifted her hand, gesturing to the lush green beauty that surrounded them. "You must have. You came back."

"I came back because Fisher Falls is on the verge of a construction boom. Business, Darby. That's all it was."

"Now you sound like my brother again."

"What does he do?"

She shook her head slightly. "How do you know we're on the verge of anything, much less a construction boom?"

"Trade secret."

"In other words, you're not going to tell me."

"You tell me something about your brother, instead of avoiding it, and I'll tell you about G&G."

Darby stopped, pointing at the restaurant sign. "Well look at that. We're here."

Garrett wrapped his palm around her slender finger,

feeling the little jerk she couldn't hide. Darby no longer looked like she was going to pass out, but she was far from relaxed, despite the effort she'd been making to convince him otherwise. "You're shivering."

She looked up, above their heads. "We're standing in the shade."

"Don't do that, Darby."

She slid her hand out from his, her fingertips fluttering nervously to her throat. "I was just a little unnerved in the elevator. That's all." She tried to step around him toward the rustic-looking restaurant, but Garrett shifted, blocking the path.

"*Unnerved.* Seems a puny word to me. You got claustrophobic. You don't have to hide it."

"I'm not. I just…just— There were so many people inside the elevator. I…I was fine when we arrived, you know."

He wouldn't go quite that far, but it was true enough. She hadn't been ready to climb out of her skin. "There were only a few people on the elevator when we took it up to the courtroom," he allowed. "So it's just overcrowded small places that get to you?"

Her cheeks were red, her eyes embarrassed. Evasive. "Something like that."

Embarrassment he could understand, even though it wasn't necessary. The evasiveness was another matter.

"Does it have anything to do with this?" He rubbed his thumb gently over her throat, and he felt her nervous swallow. "The injury to your vocal chords?"

"Why does it matter?"

"It still affects you."

"So?"

He kept his patience with an effort. "So I'm interested in—"

Her eyes widened.

"—in your...welfare," he finished, taking his hand from her smooth neck and pushing it into his pocket. Everyone was entitled to their privacy, he reminded himself. Wondering when the hell he'd forgotten it. "You've helped me out. I owe you."

"No." She shook her head, her expression growing even more pained. "You don't owe me anything, Garrett. You really don't."

She might as well have posted Keep Away banners around herself. Unfortunately, Garrett couldn't remember why he should be glad of that.

He looked at her mouth. What he did remember was the way she'd tasted. Of sunshine and cold water from the hose. Of smiles and laughter from kids who were hardly even old enough to know they had little reason to laugh.

"Well, I hope that doesn't mean you've decided against lunch." He lifted his chin toward the restaurant. "Now that you've made me hoof it all this way."

"*Made* you—" Her mouth snapped shut. "You're teasing me again," she finally said.

"Maybe."

She sighed noisily. But he could still see the twitch at the corner of her soft lips. "Why?" she asked tartly. "Why do you do that?"

He shrugged and nudged her toward the restaurant. "Because I'm beginning to think you have had as few smiles in your life as I've had in mine."

Chapter Nine

Darby shook her head when the waiter offered her coffee and watched him fill Garrett's ivory cup. "I don't know how you can just sit there so relaxed when Mayor Carson is right across this very dining room glaring at us."

"His presence is bugging you a hell of a lot more 'n it's bugging me."

"Obviously."

The corner of Garrett's mobile mouth twitched. "But it does show that this town ain't big enough for the two of us," he added.

She twisted the linen napkin in her lap another knot or two. The small table she and Garrett shared was next to the window, and she shifted the last available inch to look outside. The mayor had come into the restaurant after Darby and Garrett had already been served. "I've always hated being watched." She shifted again, uncomfortable.

"Then you should walk around with a bag over your head," he suggested.

Pleasure darted guiltily through her. Three months ago she'd hacked off her waist-length hair with sewing shears and begun dressing in the most bland clothing imaginable. She'd wanted nothing to connect her to the woman she'd been. The woman who wore only vibrant, couturier clothing because her father expected it was no more.

"You said you wanted to talk about the kids," she reminded them both. "That was the whole point of this lunch. Wasn't it?"

"Which you ate very little of," Garrett pointed out.

"It was enormous." She'd dutifully poked and prodded at the elaborate mound of chicken and lettuce and fifty other ingredients because Garrett expected her to, not because she'd had any real appetite. The day's activities had taken care of that. "The children...?"

Garrett's large hand eclipsed the delicate china coffee cup as he lowered it to the saucer. "You heard the judge," he said as he signed the credit slip and pocketed his gold credit card. "He's not happy at all that I'm single. That I show none of the makings of a 'family' man.

"My only edge over Caldwell is that I'm not old enough to be their grandfather. I've only been awarded temporary custody. Six weeks to prove—or disprove, as Caldwell over there obviously hopes—my suitability as a guardian."

"I don't think that's necessarily a bad thing."

His lips twisted. "So you think I'm a bad bet, too."

"I didn't say that. Garrett, honestly, I don't think that at all." Stunned, she sat forward, pressing her hand over his. "Do you?"

He was looking at her hand on his. Which made her look at her hand on his. Swallowing, she sat back in her chair, pressing both her hands against the twisted cloth in her lap. "Do you?" she asked again.

"I didn't plan to be in Fisher Falls that long," he said instead of answering.

"Oh." She wasn't sure where the flood of disappointment came from, but she knew she didn't like it. "I didn't realize. I, um, I thought you'd moved here. You know, permanently. To run that construction company."

"I own that construction company. And I'm only here to get things up and running. Once that's underway, I'm gone, leaving one extremely competent team behind."

"Own?" She blinked. "Well. Don't I feel the fool."

"Why?"

"Ah…because. I didn't know."

"We could feast on all the information we don't know about each other." He stood. "I asked the hostess to call us a taxi. I imagine it's here by now. You ready?"

Her stomach clutched a little. She dropped her napkin on the table and rose. He took her elbow, and she started.

"I thought you'd relaxed over the lunch you didn't eat." He guided her through the dining room toward the entrance.

It was only because she was no longer accustomed to a man escorting her around, she told herself. Not because it was Garrett's hand on her arm. "I did relax. And I did eat. I just didn't eat as much as you."

His lips tilted, amused. But the faint grin died when Caldwell appeared in the doorway.

The older man's angry eyes took in them both. "I won't let you steal my grandchildren from me."

"You're showing a decided lack of sportsmanship, Caldwell."

Darby caught her breath. "Garrett—"

"And you." Caldwell turned his attention to Darby, and the cautionary words died in her throat at the torment in the mayor's eyes. "How much is he paying you to keep up this story of yours?" he demanded. "I'll triple it."

She stiffened. His offer stung like a harsh slap. "My integrity is not for sale, Mayor Carson."

"Is anything else about you for sale?"

She stared at him. "I beg your pardon?"

Garrett's expression frosted over and he stepped close to his father, topping him by only an inch in height. "You might want to apologize while you can, Mayor."

"I have no intention of apologizing. What you two are doing is criminal. Amoral. Taking advantage of Elise's death. Cavorting in front of innocent children, then abandoning them to God only knows who while you play footsie—"

"Watch it, old man. That's your future daughter-in-law you're insulting."

Darby blinked, staring at Garrett. "What are you—"

Garrett's arm slid around her shoulder, and she found herself pulled snugly and securely against his warm side. The words died in her throat.

Caldwell was staring at them both. "You're getting married?"

"As soon as it can be arranged."

She couldn't believe what she was hearing. "Garrett, I—"

"It's all right, darlin'. There's no point in keeping it a secret. Caldwell *is* family, after all."

"You didn't say anything about this in court today. This is just another part of your plot to keep my grandchildren from me."

Beside her Garrett shrugged, and her temper finally flared. "I'm appalled at both of you! You—" she poked Garrett in the chest with a furious finger "—are acting as if this is some great big game, just as I expected all along. And you—" she turned to point at the mayor "—are just as bad. The only family those poor children have left are the two of you, and look at the way you are behaving! Maybe the judge shouldn't choose *either* of you."

The flash of anger drained away, leaving an aching heaviness in its wake. If it weren't for her, these two men wouldn't be using the children as the rope in their personal tug of war. "And I shouldn't be involved at all," she finished. She turned on her heel and ran over to the waiting taxi, slipping into the backseat before anyone could stop her.

Garrett watched the cab drive away. "That was low, Caldwell. Even for you."

"What is low, Garrett, is what you're doing. If you want to take me on businesswise, you go right ahead. Castle Construction is more than a match for G&G, and you know as well as I do that this town isn't large enough to support two major firms. But I won't let you steal away my grandchildren like this."

"The court decided it. So I suggest you learn to live with it." He started down the sidewalk. Darby had used the taxi, so he'd just walk back to his truck, still parked near the courthouse. "As for Fisher Falls being large enough for only one of us?" His lips stretched in a cold smile. "I'm counting on it."

He turned and strode down the driveway, the pleasure that he'd felt on the walk to The Overlook gone. And that lack had nothing to do with Caldwell's pain-in-the-ass comments. It had everything to do with Darby's absence, and the look in her sky-blue eyes when she'd run away.

Disappointment.

By the time he'd retrieved his truck and driven back to his rental, he'd convinced himself that Darby would be packed and gone from the house. So the sight of the pathetic green monstrosity she drove still parked at the curb was a distinct relief. It was right where he'd had it returned late last night.

He strode inside, stopping short at the sight of Carmel standing in the living room. She was all but wringing her hands together. "Thank goodness you're finally back."

"What's wrong? Where are the kids?"

Carmel looked toward the staircase. "Wonder of wonders, they're all taking naps. They're fine. It's Darby. She's gone."

"*Gone?* What do you mean *gone?* Her car's parked outside."

"It wouldn't start."

"How long ago? I was only a half hour behind her, at the most." He took the stairs two at a time, bursting into the master bedroom.

The bed was neatly made, Darby's wide-brimmed

straw hat sitting on the foot of it. The cribs lined up like stalwart soldiers against the wall, guarding the sleeping tots who lay inside.

He went into the attached bathroom. She'd left behind a bar of soap, sitting in the soap holder on the edge of the sink. He touched the smooth, dry cake, but that one touch was enough to leave the tip of his finger smelling like vanilla.

Like Darby.

He turned to see Carmel watching him, her eyebrows raised. He shoved his hand in his pocket and went out into the hall, softly closing the bedroom door behind him. "How long ago?" he asked again. "Did she say where she was going?"

"About twenty minutes ago. And I'd assume, home."

He muttered an oath. "Did she say anything else?"

"Other than that you and Caldwell are two of a kind?" Carmel shook her head. "Not much."

"Two of a kind. God." The idea was repugnant, but not one he hadn't thought more than once himself. "Listen, Carmel. I need you to do me a favor."

"No. No way. Uh-uh. I've got work at the office. Remember the office? G&G? The reason why we're holed up here in this town that's right out of a Norman Rockwell?"

"It shouldn't take me more 'n an hour." He looked at his watch, calculating. "Better make it two. Or three."

"I'm not staying here with those children while you go chasing after Darby." She followed furiously on his heels when he headed back down the stairs. "She's not the only person in town who can watch them!"

"I don't want anyone else."

"But—"

"Carmel, please. Call Hayden. He'll come and help you."

Her expression tightened. "I don't need your attorney's help."

"Then don't call him." Garrett didn't care. "Three hours." He left the house on Carmel's muttered Spanish. She was cursing his ancestors, his future progeny and all points in between.

He started up his truck and drove back toward the center of town. He caught up to Darby on Riverside. The same road they'd walked earlier on the way to The Overlook.

Her soft-sided overnight bag, its long strap slung over one shoulder, bumped against her hip with each step she took. He slowed his truck, pulling up beside her.

The look she gave him should have singed the hair off his body. She angled her head, adjusting the wide strap on her shoulder, and trudged on, ignoring him. He sighed and took his foot off the gas, the powerful engine creeping along.

"You've got a long way to walk before you get to Georgie's place."

"One foot in front of the other."

Her voice was as cool and imperious as a princess. Totally at odds with her screwball haircut and mutinous chin. "We never did get a chance to talk about the kids."

She shot him an incredulous look. Her mouth parted, as if she was searching for words. But none came. Her lips tightened and she faced forward again, her steps quickening.

"I know you're angry with me, but I didn't think you'd take it out on the kids."

She stopped. His foot hit the brake.

"Don't do that," she said tightly. "Don't use the kids to manipulate me into doing what you want. It's…it's… unworthy of you."

Unworthy. Which just went to show how little she really knew about him. "I'm sorry." And he almost was. Only because he hated, really hated, the look of disappointment that was still clouding her pretty blue eyes. He pulled up to the curb and shut off the engine, climbing out.

She backed up warily, not stopping until she bumped the waist-high stone wall behind her.

He lifted his hands peaceably. "Come on home, Darby."

"Home?" Her eyebrows skyrocketed. "I don't have a home. Certainly not one with you. *How* could you tell your father that you and I are getting married? How could you lie like that?"

"It wasn't a lie." He moved across the sidewalk. "It's the perfect answer, Darby. You love the kids."

"I don't—"

"Of course you do." He swallowed his impatience, knowing that it was definitely not the time or place for that particular flaw of his. "It's obvious. And they love you. You've already admitted that you're not involved with anyone else."

"Oh, so *obviously* I must be available for something as insignificant as *marriage?*" She shook her head. "I cannot believe you."

"Don't put words in my mouth."

"Don't go around telling people that I'm going to be your wife!" Her voice rose with each word. She colored and pressed her hand over her eyes.

Her shaking hand, he noticed.

"Let's go somewhere where we can discuss this," he suggested quietly.

Her hand dropped. "There is nothing to discuss."

"Then give me a chance to explain, at least."

"I can't marry you."

"Can't? Not won't?"

Her lips twisted. "Won't then. The very idea is ridiculous."

"Why?"

"Why? *Why?*" Her hands lifted. Pushed through her red-blond-brown hair. "We've known each other for only ten days! The other proposals I've received at least came from men I'd known more than two weeks."

"Proposals with an *s*. How many does that mean?"

"Three. But only one did I take seriously, and for all his faults he at least had the decency to ask me before announcing it to all and sundry."

"I thought you said there was no one."

"There isn't." She turned away from him, staring out over the fence, out over the rocky drop-off to the jewel-green valley below. "There hasn't been for two years."

"He's the one you're running from, then."

Her spine stiffened as if rebar had just replaced it. "Why on earth would you say something like that?"

"You're not denying it."

Her jaw worked. "Of course I'm denying it."

"What brought you to Fisher Falls, Darby?"

"Georgina Vansant," she answered tightly. "Are these the standard questions on the job application for a prospective Mrs. Garrett Cullum?"

"And the joker who proposed to you had nothing to do with it?"

"The *joker* was my fiancé. Until he decided he preferred his ex-wife, the mother of his children, over me."

It was so far from what he'd begun to suspect that Garrett couldn't think *what* to say.

Her eyes glistened, her expression pained. "What? No smart answers? No quick retort? No smooth thinking to turn that to your advantage?"

He wasn't used to tenderness. Feeling it. Expressing it. That wasn't what his life had been about. But the sight of the silvery tear slipping down her smooth cheek nearly undid him. He wanted to wrap her in cotton. Protect her from any more pain. "What—" he had to clear his throat "—what happened?"

"That's none of your business." She stepped around him, heading once more along the road. "It's none of anyone's business."

Garrett slammed his palms against the wall. The rough, aged stone scraped him. Cut. It was nothing compared to watching Darby walk away from him. Again.

Had he ever made such a mess of anything in his life?

Everything he said was wrong.

Everything he did was wrong.

He'd started out just wanting a caring nanny for his sister's kids so his conscience would let him sleep at night.

When had he managed to so completely screw it all up?

He crossed the sidewalk, reaching for the truck door just as Darby crossed the street to head up the mile-long private road of the Vansant estate.

As she did, a white van came barreling along the road, screeching to a halt as it passed Darby. A man jumped out the passenger side door and approached Darby.

Garrett saw her shake her head, try to walk around the man. That's all he waited to see. He jumped behind the wheel, gunning the engine, heading for the private drive. His truck easily bumped over the curb, and he cut in front of the television station van.

He saw the flash of Darby's pale, startled expression. The frustration on the face of the news anchorman's. "Get in," he told Darby harshly.

"I just want a comment for tonight's segment," the newsman shouted after them. "We're running a report of the accident investigation!"

Apparently, Garrett's company was less objectionable than the newsman's, because Darby ran in front of his truck and scrambled up into the passenger seat. He drove around the van, heading up the drive toward the estate.

"Go to the gatehouse."

He looked over at Darby. Her husky voice had been barely audible.

"Where?"

She pointed. He took the right fork in the road, heading away from the grand main house, moving at a fast clip between the high hedges and the vibrant rows of summer flowers.

There, at the end of the road, was a small building. The gatehouse. He parked in front of the door, rounded the truck and opened Darby's side.

She was trembling. Staring at her hands.

"I hate reporters." Her voice shook. "Vultures. All of them. Why can't they let people be? Why does everything have to be a damn story?"

He started to reach for her but didn't. "Darby."

She didn't look at him. Her hands still rested in her lap. Pale, pale hands. Palms up against the white fabric of her floaty dress.

"I'm out of my element here," he admitted. Claustrophobic in a crowded elevator. An ex-fiancé she was not running from. An absolute aversion to reporters. "Tell me how to help you."

Her long, elegant fingers curled into small fists. "I don't need your help. I don't need your marriage proposal. Such as it was." She shifted, sliding out of the truck and walking past him toward the gatehouse. "I don't need anyone."

Chapter Ten

Marry him.

The idea was insane.

Darby's hand shook so badly she could barely fit the door key into the lock. When she finally succeeded, she practically threw herself into the haven that Georgie had allowed her when she'd arrived in Fisher Falls.

She didn't know why she didn't close and lock the door after her.

To do so would surely have kept Garrett out. Which was only the sensible thing to do.

She dumped her overnight bag on the tile floor and moved across the square room to the other side, where windows overlooked the edge of the Vansant property.

Wild, wooded.

It was the sight that she'd wakened to for the three months that she'd lived in the gatehouse. Only from the rear of the main house was the view different. The windows there overlooked the beautiful waterfall that gave the town its name.

She had never had someone inside the gatehouse. Not even Georgie visited her down here.

Now *he* was here.

Walking through the door and closing it behind him

as if she'd invited him. As if he had every right, every reason to be there.

Darby turned around, pressing her palms flat against the cool windowpane behind her.

"Everyone needs someone," he said. His intent gaze drifted over the cozy interior of the gatehouse. Noting everything, she felt sure. From the blue-and-yellow chintz sofa to the mini-kitchen against one wall with the pale-yellow sink and tiny refrigerator.

"Not everyone." Her father, for one. Dane for another. "If you had just let the mayor take your nieces and nephews, you wouldn't need anyone, either." Dammit, she hadn't meant to bring that up. She'd meant only to get him out of there. Out of her only haven.

That she would now forever remember him invading.

She realized he was looking at the shelves surrounding the small television in the corner and deliberately moved into his line of vision, drawing his gaze away from the small collection of photos she'd placed there. "Why, Garrett? Why me? You don't even know me. Why tell your...tell the mayor such an outrageous lie?"

"I told you. It doesn't have to be a lie."

Her hands pressed to her stomach, but nothing could take away the ache she felt deep inside. "It cannot be the truth."

"There are five good reasons for it to be the truth," he said. "Regan, Reid, Tad, Bridget and Keely." He nudged her down onto the sofa, sitting beside her. The fluffy, flouncy, feminine fabric made him look even darker. More dangerous. "Listen. It's the perfect answer. Consider it a job, if it makes you feel better."

"A job," she echoed.

"A few years as my wife. At least until Regan and Reid are both in elementary school. You'll be well compensated."

"Well, golly. I guess I should just leap right at that delightful offer." She jumped to her feet, moving away from him. Far away, where she could think clearly again. "Between you and your father, one would think I'd do anything in exchange for the almighty dollar."

"I'm not trying to insult you."

She smiled humorlessly. "I'd hate to see how well you could accomplish it if you *did* try."

He leaned forward, resting his arms on his thighs. Somewhere along the way he'd gotten rid of his suit coat and rolled up his shirtsleeves. He linked his fingers together, looking as casual and easy as if they were discussing the color of rice.

Since she figured she had as little hope of rousting him from the gatehouse as she did of turning back time, she focused on the way the afternoon sunlight glinted on his gold wristwatch.

"Darby, all I'm trying to do—badly, I admit—is be fair. I don't expect you to go along with us and get nothing in return."

"Well. It's a change of pace, I admit," she said wearily. Bryan hadn't wanted to marry her, after all, no matter how much money her father threw his way. Now Garrett was offering to pay *her* to gain a more permanent caretaker for his nieces and nephews.

At least for a few years, according to him.

"Why marriage?" she asked. "You started out wanting a nanny. What happened to that?"

"You heard Caldwell. He's not going to stop this… campaign of his until he wins."

"Wins!" She turned on her heel, crossing to the kitchenette. "There you go again. Acting as if it is some contest to be won. Are either one of you thinking about what the children need? What the children want?"

"That's why I need you. Because you *do* think of the children. First. Not as an afterthought, or as an obligation. But because you actually do care for them."

She shook her head. "No. I can't do it. I agreed to… watch them for this week. Remember that agreement?" It seemed like ages ago, but it truthfully had been only one week. "Find somebody else."

"Where am I going to find anyone who cares as much for them as you do?"

She raised her arms, turning around to glare at him. "Hire someone off the street. It's practically what you've tried to do with me!"

He just looked at her.

And she wanted to turn around and run. Run away. Just as she'd done three months ago.

Only running had led her to Fisher Falls and that, in turn, had led Phil Candela there. To that corner outside of Smiling Faces at the same moment as Elise and Marc Northrop. Running had caused this situation.

And already her arms felt empty from being away from the children.

Oh, God. It was that kind of thinking that had gotten

her involved with Garrett and his "fearsome five" in the first place.

"No," she shook her head. "No. No way."

He rose from the couch, walking toward her. "What are you afraid of?"

She backed up. Bumped the yellow tiled counter behind her. "Nothing."

"Tad, Bridget and Keely are so young they'll think of you as their mother. Reid, too, most likely."

His green eyes saw too much. She held his gaze with an effort. "But I'm not their mother," she said carefully. "I never will be. They're your nieces and nephews, and even if I did agree to this ridiculous idea that you've come up with, that wouldn't change. Somewhere down the line, whether it's when Regan and Reid are finally in school or not, you'd decide you didn't need me anymore, or…or you'd want to marry someone else for real." Her throat was tight, the words emerging with difficulty. "And I'd be lost."

His eyes gentled. "You won't be lost, Darby."

"You don't know."

"I know what I can promise. There isn't going to be someone to come along that I want to marry 'for real.' I never planned to marry at all. Until now."

"Garrett, please. A man like you—"

He waited.

And she was suddenly, painfully aware of the silence surrounding them. "Well. I mean, there must be women in your life or who will come into your life. You'll date and…get involved."

"I'm already involved," he murmured.

"There you go, then." She forced a smile. "Get her to marry you."

"I'm trying to."

That silence, that intimate, seductive silence twined around them again. "You and I—" She swallowed. "We're not involved."

"Feels like we're getting there to me."

She moistened her lips. "If that were true, which it *isn't,* you're already setting things up to fail. Planning a marriage that will last only a few years. That's no way to live. Believe me. I know."

He touched her shoulder, his hand warm and hard and indefinably gentle. "How do you know?"

She hunched, trying to move out from that tempting touch. She didn't succeed. And the loose strap slipped off her shoulder, stopped only by Garrett's long fingers. "I just do," she said irritably.

His head tilted, the corner of his lips deepening. "Something wrong?" he asked mildly.

She stalled her motion to adjust her dress strap. "I don't like being crowded."

"Ah, Darby. How many words that come out of your mouth are actually true?"

She flinched. "Then you surely wouldn't want such a compulsive liar to be your convenient wife."

"Darby?"

"What?"

"Shut up."

Her lips parted. His head lowered, his mouth fitting over hers. She caught her breath. Breathing him. Inhaling him. His scent. His taste. He was intoxicating.

She frowned, grappling for sense, twisting her lips from his. "Garrett—"

His kiss ran along her jaw, touched her ear.

She moaned and angled her head away again. He merely transferred his attention to her shoulder. The shoulder that was bare of the dress strap. "This isn't, ah, sensible."

"I find it remarkably sensible." He slid his palm against the small of her back, lifted her hand and pressed his mouth to the tender skin in the crook of her elbow.

Her fingers curled. Her knees sagged. He kissed her jaw again. Driving her mad. "I don't do this sort of thing," she protested desperately. And shocked herself right down to her core when she thrust her fingers through his hair and drew his mouth back to hers.

His arms tightened around her, pulling her close. Ever closer. She couldn't seem to remember why this was wrong. Not when he felt so good. Not when his hands, so sure, so wonderfully male, so perfectly him, slid over her hips, lifting her.

She gasped, but he was setting her on the tiled counter, stepping between her knees, his touch burning through her dress. No, not through her dress. On her skin. Her knees. Her thighs. Her—

"No." Darby pressed her hands against his chest. His bare chest. Had she done that? Had she unbuttoned his shirt like that? Pulled it free of his trousers? She yanked her hands back, folding them together, determined to keep them under control. "We can't. I can't. I'm your... nanny."

"Fiancée," he countered. "And not just for convenience. We'd have a real marriage. It wouldn't be a name-only thing."

He ran his fingertip along the neckline of her dress, and she wondered if her heart would just burst right out of her chest it beat so hard.

"We could try it," he continued, "if it makes you feel better. But I'm telling you right now, it wouldn't work."

"No." She caught his wandering finger.

A muscle ticked unevenly in his jaw. "No?"

He very deliberately stepped back from her, holding his hands slightly out from his sides.

She covered her eyes for a moment, shaking. "You don't know who I am."

"I know enough."

"No, Garrett." She looked into his eyes. Feeling herself becoming absorbed by that deep, dark green. "You don't. I'm—"

"I know this." With one smooth swoop, he took her lips with his.

Her head reeled. He touched her nowhere else. Just his mouth on hers. His lips rubbing ever so gently across hers. Then he straightened. She swayed, feeling bereft.

"The first time I saw you," he said roughly. "I knew that. But I figured it was smarter to ignore it."

"And now?"

"I can't ignore it anymore." His gaze felt like a caress on her skin. "Can you?"

She slid off the counter, yanking her dress strap into place. She walked across the room. Back to the windows and that wild, wooded view. But sudden tears obscured it, and she closed her eyes, pressing her fists against her temples.

"Bryan had two children. *Has* two children." She swallowed. How easily she saw them in her mind. "Bobby was six, then. Amy was four. Bryan had custody, you see. We were going to be a family. The four of us. I was finally going to have the kind of life I'd dreamed of. A family who was together. Who stayed together. Forever."

She felt Garrett behind her. His hands closed gently over her shoulders, and she just wasn't strong enough to resist. She leaned back against him, sighing. Beneath her cheek she felt the hard contours of his bare chest and knew she should move away. She just couldn't quite make herself do it.

"What happened?"

"I was wrong. He changed his mind. I lost them all. And now you're suggesting I walk into the same situation."

His thumbs smoothed over her skin. "It's not the same."

"Close enough," she whispered. There *were* a lot of differences between the two situations. But the bottom line was one and the same. "I couldn't bear to walk away from your 'fearsome five.' And sooner or later, I'd have to."

"What if I guarantee that won't happen?" His words whispered over her forehead.

"Oh, Garrett. There are no guarantees. You of all people should realize that."

"What I know is that every time I follow my gut, I land on my feet. It got me from being a fifteen-year-old delinquent to where I am today. And my gut is telling me this is the right thing. I knew it the second I said it."

Her lips twisted. "I remember my anatomy classes. That's not your gut talking."

His hands turned her around until she was facing him. "Yeah. It is. Even if I wasn't battling the urge to lock ourselves into a bedroom for about a month of Sundays, I'd still think this was the answer for us both."

"I'm not looking for any answers."

"That's because you're afraid. Of being hurt again."

She opened her mouth to deny it. But what was the point? She *didn't* want to be hurt again. She didn't want to love someone else's children, envision a life together, plan for it, only to have it all yanked away. "You're not afraid of ever being hurt?"

"It takes a heart to be hurt, Darby."

She looked at him. This man who was fighting tooth and nail to make sure he followed through on his sister's last wish. "You…don't think you have a heart," she realized sadly. "Why would you think that?"

"Whether I like admitting it or not, I am Caldwell's son."

"And he's heartless, therefore you must be, too," she concluded softly.

He was wrong. About himself. And, she suspected, about Caldwell, too. A heartless person couldn't fake the pain she'd seen in the mayor's eyes. But she knew Garrett didn't want to hear that from her.

"The children need you, Darby."

"What about you?" She couldn't believe the words came out of her mouth. But there they were. Hovering in the air between them, large as life.

His green gaze drifted to her lips. "I think we've established how I feel about you. One way or another you're gonna end up in my bed. I might as well keep it good and proper."

She didn't know how she could feel such sadness for someone and still want to bean him on the head. "Killing two birds with one stone, as it were. Satisfying your—" her cheeks heated "—urge and the judge all in one."

"It's more than an urge," he said, amused. "And I don't think you'd be terribly disappointed, either."

"Pretty confident, aren't you?"

"You want me to lie and tell you I think we'll be awful together?" He flicked the tail of his shirt. The shirt *she'd* yanked from his trousers. The shirt *she'd* unwittingly unbuttoned.

She flushed hotly.

He moved away from her, glancing around. "I need a piece of paper."

She frowned, started to reach for a drawer where she kept a small collection of note cards. But he'd already pulled a paper napkin from the holder on the counter by the sink. He sat down on the sofa, scrawling rapidly on the napkin, using the silly sparkly pink pen she'd brought home from one of the birthday parties at Smiling Faces. Then he held the napkin out to her.

She automatically took it. "What is this?"

"Terms."

She read. And had to sit down, herself. "A pre-nup."

"More or less."

She looked at the sparkly pink scrawl again. It was brief and to the point. Only he didn't specify that, in the event of the demise of their marriage, what was his would remain his and vice versa.

What he did specify was that she would retain joint custody of the children. And lifetime support.

For a moment she thought she might be ill.

"It's only fair," he said evenly. "You're the only reason I've got a chance at fulfilling Elise's wish. You're the one who cares most about them. Sometimes I even get the feeling that you're the one who is hurting the most over the accident." He reached out and brushed his thumb over her cheek. "You're the only one who has cried for them."

She carefully set the napkin on the coffee table. "You said you'd remain in Fisher Falls until the judge makes his final decision."

"Yes."

"If I agree to stay on as their nanny until then, will you stop talking about this marriage business?"

"Probably not."

She laughed brokenly. "You're relentless."

"Usually. Until I get what I want."

"And you want me."

His eyes darkened. "Oh, yeah."

"I meant as your wife."

"The only way the nuns would have approved."

"I *meant* to...because of the children."

"I couldn't have said it better."

Her lips tightened. "Don't tease."

"Sorry."

He didn't look it. He looked hard. Relentless. Only when her gaze was caught in his did she see more. His edginess. His tension.

It would be so easy to tell him yes. To just agree. To go along with the flow. And it would be so very, very wrong. He didn't know who she was. If he did, he would have every right to boot her right out onto the street.

"I'll stay on as their nanny until you're ready to leave Fisher Falls," she said shakily. "But if you're set on finding a wife, you'll have to look elsewhere."

"You'll change your mind."

"No. I won't."

He smiled faintly and finally, *finally,* began buttoning his shirt. "Time will tell, won't it?"

Chapter Eleven

"Look at this. You're not going to believe it!"

At Darby's outraged gasp, Garrett looked up from his computer, barely managing to move the keyboard out of the way before she slapped the newspaper down on it. Twenty minutes ago she'd been cleaning up the kitchen after breakfast. Now she looked poleaxed. "What don't you believe?"

"Look at it!"

He glanced briefly at the section heading. The Leisure section. "I quit reading the comics after Charles Schultz died. No more Snoopy."

She made an impatient noise and jabbed her finger against the paper. "This."

This was a grainy long-distance shot of a man in a dark suit and a woman in a floaty white dress. "That's us," he said, surprised. "At the courthouse yesterday." He'd had his arm around her shoulder because she'd still been shaky from the elevator.

"Read the caption," she gritted.

Wedding Bells Ringing? Millionaire developer Garrett Cullum escorted his mystery woman in white from the Fisher Falls courthouse yesterday, quashing hopes of wishful young women everywhere.

"Wishful women everywhere," he repeated, amused.

"It's not funny."

He shrugged. "It's a gossip column. That's what they do. Gossip."

"People have *seen* that."

"Around here, maybe. But the *Fisher Falls Gazette* isn't exactly the *New York Times*." The photo didn't carry a credit, he noticed. "Just think. Some person without a life was actually sitting outside the courthouse with a camera. Probably in the park across the street, from the looks of it."

"What if it gets picked up. You know? One of the news wires?"

"It's a poor-quality photo from a backwater town in northern Minnesota. I think the world will live if it isn't."

"Garrett!"

He pushed the paper aside and looked at her. "Why are you panicking over this? Nobody pays attention to gossip columns."

She flopped her hands impatiently. "Yes, they do. 'Millionaire developer'? What's that about?"

He shrugged. "I do own G&G Construction and Development. And my bank account is fairly healthy these days."

"Great. More jokes."

"My banker smiles every time I see him." Her skin

was paler than normal. "You really have a thing against reporters and such." Vultures, she'd called them.

"I just like my privacy. Why on earth didn't you say you were well off?"

"Sorry," he said shortly. "I'd have let you run a credit report on me if I knew it mattered so much. You're not the only one who prizes their privacy. Which is why I choose to keep a low profile." He leaned back in his chair, watching her closely. "But I'm not turning gray over one blurry photo. You're not even identified, Darby."

"Thank God for small favors," she muttered.

Since they'd returned to the house yesterday, there hadn't been one moment when Darby hadn't had one or more of the kids attached to her hip or wrapped around her leg. If he had to make a guess, she'd been deliberately avoiding him. And now she was practically tearing out her hair over a blurry newspaper photo. To say she was regretting what had happened the day before was putting it mildly.

"Obviously the notion of being witnessed in my company is on a par with being cornered by a reporter for you." He pushed the paper back toward her and moved his computer keyboard into place.

Darby struggled with the panic that threatened her until she wanted to scream at it and Garrett's logic that told her she really was overreacting.

Then he shoved away from his desk and strode past her toward the front door. "I'm going to work. Stop worrying," he said flatly. "Your face is hardly visible with that enormous hat you were wearing. Nobody'll recognize you."

He went out the front door, leaving her staring after him. He was annoyed.

No. He was hurt. She'd hurt him.

Regret came swift and hard, and she rushed out the door after him, but he was already driving down the street in his truck.

She might have left her old life behind, but she was still piling one mess right on top of another. Sighing, she went back inside, just in time to rescue the ringing telephone from Regan, who had a habit of answering the phone and promptly hanging up on the caller.

"Hello?"

"You go and get married without even telling me?"

Georgie. "I'm not married." She hastily caught Keely from climbing into the cold, empty fireplace and redirected her toward the soft blocks that Bridget and Tad were playing with.

"So what was that picture in the paper all about, then?"

"I told him that people read gossip columns." She sat on the edge of the couch. Keely turned her attention to Darby's shoelaces. "You must be having a good day."

"You're avoiding the question. But I'll let you, for now. I told Karl to swallow that pain medicine himself. If I'm really going to have only a limited number of days left, I'm choosing to be lucid for them. Bring the children over, dear. Spend the day here. I'll have Cook fix all your favorites for lunch. Please."

"I'm currently without wheels. My car won't start, and Garrett's already gone to work."

An excuse that mattered little to Georgie. And a few minutes later Darby hung up the phone. She'd never been able to say no to Georgie.

"I remember Garrett's mother. She was a pretty one." Georgie had talked Darby into fixing her hair, and she was looking at the results in a gilded hand mirror. "Yes, that looks quite nice, dear. Where was I?" She handed the mirror to Darby. "Oh, yes. Bonnie Cullum. She worked for the Carson family, as did her mother before her. I always thought it odd how she kept working for the Carson family even after, well, after she had the baby."

Darby glanced out the window as she put the mirror back on Georgie's dresser. On the grass below she could see Karl and Lucinda—Cook—playing with the children. "What happened to her?" She felt almost guilty asking Georgie for information. But her aunt had brought up the subject all on her own.

"You know, I was never sure, or maybe I'm so old now that I've forgotten." Georgie's bright gaze settled on Darby. "I'd heard that her death affected Caldwell Carson very deeply," she went on. "Now there's a man who hasn't had a happy life. I don't like to speak ill of the dead, but his daughter…that Elise. She was quite a piece of work. A more spoiled woman I'd never met. Unless it was her mother, Caldwell's wife. I can't imagine either of them bringing Caldwell much more than misery."

It was a far different picture than Garrett would have painted. "Do you know him well? Mayor Carson?"

"Well enough, I suppose. He took over his family's business after his father practically ran it into the ground. Drink, you know. And it was a good thing he did. This town needed the employment. But I suspect he sacrificed his own happiness in the process. Now, stop watching and worrying out the window. The children will be just fine with Karl and Cook. Sit down here with me."

Darby swallowed. They'd had lunch. They'd primped with powder and pots of expensive makeup. They'd styled hair and Darby had even read aloud from the latest spy thriller Georgie was reading. But now it was time to face the music. Georgie-style. She sat in the chair next to the lace-draped bed. "Are you sure you don't want a manicure, too? I'd be happy to give you one."

"Stop fussing, dear. You're worse than Molly Myers. She came by yesterday to visit. I understand she was none too pleased when you told her you were not returning to your job at Smiling Faces."

"She did you a favor by hiring me in the first place. I think she was mostly worried that I'd expect her to hold the position open for me. When I, um, need it again."

Georgie looked at her for a long moment. "And you don't plan to need it again. Does that mean you're ready to go back home now? Or does it mean there's more to that newspaper photo than speculation? I'd love to think you'd be staying in Fisher Falls because you'd fallen in love with a man like Garrett Cullum."

"You know I'm not interested in marriage."

Particularly the kind Garrett had proposed. "I just work for the man."

Georgie's lips thinned impatiently. "I don't have time left on this earth to listen to nonsense. Karl saw you and Garrett in the gatehouse yesterday. He was gathering leaves for me. You know how I like the scent of the outdoors in here with me. He says you two looked quite, ah, cozy."

Darby's skin heated. "I'm sure Karl exaggerated."

"Pooh. Garrett is a real man, Darby dear. Nothing like that mealymouthed Bryan. The only time that pup ever stood up to anything was when he left you standing at the altar. Now, I know you were embarrassed by that, but really, dear, it was for the best. Wasn't it?"

"I was a little more than embarrassed, Georgie."

Her aunt's expression softened. "I know. You were so attached to his children. But don't forget. I remember when you and Bryan first started seeing each other."

"At the Schute Clinic," Darby murmured. "You were there for weeks. Making sure your endowment was being properly used." Despite Georgie's age and declining health, she'd been a holy terror when she'd arrived at the acclaimed pediatric clinic, cowing doctors and nurses and administrators alike.

"I was there to see *you,* darling. I know how hard your father made it for you to get through nursing school. My nephew is terribly hardheaded about some things. But you did it, and you found your own place at the Schute Clinic with no help from any of us. I was so proud of you. Every child who passed through the doors on your shift loved you. I was delighted when you told me about Bryan.

"But then I saw you two together. And, well, Darby dear, there was just no *passion* between you. And I must say, sometimes there is just nothing more important than a grand, sweeping passion. The kiss and touch of a man that makes you forget your own name. The kind that goes hand in hand with love you never expected to find."

Her eyes seemed lost in memories. Then she focused point-blank on Darby. "You know I'm delighted that you came here to me when you felt you had to get away. This big old place will be yours once I'm gone, after all. But you really are so much stronger than you think you are, darling. I hope you're finally beginning to realize that."

She tutted impatiently. "I could *almost* feel guilty for not admitting that you were here, safe and sound, when your father called, looking for you. Quite *obviously* he didn't believe me, or his security man wouldn't have been in Fisher Falls. But then he and I have been on opposite sides of the fence his whole life."

"Because he's one of the few people in this world who doesn't agree with everything you say," Darby pointed out dryly. Her father and Georgie were very much alike in that regard. It was no wonder they couldn't agree on anything.

"Well, he's been an overprotective fool where you're concerned."

"As long as nobody knows who I really am, Daddy

has no need to worry. Nobody has any interest in the very ordinary Darby White."

"From the looks of that photo in the paper this morning, Garrett Cullum has plenty of interest in the woman his arm was around, regardless of her name."

"He just needs someone to help his custody case against Mayor Carson."

"Are you sure that's all?"

Darby sat back in the chair, wrapping her arms around herself, not letting herself think beyond that. "It doesn't matter, in the end. Three people, including his sister, died because of me."

"They died because of an automobile accident," Georgie corrected gently. She leaned her head back against her pillows and sighed tiredly. "You've always been too hard on yourself, dear. Always taking responsibility for what other people have done. Do you ever wonder why two cars would collide like that on a perfectly clear day on an otherwise quiet corner?"

Darby knew she should go to bed. Bridget had a habit of waking at 3:00 a.m., an hour that came far too quickly. It wasn't as if she wasn't tired. Their visit to Georgie had gone as smoothly as it could go, considering the planning it took just to travel down the street with five kids, much less go out for the entire afternoon. But it was all worth it, just for the smile on Georgie's face when they'd arrived.

Yet now, with the children bathed and finally all asleep, Darby found herself sitting in Garrett's swivel chair, staring at his computer.

It had a dedicated phone line, she knew. Garrett did a lot of work online. She settled her hand over the mouse. The screensaver—a whirling eddy of greens and blues— disappeared and there it was. The little picture that, if she clicked on it, would connect her to the Internet.

She could send an email to her brother. Let him know she was okay. Just a quick hi and bye. He'd certainly pass on the message to their father.

Her fingers curled and she sat back. No. She wasn't ready yet. Maybe someday. When she knew that she could stand firmly on her own two feet and not let them take over her life again.

She wasn't that strong yet. If she were, she wouldn't have been so terribly tempted to fall in with Garrett's proposal.

Her pulse quickened. Oh, had she been tempted.

And sitting here in his chair, in his den that was the only room in the house that was simply, purely, *him,* she felt that temptation flood through her all over again.

Not even Bryan, whom Darby had still loved after she'd learned that their engagement had been arranged by her father, had made her feel the way Garrett did.

When Bryan had suggested they wait to make love until after the wedding ceremony, she'd been touched by his romantic, old-fashioned chivalry. Only afterward, after her life had blown apart, did she realize why he'd always been so circumspect.

As Georgie had observed. There had been no *passion.*

She left the den and the temptation of the computer and went out into the backyard, sitting on the step in the dwindling twilight. She propped her chin in her hands, listening to the sound of the crickets and the low rumblings from the sky.

Another thunderstorm was brewing.

Garrett hadn't come home for dinner. There'd been no message on the answering machine about his plans.

He'd been supportive and she'd behaved like an idiot. All over a photo that, in all likelihood, wouldn't be noticed by anyone beyond the city limits of Fisher Falls.

She pushed to her feet, nodding to the neighbor man who was standing on a ladder next door replacing a lightbulb. He waved and said he hoped they got some rain out of all that noise tonight. She smiled and agreed and told him good-night before she went back inside the house.

Something so simple. One neighbor talking to another. But until she'd found refuge in Fisher Falls, it was something that Darby had never before experienced.

And with each passing day, the thought of giving it up again only grew more painful.

Garrett stood in the dark house, staring at the still shadow on the couch. If Darby wanted to sleep on that thing, who was he to stop her?

He got himself a cold beer, then went into the den, replacing the clothes that had gotten wet from the rainstorm for a pair of old sweatpants. He flipped through the mail that Darby had left on his desk. He drank his beer halfway down.

Maybe she hadn't intended to fall asleep down here. The couch was too damned lumpy to get a decent night's sleep. He ought to know. The pullout in the den wasn't much better.

He'd go wake her. Then she could go upstairs. Someone should be making use of that brand-new mattress up there.

He set the long-neck on the desk and went out to the living room. She was curled into a tight ball. As if, even in sleep, she needed to keep the world at bay.

"Who are you, Darby White?" he murmured.

She slept on.

Cursing himself for a fool, he leaned over and slid his arms beneath her gathering up the ghostly white robe twisted around her and lifting her easily against him. She was so incredibly leggy that he was continually surprised at how small she really was.

She sighed and turned her face trustingly into his shoulder. Her breath whispered over his skin. He swore under his breath and headed for the stairs. They were so narrow he had to turn sideways to carry her up and even then he managed to crack his elbow against the wall.

"Mmmm." Darby's arm glided over his arm, up his chest, around his neck. "You're home," she whispered huskily.

Garrett grimaced. She was probably dreaming about the idiot ex-fiancé. The door to his bedroom was ajar, and he nudged it wider, carrying her over to the bed.

He shifted her in his arms, yanking back the covers before lowering her to the sheet. Her hands linked behind his neck and she made a protesting little sound. A sexy little sound that went straight to his gut.

"Come on, Darby," he murmured in a low voice. He looked at the cribs. The babies were all soundly sleeping. He wanted to keep it that way. "Time for bed."

He unlatched her slender fingers from his neck, only she twined her fingers with his, drawing their hands toward her, making that same sound again.

God. He was a glutton for punishment.

The belt of her robe was doing a rotten job of holding the robe together. And the silky nightgown underneath did a rotten job of not clinging to her lean curves. And the nightlight she'd plugged into the wall did an excellent job of illuminating it all.

He slid his hands out from hers, telling himself that he wasn't noticing the jutting curve of her breast against his knuckles.

"Garrett."

Her velvety voice whispered to him so faintly he wondered if he'd made it up in his head. He lowered his head, still leaning across the bed. *Get a grip.* He started to straighten, but her arm slid across the cool sheet toward him, her palm turned trustingly upward.

"I'm sorry," she whispered, just as quietly. Her eyes were open. Just.

"For what?"

Her head moved faintly. "Everything."

The word sighed over him. Knowing he'd be smarter to let it go, his knee settled on the bed, anyway. She turned toward him. Smoothly. Warmly. Lifting her head toward his. Pressing her soft lips against his.

Want, never far when she was near, settled deep inside him. He kissed her. One kiss wouldn't kill them.

Her mouth parted, her tongue shyly flicking.

One kiss only was gonna kill him.

He pushed at her robe with the faulty, lackadaisical tie belt. She twisted and kicked it away. Then her arms, satin-smooth, strong, female, wrapped around him and he was only too willing to follow.

He rolled, pulling her over him, filling his hands with her slender hips, running his palm beneath the hem, finding another scrap of satin beneath, then just the warm sleek curve of her back. She arched against his hand, supple as a cat. Her fingers flexed against his scalp, her breath becoming his.

"Your hair is wet," she murmured.

"The rain." The stringy things that held up her night-gown slipped so easily away as he drew the fabric up. Over her head.

She sat up and the nightlight gleamed like gold over her ivory skin. He could see the pulse beating in her neck as her arms crossed over herself. Her eyes were dark pools in the pale oval of her face.

The raging fire inside him eased in the face of her shy modesty. He sat up against the pillows and gently took her hands in his, uncrossing her arms. Her fingers curled, unsteady. "I want to see you," he murmured. She was beautiful. He pressed his mouth to her collarbone. Rubbed his fingers over her slender torso. Dipped into the gentle valley between her breasts. Grazed over the tight nipples.

She trembled wildly against him as he tasted each curve. So sweet. So creamy. So— *"Mamaaaaaaa!"*

The sobbing scream jerked his head back. He

swallowed a curse as Darby suddenly scrambled off him, yanking on her nightgown, throwing her robe over her shoulders. "Reid," she mumbled and darted out of the room.

Garrett thumped his head against the wall behind him. A crying kid. Better than a cold shower.

He wondered how parents ever managed.

He could hear Darby's low voice murmuring to Reid. Then one of the triplets started crying.

He rolled out of bed and stepped over to the cribs. It was Bridget. Sitting there, rubbing her eyes, her mouth pouting as she cried softly.

Then she held up her hands to him, clearly expecting him to do something. In the other room he could hear Reid, still upset.

Garrett reached into the crib and picked her up. She snuggled close against him, her crying miraculously stopped. She babbled nonsensically.

"Yeah," Garrett muttered, carrying her with him downstairs before she managed to wake up her brother and sister with her chatter. "That's a woman for you. Always giving a guy a hard time."

Chapter Twelve

Darby woke with a start. She was lying in Reid's bed, where she'd fallen asleep with him, and sunlight filled the room.

There was no sign of either Reid or Regan.

She blinked, feeling positively blurry in the head, and climbed out of the narrow bed. The bedside clock in the other bedroom told her it was nearly ten in the morning, and shock propelled her downstairs.

The triplets were safe and sound, dressed in colorful shorts and shirts and contained within the safe zone of the living room thanks to the baby gates she'd borrowed from Smiling Faces.

Keely was standing all on her own, and Darby smiled, delightedly kissing the tot on the head. Then she stepped over the gate into the kitchen to find Regan and Reid sitting at the table, both studiously drawing on big sheets of white paper. Drafting paper, she realized, and finally focused on Garrett, who was also sitting at the table.

Her entire body went into a slow burn. "I'm... sorry," she fumbled. "I overslept."

"We managed. Surprisingly enough." He set aside the sheaf of papers he'd been studying, placing them on the counter where curious little hands couldn't reach.

"Carmel has the office well in hand. She loves to lord it over me and tell me that I'm basically unnecessary."

"You're not."

His smile was brief. "I need to talk to you."

Her stomach twisted. She'd practically thrown herself at him last night. Right there in the same bedroom as the sleeping babies. No matter what kind of arrangement he'd proposed with her, behavior like that was simply outrageous. He had every reason to be appalled.

He was standing by the back door, his expression unreadable. And her stomach did more than twist. It seemed to fall right down to her feet. Lower. Through the floor. "What is it?"

He drew her outside, where the sun shone brightly, all evidence of the rain from the night before gone. "I got a call this morning," he said quietly. His eyes were gentle. Utterly serious. Her heart simply stopped.

"My father—"

He frowned a little, shaking his head. "A guy named Karl."

Sudden tears lodged in her throat.

"They had to take Georgie to the hospital last night."

"No." She shook her head. "I was with her yesterday. She was good. We had lunch. Crab salad for us and chicken fingers for the kids." Her voice broke.

"I'm sorry, sweetheart. I know you're very close to her."

Darby brushed her fingers over her cheeks. "I have to go see her. She'll be mad if she finds out I was crying. Tell me it's a waste of good water."

"That sounds like the Georgina Vansant I know. The one who offered me a job when no one else would."

She managed a shaky smile. But it didn't last. "I don't want to lose her, Garrett. I know it's going to happen one day, but I'm not ready yet," she whispered. "I'm sorry. I shouldn't complain. Not after your sister...and all."

He pulled her against him, tucking her head beneath his chin. "I wish I could tell you that losing Elise hurt me this much. That there was that much caring between us. But there wasn't. And I think that's what hurts the most."

Darby caught back a sob.

She felt him kiss her forehead. "Georgie is wrong about one thing," he said gruffly. "It's not a waste of water."

Her arms crept around him, and he held her while she cried. Then, once she collected herself and got dressed, he loaded everyone into his truck and drove Darby to the hospital himself.

Unfortunately there wasn't much any of them could do when they arrived. Georgie was in the Intensive Care Unit, and Darby was allowed to visit her for only a few minutes once each hour. Darby spent her few minutes with her aunt reading aloud to her. Georgie was unconscious, but Darby knew that her aunt was somehow, somewhere, listening.

Halfway through the second hour, the children were going mad from being confined in the waiting room. The only saving grace had been that the seven of them were the only ones in the room, so they'd been free to be as noisy and rambunctious as Darby and Garrett could stand.

But now Darby caught Keely from crawling out of the waiting room and popped her back in the stroller with her brother and sister.

"They need lunch," Darby told Garrett. She'd been so panicked over her aunt, she hadn't thought to make sure the supply of cereal inside the diaper bag was enough. "I'll just have to come back and visit Georgie later tonight. Maybe after the children are in bed."

He shook his head and nudged her hands away from the padded stroller handle. "You don't want to leave," he said. "I can see it on your face. I'll take them home now. When you're ready, give me a call and I'll come back and pick you up."

"I don't want to make more work for you."

"Why don't you let me worry about that."

"Garrett—"

He brushed his thumb over her lips. "Everyone should have a friend as true as you," he murmured.

His easy support made her want to cry. There was so much that wasn't true about her, and she hated that as much as she hated the fear that had been motivating her for months now.

She caught his hand between hers, noticing the way his sun-bronzed skin looked in comparison to her pallor. "I'm not just her friend," she admitted after a long moment. "Georgie is my great-aunt, Garrett."

His expression didn't change. "Okay."

"You don't want to know why I didn't mention it before?"

"Was there a good reason?"

She swallowed. "I...needed to get away," she faltered. "From everything."

"That ended up being our good luck."

"Oh, Garrett."

He glanced at the children. Regan was watching them openly. Reid was picking at a loose thread on his shirt. "Darby, I know I'm not the best at some things, but...if you want to talk. You know." His mouth twisted crookedly. "Hell, you already know most of my secrets now. Least I can do is return the favor."

She chewed her lip. "Garrett, I—" She couldn't do it. She couldn't tell him, right there in front of the five children, that she'd been responsible for their parents' death. She was the absolute worst kind of coward.

"Miss White?" One of the nurses appeared in the wide doorway of the waiting room. "Mrs. Vansant is coming around. She's asking for you."

Darby's mouth parted. She looked back at Garrett, unbearably torn.

"Go on, Darby." He lifted his chin toward the door and told Regan and Reid to gather up the magazines they'd scattered about. "Call when you want to head home."

Home. All she'd ever wanted and the one thing she'd never seemed to really have.

"Thank you," she whispered. Then she stretched up and pressed a quick, trembling kiss against his lips, before following the nurse back to Georgie's bedside.

* * *

Three days later Garrett sat in the kitchen of his dumpy little rental house and scooped goopy chunks of pears into three hungry mouths, and wondered what the hell had become of his life.

What had happened to the guy whose house—designed and built mostly by his own hands—had won architectural and design awards? The guy who did deals; who traveled around the country on a moment's notice; who enjoyed the company and charms of tall, curvy blondes; who answered only to himself and liked it that way?

Keely patted his cheek with her little hand and talked nonsensically. Tad was kicking his legs, grinning and displaying the sharp edges of two shiny new teeth. Regan was picking up the sipper cup that Bridget had thrown to the kitchen floor. Reid was standing on the chair seat behind Garrett, sprawled over his back like a wet blanket as he seemed to find great interest in the shape of Garrett's right ear.

The phone rang, and before Garrett could disentangle Reid from him, Regan bounced over to the wall phone. "Regan, wait—"

Too late. Regan picked it up. "Hello!" she greeted cheerfully, then promptly pushed the phone back on the cradle. She turned around and beamed at Garrett, then bent down and picked up Bridget's sipper cup when it went sailing again.

Garrett shook his head and laughed wryly. He guessed if it was important, the caller would try again.

He didn't know how to describe his life now, except

to say it was *definitely* different. And, honest to God, he couldn't wait for Darby to once again be more than an in-and-out visitor in this new, unrecognizable life of his. Since Georgie seemed to be improving, he hoped that'd be soon.

Which just went to show what a selfish soul he really was.

He finished feeding the triplets, which wasn't as much of a disaster as some of his attempts, then cleaned them up some before sticking them on the floor in the living room where an assortment of baby gates kept them corralled with their toys and away from hazards. Then he turned to the two older ones. "Bath time," he announced.

Reid yelled and ran out of the room.

"I don't want soap in my eyes no more," Regan said, her smile gone as she warily eyed him.

Garrett grimaced. "I don't want that anymore, either," he assured. When he'd inadvertently let shampoo suds drip into her face the evening before, Regan had let the entire neighborhood know with her crying just how much it stung.

"Darby doesn't get soap in my eyes."

"I know, peaches." Garrett blew out a breath. "Tell you what. If Darby gets home from the hospital in the next hour, then you can have her. But if she doesn't, then we'll have to muddle through together."

Satisfied, Regan ran off, yelling for her brother. Garrett turned to the kitchen and restored it to some semblance of order. Then he attacked the laundry that was threatening to take over the minuscule laundry room.

Darby had done a good portion of it, and there were neat stacks of clean, dry and folded clothes, along with the two baskets of stuff from the toddlers.

It seemed as if they went through a drawerful of items per kid each day.

There was no point in grumbling over it, though. Staring at it wasn't going to make it go away. So he dumped some detergent in the washing machine and shoved it full to bursting, then grabbed up an armful of the clean things and carried them upstairs. He didn't even realize he had a handful of Darby's clothes until he'd shoved the top half of the piles into what he hoped were the right drawers in the kids' dressers.

One minute he was holding miniature socks, T-shirts and shorts and the next, he was holding a bundle of filmy, lacy things. He stood in the master bedroom, staring at the lingerie in his hands and damn near broke out in a sweat. It was crazy. He was not some pimple-faced teenager, faced with his first sight of a woman's panties and bra.

Garrett's fingers closed around the frothy, delicate things. His gaze fell on the bed that Darby slept in each night.

Then he heard the latch of the screen door from downstairs and Darby's sexy, husky voice as she greeted the toddlers. He strode around the bed and yanked open the drawers of the small chest there that he figured Darby was using for her own, since the other dresser in the room was filled with baby stuff. He started to shove the lingerie into the second drawer, thinking that the sooner he got out of there, the better.

But the colorful magazine cover inside the drawer caught his eye, and he went still for a moment.

Her hairstyle was different, but there was no mistaking that color. Very aware of the sound of Darby moving around downstairs, Garrett dropped the bundle of lingerie into the drawer. The satin and lace bits covered the magazine, and Garrett almost wished he hadn't seen it at all. Because even as one puzzle piece was fitted into place, it seemed to make him more aware than ever of the other pieces still missing.

Standing at the base of the stairs, Darby looked up the staircase. "Garrett? Are you— Oh, there you are."

He'd appeared on the landing, looking particularly tall and broad from her angle below. "You're earlier than I expected," he said as he started down the stairs. "How's Georgie tonight?"

"Pretty good, actually. She's scheduled for surgery tomorrow morning. Once she decided she wanted to go for it, the surgeon saw no reason to delay." She looked at him. She would like to rest her head against that wide chest. Instead, she went into the living room, busying herself with straightening the cushions on the couch and adjusting the skewed lampshade.

"That's good, right?"

"Well, yes. Georgie isn't young, of course. But her surgeon is optimistic. And Georgie is determined." She stepped over one of the baby gates and sat down on the floor to lift Tad into her lap. He gave her a toothy grin, and Darby's heart suddenly felt lighter.

Feeling the steady weight of Garrett's gaze, she

glanced up at him. Then hesitated. "Is something wrong?"

"No."

Whatever he said, she could guess. "You should have found someone else to watch the kids," she told him, even though the notion made her feel empty inside. "The past three days, I know I've barely been here. That's certainly not what you hired me for."

He sat down on the arm of the couch and stretched out his legs, his eyes never leaving her face. "When are you going to get it through your head that I don't want to hire somebody else? Nothing's changed," he seemed to stress the words, "as far as I'm concerned. I want you to marry me. Remember?"

As if she could forget. "Garrett, I've already told you that I can't."

He lifted his hand. "Let's not get into that just now," he suggested smoothly. "So your aunt was in good form today, then?"

Darby kissed Tad's head and let the squirming boy go. She folded her hands in her lap and looked at them. Since Darby had admitted to him that Georgie was her great-aunt, he hadn't once referred to her that way. It struck her as…odd. But then, the entire situation they were living in was hardly the norm.

She looked up as Regan and Reid came racing down the stairs, chasing each other and whooping at the tops of their voices. At least the children seemed normal at the moment.

It did little to ease her conscience, however.

"Yes, she was." She focused on Garrett's comment

about Georgie. "She made me promise not to wear white tomorrow if I 'insist' on being at the hospital while she's in surgery."

"Oh, yeah?"

"She doesn't want me reminding her too much of angels."

"You do seem a little angelic," he murmured. "Look at the way you've helped save us."

Darby shook her head. "I haven't."

His lips tilted. "So. What does she prefer you to wear? Red?"

"Well. Yes, actually." She felt silly admitting it. "How did you know?"

He shrugged easily. "Seems like a Georgie color. Do you even own anything that isn't white or tan?"

Darby waved her hand at the narrow garment bag she'd left by the front door. "I scrounged up a dress from my closet at the gatehouse. She also made me promise to personally go by her house tomorrow and check on her houseplants. Since she's been in the hospital, there hasn't been a need for her staff to go the house, and she's pretty attached to her ferns and such."

"What time is the surgery?"

"Nine."

"I'll go with you."

Darby's throat tightened. "I—" She looked at him and the automatic refusal of his offer died, unsaid. "Thank you." Then, because of the steady way his mossy-green eyes kept watching her, she plucked Bridget off the floor and stood. "Diaper time," she announced.

She stepped over the gate, waiting for Garrett to move

his outstretched legs, but he didn't. She moistened her lips and stepped over them, as well, making the mistake of glancing at his face as she did so.

Her breath stalled. She nearly tripped. He put out one long arm, catching her hip, steadying her and Bridget.

"Garrett—" She didn't know what she wanted to say.

His gaze dropped to her mouth. The fingers on her hip flexed. She felt herself leaning just a bit closer to him.

Closer.

The phone rang and Darby jerked back, catching her breath. Garrett muttered something about "racing Regan" under his breath as he straightened and strode into his den.

She heard him answer the phone. Then the low tone of his voice. Business. Naturally he'd have to handle a lot of business at home. In the evenings; whenever he could fit it in around caring for the children the way he'd been doing the past few days.

She blew out a long breath and focused on the tot in her arms. "Your uncle is a good guy," she murmured as she carried Bridget upstairs for a fresh diaper.

When she came back down, Garrett was still on his phone call.

It was just as well. She needed to remember that she *wasn't* Garrett's devoted fiancée. She was nanny to his fearsome five and the fact that she couldn't look at him without thinking of the night he'd carried her up to bed was something she'd just have to get over.

She settled Bridget back on the floor with the other

two and rounded up Regan and Reid for their baths and bedtime story.

Once that was accomplished and she'd settled the babies down after snuggles and a last bottle, she headed for the laundry that she'd left early that morning.

Only the stacks she'd expected to see still sitting on top of the dryer were gone. She opened up the washing machine to find a wet load waiting. She transferred it to the dryer and turned to find Garrett standing behind her.

She stepped back, bumping against the appliances behind her. "You startled me."

"Sorry. I put the clothes and stuff away already."

"Oh. Right. Thanks."

"Here." He held out a wad of bills. "Your pay."

"I've barely done anything to earn it since Georgie went into the hospital. You've even arranged for that second truck that I've been using. I don't think I should accept it."

He pushed the money into her hand, despite her protest. "Unless you're ready to call a justice of the peace and be done with it, you'll accept it."

She rolled the cash into a tube, closing her fingers around it. "Garrett, this marriage thing, it's not going to happen."

"Why?"

"We've already been through this."

"You can do better than us, I know."

"No! No. You know that's not what I think. Garrett, you're a good man. A...decent man. Any woman would be lucky to have you and the children for her own, but—"

"Not you."

"Yes. No." She shook her head, feeling overwhelmed and confused and sad. "I thought you didn't want to get into this."

"I didn't while the kids were right there. But they're all in bed now."

"Which is probably where I should be, too," she said hurriedly. "I'll finish this stuff up in the morning. It's just towels and things. It won't harm them being in the dryer until then. It shuts off automatically, you know."

"Are you afraid of me?"

Her jaw dropped. "Afraid? No. Should I be?"

"Then why are you acting like a long-tailed cat in a roomful of rocking chairs?"

She gave a breathless laugh. "My father uses that expression."

"Does he?" Garret stepped closer. "If you're not afraid, then why can I see your pulse beating in your throat?"

She lifted her hand, pressing it against that betraying sign. "Look, Garrett. About the other…that night. I shouldn't have—"

"Why not? We're adults. I want you. You want me. What's more simple than that? I'd rather this place had another bedroom for us to put the cribs in, but we'll be more careful next time."

Her skin heated. "Next…time."

He cupped her chin and raised it. He kissed her lips,

gently, tantalizingly. "Next time. You know this is where we're headed, Darby."

"But I can't marry you."

"Yes, you can." His words were a whisper over her mouth. "It'll be fine, Darby. I'll take care of everything."

She sighed, sinking so easily into his kiss. So seductive, so tantalizing. Making her want more and more.

I'll take care of everything.

His words finally sank into her muddled brain. "No." She wedged her hands between them and pushed him away. "No! I don't need you to take care of everything. I don't want someone running my life for me. I want to make my own decisions, my own choices, my own mistakes!"

She stared at him, shocked at the words that had tumbled from her mouth.

"We all do, Darby," Garrett said quietly, as if he could see straight to her soul and recognized all the fears that drove her. "I meant that I'd take care of finding a justice of the peace. But whether or not we find a JP before or after makes no difference to me."

There was no mistaking his implication. "You seem to think that's a forgone conclusion. Our, ah…"

"Making love," he supplied. "Sooner or later, Darby, it is."

She wanted to disagree. But the denial wouldn't quite come to her lips. So she just stood there, feeling awkward and much too aware of his appeal.

He watched her for a long moment. Long enough to make her brush her fingers through her hair. Long enough to make her wonder if she'd buttoned her blouse crookedly.

"You've been under a lot of stress," he finally said, and something about the way he said it made tears suddenly burn behind her eyes.

"That was Hayden on the phone earlier," he went on. "I've got to go into the office for a while. I'll be late getting back. Don't leave for the hospital in the morning without me. And—" he brushed his thumb over her lips when she started to speak "—I'll arrange for child care, too. Not that I think you're incapable of doing it yourself," he added with a faint smile. "Okay?"

She managed a smile herself and nodded. She even managed to hold her composure together when he ducked his head and pressed a hard, fast kiss to her lips.

But once he was gone, she slid to the floor in a quivering mess and pressed her forehead to her knees.

The man sure knew how to kiss. It was enough to make her forget her own name.

Chapter Thirteen

Darby walked through the central corridor of Georgie's grand old house carrying the filled watering can. She tipped it gingerly over each potted plant. The last thing she wanted to do was drown one of Georgie's precious green things.

She looked over at Garrett, who was running his hand across an inlaid door, his expression appreciative. True to his word, he'd driven Darby to the hospital. He'd visited with Georgie before she was rolled out of her room. He hadn't left Darby's side for more than a few minutes at a time since.

She tipped and watered. "How was Carmel faring with the children when you phoned?"

"Better than she admits, I suspect." He moved to her side of the wide hallway, touching the wall, crouching down to look at something near the floor.

"Well. It was very nice of her to stay with the children while Georgie had her surgery." She moistened her lips. "I do appreciate your support today. But I really can handle watering Georgie's plants by myself." She jiggled the oversize plastic watering can.

He stood and took the can from her. "Did they teach you these manners in finishing school?"

She jerked, startled. "What?"

He grinned slightly. "You are pretty polished."

Darby rolled her eyes. Since the watering can weighed a small ton, she let him take it and led him into the sunroom where she sat down, nudging off her shoes with relief. She'd have much preferred her usual tennis shoes, but with the red dress she'd worn per Georgie's instructions, they would have looked ludicrous.

Garrett poured water into the pots, and Darby, realizing she was watching him much too closely, looked beyond his dark head, through the sparkling windowpanes where the falls were visible in the distance. It looked like a rippling veil tumbling over the sheer rocks.

"Georgie's bedroom upstairs has the same view as this room," she murmured. "She loves it. So do I."

Garrett set the can down and closed his hands over the back of her shoulders, staying her when she jumped a little. "Her surgery went well. She'll be back talking to her plants and admiring the view before you know it."

"Yes." Darby smiled faintly. "And ordering Karl and Cook and everyone else around." His massaging fingers felt much too good, and she shifted away. Stood. "Speaking of orders, there are probably a dozen plants upstairs, too. She'll have my head if I neglect a single one of them."

"Relax. I'll finish watering the plants. I've wanted to explore this great old place since I was a kid. It'll give me a chance." He shrugged out of his black suit coat and dropped it haphazardly on a chair, picking up the watering can again as he left the room.

Darby watched him go, chewing the inside of her lip. She picked up his jacket, only intending to straighten it from the wrinkled heap he'd dropped it in. But the fine fabric smelled of him, and her fingers tightened around the garment. Hugging it to her, she moved blindly about the sunroom. Remembering the first time she'd come here three months ago.

Despite their family connection, Darby had never visited Georgie in Fisher Falls. She felt bad about that now. But her aunt had traveled so much. She'd always seemed to enjoy descending upon them in Kentucky, where she and Darby's father would battle over everything from the color of the sky to the price of the company stock.

Yet, when Darby had needed a place to go, Georgie had been here. Her aunt had sat right here in this very sunroom, dragging Darby's garbled tale out of her, clucking and tutting just when Darby had needed it. She'd given her a place to stay. Helped her find a job that Darby could enjoy, since she couldn't possibly find a nursing post without her name being traced.

Holding Garrett's jacket to her cheek, she leaned against the window. She'd thought she was all cried out. She'd made it through Georgie's long surgery without wasting one bit of good water. But now the tears seemed far too easy. Far too close.

She closed her eyes and wiped her cheek.

"I always figured you'd look great in red. I don't think I told you that, yet."

Embarrassed that Garrett had caught her nuzzling his jacket, she quickly smoothed it and folded it over her arm. "Why red?"

"It's about as far from your usual palette of whites as it can get."

She lay his jacket over the back of one of the rattan chairs and flicked her hand against the silk sheath she wore. "Georgie obviously agrees with that. She told me once that she wants everyone to wear red to her memorial...once she's gone." Her eyes flooded and she turned away.

"That's not going to happen anytime soon," Garrett said quietly.

She dashed her fingertips beneath her eyes and turned to face him. He'd been a rock for her, just as much as Georgie was. "I think you try to hide it, but you're a nice man, Garrett Cullum. And I couldn't have gotten through the last few days without you." She stretched up and pressed a kiss to his cheek.

He closed his wide palms over her shoulders, bare below the tiny cap sleeves, and the moment slowly stretched into infinity.

His thumbs drew gentle circles on her skin.

"Garrett—"

His lips twisted. "I know. It's not the time. Or the place. You're exhausted. But I'm...short on willpower at the moment."

Passion. Just like Georgie said. She'd approved of it, despite knowing everything there was to know about the situation. But as Darby looked at Garrett, she realized with a startling moment of clarity that it was so much more than mere passion.

It was love.

Maybe on any other day, at any other place, she could have kept her defenses in place against the realization.

But it wasn't any other day.

It was here. And it was now. And denying the emotion that churned inside her heart, crying for release, was more than she was capable of.

"So, I think I'll head on out now," Garrett was saying wryly. "Do you want to come or stay here?"

"Why would I stay here?" she asked faintly.

"I thought maybe you'd want some time to yourself now." He reached for his jacket. "If you need a break from everything, I understand."

"What about the children?"

He looked at her for a long moment. "Nothing's changed, Darby. We'll still be there."

She drew in a shaky breath. "Actually, there is something I need."

He waited.

"Some...time to ourselves."

A muscle in his jaw flexed. "Ourselves," he repeated after a moment. "You and me."

She moistened her lips. Nodded. Her heart felt as weightless as the water must when it tumbled over the rocks, creating that beautiful, magnificent, awesome waterfall. "Unless you're averse to that."

He smiled grimly, shaking his head once. "Darby, if you and I are any more alone, you know what's going to happen."

Her chin tilted. "Yes. I know."

He studied her through narrowed eyes, and time

seemed to stall. To hang like a physical thing, taut and expectant, between them. "The gatehouse?"

She shook her head. "Here. Right here. Right… now."

"Georgie—"

"Would be the first one to applaud. Trust me on that. We're alone. Karl and Lucinda won't be back until Georgie recovers and comes home."

He smiled faintly. Tossed his jacket back onto the chair. He held out his hand. "Come here."

She put her hand in his.

"You're shaking." He stepped closer.

"I've…um…" She jumped a little when his fingers grazed her neckline, then slowly, unerringly, drew the zipper down along her spine. "Um, I've never done this before," she admitted in a rush.

His fingers halted on the zipper. His eyes darkened. "Never?"

"Never." She pushed her tongue against her teeth for a moment. "Have you changed your mind now?"

He snorted softly. "Not on your life."

"Well. I might not be any good at—"

"Darby?"

"What?"

"At the risk of telling you what to do, put your mouth here—" he tapped his lips "—and be quiet."

She stretched up to him, following instructions to the letter.

Her dress slithered to the floor, and he lifted her out of it, carrying her over to the cushioned love seat.

He settled her on it, then straightened, reaching for his tie.

Darby's throat tightened as he yanked it free and flicked open the buttons of his white shirt. It billowed open, harshly white against his chest. "You are a construction guy aren't you," she murmured, watching the sun-bronzed play of his muscles when he pulled the shirt off and tossed it aside.

"Yes, ma'am."

She knew she should feel decadent sitting there wearing nothing but her undies and hose, but she didn't. In fact, she was almost disappointed that he stopped undressing after his shirt.

Outside the sunroom a breeze drifted by, jingling the wind chimes that Georgie collected and hung around her house with a generous hand.

Like delighted laughter.

She tilted her head and stood. Boldly pressed herself against him, feeling more wonderfully feminine than ever before. She kissed his chest, exploring his hard muscles with her palms, going breathless all over again at the way he went still and tense when she touched him.

"Don't stop." His head curved over hers. His lips burned on her shoulder. Somewhere along the line he'd unclipped her bra and it fell, unnoticed.

His hands knew no boundaries. Hard with calluses that ought to have been out of place on a millionaire developer but weren't, they were infinitely gentle, indescribably seductive.

He pushed the cushions from the love seat onto the

fluffy hand-tied rug and drew her down to them. She followed, mindless with need.

He unrolled her nylons with agonizing attention, and she watched them drift from his hand to the floor.

Then his hands settled around her ankles and she exhaled shakily. She caught the gleam of his white teeth as he smiled fiercely, utterly male, utterly aroused.

He rubbed the ache from her tender feet, seemed to find her ankles fascinating and her knees even more so.

She didn't even think to protest when he delved wickedly beneath the edge of her panties.

Again and again she restlessly reached for him only to have him elude her touch with a faint smile, his mossy-green eyes filled with intent as he taught her the wonder of a man's hands on a woman's body.

Finally his name burst from her lips, and she twisted against him in a paroxysm of need, twining her legs around his, wondering faintly when he'd gotten rid of his pants. "Please."

He kissed her deeply, finally settling hot and heavy and wonderful against the cradle of her hips. He made a low sound, deep in his throat. A sound that twined around her heart. "Open your eyes, Darby."

She did, and his hard, beautiful face filled her vision. And she felt him there. And even though she was a trained nurse, she suddenly couldn't imagine how such a thing could possibly work. "Garrett—"

He inhaled sharply, pressing his forehead against hers. "You don't know what your voice does to me," he said roughly. "Say it again."

"Garrett," she whispered.

He groaned.

She arched against him, needing more. "Garrett. Garrett. Oh." And then she could say no more.

And everything worked beautifully.

Because of him.

"It's getting late." Darby sighed as Garrett's long fingers smoothed up her spine. She pressed her cheek against his chest. "We should probably get back."

"Probably."

Neither made a single move.

Darby scooted upward, propping her chin on her hand. "We should."

"Right." His grin was slow.

Darby laughed softly.

He pulled her over him, and his warm hands cupped her hips. "So tell me why you hadn't done this before. The guy you were engaged to was a bigger jerk than I thought if he managed to keep his hands off you."

"Maybe he was a gentleman," Darby said primly.

"Something I'm definitely not."

"You're not like anyone I've ever known," she admitted honestly. "I wish—"

"What?"

She tucked her head against his neck, breathing in his scent, committing it to memory so she'd never, ever forget this moment. "I wish that we could have met under different circumstances."

"Why? We'd still be the same people."

"I know."

"For a long time, there, I wanted to be somebody other than who I was," he murmured. "Anybody other than Caldwell's bastard son. Couldn't change it when I was five or fifteen or twenty-five. Finally I quit caring."

She didn't think he had quit caring, at all. "My family is…difficult to take, too," she admitted huskily. "My parents are divorced. Mother lives in New York. Dane, my brother, gets along with her better than I do." She smiled wryly. "Actually, he gets along with all females better than anyone I know."

"Has it been a long time since you've seen them?"

"Nearly four months," she admitted. "My father… we had a disagreement. I wanted to move out. Live on my own. I'm twenty-six years old, for heaven's sake. You would have thought I'd suggested shaving my head and joining the circus."

"Why didn't you do it anyway? Move."

"I couldn't afford it. My father used his influence with my employers, and I lost my job." She closed her eyes. She'd been furious with her father when she'd learned the truth. Dane had shrugged and told her to stop expecting the old man to change his stripes.

Dane had also thought she was crazy for remaining in the house after she'd learned the truth of her father's machinations in her engagement to Bryan.

"I was a nurse at a clinic specializing in treating pediatric cancer patients," she said.

"Sounds grim."

She shook her head. "The children I worked with had fifty times the courage that I did," she murmured. "Anyway, I had trouble finding another post." Thanks again to her father's meddling. "I think my father believed that as long as I couldn't find a job, I'd have no choice but to stay under his roof."

"Controlling."

"You have no idea," Darby murmured.

"And you ended up here, in Fisher Falls with your aunt."

"Great-aunt. On my father's side. They don't get along." Darby had a sudden thought that Garrett might mention something to Georgie. "She hasn't told him about her health or the surgery. She doesn't even like to talk about him."

"Neither do you, much," Garrett pointed out. "Do you feel a strong need to get back to the children now or not?"

Every thought flew from her mind as she looked into his hard, beautiful face. "I—"

"Good." His smile flashed as he suddenly rolled, pulling her beneath him, his intentions as obvious as the arousal he couldn't hide.

Darby twined her arms around his neck, opening her mouth to his. *I love you* hovered on the edges of her thoughts, but she managed to hold back the words.

And a few moments later she couldn't think at all.

Chapter Fourteen

"Are you sure you don't want to go to the carnival with us? It's the last day."

Garrett looked up at Darby from the pile of letters Carmel had brought by before lunch for his signature. Since Georgie's hospitalization and surgery two weeks before, he'd continued working more often at home. The elderly woman was now recuperating well in a private care center on the other side of town, where Darby visited a couple times a week.

"I can't," he said. The stab of regret he felt surprised him, and he tossed down his pen in favor of tugging Darby onto his lap. "Carmel has set up more interviews for hiring staff this afternoon, and then I've got a meeting with Hayden and the Nielson Farms folks to finalize the deal with them."

"I still find it hard to believe that Fisher Falls is going to be the new home for a gourmet ice-cream manufacturer."

"And G&G, who won the contract right out from under Castle Construction's nose, will get fat and happy building their plant, the new housing development, the—"

"Yeah, yeah." She looped her arm around his neck, resting her forehead against his. "You millionaire developers are all alike. Brag, brag, brag. It's all you do."

"All?" He kissed her. Caught her soft lip between his teeth and felt her smile.

Just that easily Garrett wanted her. He put his hands on her hips and bodily lifted her until she faced him, then he lowered her once again onto his lap. His swivel chair rocked precariously.

Her eyes widened. "Garrett! It's the middle of the afternoon."

"So? We've got time." He yanked her skinny little pink top out of her shorts and pushed his hands beneath. He liked the fact that she was starting to wear some colors, almost as much as he liked the way they fit her sweet, sexy body. "You don't have to pick up the minis from Smiling Faces for another half hour."

"Hour," she corrected breathlessly.

He smiled slowly and pulled her shirt over her head, tossing it carelessly onto the desktop. "Even better."

"One might think that you wanted—oh, my."

When had he ever thought her too bony for his tastes? She was perfect. Nothing went to waste on her slender body. Her coral-tipped breasts fitted his palms as if they'd been made for him. And they tasted... perfect. He lifted his head, catching the look on her face. Heavy lidded, her eyes glowed like little blue flames. "What were you saying?"

"Huh?" She blinked. Made a face at him, then somehow managed to move her legs on either side of him in the chair so that he felt as if the back of his head would blow right out. "Something wrong?" Her sexy voice was as innocent as he'd ever heard it.

He closed his hands around her hips, but she still managed to rock against him. "You're a witchy sprite."

Her lashes lowered and the tip of her tongue slowly ran along the edge of her pearly teeth. "What I was going to say, before you so…rudely…interrupted me, was that one might think you have ulterior motives for wanting the kids to start going to Smiling Faces again for a few hours each week."

"It was your idea," he reminded. "I just went along with it." He rubbed his thumb over her nipple and watched her eyes glaze.

Her throat worked, and she dug her fingertips into his shoulders. "It's good for Regan and…and Reid to, uh, be with other children their—" she groaned breathlessly "—ages. And the triplets are—"

He knew all the reasons she'd worked so hard at getting Regan and Reid to willingly return to Smiling Faces. Dealing with separation anxiety was only part. She was getting the kids prepared for when she was no longer their nanny. He understood what she was doing, but it didn't mean he had to like it. And even though he hadn't pushed the marriage thing lately, it didn't mean that he'd given up the notion.

He was incapable of love, but that didn't mean he wanted Elise's children to grow up without it the way he had. If Darby was his wife, he could make sure that didn't happen.

All good and fine thoughts, none of which were paramount in his mind at that moment. "I don't know what it is about you," he muttered, sweeping his arm across his desk to clear the surface. Half a dozen file folders and their contents tumbled to the floor in a shower of white and manila. "All the women I've known, and you're the only one who can make me forget everything but this." He tumbled her back onto the desktop, cradling her head with his hands.

She stared up at him, her mouth parted. She tugged impatiently at his shirt. "Have there been many?"

He straightened enough to tear open the buttons, then slid his arm beneath her, pulling her flat against his chest, skin to skin. *Oh, yeah. That's it.* "Many what?"

"Women," she laughed breathlessly.

"Enough," he said truthfully. "Dammit, where is the zipper on these shorts!" They looked like a little skirt from the front, and from the back they'd driven him nuts with the way the pink garment hugged her rear.

She twisted a little, pulling his hand to the fastening, hidden beneath the skirt flap in the front. He loosened his grip on her, a little regretfully, to yank it down, dashing her clothes away.

"What were they like?"

"You're lying naked on my desk and you want to know what my 'other women' were like?"

"Yes," she said primly. Then ruined the effect by sliding her sleek knee slowly along his side.

"To a one, they were tall, stacked, long-haired blondes." He caught her knee, lowered his head and kissed the curve of it. Thoroughly enjoying the broad daylight filling every corner of the house, thoroughly enjoying the fact that they had nearly an hour all to themselves.

Not that the shower they'd taken together in the middle of the night last night had been at all unsatisfactory. Or the other times he'd managed to get her behind a closed door during nap time. Or the—

"Ah-ha. Just like Beth."

"Who?" Garrett mumbled as his mouth moved against her taut thigh.

Darby laughed softly and tugged him over her, fingers fumbling with his straining fly. "Come here. We're wasting valuable time with this infernal chatter of yours."

Three hours later Darby was glad that she'd decided to leave the triplets at Smiling Faces as she took Regan and Reid to the park where the Summer's End Festival was being held. Not that it felt like the end of summer was nearing, considering how hot and humid it was outside. She knew the babies would have been miserable in the heat.

Regan and Reid had already ridden every one of the kiddie rides. Twice, with no regard for the sweltering afternoon. They'd also tossed pennies into glass dishes, bean bags through holes cut into an enormous smiley face and whipped-cream pies at a giggling, red-nosed clown.

Now the snow cones she'd purchased for Regan and Reid were dribbling over the edges of the white paper holders, leaving sticky blue and red stains on their hands, their faces and their clothes. But their smiles were wide and carefree and two pairs of brown eyes gleamed with excitement.

Darby couldn't wait to tell Garrett what a good time he'd missed.

"I wanna go on that!" Regan pointed.

She swallowed a jolt of dismay. "The Ferris wheel?" She hated the Ferris wheel.

"Me, too. Me, too." Reid jumped up and down.

Darby looked around. "How about the boats over there? They look fun, don't they?" And since they were contained in a man-made pool, they didn't rise above the ground more than five feet.

Regan's expression fell. Her eyebrows drew together, but rather than stomping her feet and demanding, she looked up at Darby. "Please?"

Ohh. Darby's shoulders sagged. She looked from Regan and Reid to the Ferris wheel and back again. She just couldn't do it. As much as she didn't want to disappoint them, there was no way on this earth that she could make herself climb into one of those swinging buckets and lift off from the ground. No way.

"I'm sorry, sugar-pie. But I don't think so." She sighed and looked around. "Let's go sit on that bench for a few minutes and decide what to do instead. Okay?"

Regan made a face, but she took Reid's snow-cone-sticky hand in hers and sat. "Regan, I'd take you on the Ferris wheel if I could," she said gently. "But I—I'm afraid of heights. And I can't let you two go on it alone."

"My mommy was 'fraid of being by herself. She

yelled at my daddy 'cause she was 'fraid. Are you gonna yell now?"

Darby brushed Regan's hair away from her forehead and cupped her round cheek. Poor Elise. She and Marc would never be alone now. "No, sugar-pie. I'm not going to yell."

"Perhaps I could be of assistance."

Darby frowned and craned her neck around, looking behind them at the voice.

"Grampy!" Regan squealed and climbed over the back of the bench, dropping her icy treat onto the ground as she launched herself into Caldwell's arms. Reid was only a second behind, and Darby just stared, not knowing quite what to do.

"I'll take them on the Ferris wheel," the mayor offered. If it bothered him that Reid's snow cone was smashed up against his designer polo shirt, he didn't let on.

"Mayor Carson, I really don't—"

"Please."

It didn't look as if the word sat easily on him. But his green-brown eyes were steady on hers, and Regan was nodding enthusiastically.

If Garrett were there, she knew he would flatly refuse. Torn, she chewed the inside of her lip.

"You can sit right there on the bench and watch us the entire time." His lips twisted, and in that moment he looked so much like Garrett that she felt herself softening.

"All right," she agreed reluctantly, and was rewarded

by Regan's yippee. "One ride," she added as she took Reid's melting snow cone from him.

She handed their remaining tickets to Caldwell and sat down again to watch. The mayor set the children on their feet and they held both his hands as they walked over to the small line at the wheel. Within minutes they were sitting in one of the buckets and Darby couldn't help but smile as Regan and Reid waved to her. She waved back.

Up they went on the Ferris wheel. Until they seemed to be tiny dots against the sky. If it were she up there at the peak of the wheel, she would be as panicked as she'd been on that overcrowded elevator at the courthouse.

The wheel began turning again, stopping occasionally. As their bucket lowered, Darby could see the excited expressions on the children's faces. She could also see the completely devoted expression on their grandfather's face.

Sighing a little, she sat back against the bench and watched while the wheel went around and around. Then the children were racing pell-mell toward Darby, chattering a mile a minute.

Caldwell followed more slowly and stopped several feet away from Darby. His eyes lingered on the children, but he seemed to realize that her allowances could only go so far. "Garrett was right when he said I owed you an apology. I was distraught and I was unkind to you. It was uncalled for."

Darby gathered her wits. Caldwell's son hated being his son. And yes, Caldwell had insulted her that day at the courthouse, but what she'd done was so, so much worse. "Losing your daughter has been a terrible tragedy."

"A tragedy," he repeated, his expression pained. "Yes, it was that." He was silent for a moment and the festive sounds of the carnival surrounded them. "I'm fighting Garrett the only way I can," he said suddenly, startling her even more. "I know, given the chance, he will remove them from my life as completely as he's removed himself."

She was totally, utterly, out of her depth. "Mayor Carson, I think Garrett is the one you need to say this to. Not me."

"He's out to ruin the company that has been in my family for generations. He isn't interested in what I say." His smile was thin, his eyes unreadable. "You're his fiancée. I'm sure he's told you what a failure I was as a father."

A group of women dressed in business suits strolled by eating cotton candy. They called out to the mayor with a wave. He waved back, smiling, greeting them all by name. Then he turned back to Darby and his smooth mayoral smile faded. "Fact is, a lot of us failed Garrett, and to my…shame, I let it happen. But he's made a success of himself despite us." There was a touch of pride in his face at that.

Darby shifted on the bench, beyond discomfort with this entire dialogue. "Mayor…" She didn't know what to say to him. And his expression seemed to indicate that he understood.

He crouched down and held out his arms to hug

Regan and Reid. Over their heads he looked at Darby. He glanced back at the Ferris wheel. "Thank you."

She managed a smile. Then felt something sad tear inside her when she heard Regan's soft voice.

"I love you, Grampy," the little girl said.

Caldwell's eyes closed. "I love you, too." Then he cleared his throat, straightened to his feet and walked away.

He didn't look back.

After that the children seemed subdued. They didn't protest when Darby suggested they head to the truck. She strapped everyone in and drove carefully to Smiling Faces for the babies and then home in Garrett's new truck. Her poor green car was still sitting at the curb, deader than a doornail. Garrett wanted to have it towed for scrap, but so far she'd refused to let him arrange it.

Before long, she knew she'd need the car again.

But she didn't want to dwell on that depressing thought, and she took the sticky children inside the house.

It was definitely time for baths.

Maybe while she was washing them up, she could wash away the memory of Caldwell's face when he'd walked away from his grandchildren.

"My mother used to make meat loaf like this," Garrett said.

Darby's fork halted midway to her mouth. She contained her surprise that Garrett had voluntarily mentioned his mother. It had seemed to be one of those off-limit topics. "It's the recipe from the box of rolled oats. Probably been printed on it for years."

"Probably." He reached out and pushed Reid's glass away from the edge of the table in a move so automatic that Darby wanted to smile.

"So did you have fun today?" he asked. His words were directed at the children, but his gaze focused on Darby, sending another message entirely.

She felt her cheeks warm, and quickly rose, beginning to clear the dishes as Regan and Reid chattered about the rides. The cotton candy. The snow cones. She'd promised herself that she would tell Garrett about running into the mayor. After dinner. When the children were settled so they wouldn't have to witness the explosion.

She knew she was taking a chance. But so far, neither Regan nor Reid had mentioned their grandfather. It was cowardly, she knew, but their dinner together had been so pleasant that she'd kept putting off the inevitable.

She began loading the dishwasher and turned back to the table only to find Garrett handing her the last remaining stack of plates. She stuck them in the sink to rinse them.

"I had a fun and exciting day, too, today," he murmured over her shoulder and she accidentally squirted the counter with the sprayer.

"How could inking the deal with Nielson Farms be anything less?" She leaned over to put the plates in the dishwasher, and Garrett's arm sneaked around her waist, lifting her right off her feet.

She gasped and wriggled her legs, but he held her high. "Garrett!"

Regan and Reid goggled. Tad and Keely squished their cooked carrots under their fingers, and Bridget's round little face split into an enormous yawn.

It was so wonderful that she fell a little bit more in love with them all. With one in particular.

"Did you or did you not have fun today?" Garrett demanded, mock fierce, against her ear.

She giggled and covered her mouth with her hand, unable to believe such a silly sound had come from her.

"Well?" His eyes crinkled. "I need to know. You know. For future planning and all."

She threw her arms around his shoulders and nodded, giggling some more. "I think going to the carnival should be an everyday affair."

"Are you gonna get babies in your tummy like my mommy?" Regan's voice broke over their silliness.

Darby's mouth parted. She caught Garrett's look. He set her on her feet, and she tugged her shirt firmly about her hips. "Why would you ask that?"

Regan watched her, seeming way too old for a four-year-old. "Daddy kissed Mommy in the kitchen, and she got the babies in her tummy," she said seriously. "Are you?"

Darby shook her head. "No, sweetheart. Not anytime soon." Aside from that first time at Georgie's... and earlier that afternoon in Garrett's den, they'd taken precautions. The last thing they needed was to increase the ratio of children to adults here. Knowing the truth of that, however, didn't keep her from a lingering, torturing vision of having a baby. Garrett's baby.

"How come?" Regan persisted.

Darby stared at Garrett, silently asking for assistance. He shrugged his shoulders. Then, when the doorbell rang, startling them both, he grinned, unashamedly relieved. "Saved by the bell," he murmured, and went to answer the door.

"Because we're not married," Darby answered Regan hurriedly. She started cleaning up the high-chair trays. The children were obviously only interested in playing with their food. "Now, let's get you guys into your pj's and I'll read you a story before bed."

Since Regan and Reid both loved their nighttime stories, they hurried out of the kitchen. Darby quickly wiped up the triplets' hands and faces, then set them on the floor. They crawled like fury for the living room and their favorite toys.

She reached for the dishcloth to wipe down the table and heard Regan's and Reid's delighted squeals. She started to smile, but stopped when she heard Regan's voice.

"Grampy!"

She clenched the wet dishcloth. Knowing she couldn't hide out in the kitchen, she walked out into the living room, taking in the tableau at a glance.

Garrett, standing in the doorway, stiff as a statue.

Caldwell, carrying a large cardboard box under one arm while his free hand tousled Regan's blond curls.

Regan, who chattered happily about riding the Ferris wheel that afternoon with her beloved Grampy.

Garrett cast her one long look. A look totally devoid of amusement. Of laughter. Of trust.

She sighed and reached for Keely before the tot could climb into the fireplace again. So much for putting off the explosion. She should have told him what had occurred that day as soon as he'd walked in the door.

She saw Caldwell look from his son to her and back again. "These are some things of Elise and Marc's that I thought you should have," he said after a tense moment. "The new owners are moving into their house soon." He pushed the box toward Garrett, who didn't make any attempt to take it from the older man.

Darby's stomach tightened. A more stubborn person she'd never met.

Finally Caldwell just set the box on the floor inside the door. "Well. Good night."

"Can Grampy read us our story?"

Garrett shook his head, his eyes flat.

"Please, Uncle Garrett?"

Darby held her breath.

Then Garrett muttered something unprintable and strode through the living room, into the kitchen and out the back door.

"I guess that's a no," Caldwell murmured, after the screen door slapped shut.

"No," Darby corrected softly. She knew if Garrett had wanted to say no he would have, and that would have been that. He never would have just walked away from the situation. She stared through the kitchen at the closed screen door. "I don't believe that was his answer, at all." And it made her realize, just then, how well she was coming to know this man who'd captured her heart.

Chapter Fifteen

"He's gone?"

Darby didn't need to ask who Garrett meant. She nodded and, since he hadn't frozen her out with a cold look when she'd tentatively stuck her head outside the back door, pushed the screen door wider and walked out onto the porch.

"Is there anything else you did today that you haven't told me about?" He was sitting on the wood-and-wrought-iron bench, one boot propped against the railing opposite him. Even his voice was deceptively smooth. But the rhythmic ticking in his jaw betrayed him.

She shook her head, feeling a bit the way she had the first time she'd told her father that yes, she was still going to nursing school even though he'd promised to cut her off financially if she did. And because she felt that way, her spine stiffened.

"The carnival was in a public park, Garrett. What was I supposed to do? Grab up the children and run screaming for the car as if he's some monster? I'm sorry I didn't tell you right away. All he did was take Regan and Reid on the Ferris wheel, and all three of them loved it."

He didn't answer. His eyes were flat. "I don't want him around them."

Impatience swept through her. "Why not? Garrett, he loves them. Surely even you can see that."

"He's not capable of love. No more than I am."

"Why?" She wrapped her fingers around the metal railing. "Because he never acknowledged you as his son?"

"Because he took my mother's heart and stomped it into the dust," he said unemotionally. "Her family had always worked for the Carsons. When she was sixteen she became a maid there herself. Working before and after school. Even after I was born she stayed on. And after she banished me to New Mexico, she still worked there. And Caldwell, he just…let it continue."

She frowned. It did sound odd to her, but not enough to explain Garrett's deep distrust. "I still don't understand."

"Yeah, well, you don't have to understand," he said flatly. "It's none of your business."

She jerked back. He was right, of course. It wasn't her business. But—

"Wait a minute! You asked me to marry you! Said I would be their…their *mother.* And it is 'none of my business'?"

His eyebrow peaked. "Are you finally accepting my proposal, then?"

"And what? If I say yes, you'll let me in on the big secret about your father, and if I say no, I'll just have to be content with my curiosity?" She stared at him. Loving him. Hating him. Hating herself. Because he'd offered her nearly everything she'd ever wanted in life, and she had no hope of accepting it.

It was probably just as well that he hadn't offered her his heart.

Garrett's jaw was white with tension. "My mother worked there until she got into Caldwell's wife's medicine chest and swallowed too many of her tranquilizers. And Caldwell didn't even trouble himself to attend her funeral. *Now* do you get it?"

She pressed her hand to her heart, horrified. "Oh, Garrett. I'm sorry. I didn't know."

"Nobody knew," he said flatly. "Except Caldwell… and Elise. I came back from New Mexico for the funeral, and Elise couldn't wait to tell me."

"How old were you?"

"Eighteen."

She swallowed and folded her hands together. If only she could hate him. Then when she had to walk away it wouldn't feel so much like dying.

But his mother, it seemed, had been as responsible for Garrett's unhappiness as Caldwell had been, and Darby had to make him see reason about the children. "You're their legal guardian, Garrett. I know the mayor says he wants guardianship himself, but I think it's more knee-jerk than anything. It's not as if he's going to kidnap them or something from you. You can't pretend he's *not* their grandfather just because you pretend he's not your father. The children lost their parents. Don't make them lose the rest of their family, as well."

She watched him. Waited painfully for him to say something. He just sat there like a stone, watching her back. And the last little bit of hope inside her, the wishful kernel that wanted to believe there was some miraculous way that everything could work out, shriveled.

They really didn't know each other at all. Despite everything. And she was even more guilty of that fact than he was.

"You're right," she said stiffly. "It is none of my business. I am only the nanny. The temporary nanny." She turned on her heel and yanked open the screen door.

"Darby."

Just that. Her name. And her feet stopped. She looked at the screen, knowing she should leave before things got even worse, but unable to take…one… more…step. "What?"

"When I told you that Karl had phoned. About Georgie going into the hospital. Do you remember your first thought?"

Her throat tightened and she let the screen door close again.

"Your father," he reminded evenly. "You thought something had happened to your father. Even before thinking of Georgie, regardless of this feud you've got going between you and your family, you thought of your father."

"Your point?" she asked tightly.

Garrett looked at Darby. Explaining didn't come easy for him. But he knew if he didn't, he could write off his chances. With her. With the kids. He might as well give up and let the old man have the fearsome five, because without someone in their lives so filled with loving the way Darby was, his nieces and nephews were no better off with him than they would be with Caldwell.

But he would never give up. Not on this.

So he had to make her understand.

"There must have been some point in your life, growing up, when you knew who you were." She seemed to pale, and he stifled an oath, pushing impatiently to his feet to move down the steps to the grassy yard. He understood a lot more about her than she thought he did, if she would only open up and let him in on her own share of secrets and the past she was running from. "You had a home...with your parents—at least until they divorced. And with your brother. I didn't."

"Lots of people grow up in single-parent families."

"I grew up with a father who acted as if I didn't exist and a mother who put everything aside, including me, in favor of *him*. It didn't matter that the guy was married. Not to him. Not to her. Twisted, if you ask me. I never did know why she even chose to have me, much less keep me."

He smiled grimly. "And then there was Elise. My half sister. Pretty, blond-haired, brown-eyed Elise. She was a year younger than me. We went to the same school. She had everything. Caldwell. Her mom. My mom."

"Garrett—"

"Don't. Don't look at me with pity in your eyes. It was a long time ago, but you might as well understand why things are the way they are."

She sat down on the step, clasping her knees close with her slender arms.

"It wasn't until I was ten that I really started to grasp

it. I was in a lot of sports. Baseball. Soccer. Basketball. Whatever season it was, I was in the after-school program. I liked it. Better to be there than go home to an empty house."

He closed his eyes for a minute. Remembering that house. It hadn't been a hovel by any means. Caldwell wouldn't have allowed that. It had been comfortable and well furnished, but it had still been empty. Empty because his mother was always at Caldwell's stone mansion.

He dragged his thoughts back in line. "Anyway, at the end of the baseball season, the coach had a party. Where the trophies are handed out. You know. Most improved player. Stuff like that."

He shoved his fingers through his hair and laughed grimly. "It's been a long time since I even thought about this," he admitted.

"What happened?"

"All the parents were there. Except mine."

"You mean Caldwell."

"I mean my mother," he corrected flatly. "She'd chosen to be at Elise's birthday party, instead. The coach finally gave me a ride home from the pizza place where the party was held when it became apparent that nobody was coming to get me."

"Oh, Garrett."

"Elise made sure that everyone at school knew that my own mother preferred to cut cake and wash dishes at her birthday party than to see me get my stupid trophy for most valuable player. I wouldn't even care so much about that except the only fun Elise seemed to get out of it wasn't her birthday party, with the fifty guests and the pony rides and the clowns, but getting to rub my nose in what she had that I didn't."

Darby rose, silently walking over to him. She folded his hands in hers.

"She was a spoiled brat, and even with the attention of her parents and my mother, she was no happier with her life than I was with mine."

"What happened to Elise's mother?"

He looked at their hands. His looked big and clumsy and brown against her ivory ones. "She went back to England. That's where she was from." His lips twisted. "Came from some rich family over there with titles and God knows what. Elise stayed here in Fisher Falls until Caldwell bought her way into college. As far as I know her mom never divorced Caldwell."

"Then the children *do* have more relatives."

Garrett shook his head. "Hayden did a thorough search. Marc grew up in an orphanage. Elise's mother died several years ago. There's only me. And Caldwell. And I'll be damned if I'll let him do to them what he did to us."

"So you'll ostracize him from the children's lives, instead. Just the way you felt ostracized yourself. When your new office is up and running here in Fisher Falls and the judge gives his final ruling in a few weeks, you'll take them away and never give him an opportunity to see them again." Just as the mayor feared.

"Don't make it sound as if it's some cruel thing. They'll survive. They'll thrive, thanks to you."

Darby looked into his face. "They would thrive, thanks to you, if you let yourself."

"Dammit, Darby, I don't love them. I never will. I don't have it in me. I'll make sure they have everything they need in life, but I can't give them love. I can't give *anybody* that. I wanted them only because I knew it would make the old man crazy."

He really believed it, and her heart broke for all of them. For the boy he'd been, standing on the outside looking in. For the man he was, hard and driven and unwilling to acknowledge his own needs. "I think you're wrong. I think you're infinitely capable of loving."

"Why? Because you and I have great sex?"

She flinched at his harsh demand. "Whether you admit it or not, you have a great deal of compassion. Tenderness. And not just in bed with me."

She swallowed past the gargantuan knot in her throat. "What will you do if the judge doesn't award you permanent custody? It could happen, you know. Or if you do get it, Caldwell could petition for visitation rights. Grandparents have been doing that, and succeeding. What are you going to do then?"

"Then I'll take Caldwell back to court until I *do* win. The only reason I brought G&G to Fisher Falls was because I knew we could put Castle Construction out of business for good. My resources will outlast Caldwell's. And in the end, I *will* win." There was no doubt in his expression. "I always do."

"And the children will grow up being at the center of this war between you and their grandfather, all so that you can sleep at night, knowing you have finally *won* this little—" she turned away from him, waving her hands impatiently "—revengefest against your father."

"They'll live."

"Like I lived." What could she do to make him see the awfulness of his reasoning? "From the time I was nine until I turned thirteen, my parents waged a war against each other for custody of my brother and me. They dragged up every possible, hideous thing they could throw at each other, whether it was true or not.

"And they did it thinking that none of it would affect Dane or me. But they were wrong. Newspapers, friends, television. Everywhere we turned, there it was. The great battle for the—"

Dear God. She'd almost said it. For the Rutherford kids. The heirs to a transportation empire.

"For the what?"

She realized her cheeks were wet. "For the two of us." She turned away from him, wiping away the tears.

The evening had darkened. Crickets chirped to life. The outside light next door flicked on, casting half its glow into Garrett's yard.

"And when you were engaged to the joker, you thought you'd have a life that erased the past."

She didn't deny it. But she'd come to realize that it wasn't losing Bryan that had hurt so badly, but losing the dream of a perfect life where divorce had no place. Where custody battles didn't exist.

"I don't know why Elise said what she did," he admitted. "But maybe she'd realized the same things I had. And she—hell, I don't know—gambled that I was a better bet than our old man. Marry me, Darby." His voice was low. "Come back to New Mexico with me. You'll have the children."

"But none of us will have your love." And she knew she wanted it. With every fiber of her soul, she wanted Garrett's love. She wanted it all. She wanted to know that his nieces and nephews had his love.

Even *want* wasn't the right word.

She *needed* it. For herself. For the children. But most of all, for him. She looked back at him, waiting for a response.

He said nothing. And that was answer enough.

She was caught so thoroughly in a web of her own making that she honestly didn't know which way to turn.

She couldn't tell him that she didn't want to marry him, because she did. She wanted to make a life with him and the children. She couldn't bear the idea of leaving them.

But she couldn't marry him without telling him the whole truth about herself. And once he knew who she was, he wouldn't want to marry her, anyway. He wouldn't want her anywhere near the children. Because her presence in Fisher Falls had brought more harm to their family than anything Caldwell or Garrett could ever do.

"What are you thinking?"

She folded her arms around herself, chilled. "That no matter what we try to do, life is never cookie-cutter perfect."

"Did you think it would be?"

The ache inside her went too deep for tears. "I kept

hoping." And in her search she'd only made things worse.

"I guess that was a lesson I learned a lot younger than you. The only person we can count on is ourselves, and happily ever after exists only in books."

"I don't want to believe that, Garrett." She drew in a long breath. Let it out slowly. "I love you."

"You love everyone. I've seen it. In everyone you meet you find something about them to care about."

"I'm not talking about caring. About one human relating the best way they can to another, which you know very well *you* are more than capable of. For heaven's sake, Garrett. Carmel and Hayden are loyal to you to a fault. Do you think that is only because you pay them for it? It's because of the caring among you."

He so easily discounted her profession of love, but she wouldn't let it hurt her. Not yet. There would be plenty of time for that.

The rest of her life.

"I'm talking about *love*." She stressed the word. "I love you. Maybe you think that doesn't exist, but I'm telling you that it does."

"Just because your first time was in that sunroom at Georgie's house with the falls running outside doesn't mean the legend has come true."

She'd been wrong. The ache wasn't too deep for tears. She looked at him in the half-light, her vision glazed. "This isn't about a silly legend. It's about what's in my heart. And one day, oh, God, one day I pray that you let someone get past the walls you've built around your heart. That you let yourself love someone back. Because in the end it doesn't matter how perfect the cookie was. How much money you have in the bank, how many houses you've built or how many reporters you've managed to elude. The only thing that matters is love. Love between a parent and a child. Love between a man and a woman."

"I didn't say that I think love doesn't exist."

"No," she agreed softly as she turned to go back into the house. "You think you can stand back from it and let other people feel it. But until you step forward, and get right in the muck of all those emotions, it won't matter how tidily you provide a caring parental figure for those children or how much you provide for their physical needs. They'll still grow up looking at you and wondering what they've done wrong that you don't love them back."

"Daaaarby!"

Garrett sat on the lumpy sofa in the living room and heard soft footsteps overhead. Darby. Going to Reid again. It had been weeks since the boy had wakened like that. He'd actually begun to hope that the restless sleeping episodes might be over. That Darby's steady attention to the kids was having its effect.

Reid was still crying, and Garrett stood up, heading to the stairs. His bare toe painfully jammed the box that Caldwell had left by the door, and he swore under his breath, shoving it out of his way. Damn Caldwell, anyway.

He went up the stairs, stuck his head in the second bedroom. He could see Darby sitting on Reid's bed in the dark, holding him in her lap. He could hear her humming softly. And then he heard something else. Reid humming, too.

He cupped his hand around the doorjamb and stood outside the doorway, looking in.

Where he'd always been.

I love you, she'd said.

Darby could say whatever she wanted. Believe what she needed to believe. But no one had ever loved him before, and he couldn't let himself fall into the trap of thinking that she really did. Because as soon as he did, she'd come to her senses and go back to the life she'd been running from. The life she didn't feel she could fully share with him, despite her pretty words of love.

"Garrett?"

He realized that Darby was looking at him from within the darkness of the room.

His jaw ached. He consciously relaxed. "Yeah. I wanted to make sure Reid was okay."

She stood up from the bed, walked soundlessly toward him. God. She was such a bitty thing.

"He's asleep." She stayed inside the room, leaving a few good feet between them.

"He called your name this time. In his sleep he cried for you."

She made a soft sound. "Yes."

"You're crying," he realized. He reached for her,

pulling her out into the hallway. Her robe swished, revealing her bare toes. "Because of Reid?"

"Because of us all." She wiped her cheeks. "I can't do this anymore, Garrett. It's wrong. You don't know—"

"Do what? Go to a crying kid at two in the morning?"

"No. Yes." She pushed her hands through her hair, turning away from him. "All of it."

His gut ached. "Well. That didn't take long. Six, seven hours, to come to your senses." I love you. What a damn joke.

"What?"

He pushed his hands into the pockets of his jeans, because if he didn't he was going to do something stupid. Like reach for her and tell her anything so long as she didn't take back her love and go away. It was better that he put the distance between them.

"I'll be gone early in the morning," he told her abruptly. "We're checking out some property in Colorado."

"But it's Satur—"

"We have to move fast on it. If words get out, they'll jack the price up."

"You, um, didn't mention a trip before."

"It didn't come up."

"How long are you going to be gone?"

He shrugged. "Day and a half, maybe."

"I...see," she said faintly. But he knew she didn't.

"Carmel will know how to reach me if you need anything."

"I'm sure we'll be fine."

He nodded, thinking that she should have added *without you*. But even if she'd come to her senses about loving him, it just wasn't in Darby's nature to be so cold.

No matter how true the words would have been.

Chapter Sixteen

"Stubborn…pigheaded man. Can't see beyond the nose on his stubborn, handsome face."

In the weeks since Darby had moved in with Garrett and his crew, she'd gotten into the habit of mopping the tile floors on Saturday mornings. Just because her life was falling apart around her ears didn't mean the floors didn't need a good cleaning.

Now her nose ran and her eyes watered. From the smell of the floor cleaner she'd dumped into the water, she assured herself. That's the only thing it could be, because she was tired of crying over that big…dumb… man.

"I see he's got you swabbing the decks now."

She nearly jumped out of her skin at the voice behind her and turned to see Hayden Southerland outside the front screen door. Her in-the-cellar stomach took an even deeper nosedive.

She stuck the mop in the bucket and moved to the door, flipping loose the latch. "Hayden. I figured you would be with Garrett."

"He's not here?"

"No." Twenty floors underground. That's where her stomach was now. "He went to Colorado," she said, feeling awkward. Stupid. She knew that Garrett unfailingly included Hayden in his business plans. "He said he was looking at a property there."

"Right. Of course." Hayden was nothing if not smooth. He tapped the manila envelope he held against his palm. "I didn't really need him, anyway. I can give these to you just as easily." He handed her the envelope.

"What is it?"

"The prenup. You guys just read it through, make sure everything is covered the way you want, and if it is, sign whenever you like." He smiled faintly. "As long as it's before the wedding. Speaking of which, have you set a date yet?"

"Ah, no. No. Not yet." She stared at the envelope.

"It'll be a big event when you do."

"Why?"

He laughed. "Because as long as I've known Garrett, he's been anti-marriage. Guess it took a petite redhead to change his mind after all those tall blondes."

Not exactly. What it had taken was five orphaned children. She was only a by-product, as far as Garrett was concerned. "I'll pass these on to Garrett." She made herself smile casually. "Thanks for bringing them by."

"Sure." He started to leave, but paused. "You know, I still can't help thinking we've met before. Where did you say you came from?"

She hadn't. Which he knew perfectly well. But he was Garrett's attorney and his friend, and she couldn't blame the man for being naturally curious. "I think I'd remember meeting a man like you." Her smile was polished, her delivery smooth. And as insincere as anything she'd said in weeks. Months.

The corner of his lips lifted, and she knew he hadn't been fooled for a second. "Well. Have Garrett give me a call when you see him."

"Will do." She kept her smile in place until Hayden climbed in his low-slung black car and roared off down the street. Then she latched the screen door again and slapped the envelope down on Caldwell's cardboard box that she'd stuck on the stairs so it wouldn't get wet when she mopped the foyer. But when she did, she knocked the box off the edge and it tumbled on its side, dumping the contents out onto the damp floor.

"Oh, sure. Make more of a mess." She crouched down and righted the box, reaching for the items that had fallen from it. Several children's books. A blanket. A jewelry box.

She shifted until she was sitting on a step and flipped open the small pink-and-white box. The little ballerina inside spun, the music tinkling merrily.

"What's that?"

Darby looked up and drew Regan next to her. She touched the strands of brightly colored beads inside the box. "These were your mother's," she told Regan gently. "Your grandpa brought them over for you to have."

The little girl chewed her lip for a minute, then stuck her fingers where Darby's had been. She drew out a pink-and-white beaded necklace. "Can I wear it?"

"Yes." Darby undid the little clasp and fastened it around Regan's neck.

"Am I pretty as my mommy?"

Darby smiled shakily. She started to speak, but someone beat her to it.

"Prettier," Garrett said from the doorway. He pulled open the screen and stepped inside the house.

Darby could only stare at him. "Fast trip to Colorado."

"Plans changed." His smile wasn't much of one, but it wasn't a snarl, either. And when he looked at Regan, preening with her pretty, little-girl necklace, his expression gentled. "What have you got there?"

She took the jewelry box from Darby's numb fingers and held it up. "See? Do I get to keep it all?"

"Looks like."

Regan whooped. She started to run back to the kitchen, but turned around and trotted back. "Does Reid and the babies got any presents, too?"

Garrett looked at the tumbled things on the floor. "I don't know. Probably. Let's look."

Darby scooted up a few steps, quickly giving Garrett a place to sit, drawing her legs close. Then she watched as Garrett, Mr. I'll-provide-for-them-but-never-love-them reached for the books she'd already put back in the box.

He held them out for Regan. "More bedtime stories for you guys."

Regan plopped down on the tile and set the books in her lap. "What else?" Her eyes danced. She reached for a thick album lying facedown, and Garrett helped her pick it up.

"It's a scrapbook." He flipped through several pages. "Report cards from school. Some old pictures and stuff. Look. That was your mommy when she was just a little older than you."

Darby looked over Garrett's shoulder to see him pointing at a school class picture.

Regan peered. "She was little."

"Yes, she was," Garrett murmured.

"Was you bestest friends with her like me 'n Reid?"

Darby saw Garrett's shoulders go still. "Not quite like you and Reid," he said after a moment. "Look. This must've been her baby blanket." He plucked the soft-blue receiving blanket out of the box and flicked it open over Regan's crossed legs, making her giggle.

"What's this?" Regan pointed to the corner.

"Initials. Should be your mo—"

Darby sat forward when Garrett's words cut off. "G. C. C.," she read softly.

Garrett suddenly stood. He grabbed up the manila envelope that had his name printed on the outside. "What's this?"

"Papers from your lawyer."

"Uncle Garrett, can I give the blankie to the babies?"

"Yeah. Sure."

Regan popped to her feet and skipped into the kitchen bearing her assortment of treasures.

"That was your blanket, wasn't it," Darby murmured. "Garrett C. Cullum. *C* for what? Caldwell?"

"Carson." He bit out the word.

She nodded, chewing her lip for a moment. "Saved all these years."

"It's just a blanket," he said tightly. "Stuck in a box

with a bunch of other old junk that doesn't matter to anybody but a bunch of little kids."

"It looked handmade to me," she observed mildly.

"So?"

"So-o-o nothing. Just seems kind of interesting that it's in the stuff from Caldwell. Maybe he wasn't as oblivious to you as you thought." She didn't wait for a reply to that, but jerked her chin toward the sturdy envelope that he'd crumpled in his grip as she stood, also.

"Your attorney is a little behind the times." Her voice was smooth. "He seems to think you and I are getting married."

She descended the few steps and bent down to pick up the rest of the books that had fallen from the box. They weren't children's books, though. They were three lined journals filled by a slanting feminine hand. She held them out to Garrett. "Looks like Elise kept a diary."

He eyed them as if they were serpents. "I don't want 'em."

"Well, your…the mayor must have had some reason for sticking them in here. Maybe Elise wrote about the children or something." She pushed the slender tomes into his free hand. "Maybe you'll find some understanding of her."

"I don't want to read her damned journals."

"Afraid of what you might find?" She regretted the words as soon as she said them. "Oh, Garrett. Whether you read them or not is up to you. But you can't throw them away. The children might want them someday."

"Fine." His tone was clipped. "I won't throw them out."

She considered that quite a concession. She quickly tipped the last few items—an old pocket watch with the engraved name Northrop nearly worn away; a leather folder containing Elise's and Marc's diplomas; a padded case—back into the box and started to fit the lid back on.

"What was in that last case there?"

She removed it again and handed it to Garrett. "I don't know. I didn't look." She took the box and set it inside the door to Garrett's den. When she returned, he was looking at the opened case.

Leaving him to it, she plucked the mop out of the bucket, wrung it out and dashed it over the faint footprints she and Regan had left with their bare feet.

"I thought I made it clear that I didn't expect you to do that sort of thing."

"Who do you think has been keeping the house clean all this time? Fairies?"

"There are cleaning services."

"Maybe I like taking care of a house," she said bluntly.

He laughed shortly. "Come on, Darby. What woman wouldn't want to give up mopping and dusting given the opportunity? Except my mother."

Darby ignored that last bit that he'd tacked on with grim sarcasm and focused on the first part. "One who was never given an opportunity to do it before!" She slammed the mop back into the bucket, making the water slosh. She didn't know where the sudden anger came from. But it was just there.

"You like cleaning a house," he said slowly. Skeptically.

She propped her hands on her hips and looked at him. So strong and intense and capable. So stubborn and deliberately alone, even when he was surrounded by people wanting to love him.

Yes, she did know where her anger came from, and there wasn't one darned thing she could do to correct the situation.

"I like taking care of a home," she corrected tightly. And not just any home, she knew. *His* home. Children or not. "I like feeling needed, and yes, that's something new to me, too."

Her eyes drifted from his face to the padded case in his hand. All the frustration and anger inside her dissolved, leaving her feeling drained. "Those are wedding rings." Two gold bands, one wide and plain, the other studded with a trio of enormous diamonds. "Elise and Marc's."

"Yeah. I remember Elise flashing the thing when we ran into each other at the deli."

Her chest was tight. "I have to tell you something," she whispered.

He squeezed the case shut. "Don't bother. I already know what you're gonna say."

Her lips moved, but no words emerged. Then her throat unlocked enough for a croak. "You...know."

"You don't want to marry me. You don't want to watch the kids anymore. You want to forget about the love you claimed to have for us all, keep on moving, never getting involved, never trusting anything or anybody long enough to even open a goddamned checking account."

She swayed. "You're the one who doesn't get involved."

"I'm involved up to my eyeballs," he said savagely. "I couldn't even get on the flight to Colorado this morning because of you and the kids. Because I didn't want to come back and find that Caldwell had gotten to you, or because you'd decided to cut your losses and run."

"Run?"

"Like you were doing when you came to Fisher Falls. What'd your father do? Beat you?"

She frowned. "Beat? No! No, he didn't beat me. You say you were ignored by your parents. Well, I was suffocated by mine. I met only those whom they wanted me to meet. My friends were chosen for me. My...my *life* was mapped out, planned out, bought and paid for."

Even thinking about her life before she'd escaped made her feel panicky and trapped. She moved past him to the screen door, pushing it open. Where she could feel the morning sun on her face. Where she could breathe the green, open space.

"Even after their divorce and my mother moved away to New York," she whispered, "it was the same whether I was at home or with her. Drivers who had bulges under their jackets because of the weapons they carried. Security systems on the houses. The cars. Bodyguards I wasn't supposed to know about, but I *did,* following me everywhere I went. Finishing school. Nursing school."

She pressed her hands to her eyes, trying in vain to block out the memories. "Do you know what it's like,

Garrett, to have every move you make documented by somebody? By the people who are supposed to be protecting you from harm? By the reporters who want a photo of the poor little rich girl? By the…men who think if they smile pretty enough at you they can convince you you're the love of their life when all they want is a chance at Daddy's millions?"

"Is that what happened with Bryan?"

"No. Bryan Augustine was actually *offered* millions to make me his wife. Only I didn't find out about that until after he'd decided on our wedding day that I wasn't worth the money after all, because he wanted to reconcile with his ex-wife."

Her eyes burned. "All I wanted was to be left alone. To live my life outside of a fishbowl for once, outside of my father's world. I wanted to walk down the street and have someone smile at me just because. I thought I'd been careful enough. I changed my looks. I gave up nursing and lived on what I earned at Smiling Faces. I didn't sign any leases, didn't get any parking tickets, didn't even get a library card, renew my driver's license or join a church."

Her voice was hoarse. "I never meant for anything bad to happen, Garrett. You have to believe me. I'd take it all back if I could. I'd go home and never try to escape again if only I could."

Tears streamed down her cheeks. "But I can't. I can't take back my love for you. I can't bring back Elise and Marc."

"Nobody's asking you to."

"That's because you don't know the truth. It's my fault. All of it."

"What is?"

"The accident," she whispered. "Phil Candela was looking for me. He was my father's head of security."

"At Rutherford Transportation," he murmured. "They're into everything. Shipping. Airlines. Trucking."

"Rail, oil, manufacturing," she added tiredly. She could have gone on. But what was the point? Rutherford Transportation said it all. She drew in a long breath, let it out slowly, wondering why it felt like such a relief to admit it, knowing that it signaled the end of her dreams.

"I didn't mean to love you, Garrett. I'm sorry. I tried so hard not to."

"Darby—"

"My real name is Debra White Rutherford. Darby's the nickname my brother gave me when I was little. And if Phil Candela hadn't been searching for me on behalf of my father, your sister and her husband would still be alive. And so would Phil."

Feeling curiously calm, she walked down the three steps of his front porch.

Garrett handled multimillion-dollar deals every week, but he didn't have one damned clue how to handle this.

Darby was walking across the lawn, her bare feet sinking into the neatly groomed grass. He hadn't mowed it. Which meant that she probably had.

Another thing she'd grown up never having to do.

He strode across the lawn and caught her arms. "Where do you think you're going?"

She shrugged, her eyes glazed. "What does it matter? You can't want me to stay here."

He stifled an oath and steered her off the sidewalk and back onto the grass. "You don't even have on shoes," he muttered.

She strained against him. "Garrett, please. I can't bear this."

"Tough. I'm not letting you go." He pulled her back inside the house, into the den. The kids were still occupied, thankfully. "I saw the magazine, Darby. The one you keep in the drawer upstairs."

She jerked. Went still.

"When Georgie first went into the hospital, before her surgery. I put away some laundry and some of your things were in the load with the kids' stuff. When I put them away in the drawer, I saw the magazine." He grimaced, remembering the jolt it had caused him to see Darby's face staring at him from the glossy pages. Every single unusual thing he'd ever noticed about her had suddenly made so much sense. "I've known who you really were ever since."

She sank down onto the sofa. "And I was worried that Hayden had recognized me, but you've known for days. Why didn't you say something?" she whispered.

"Why didn't you?" He sighed roughly. "Because you've been blaming yourself for the accident," he answered his own question. "Dammit, Darby. It was pretty apparent that you were hiding from something. When I saw the magazine, well, I didn't know what to think, to be honest. It's hard for me to picture you as that... American princess."

"I'm not."

"That's how every article ever printed about you refers to you. But you know how to bake meat loaf, for God's sake."

"I learned how to cook from a woman I met in college," she said dully. "Susan thought it was hilarious that I didn't know how to boil an egg. My father's housekeeper, Marlene, was scandalized every time I ever tried to even enter the kitchen." Her lips twisted. "The only reason Susan was in the same classes as I was, that she...befriended me...was because my father had paid her to be there. I thought she was an older woman who'd decided to go back to college and get a degree. But she was only a bodyguard."

"Bodyguards don't get paid to help another person learn how to cook. Maybe she really did like being your friend. Did that occur to you?"

"After I graduated I never saw her again. That's what I know," Darby said flatly.

"Well, I don't know your father, and he doesn't know me. I'd hoped that you'd tell me, someday, about yourself. But it didn't change anything. Not for me. Heiress or not, you are still the woman who cares the most about my kids."

Her hands were trembling and he sat down beside her, pulling her toward him. "If I'd known you were blaming yourself for the car accident—ah, Darby. It was an *accident*. Don't make it worse by walking away now!"

Darby was trembling so badly she could feel her teeth chattering. "I can't stay. Surely you can understand—"

He gave her a hard, searing kiss, silencing her. "I understand that," he said evenly. "I understand that those kids in the other room need a mother, and dammit, Darby, you *know* you're the best woman for the job."

"You still want me to marry you?"

"I haven't heard anything to make me change my mind," he said flatly.

"But my family—"

"Could buy and sell me a hundred times over."

"Nobody could buy you. But word would get out."

"So? Let it."

"Garrett, you don't know what it's like. If it's not my father thinking he can engineer everyone's lives to suit his purposes, then it's the reporters who regularly camp out, outside my family's home, waiting for a shot of us coming and going. Some don't even wait. They climb fences and disable security cameras in order to get a closer view."

"Is that why you came to Fisher Falls? To get away from the media attention?"

"To get away from that. To get away from my father. He's…impossible, Garrett. He refuses to believe that I am able to live my own life safely." She pressed her fingertips to her throat. "Honestly, Garrett, his worrying over me wasn't healthy for any of us."

"Because of the kidnapping."

Darby looked away. "You really do know."

Garrett sighed. "I remember when it happened. It

was big news, Darby." She'd been only eight or nine. Little. Stolen right out in plain sight, in the confusion of a crowded elevator. The entire country had been outraged. The president himself had promised retribution. And when she'd been found, days later, gagged and bound on the roof of some abandoned warehouse, her photo had been on every magazine and newspaper in the country.

"The kidnapping wasn't even for the ransom," Darby said. "It was a reporter who did it. Alan Michaels. He'd thought he would make a name for himself when he 'rescued' me."

"He was insane."

"Michaels has been institutionalized ever since, but Daddy still considers him a threat to me. He blamed my mother for not keeping me in better sight. It was the start of the end of their marriage."

"And your father has tried to keep you in a protective, gilded cage ever since."

"I didn't want to hurt him, Garrett. But when he made the administrator at the Schute Clinic fire me, I couldn't take it another second."

"Why did he do it? The administrator, I mean."

She shook her head. "I don't know. Not even Georgie, who supports the clinic with enormous bequests, could sway the clinic administrator. And then one of the local papers got word that I'd been dismissed, and speculation took off—everything from having an affair with the sixty-year-old married administrator to stealing drugs from the pharmacy. I couldn't take it anymore. I had to get away."

"Why didn't you correct them? Issue your own statement or something. Hell, you could hire a public relations firm to put out fires like that for you."

"And just have more people telling me what to wear, where to dine, whom to associate with, what to say in public? No, thanks. And what would I say in a statement, anyway? My father had me fired because I finally wanted to move away from home?" She hopped to her feet and paced. "Nobody would believe me. I mean, who lives that way? It's ridiculous! I'm ridiculous!"

"I believe you," he said evenly. "I don't find you ridiculous. I don't give one good damn who your family is. You've proven that you can make a life on your own without them, whether you recognize that fact or not. I still think you should marry me."

"Haven't you listened to anything I've said?"

"Have *you* listened to what I've said? The accident wasn't your fault any more than it was mine. You love my kids and they love you. What else is there to care about?"

"The future," she said huskily. "Love. Even if I thought the day might come when I could hold those children in my arms and *not* feel guilty about the loss of their parents, I can't marry you just to provide a mother for them. I can't stand by and watch you close them off from their grandfather and just keep my mouth shut about it because you disagree. I can't do any of that."

"So what are you going to do?" he asked flatly. "Run away again?"

She flinched. "I told you that I'd help you with the children until you were finished with your business here in town. Unless you are…firing me, that's what I intend to do."

His dark-green gaze bored into her. "All right, then, Darby. You're fired."

Chapter Seventeen

Darby stared at Garrett, shock sweeping through her. On top of everything else, it was just too much. "All right. Fine." She pushed out the words, then turned and ran past the mop and bucket, up the stairs and into the master bedroom.

She slammed the door shut and stood there, shaking like a leaf. He'd fired her.

After all they'd been through, he'd fired her!

She yanked open the drawers beside the bed and shoveled the clothes up in her hands, pushing them haphazardly into the overnighter that she dragged out from beneath the bed where she'd stored it. She opened the minuscule closet and pulled out the red dress she'd worn that unforgettable day and balled it up, adding it to the mess in the soft-sided bag. Shoes. Toiletries. Everything went into the bag with no regard for neatness, no regard for anything but getting the job done as quickly as possible.

She turned back to the small dresser and stared into the drawer at the folded-open magazine. It was the only item left inside the drawer.

She snatched it up, looking at the engagement photo of her and Bryan. For the life of her, she couldn't remember what it was that had attracted her to him. He'd been easygoing, true. And they'd had some fun times together.

But he was nothing like Garrett.

Nobody was like Garrett.

Her eyes burned, and she took the magazine into the bathroom and deliberately dropped it into the small trash container sitting on the floor beside the sink.

Then she shoved her bare feet into her tennis shoes and picked up her bulging overnighter. Going back downstairs took nearly every bit of strength she possessed. Walking past Garrett, who was standing by the couch, his eyes unreadable, took another chunk.

Kissing the children goodbye and not breaking down sapped the rest of her strength.

She turned and went to the entry, staring through the screen door. Her car. It was still sitting at the curb, it's engine deader than a doornail.

Well, she'd walked before, she would walk again.

"You're really going to leave. Just like that. Walk away," Garrett said, coming up behind her.

She stiffened and pushed open the screen. "What's the difference?" she asked painfully. She couldn't look back at Garrett. Not if she wanted to keep from collapsing at his feet and begging for a little more time. "I can do it now, or you can do it in a few weeks after the custody hearing when you'll be free to go back to your home in New Mexico. Either way this ends the same."

She stepped down the three steps, feeling older than her years, and walked away. Past the Suburban that he'd bought brand-new so he'd have a reliable way to transport his fearsome five. Past the second truck he'd bought so she would have something reliable, too.

She headed down the street, moving blindly.

She knew she'd go to the gatehouse. But it no longer seemed the haven it had once been. And running again didn't seem like the answer it had been four months earlier.

Tears blinding her, she reached the corner and started to cross the street, jumping back at the sharp toot of a horn.

She stood there, shaking, aware of a car stopping right there in the middle of the street where she'd nearly walked right under its wheels, and the driver getting out.

"Darby?"

She focused with an effort. "Mayor Carson," she whispered. "What are you doing here?"

His eyebrows drew together. "You're crying."

She brushed her hands across her cheeks.

"Where are you going?" He slid the strap of her suitcase off her shoulder and pushed a clean handkerchief into her hands.

Kindness from Caldwell Carson was the last thing she deserved. She shook her head, unable to speak.

He sighed faintly, then took her arm and pushed her into the front seat of his stately sedan. He rounded the car and climbed behind the wheel. "What's Garrett done now?"

She wiped her eyes. "Nothing. All he's done is love your grandchildren!"

"I know."

"Then why are you trying to take them from him?"

"Why are you walking away from that dinky little house he's rented with a suitcase and tears running down your face?"

"Because I love him and…and it's impossible."

"Love seems to be that way," Caldwell murmured. "Where can I take you?"

"My great-aunt's house. Georgina Vansant's."

Caldwell looked at her. "Georgina is your great-aunt?"

Darby nodded. She looked down the street as the mayor drove away. She watched until her poor green car and Garrett's tidy little house was no longer in sight.

"Roth Rutherford is my father," she admitted dully.

The car jerked a little. "What?"

"I'm Roth Rutherford's daughter, which means you probably also realize that your daughter's accident was my fault," Darby whispered.

"What are you talking about?"

"The other driver was in town because of me. Phil Candela. Because he was looking for me. If I hadn't been hiding out in Fisher Falls from my family, none of this would ever have occurred."

At that Caldwell swerved to the curb and practically stood on the brakes. Darby pitched forward, nearly hitting her head on the dashboard.

Caldwell's arm caught her shoulders and pushed her back against the seat. "You think *you* had something to do with Elise and Marc's accident?"

"I'm so sorry. All I've done by coming to Fisher Falls is hurt people. I never meant any of it to happen."

Caldwell suddenly took off again, his foot heavy on the gas as he drove rapidly through town. Darby twisted her hands together. "Mayor Carson, I—"

"Call me Caldwell, Darby. You're going to be my daughter-in-law, after all."

She frowned and stared at him. "I'm not marrying your son. Surely you can understand how wrong it would be."

"It would be the only right thing in this whole damned mess," he said shortly.

"I don't understand."

His lips tightened. "You will." He turned up the drive next to Georgie's and parked in front of the entrance to an ornate, stone mansion. He climbed out of the car, came around and opened her door, waiting.

A jolt of nervousness penetrated the ache inside her. "Why are we here?"

"To get some things straightened out," he said heavily.

She climbed out of the car warily. Accompanied him through the heavy door and along a cool, shadowy corridor where their footsteps echoed hollowly.

Caldwell turned into a spacious study. The walls that weren't lined with stuffed bookcases were filled with framed photographs. He went to the telephone on the desk and picked it up, dialing quickly. Then he gestured toward the red leather chairs in front of his massive desk, but Darby avoided them. She looked around, thinking that Caldwell's study was very much like her father's, only on a smaller scale. She glanced at the photographs hanging on the wall, stopping over a collection of a teenager wearing a baseball uniform.

It was so obviously Garrett when he'd been young.

She started when she heard Caldwell speak Garrett's name into the phone and turned around to look at him. His phone conversation was short. He dropped the phone back in its cradle. "Garrett is on his way."

Garrett sat in his truck and stared at the lines of the stone mansion sitting on the hill.

Caldwell's mansion.

Coming here had been about as appealing as drinking mud, but when Caldwell had said that Darby was there, he'd known he had no choice.

He blew out a harsh breath and climbed out of the truck, striding up the wide steps to the massive front door. He pushed his finger relentlessly against the buzzer.

He didn't know what Darby was doing here, but he'd collect her and they'd get the hell out of there.

After a long moment the door swung open and Garrett's father stood there. Caldwell looked behind Garrett, as if expecting to see more.

"You didn't think I'd bring the children, did you?" The children were safe and sound at home with Carmel at the helm.

"I'd hoped," Caldwell said stiffly as he pushed the door wider. "But it's probably just as well. At least until we get some things resolved."

"Only thing I want resolved is getting Darby out of here. What did you do, snatch her off the street?"

"Garrett."

He looked past Caldwell to see Darby standing there. He brushed past the older man and closed his hands over her shoulders. "Are you all right?"

"I'm fine."

"What are you doing here?"

"Come into my study," Caldwell said. "And I'll try to explain."

Garrett met Darby's eyes. "Let's just get outta here."

"I think you should stay. Hear him out," she said softly. She held up her hand, and Garrett realized she was holding a framed snapshot. "Look."

He took it from her, and his jaw tightened as he recognized himself.

"There are dozens just like this in his study," she murmured. "Please, Garrett. At least listen to what he has to say. He's making an effort. Can't you?"

He grimaced. "Fine." He wrapped his hand around hers and pulled her along with him as he followed Caldwell into the study. Caldwell started to move behind the wide slab of a desk, but changed direction and sat instead in one of the red leather side chairs situated in the corner of the room.

Garrett looked at the other chairs. He didn't sit.

"You haven't read your sister's diaries," Caldwell said.

"I'm not interested in what she had to say," Garrett said flatly. "What does that have to do with anything?"

"If you'd read them, you would have realized that Elise and Marc were getting a divorce."

Garrett stilled. Darby made a distressed sound.

"She and Marc had been having trouble for years. She wasn't what you would call a...devoted mother." Caldwell looked at Darby. "I have never seen the children as happy as they've been in the weeks since you've been caring for them with Garrett."

Darby's hand tightened around Garrett's.

"I made a lot of mistakes as a father," Caldwell continued. "But I've been a good grandfather. The children have spent a lot of time here with me. Elise...she left them here a great deal. I honestly thought that they belonged with me, Garrett. Until I saw for myself how devoted Darby is to them. When I took them on the Ferris wheel, all Regan and Reid talked about was their uncle Garrett and Darby. They were happy. Finally."

Darby sank into one of the chairs. "I don't understand. Elise and Marc seemed devoted to the children."

"Marc was," Caldwell agreed sadly. "Elise...was troubled. She wasn't delighted when she learned she was pregnant again. And when it turned out to be triplets, she was even more unhappy."

"But she didn't even use Smiling Faces full-time for the children."

"No, she didn't," Caldwell agreed. "Because of the way it would 'look' to her friends. She left them here. Fortunately, I have enough household staff that, even if I wasn't here, the children were safe and cared for. I'd agreed to pay for a live-in nanny for them, but Marc flatly refused what he considered more charity from me. Marc had finally had enough of Elise's irresponsible ways. A few weeks before the accident happened, he'd filed for divorce and for custody of the children. Elise was my daughter, but I believed that Marc was doing the right thing. She was livid with me when I told her so."

"So what's that got to do with us," Garrett asked bluntly. "Elise was angry with you because you supported Marc on the divorce, so she was trying to get back at you by saying she wanted me to raise her kids?"

"Garrett." Darby shook her head, her expression pained. "You don't know how badly off she was. I honestly don't think she was in any condition to be scheming."

"We'll never know," Caldwell said. "She was extremely angry with me, but she was angry with Garrett, as well."

"She hated me," Garrett said flatly. "She always did."

"She was jealous of you," Caldwell corrected. "She wanted me to change my will. But she had no need of inheriting any interest in Castle Construction. She had already inherited a fortune from her mother."

"Yet she and her husband lived in a house that you owned."

"Your sister wasn't very prudent where money was concerned. Marc was on the verge of bankruptcy because of her lavish spending habits. She'd have sold off Castle Construction for a quick buck without a second thought." Caldwell's gaze rested on Garrett. "The company is your inheritance, Garrett. I wrote it in my will when you were born. I never intended for that to change. Elise, unfortunately, didn't believe that I'd hold to that decision."

Garrett kept a tight rein on the emotion rampaging inside him. "I don't want it."

"Then you can sell it off. You can absorb it into G&G. You can do whatever you want, once I'm gone. It'll be your right. If it makes you feel better to think about doing that, then go ahead. I don't expect you to feel any sentimental attachment to Castle Construction even though it is part of your heritage. I was a rotten father to you, Garrett."

"So why were you?" The words came out without Garrett's permission. His hands curled. "Never mind," he said curtly. "I don't care anymore."

Caldwell winced. "I'm sure you don't. But there were reasons, Garrett. Reasons you knew nothing about."

"Well maybe you'd better tell me them once and for all."

"Will you believe what I tell you?"

Garrett's jaw tightened even more. "I don't know," he said truthfully. "But I'll be damned if I'll let your past screw up my future…or those kids' futures."

"Then you might as well sit down," Caldwell said wearily. "Because it's a long story."

Darby chewed her lip. She wanted to go to Garrett and put her arms around him. She wanted to kiss away the deep frown marring his beautiful face.

But she couldn't. It was good that Garrett and his father were trying to resolve their differences. But they didn't need her sitting in the middle of it. "I should go."

"No." Garrett's hand closed over her shoulder, keeping her in place.

"Garrett, this is between you and Caldwell."

"He's right," Caldwell said. "You should stay. It concerns you, too. I will drop my suit contesting Garrett's custody of the children as long as I know that the two of you will be together when you raise my grandchildren."

Darby exhaled shakily. "I can't marry Garrett just to provide a new mother for the children."

"Why?" Garrett asked.

She rose to her feet and stared at him. "Garrett, we've already been through this! You and Elise and Caldwell are perfect examples that secrets can't be kept for good. They fester and they hurt. One day they'll learn that I was responsible for the accident that took their real mother."

"You weren't responsible for the accident, Darby," Caldwell said.

"Why? Because I wasn't driving one of the cars? Phil Candela had no reason to be in Fisher Falls unless he'd discovered a lead on *me*."

"But the fault wasn't his," Caldwell countered gently.

"What?"

He sighed. "As mayor, I have some influence with the police department. I didn't have them change the facts in the police report or anything, but I was able to keep them from issuing the full details of the accident in any statements. There was only one person responsible for the accident, Darby. And that person was my daughter."

"Elise?"

"She was driving. Speeding. No attempt to stop at the red light. Candela was lawfully in the intersection, and she hit him. His car was the only one there. If she hadn't hit him, she'd have driven right through the windows of Smiling Faces. The police determined that there would have been no way for her to stop in time. I couldn't see it serving any good purpose for that information to get out, so I had everyone put a lid on it. Had I known you were blaming yourself, I could have cleared it up weeks ago."

Darby swayed, and Garrett caught her against him.

"If you want to focus on the fact that Candela was there, at that moment, at that time, because of you, then you should realize that his presence in that car probably saved a lot of children inside Smiling Faces."

Darby's eyes filled. "Molly's had been at capacity for months," she admitted. "And I was standing right there, right in front of the windows. We were playing London Bridge and we heard the crash. Right there."

"Then he saved you, too," Garrett murmured against her temple.

"Just as my father would have expected from the head of his security." She wiped her cheeks, looking up at Garrett. "I should have told you who I was, right from the first. I know that."

"You didn't because I wielded the kids' welfare over you. I knew you had a price. And I could see in your eyes that it was believing the children needed you. I took full advantage of you. You're a woman full of love and compassion, and I haven't done anything to deserve you. But I still want you to marry me."

She frowned and glanced at Caldwell who was watching them. "No. I'm sorry, but I...I can't. I simply can't." Then, because she couldn't bear the fierce frowns on the faces of the two men, she hurried out of the room.

Chapter Eighteen

Garrett paused on the hillside and watched Darby staring out at the waterfall. The wind was picking up again, blowing her feathery hair about her head and making the skirt of her sundress flatten against her legs.

He figured they would have another thunderstorm that night. As far as he was concerned the night could split apart with thunder. It suited his mood just fine. He didn't know if he believed all that Caldwell had said after Darby left the room. But he supposed it was as easy to believe as to not.

He strode across the grassy hill toward her. "How many times are you gonna walk away from me?"

She whirled around, her face pale.

"I hope you don't plan to do it a lot, because I gotta tell you, sweetheart, it's not my favorite view of you. Even if you do have a world-class rear end. Running is just not an option for you anymore."

"I wasn't running anywhere. You fired me, remember?"

"I fired you because I wanted to shake some sense into you! I wanted you to get mad. To get your back up. To realize that you are *not* incapable of running your own life, of making decisions, of being exactly the person you are!" He breathed roughly and lowered his voice. "I fired you so we could have a fresh start. I wasn't going to let you out of my sight for long. I had no way of knowing that you'd run into Caldwell before we could get things settled between us."

Darby wrapped her arms around herself. She wanted, so badly, to lean her head against Garrett's hard shoulder. But if she weakened now, she'd never find any strength again. "It's hard to take in. What Caldwell said. Elise seemed so devoted to her children."

"That whole family has always been expert at not being what they seemed. Caldwell married his English wife because of the money she brought to their union that would save Castle Construction from ruin thanks to *his* father, but he didn't love her."

"Georgie said he'd sacrificed his own happiness," Darby murmured.

"Then there was my mother," he continued evenly. "Working around his house, being sweet and understanding and everything that his unloving wife wasn't."

His lips twisted. "I was the result of *that*. But if he acknowledged me, his wife would've pulled her money back out of Castle Construction, and the entire town would've suffered because of the loss of jobs. Caldwell wouldn't fire my mother from his staff, though, even though his wife was livid about it all, because my mother threatened to disappear with me for good. He says he never slept with her again. And the next year, Elise was born."

"You believe him?"

He looked back over his shoulder at the stone house. "Who the hell knows. It makes as much sense as anything I've ever come up with. She wasn't a prisoner in Caldwell's house. His wife had to hate her being there. My mom could have left anytime she wanted. She never did."

"But she did end up sending you away from Fisher Falls. To New Mexico."

"Probably the smartest thing she did. Not that I thought so at the time. But it got me out of the...weirdness here. Caldwell says he was glad by then, too. He knew my mother wasn't...stable. And then here I've been, prepared to take his grandchildren away, too, where he'd never have access to them again."

"Oh, Garrett." Forgetting everything but him, and the confused, angry boy he must have been, she pressed her hands around his.

"It sort of makes sense," he said. "My mother was obsessed with him. When Caldwell's wife left and went back to England, she probably expected Caldwell to make his move on her again or something. When he didn't, she swallowed a bottleful of pills."

"And I thought my family was tough to take." His lips were inches from hers, and she drew in a quiet breath, putting some distance between them. "So what happens with the custody case?"

"Without Caldwell challenging my guardianship, there is no case. You were right about him. Caldwell just wants to be a grandfather. He called the judge a few minutes ago. The kids are mine. For good." There was no mistaking the true relief in his expression.

"You'll be a good parent, Garrett," Darby said quietly.

"I'm going to try." His gaze was fierce on her, and she looked away.

"So you'll be going back to New Mexico soon," she finally said.

"Is that what you want?"

She frowned. "That was your plan. Get G&G up and running so it could take down Castle Construction. Go back to New Mexico. All in a day's work."

He looked around. Back to the house. "Plans change. G&G and Castle will find a way to work together."

"And it's all changed because of the children."

"Yeah." His gaze settled on her once again. "And you. Caldwell and I are never going to be best buds, but I'm willing to meet him partway for the sake of the kids. So why won't you marry me? We know the truth about the accident."

Darby brushed her hands through her hair and turned around, staring sightlessly at the magnificent view. "Because I need it all. I can't go into a marriage expecting it to end in a few years. I can't fool myself into thinking that being the children's new mother is enough for me. Not now. Not anymore."

"Forget the prenup. We get married, we stay married. Period. You want me to say I love you. Admit it."

She closed her eyes. Oh, Garrett. "I want you to *feel* it," she corrected. But he didn't. He wouldn't let himself. She walked closer toward the waterfall, leaned her elbows on a jagged wall of outcropping rocks. She could feel the spray on her face. Or maybe that was just more tears.

"I'll tell you what I feel," he said. His voice was

low, and she looked back to see him walking toward her, looking fierce and male. "You smile at me, and it makes a hell of a day suddenly go away. You laugh and push your fingers through your hair, and I find myself laughing, too. You sing to my kids, and it makes me so damn glad that they're not going to have the childhood that I did."

He took a step closer, and she could see the pulse beating in his corded throat. His voice dropped even lower as he pulled her around to face him. "You make love with me, and it's like I'm not even owner of my own soul anymore, because you've taken it over and turned it into something I can't recognize. And then you turned and walked away from me, from us all, when I stupidly said you were fired, and it felt like you'd yanked my insides out with a grappling hook. I don't know if that's love. All I know is it's something I've never felt. Not for anyone." He ducked his head, pressing a hard, fast kiss to her mouth.

She tore away. "I'm a coward, Garrett! Don't you see that? I couldn't stand up to my father and insist that he let me live my own life, so I ran instead. What kind of wife would I be? What kind of mother?"

He pulled her back into his arms. "Being a coward would have meant staying in that protective cage that made you miserable. You did what you believed you had to do. That wasn't the work of a coward. You can do *anything* you put your mind to. And I think it's time we both let the past be the past. The only thing that matters is now. And what we make of the future. You're the only woman I've ever wanted as my wife. You're the only woman who can love my kids as well as you do."

She sucked in her breath at the feel of his warmth against her. "I don't want to make a mess of this," she whispered. "I don't want to keep hurting people."

"Then stop hurting yourself first. Stop blaming yourself for being who you are. There're five kids anxiously waiting for me to bring their Darby back home where she belongs. And there's one man who's never gonna figure out how to let his heart out of its cage if you don't take pity on him. You're our only hope, Darby."

She looked into his eyes, those deep mossy-green eyes. And finally saw the truth. Her knees went weak, and her heart seemed so full that it might burst. "Do we really have to go back to New Mexico?"

He smiled faintly. "Sweetheart, I'm the boss. I can go wherever I want to go. And God help us but Caldwell has actually admitted he's wanted out of Castle for years, but responsibility kept him at it. He wants to focus on being the mayor."

"So what are you going to do?"

"Buy him out or something. I don't know." He cupped her face in his hands. "You don't want to leave Fisher Falls, do you?"

She sighed shakily. "It's the first place I've ever really felt at home. And I...I really think that Georgie needs me, Garrett. Once she's well enough to leave the care center, I want to be here for her. She's told me time and again that she wishes her house would be filled with children's laughter. I can't imagine any better medicine for her than her living to see that become a reality."

"What are you suggesting?" His eyes were filled with light, as if he already knew.

She smiled at him. Loving him so much that the world really did seem suddenly full of possibilities. Thunder rolled over their heads, and a gust of wind dashed a spray of water over their heads. "Will you marry me," she asked, raising her voice above the noise. "Despite the family that comes with me?"

His lips slowly curved. "If you'll marry me, despite the family that comes with me."

Laughter bubbled from her. "I can't think of anything more wonderful."

He swept her up in his arms and carried her away from the rocks. Away from the waterfall.

"Where are we going?"

He strode steadily toward his truck. "To visit Georgie and tell her the news," he said. "Then I'll know that you're not going to change your mind and back out on me."

Darby pressed her palm alongside his bristled jaw. Oh, she did love this hard, bristle-faced man. "We can tell Georgie later," she told him softly, surely.

"Okay. We'll go pick out a ring, then. Right now." He yanked open the passenger door of his truck and set her inside on the seat.

She laughed softly. "Garrett, *later*. I'm not going to change my mind about becoming your wife. I promise."

His movements finally slowed. "What is it that you want to do then?"

She looped her hands around his neck and tugged

his head down to hers. "Take me home, Garrett. Take me home to our kids."

He kissed her, long and slow. "I never thought I'd say this, but I like the sound of that."

"So do I, my love. So do I."

Epilogue

One Month Later

"Are you ready for this?"

Darby stared out the car window as they approached the gated entrance to the Rutherford family estate in Kentucky. She pressed her lips together for a moment, then nodded. It may have taken her a month, but she *was* ready. Georgie was recuperating well and was back home. The children were happy and healthy and recovered from a brief bout with summertime colds.

There were no more reasons for Darby to put this off. It was time. And she knew it right down to her bones. "I'm ready. See that van there? The one parked across the road in the trees? Two reporters inside. Names are Fitzpatrick and Gonzales. They are always there."

Garrett closed his hand over Darby's. "Want to stop and give them a scoop?" He lifted her hand and kissed the delicate diamond ring on her finger.

She laughed softly. "Not likely."

He enjoyed the light of battle in her eyes. He slowed and turned the vehicle into the wide, curving drive, pulling to a stop next to the security guard who stepped forward from a small enclosed booth.

Darby leaned across Garrett and smiled at the guard. "Hello, Sims. Is my father or brother about today?"

"Yes, ma'am." Sims eyed her with surprise. "Shall I call ahead or—"

"We'll surprise them," Darby interrupted. "Thank you, Sims."

The guard nodded and stepped out of the way as the enormous iron gate slid open.

"Good grief," Garrett muttered as he drove the rental car through.

"I warned you," Darby murmured at his side. "There's still time to back out, you know."

"And lose out on marrying an American princess?" He grinned at her, seeing the way she rolled her eyes. He was glad to see the humorous light in her eyes again. She'd been growing increasingly tense since they'd left Minnesota early that morning.

"Do you think Caldwell and Lucinda will really be all right with the children this week? I'm not sure we should stay here in Kentucky quite as long as we'd planned."

"They're fine," Garrett assured her, though he wasn't all that delighted leaving his kids in Caldwell's care, even with Lucinda's help. Georgie's cook-cum-housekeeper had been delighted with Georgie's instructions to care for the wee ones. Not even the mayor had the nerve to disagree with Georgina Vansant. But Garrett had to admit Caldwell was making an effort, and for Darby's sake Garrett would hold up his end, too.

"Georgie…"

"…can't wait for us to get back so we can finish ironing out the details for the wedding and so she can give me more orders on work she wants done around the house," he suggested.

"You're sure you don't mind living there with her?"

He grinned at her. "She keeps things lively, that's for sure. Gives me some idea of what her great-niece will be like in another sixty years or so. She's happier than all of us combined at having her house filled with more than wind chimes and plants."

He braked and parked their rental car behind a dark blue sports car. He looked at Darby, who was staring at the house. "You can do this," he said softly.

She looked back at him, smiling quickly. Nervously. "I suppose I shouldn't be angry with my father anymore. If I hadn't been so upset about being dismissed from my job, I wouldn't have left home. And if I hadn't done that, you and I might never have met."

Garrett brushed her lips with his. "Everything happens for a reason."

Darby rested her forehead against him for a moment. The silly jiggle in her chest had a lot more to do with the man sitting beside her than the two men she would soon face inside her childhood home. "Thanks for coming with me," she murmured.

"I faced Caldwell because of you," he murmured. "Seems only fair. But you're capable of doing this on your own. You always have been."

Darby smiled and sat back, releasing her safety belt. Garrett had such faith in her. "Not always," she corrected. "And I'm still glad you're here with me now."

She waited while Garrett rounded the car and opened

her door. Then she climbed out and, holding his hand, walked up to the house and in through the front door.

Marlene, the wizened little housekeeper who'd been with the family longer than Darby had been alive, appeared from one direction and gasped. "Miss Debra! You're home."

Darby went forward, hugging the woman. "Just for a visit, Marlene," she cautioned, laughing. "But definitely long enough to have some of your Derby pie."

"Marlene?" A deep voice filled the foyer. "I could have sworn I heard— Well, holy hell. Look what the cat dragged in."

Darby looked up from Marlene into the brilliant-blue eyes of her brother. "Nice to see you, too, Dane. Sweet talk and all."

He grinned suddenly and hauled her up in his arms, swinging her around in a circle before setting her back on her feet. He looked at Garrett, then back at her. "So you're finally done hiding behind Georgie's skirts, are you?"

Darby's mouth dropped. "You…knew?"

Dane made a face. "Peanut, you can't make a move in this world without us knowing about it. Georgie denied seeing you, of course, but knowing how she and Dad argue about everything under the sun, I was still suspicious. Then I got word about Phil's accident. It seemed obvious to me even before I obtained a copy of the accident report, which included a very concise account by a witness named Darby White."

Darby reached out blindly and felt the warm security of Garrett's hand close around it. "Does Daddy know?"

Dane shook his head. "I assured him you were safe, but I managed to keep your secret. Mostly because he's been leaving the business more to me while he concentrates on another horse farm he wants to buy. You and I are a team, remember?"

Darby's eyes filled. "I remember." She blinked rapidly and turned to Garrett. "Dane, this is Garrett Cullum. My fiancé."

Dane's eyes narrowed. "Well. That *is* a surprise. How did you meet?"

"Stop looking all fierce," Darby said, suddenly amused. "Garrett, this is my know-it-all brother, Dane Rutherford." She watched the two men size each other up, apparently coming to the same decision when they stuck out their hands and shook solemnly.

"When is the wedding?"

Darby stiffened and looked up the curving staircase at the gruff question. Roth Rutherford looked the same as he'd always looked. Rich and powerful and demanding. And no matter how infuriated he could make her, she did love him.

"In three weeks," she told him clearly. "On the grounds of Georgie's place."

"I should've known not to trust that old battle-ax. She was hiding you all along."

Darby continued as if her father hadn't spoken. "And if you promise to behave yourself, we'll invite you to the wedding, and I'll let you give me away. *If* you promise."

Roth slowly descended the staircase and walked toward Darby. "If?"

She swallowed, then just said what she felt. "If you can't behave yourself, you can stay here in Kentucky, and the rest of us will enjoy the festivities. I'm not going to tolerate any more of your interference in my life, Daddy. No more trying to buy my friends or pay off those you think are my enemies. I know you believe you're only protecting me, but none of us can live that way. Not anymore."

"Are you telling me what to do?"

Her chin lifted. "Yes. I am." And it was easier than she'd ever dreamed.

His tight lips slowly eased as his gaze slid to Garrett. "I suppose *you* had something to do with Debra's newfound contrariness."

"Daddy, I'm warning you," Darby began.

"It's past time Darby was a little contrary, don't you think?" Garrett answered smoothly. "But I'm not taking credit for it. She's had it inside her all along."

Roth harrumphed. "I've already cut her off from the money. Just how much do you figure marrying my girl is worth?"

"Daddy!" Appalled Darby stepped in front of her father. "That is uncalled for."

"Fifteen million," Garrett said flatly.

Darby swayed. She looked from her father's calculating expression to Dane's curious one, and finally to Garrett's. His mossy-green gaze met hers, and she melted inside.

"Fifteen million it is," Roth said. "And then you can get the hell off my property and away from my girl."

"I don't think you understood me," Garrett said quietly. "I'm perfectly happy to leave your property, but I'm not leaving Darby." He reached inside his leather jacket and pulled out a slender checkbook. He flipped it open and began writing.

"What are you doing?" Roth blustered.

"Writing you a check for fifteen mil. That was the amount we agreed upon wasn't it?" He tore out the check and extended it toward Roth. But his eyes were on Darby. "Darby is worth more than everything I own in this world, which totals just about this amount. If you want it in exchange for a life with her, you can have it. I'm coming out on top of the deal."

Darby smiled shakily. "Oh, Garrett."

"You're plumb crazy, you know that?" Roth looked at them both. "I take that check and you two won't have anything."

"We'll have each other, Daddy," Darby cut him off.

"Each other and no money," Roth grumped.

"Each other and love," Garrett assured. He brushed his thumb along Darby's satiny cheek, not even noticing when the check drifted to the floor. "I love you. I'd love you even if it weren't for the kids."

"Kids?" Roth's voice rose. "Kids? You've haven't even been gone five months! Just what on earth have you been doing?"

Darby barely heard him. She was too entranced with Garrett. "I love you, too," she whispered.

Dane sighed noisily and leaned down to pick up the

check. He tore it in half and stuck it in his pocket as he pulled his father away from the pair who seemed to have forgotten they weren't quite alone. "Close your mouth, Dad," he advised dryly. "Your girl has grown up and found herself a man as determined as you."

Roth harrumphed again. "He'd better protect her, that's all I've got to say."

Darby smiled tremulously at Garrett. They knew the truth. They would protect each other.

"Just how many *kids* are there supposed to be, anyway?" Roth's voice floated back through the foyer.

Garrett chuckled. Darby giggled. She pushed her fingers luxuriously through Garrett's dark hair and tugged his head toward hers. "He's gonna have a fit when he hears six," she murmured.

"Five," Garrett corrected.

Darby pressed her lips together and waited. It didn't take long.

"Darby?" His arms cradled her against him with such tenderness that her eyes filled with tears.

"I'm pretty sure. Do you mind?"

He slowly shook his head. "Do you?"

"I think it's perfect." Then she laughed. "It's a good thing we have plenty of bedrooms at Georgie's."

"If we didn't I'd build more myself. I meant it, Darby. Even if you and I had to start from scratch, kids and all, I'd do it."

Darby looked into his eyes and knew it was true. "Tell me again?"

Garrett's expression softened. "I love you. Not because a legend says it's so, but because I feel it." His palm settled over her flat belly. "And I promise to treasure our love for the rest of our days."

Darby covered his hand with hers. "And beyond?"

His lips met hers in a vow that nothing could ever surpass. "And beyond."

* * * * *

MILLIONAIRE'S INSTANT BABY

Chapter One

"I'm looking for a wife."

Emma Valentine turned her attention away from the tall man who'd just made the flat statement and focused on the feel of the unfamiliar, wonderful weight of the baby in her arms. Her son, barely one day old, took her breath away. All the months of waiting, of worrying, of planning. All were wrapped within the soft blue blanket, contained in the eight pounds of perfectly formed baby. She drew her finger along his velvety cheek, not wanting to wake him, but unable to resist touching.

"Miss Valentine, did you hear me?"

She bent over and pressed her lips ever so gently against her son's perfect forehead. Her son. She straightened when the door behind the man swished open and Nell Hastings, one of Emma's favorite nurses, appeared to take the baby back to the nursery.

Emma reluctantly surrendered Chandler. And only after the door had swished closed again did she turn her attention back to the man.

Her arms felt woefully empty, and she folded them across her chest, painfully aware of the sight she must present to the man who looked so flawless he could have stepped from the pages of a men's fashion magazine. She shifted gingerly in the cushioned side chair and wished she had more clothing covering her than her pink chenille bathrobe and pale hospital gown. "I'm sorry. Mr....?"

"Montgomery. Kyle Montgomery."

Emma nodded. Dennis Reid, the chief of staff at the Buttonwood Baby Clinic, had introduced him when he'd stopped by. Obviously Dr. Reid had come by with the intention of introducing this man to Emma, though she couldn't fathom why. Up until now, Emma's only contact with Dr. Reid occurred when the man went into Mom & Pop's. The diner where she waitressed was located across from the medical complex and she knew a lot of the clinic's staff.

She studied the man standing in her room, from the cuffed hem of his black pleated trousers that broke ever so perfectly over his gleaming leather boots to the white shirt flowing over an impressive set of shoulders. The button at his throat was unfastened, but Emma figured he probably had a tie in his car or his briefcase. She knew instinctively that this was a man who'd been born wearing imported suits and silk ties. Even his chestnut hair had fallen precisely back into thick waves when he'd raked his fingers through it.

"Dr. Reid was saying something about you needing assistance with a job?" she asked. It helped to look in the vicinity of his ear, she decided, rather than into his starkly handsome face. Because then she didn't feel quite so much like a wrung-out dishrag in the face of his masculine elegance.

"I don't know how I can help," she went on. "As you

can see, I'll be busy for the next little while, and after that…" She trailed off.

After that it was back to her two jobs and the worry about paying the hospital bill. She'd already determined that the tuition for her next semester of college courses would have to wait.

"I believe we can help each other, Emma."

She swallowed the dart of nervousness that rose when he crossed the room, passing the other bed—empty for now—before pulling out the chair opposite her.

Almost as if he recognized her reaction, he seemed to consciously relax his rigid stance. He sat, rested his arms on his thighs. Clasped his long fingers together. Almost smiled, but didn't quite make it. "As I was saying, I need a wife. A family."

Good gravy, he smelled nice.

The thought shocked her. She moistened her lips. "Mr. Montgomery, I really don't know what you—"

"Kyle." He halted her confused words. "And I can explain. But it's occurred to me that this isn't the best time. You're tired, and my offer might be better received after you've had some rest."

"Mr. Montgomery…" Emma tugged self-consciously at the lapel of her robe, then flushed when his startling green gaze followed the movement of her hand. She'd been blessed, as her mama termed it, with a curvaceous figure by the time she'd turned fourteen. Becoming pregnant and having a child had only increased the problem.

She swallowed and tried again. "Kyle, I really can't imagine how I can help you find your family. But you might as well tell me what's on your mind now, because I'll be leaving the hospital this afternoon and I—"

"Already?" Lush black lashes narrowed around his intense gaze. "Surely you're not up to being released yet."

She wondered if she'd accidentally been given some type of drug other than acetaminophen, because this was surely the oddest conversation she'd ever had. Mr. Mont— *Kyle* seemed distinctly annoyed. As if he suspected she was receiving inadequate care. "Women don't spend days and days in the hospital anymore when they give birth, Kyle. I'm healthy, as is my baby. Everything went just fine." Thank heavens. "And studies show—"

"I wasn't casting aspersions on the medical care you're receiving. I was just surprised." He sat back in his chair, laying one arm on the minuscule table beside it. Emma had the strongest impression he was mentally drumming his fingers against the tabletop. "Right. I apologize for the timing here, but Dennis Reid seemed to think you might be able to help me, and I'm running short of time."

"Do you think I know your wife? What is her name?"

"I don't already *have* a wife, Emma." He hesitated for a fraction of a second. Just long enough to make her stomach drop to her toes. "I *need* one. And I'm hoping you'll be her."

Thank goodness she was sitting. Because if she hadn't been, she'd have ended up on the floor. "Mr. Montgomery," she said firmly, "I don't know what Dr. Reid led ya'll to believe about me, but—"

"I'm going about this wrong." He sat forward again, bringing with him that tantalizing scent of expensive aftershave. No drugstore brands for this man. He was strictly the charge-by-the-quarter-ounce type.

He linked his fingers together again, regarding her with eyes that gave no hint of the manic mind he must possess. "Dennis said I could count on your discretion."

He seemed to be waiting, so she nodded hesitantly. The call button was just out of her reach, but if she leaned to the side, she could probably get to it. She would get to it, because she was a mother now. She *would* protect her child with every fiber of her being, and that meant she also had to protect herself. Even from a sinfully attractive madman.

"I run ChandlerAIR," he continued calmly. "Have you heard… Yes, I can see by your expression that you've heard of us. I'm in the middle of some delicate negotiations with a company we are acquiring. The founder of this company has some old-fashioned ideas about how he likes to do business." Kyle paused, as if she needed a moment to digest what he was saying.

She nodded, since she didn't know how else to respond.

Kyle's lips twisted slightly and he turned his attention to his hands. "He refuses to deal with anyone who is not the fine upstanding family man he is," he elaborated. "Acquiring this other company will benefit Chandler-AIR, but it will also help the economy here in Buttonwood. Provide jobs. Increase tourism—"

"I understand the economic benefits, Mr. Montgomery.

Surely this other man would understand that, as well, wouldn't he?" She brushed back a lock of hair and was dismayed to realize her hand was trembling.

"Payton Cummings is perfectly happy to retain control of his company as long as he needs to until he finds the right opportunity. The right—"

"Family man," Emma murmured.

"Exactly." Kyle's lips tightened for a brief moment. "I'm more determined to see this acquisition through than Cummings is. Assuming the trappings of a family man is something I'm prepared to do to attain my goals."

"But...but why me? Someone in your company, your girlfriend..."

"I don't have one."

Men who looked like Kyle Montgomery always had a woman in the background somewhere. Whether they admitted it or not. She swallowed the bitter thought.

"I don't have time in my life right now for personal entanglements," he was saying, his voice deep and smooth. "And I don't want to create any ties with my associates that might later cause discomfort."

"Discomfort," Emma repeated. It was the word so often used to describe childbirth to prospective parents. She considered it singularly inadequate to describe the reality. "But with me, a total stranger, there would be no cause for later...discomfort."

"Essentially, yes. I'm new to this area, Emma. I've bought a house and I'm moving ChandlerAIR's corporate offices from Denver. Having a family that lives here dovetails nicely with what Cummings already knows about my plans."

"Then he probably already knows you're not married."

"He doesn't." There was no room for doubt in his assurance.

She argued, anyway. "You can't know that. I've seen articles now and then about your company. About the services you offer and its success." Phenomenal success, if Emma recalled correctly. She also recalled his company being praised particularly for its progressive policies toward its employees. "I'll be the first to admit that I don't follow the business pages very closely. But even I know a little about your company. A man you're plannin' to do business with like you've described would obviously know a great deal more. Including some personal details."

Kyle nodded. "Those are valid points. But until last year when he moved to Durango, Cummings had been living in New Mexico. Our paths didn't cross. Besides which, I've always kept my private life private. Only my closest associates know much about me personally. I prefer it that way."

Emma couldn't imagine it. There were times she suspected every resident of Buttonwood knew the business of everyone else. It was almost as bad as her hometown in Tennessee. "But to suddenly produce a wife? I just don't see how you can possibly hope to fool anyone."

His eyes narrowed. "I can count on your discretion, can't I, Emma?"

She winced. "As if anyone would believe me if I

went around announcing that a guy like you walked into my hospital room one morning and asked me, a simple waitress, to be his wife."

He frowned. "For appearances only," he corrected. "I meant no offense. This is a delicate situation. Cummings already thinks I'm married. But he's been showing more interest in that area of my life, and I'm going to have to introduce him to my wife, I feel certain, before he'll close the deal."

"You told him you were married because he wouldn't do business with you otherwise?"

"I told his stepdaughter I was married when she came on to me at our first meeting."

"Oh," Emma murmured.

Kyle grimaced. "I didn't want to jeopardize my plans. It seemed, at the time, the easiest way."

"And you couldn't have just said you didn't want to mix business with pleasure?"

"Let's just say that Winter Cummings is a determined woman who doesn't necessarily hold with her stepdaddy's values."

Kyle's hand moved and Emma realized he was unclenching his fist.

"Ironically, once word reached Cummings that I'd been recently married, he was willing to meet with me himself. I wasn't going to derail the deal by getting into explanations."

She was believing every word that left his lips. He was utterly serious.

And his seriousness seemed far more dangerous than his being nuts. "Perhaps Mr. Cummings and his crew aren't the type of people with whom *you* want to do business," she suggested faintly.

Kyle smiled tightly. "I want Payton Cummings's company," he said. "If it takes a family to get it, I'll produce a family. At least for show."

Emma swallowed. "But to…to marry strictly for the purpose of a business deal? That seems so, well, extreme, don't you think?"

"It wouldn't be a real marriage," he said. "I just need you and your son to pose as my family. The two of you would move in with me—strictly business," he assured when she caught her breath audibly.

"But, sugar, it would be a lie." Her face heated as the words burst out.

Kyle felt an odd stirring when he let himself look at the young woman opposite him. Her melodic voice had been growing increasingly smooth, like warm honey. There was more than a touch of the South in this dark-haired beauty. He'd had women call him all sorts of nicknames from darling to pig, but he knew he'd never been a *sugar*. He dragged his thoughts front and center, where they belonged. "I have to consider the weight of what I'm trying to accomplish."

"Ah." She nodded, her big brown eyes studying him steadily. "The old 'end justifies the means' reasoning."

"I want to add more flights, Emma," he said truthfully. "More flights, more service, more employees. The only people who will be hurt if ChandlerAIR's acquisition of Cummings Courier Service falls through at this late date will be the considerable number of people within the Four Corners area who *won't* be able to work for me. That's four states, Emma. Colorado, Utah, Arizona and New Mexico."

"I did pass geography, Mr. Montgomery. And regardless of your motives, it still doesn't make lyin' right."

His jaw hardened. He'd had this argument with himself too many times already to want to sit here and go through it with this young woman. He'd spent too many years planning. Waiting for just this opportunity. To finally take the action that, while it wouldn't reverse the past, would go a long way toward evening the score.

If producing the family Payton kept harping on got Kyle to his goal, then produce a family he would.

ChandlerAIR would survive if the deal to acquire CCS didn't go through. His company was strong and solid because he'd devoted his existence to it for most of his adult life. But taking over CCS was an action that went beyond business.

And he had no intention of discussing his personal motives with this young woman, no matter how honeyed her voice. "I prefer to look at it as expedience. And perhaps we should agree to disagree on the point," he said.

"Might be wise," she murmured, shifting in her chair.

A fine white line appeared around her softly compressed lips at the movement, and he felt a jab of conscience. She'd just had a baby. Sitting here arguing ethics was undoubtedly the last thing she'd expected to be doing today. "Miss Valentine. Emma. Give my offer some thought." He kept his voice calm even though his impulse was to push the issue. "I'll make it worth your while."

Far from calming her, however, her face blanched. "I'm sorry, Mr. Montgomery." Her tone said she was anything but. "I can't help you." Her hands curled over the sides of the chair and she pushed herself gingerly to her feet.

He rose, automatically reaching out to assist her, but the frosty look she gave him had him keeping his hands to himself. He felt awkward and inept, something he hadn't experienced for at least twenty years. Yet watching her slowly maneuver herself to the hospital bed without offering assistance went against his grain.

"One of my sisters had a baby last year," he said.

"How nice," she murmured.

It would have been so simple just to lift her off her feet and deposit her on the bed—much easier than watching her efforts to climb into it. He looked away, shoving his hands in his pockets. When his sister had been in the hospital after giving birth, her room had been filled to overflowing with flowers, plants, balloons and assorted baby gifts. The only thing personal in this room was one small green plant with a cheerful smiley-face balloon sticking out of it.

At the rustle of sheets he let his gaze travel back to her. Emma was still bundled in the thick robe and looked as if she'd just as soon be buried in it as remove it with him present.

This wasn't going at all the way he wanted. Needed.

He started to reach up to loosen his tie, then realized

he'd left it in his car, so it wasn't a tie that made him feel choked. "Is someone picking you up this afternoon to take you home?"

She folded her arms across the top of the sheet and sighed faintly. "You're not going to go away, are you."

It hadn't been a question. He answered, anyway. "Emma, this is too important for me to go away." How many times had he removed an obstacle from his path simply because of his ability to outlast, outthink, outmaneuver?

Only this time, the obstacle in Kyle's path had smudgy shadows beneath her eyes and slender shoulders he was certain were being held straight through sheer grit. "But I can see you're exhausted. So I'll come back later when you're released and get you settled at home. We can discuss this more then."

"There is nothing to discuss. Besides, I have my car here and I'll be getting myself and my son home just fine."

"Your car is here? Did someone drop it off for you?" He pulled his hands from his pockets and wrapped them around the metal rail at the foot of her bed. Kyle had specifically asked Dennis Reid if there was a man in the picture with Emma Valentine. Reid had assured him that Emma was totally on her own. The last thing Kyle needed was some love-struck fool bumbling onto the scene.

"I drove it here," she said, surprising him into forgetting the issue of her single status.

"While you were in labor?"

"Yes," she said with exaggerated patience. "And I'll

drive it home again this afternoon. I assure you I have the proper baby seat and everything, so stop frowning."

"You have no one you could have called on?" If not the man responsible for her pregnancy, then a friend. A sibling. Someone.

Her lips firmed. "Whether I do or not is hardly your business, now is it?"

Kyle would have liked to debate that point, considering he was determined this woman would be his make-believe wife. But there was a loud rattle out in the corridor and the door swished open to reveal a young man in pristine white bearing a breakfast tray.

The orderly smiled genially at them, set the tray on a rolling cart and slid it neatly against the side of Emma's bed, turning it so the tray hung over her lap. Then he lifted the cover from the food and left.

As Kyle peered at the bowl of cooked cereal, the puny foil-covered plastic cup of orange juice and a half-burned piece of toast, he thought of the fluffy omelet, crisp bacon and fragrant coffee Baxter had served him that morning. He'd barely taken time to appreciate the food or the way it had been served—on china at the wrought-iron glass-topped table on his patio.

"Are you hungry, Mr. Montgomery?"

"No, why?"

"You're staring at my breakfast like you haven't seen food in a month." She didn't look at him as she peeled back the foil cover of the juice.

"I haven't seen a breakfast that looks like that in more than a month," he muttered. "I'll bring you back something more...appealing."

She took a healthy swallow of the juice, then picked up a spoon which she plunged into the cereal. "I like hot cereal, Mr. Montgomery. Some people do, you know." Her tone slowed like rich rolling drops of syrup. "Even rich folks, I'm told."

He smiled, genuinely amused. "You think I'm a snob."

Her hesitation was barely noticeable. "I can't imagine what you mean."

His amusement grew. "Neatly avoided and you didn't have to lie." Seeing the corners of her mouth twitch as if she was holding back a reluctant smile of her own, he decided it was a good time to retreat. On a high note, so to speak. "I'll leave you to enjoy your oats and whey," he said. "We'll be talking again."

"I don't think so. Our paths are in different neighborhoods. I doubt they'll cross again."

He shrugged easily and headed toward the door. She didn't know him yet, so she could have no idea how wrong she was. He stopped and turned. "Get some sleep after you eat," he suggested. "It'll be a busy afternoon taking your son home. What did you say his name was?"

She tilted her head. "I didn't. Which you know very well."

"He is a good-looking boy."

Her eyes softened like rich melting chocolate. "Thank you. He is beautiful."

"And his name? You've already given him one, I'm sure." He smiled faintly. "I'll bet you had his name picked out when you were only halfway through your pregnancy." She seemed like the type of woman who'd have cherished every moment she carried her child. Very much the way his sister had.

"Four months along," she admitted.

"And?"

She moistened her lips. Hesitated. "My son's name is Chandler."

Kyle absorbed that. "Well. Good name."

"I named him after a very dear old friend from my hometown," she said evenly. "A name I chose months ago, so wipe that smug look off your face."

"Not smug at all, Emma. It's just another indication that I've chosen the right woman for my wife."

"Your pretend wife," she corrected.

"That's what I said."

"Not exactly."

"You like to have the last word, don't you?"

"I'm a woman, Mr. Montgomery."

"I did notice that, *Miss* Valentine." He watched her cheeks blossom with pink. "And while I am but a humble man—" he ignored her soft snort "—I'm a determined one. Our paths *will* cross again, Emma. And again. Until I have your agreement that becoming my pretend wife benefits everyone."

Her mouth moved, but no words emerged. He smiled and stepped out into the hall. "I'll see you and Chandler later."

The door swished closed, but he heard her honeyed voice in the moment just before it did. "Good gravy."

He pushed his hands into his pockets and thought about the woman on the other side. She was perfect for his needs. He just needed to remember that his needs were *strictly* business. That her curvy body, from slender neck to trim ankles, was off-limits.

All he needed was a pretend wife. He'd keep his hands to himself. He'd keep his thoughts strictly on sewing up every last detail of acquiring Payton Cummings's company.

So that when the day arrived that he dismantled every facet of that damned company, he'd have the personal satisfaction of knowing there wasn't one thing Payton Cummings, Sr., could do about it.

Kyle let out a long breath and went in search of a flower shop.

Chapter Two

"Okay, Emma, this one is what we'll use to file for Chandler's birth certificate. Fill in the blanks, sign and leave it in the folder with the others. The state will send you the certificate once it's recorded. You can leave the folder with the nurse when you're released. Okay?"

Emma nodded and waited until the brisk I'm-from-Records-honey woman left. Then Emma looked down at the form and nibbled the inside of her lip. She'd been completing and signing forms for the past ten minutes. Financial forms, affirming that she didn't have medical insurance and including a payment agreement that would take every cent of the pay she earned from her part-time teaching job for the next few years. Medical-information forms regarding the aftermath of childbirth. Even forms to purchase sets of newborn photos.

She'd ordered one eight-by-ten and six wallet-size ones simply because she hadn't been able to resist the first photo of Chandler, his little fists pressed against his round cheeks and a snug blue cap covering his thatch of dark brown hair. But even the photos were an extravagance these days. Signing all those financial forms had brought home with a thump the responsibilities she had to shoulder. Alone.

Which brought her right back to the birth certificate

information. She rolled the pen between her fingers, looking at the empty boxes. Mother's maiden name. Location and date of mother's birth. Father's name.

The tip of her pen hovered over that last box. Father. It took much more than biology to make a father. It took love and commitment and dedication.

Yet all she had was betrayal and lies and a twelve-page legal document sitting in the closet of her apartment.

She drew in a breath and let it out slowly. Then she deliberately slashed a line through the father box before completing the rest, and placed the form, along with the others, inside the folder.

She looked at her watch and hoped the nurse came by soon with her release. She didn't believe for one minute that Kyle Montgomery would be returning as he'd said that morning. Why would he?

He had money. He had incredible looks. He could find a make-believe wife wherever he wanted, *making it worthwhile* for some other woman. Personally Emma had had enough of rich men who thought they could either buy her presence or buy her absence.

The only man she was interested in was the tiny one sleeping in his carrier right beside her.

She looked down at Chandler, feeling tears threaten. Tears of gratitude for his sweet perfection she could happily shed. But tears filled with worry and fear about the days ahead, of managing, getting by—those tears she refused to indulge.

She was twenty-six years old. When her mama was that age, she had five kids. All daughters. Another year and she had six. The year after that, Hattie Valentine had stopped having babies, because her husband went off one night and didn't come back.

A soft knock on the door caught her attention, and she pushed to her feet, tugging the hem of her cotton maternity top over her hips. Nell Hastings smiled and pushed the door wide until it stayed open on its own. "I've got your ride here, Emma." She patted the bright blue wheelchair, her eyes twinkling. "Is that all your stuff in that bag?"

She didn't wait for an answer, but tucked the handles of the big plastic sack that held bottles of water, formula samples and diapers over the back of the wheelchair.

Emma handed the motherly nurse the folder of paperwork and sat in the chair, holding Chandler in his carrier on her lap as Nell pushed her to the sidewalk outside the small hospital. Emma could see her orange car in the parking lot. She swallowed, thinking it was stupid to feel nervous about leaving the hospital. She could do this. She looked down at her sleeping son. She *would* do this. She climbed out of the wheelchair. It wasn't as if she had no friends to support her decisions. To laugh with. To cry with. She just didn't have a husband. And she'd turned down the offers of a ride home from the hospital. She'd start out as she intended to continue. Depending on herself.

"Emma, you and Chandler are going to be just fine. But you get nervous about anything, you just call. Okay?"

"Thanks, Nell. When I'm back at work, I'll treat you to pie and coffee."

The nurse patted her ample hips. "I don't need pie,

but I'll take you up on that." She helped Emma with the plastic bag and overnight case before turning the wheelchair around and heading back inside.

"We can do this, right, Chandler?" With the plastic sack slung over one shoulder, the strap of her overnight bag over the other and Chandler's carrier cradled between her arms, Emma slowly headed toward her car.

When she reached it, she had to set everything down on the ground, though, because her keys were buried somewhere in the overnight bag. Chandler was starting to stir, and she moved his carrier onto the hood of her car, humming to him while she dug blindly through her bag.

"Looks like you could use an extra hand."

Emma gasped, automatically closing her arm over the carrier. She looked across the hood of her ancient car to the gleaming late-model sports car against which Kyle Montgomery leaned lazily. Her heart was thudding only because he'd startled her, she assured herself.

"My two hands are quite sufficient," she said, flushing when the words came out sounding breathless. She swept her hand once more through the interior of her case searching, searching.

He tilted his head slightly, his eyes crinkling at the corners. Emma swallowed and pulled the case in front of her, pushing aside the clothing she'd worn to the hospital in her search. She was certain she'd dumped the keys in the bottom of the case.

"You're overflowing there."

She frowned, looking up. Right there, large as life, was her white cotton bra, D cup and all, hanging drunkenly over the side of the case. She hastily shoved it back inside, finally encountered the sharp edge of a key with her fingertip and pulled the set out triumphantly. Without bothering to refasten the zipper of the case, she hurriedly unlocked the car and dumped the two bags inside, rolled the car window halfway down and reached for the baby carrier. From the corner of her eye, she could see Kyle still leaning against his car.

He'd added the tie that had been missing that morning. Looking just as spit-polished as she'd figured he'd look. She swallowed and tried blocking him from her sight as she bent over her baby.

Though she'd practiced fastening the baby carrier into the stationary base that was already in the car, she fumbled the job. Chandler started whimpering and Emma crooned soothingly to him as she tried again. But the latch wouldn't connect.

Painfully aware of Kyle's gaze, which she couldn't seem to ignore no matter how hard she tried, she worked at the carrier again. And again. Chandler started crying in earnest. "Oh, pumpkin, don't," she murmured, trying to distract him with the pacifier the nurse had sent with them. But Chandler wasn't interested in the pacifier, and his newborn wail rose.

The panic rose in her far too easily. Her knees felt wobbly and all she wanted to do was lie down. She took a deep breath and tried fitting the carrier into place once more. What was *wrong* with the thing?

"Let me give it a try."

Emma looked over her shoulder at Kyle, who'd moved to stand behind her. His wide shoulders blocked the bright afternoon sun in a way that no man wearing a silk tie should be able to do. "I can do it."

"I'm sure you can," he said mildly. "But that's the same model I bought my sister when she had her baby. Remember, the one I told you—"

"I remember." Feeling cross, she pulled the carrier back out of the car and propped it between her hip and the open car door while she tried coaxing Chandler to take the pacifier. At last he did, his cries ceasing as his lips worked rhythmically.

"He's hungry."

"I'm aware of that." And her breasts positively ached for relief. But she wasn't going to tell this man *that*. Not that she needed to, she realized with a hot flush, because his eyes had definitely been eyeing her there. "Don't you have planes to fly somewhere or something?"

His eyes crinkled and he gently, firmly, nudged her out of the way, easily replacing her hands on the carrier with his own. "I am a pilot," he said as he leaned into the car. "But unfortunately the business end of things keeps me on the ground pretty much these days. There. All set."

He straightened and Emma could see the carrier had been transformed into a secure car seat. Naturally. She felt like bawling. "I... Thank you."

"You're welcome." He looked at her, not smiling, just being male and competent and calmly accepting the tears collecting in her eyes. This last made the urge to cry magically fade. "I'll follow you home."

His statement was oddly appealing. And as such, completely out of the question. She blinked, moved away from him and his hypnotic scent, and pushed the door closed. He either had to move or have his hip banged.

"What for? To see if I can release the carrier once I get there?" She knew she was being rude. He had helped her with the carrier, after all. But criminy, the man seemed incapable of taking no for an answer. "I don't know how to get it through to you, Mr. Montgomery, but you cannot buy me into playing your pretend-marriage game."

His eyebrows peaked. "Buy?"

"So please just go make your offer to some other woman." *Some other woman who can think straight when you look at her with those green eyes.*

"Buy?" he repeated.

Emma propped a steadying hand on the car, her attention veering from Chandler to Kyle and back again. Chandler, for the moment, seemed satisfied with his pacifier.

"Yes. Buy." Did she have a For Sale sign tattooed on her forehead that was visible only to men or something? "I'm no actress, Mr. Montgomery, and my mama always told me that anyone with eyesight could see in my face when I was telling a lie. Frankly I can't imagine what you could pay that would make attempting such a pretense *worth my while.* I'd be lying not only for your business deal but also to my friends here. So please, take your...offer to someone else."

She jingled her car keys. Decided she wasn't finished. "Better yet, Mr. Montgomery, make your business deal with this other man without lying at all. Don't you think a man who has such staunch values as you've described would prefer a man of integrity to a man who'd resort to a ruse to get his way? Just tell him how the whole misunderstanding began with his stepdaughter."

Kyle shook his head. "My integrity is intact, thanks," he said shortly. "And you are making too much of a simple thing, Emma. If the pretense bothers you so greatly, I guess I'm willing to make it a legal reality. An annulment after the merger is complete and our lives will continue on as if nothing had ever happened."

"Oh, sugar, that's even more ridiculous. I'm a complete stranger to you, but you're willing to marry me to pull off some business deal. Yet you're not willing to tell some man you don't really have a wife, after all? Have you listened to yourself? Do you know how insane that sounds?" Frankly, she thought, a woman would have to be dead to continue on as if nothing had ever happened after meeting Kyle Montgomery. And she was as insane as he was to be debating the merits of such a ridiculous scheme with him.

"I know exactly what I'm proposing, Emma. I haven't gotten to where I am in life by making foolish choices. Choosing you to be my wife, pretend or otherwise, may be a calculated risk, but it's not remotely insane."

Emma just shook her head and slowly walked around the car to the driver's side, using the car as a support to lean on as she moved. She pulled open the door, then looked at him over the roof. "It's a lovely summer afternoon, Mr. Montgomery. Take a walk in the park over there between the buildings. The flowers are beautiful this time of year. Or go across the street to the diner and tell Millie that you'd like a piece of her indescribably delicious blueberry pie. Tell her I sent you and that it's on me, even. But please, please, give up this ridiculous plan of yours. I can't be a part of it."

"You *refuse* to be, you mean."

"Is there any difference?" She squinted into the sunlight. "My integrity isn't for sale."

"If I thought it was, Emma, I wouldn't have decided you were exactly the person I needed to help me." He stepped closer to the car, pinning her with his intense gaze. "When I said I'd make it worth your while, I merely meant that I wouldn't expect you to give up the next six weeks or so of your life without some recompense. I was thinking more on the order of covering your medical costs for the baby. Establishing a trust for Chandler's future. Providing medical insurance for you and your son for the next several years, at least until you can obtain your music-education degree and become established in your career."

Her lips parted. "How did you know—"

"I know a great deal."

She closed her mouth. All a person had to do was go into the diner a few times and he could learn all the gossip he wanted about the waitresses and regular customers. Most everybody who went into the diner knew what her field of study was and how long she'd been inching toward her degree. She didn't need to start conjuring up silly notions of investigations and dossiers. Just because that was what Jeremy's family had—

She closed off the thought. She wanted to go home and get off her feet for a while, feed her son, hold him close and pretend that her body didn't ache as if it had been twisted inside out.

"Goodbye, Mr. Montgomery. It's been...interesting meeting you." She slid into the car, catching her breath at the sharp "discomfort" of the sudden movement.

As she backed out of her parking spot and drove away, she could see Kyle in her rearview mirror. His hands were pushed in his pockets, his stance relaxed. The afternoon breeze ruffled his chestnut hair.

She pulled up at a stop sign, waiting for the traffic to clear, and looked over at her son. "That man is more trouble than anyone I've ever met."

Chandler blinked his round eyes and sucked enthusiastically at his pacifier. Emma was certain he was agreeing with her.

Emma's apartment was a simple studio over the detached garage behind a big old house owned by Penny Holloman. As soon as she pulled up beside the garage and climbed out of the car, she heard Penny call from the back porch. She watched as the older woman skipped down the porch steps and started across the expansive yard.

Emma smiled with real pleasure and waved at her landlady. She reached in and unstrapped Chandler from the carrier, deciding just to leave it where it was, and carefully lifted his warm little body out just as Penny reached her side.

"Oh, sweetie, he's just a peach." Penny brushed her hands down her colorful shirt before reaching out. "Let me take him. You must be exhausted. I swear, when I had Elliot, they kept me in the hospital for a week. Was I ever glad, let me tell you. The last thing I wanted to do was get back home and start cooking three meals a day when I was a nervous wreck about doing something wrong with a new baby."

Emma's arms felt empty when Penny took Chandler into her own. But the other woman was oohing and ahhing over him, obviously delighted to hold him. Emma collected the plastic bag and her case and drew in a breath as she faced the wooden steps leading up the side of the garage to her apartment.

"I just got home myself, and I'm so sorry I wasn't able to meet you at the hospital," Penny chattered on, taking Emma's overnighter from her. "You shouldn't be carrying that," she chastised, heading up the stairs. "If I could have canceled my meeting, I would have. I feel terrible that you drove yourself home like this."

"Don't worry about it." Emma followed her landlady more slowly. Once she got Chandler fed and settled, she was definitely going to take a few of those extra-strength pain relievers her doctor had advised. "Megan agreed to, but I said no. We were fine." She made it to the landing and pushed open the door, stopping short. "Oh, my!"

Penny laughed and rested her cheek on Chandler's head. "Isn't it fabulous? Why didn't you tell me you'd met a man? Because I know for certain that good-for-nothing Jeremy St. James would never have been so extravagant."

Emma cautiously stepped into her apartment. Glorious displays of summer flowers decorated every single surface. An enormous bouquet of yellow and white balloons hovered above her small round dining table. "I haven't met a man," she murmured faintly. Cheerful daisies graced the small table just inside the door and she touched one of the blooms. "Well, nobody except… No. He wouldn't have. He couldn't—"

"Who? Kyle Montgomery perhaps? He is a handsome one. And quite determined, too."

Emma felt light-headed. She dumped the plastic bag on the floor and cautiously lowered herself to the couch. "Kyle…was here?"

"Earlier today." Penny nodded. She flipped open a changing pad on top of the table and gently settled Chandler on top of it. In seconds she'd changed his diaper and carried him back to Emma. "There you go, sweetie. You feed him and I'll get some lunch started for you."

Emma had a lot of questions, but her son's hunger was the primary need. She opened her blouse and situated her son in her arms. He latched on greedily and she chuckled and winced both at once. "Good thing you know what you're doing there, pumpkin, 'cause if it was up to me, I'd still be fumbling around."

Penny must have heard her, because she laughed lightly. "When Elliot was born, bottle feeding was the preferred choice. Herman was horrified when I insisted on nursing our baby." She came back into the room, carrying a tray with a sandwich, a cup of soup and a tall glass of lemonade, which she set on the metal footlocker Emma used as a coffee table. She nudged it within reach of Emma, then pushed the footrest she'd given Emma for Christmas the year before next to the couch.

Emma lifted her feet onto it and let out a long relieved

breath. But Penny wasn't finished. Not until she'd taken Emma's two bed pillows from the top shelf in the closet where they were kept during the day and propped them behind Emma's neck and under her knees.

"There. That's better, isn't it?" Penny patted her hand and continued moving around the small apartment, unpacking the few items from Emma's overnighter and adding the baby items from the plastic bag to the secondhand chest of drawers Emma had found. "Too bad your mother can't be here to help you," Penny said.

Emma shook her head. That was the last thing she needed. "Mama's helping my sisters back home with the grandkids she already has." She shifted against the pillows and sighed sleepily. "She doesn't understand why I'm a single mother, anyway, so her helping would have been accompanied by a lot of lectures I don't want to hear. Once a week is plenty for me."

"The only one needing a good lecture is that pimple on the face of society who left you to fend for yourself."

Emma managed to smile at the caustic description of Jeremy St. James.

"Fortunately I'm able to wholeheartedly say that I approve of your new choice," Penny went on.

"If you're referring to Kyle Montgomery, he is *not* my new choice. He's just…"

Penny waited expectantly, her eyes sparkling with expectation. "Just handsome enough to make even my old bones sit up and take notice?"

"You're not old."

Penny chuckled. "Old enough to know a perfect

match when I see one. A grown man doesn't track down a landlady at a church committee meeting to gain access to his young lady's apartment where he proceeds to fill it with every flower known to humankind if he's not totally smitten."

Totally determined, totally insane and totally off-limits. "I don't even know the man," Emma insisted. "I met him just this morning."

A fact that seemed to delight Penny even more. "Well, you certainly made an impression on him," she said. "I'll leave you to rest now, but I'll come back this evening with some supper for you."

"You don't have to do that, Penny. I can manage."

Penny stopped at the door and shook her head. "I know you can manage, sweetie. But sometimes you don't have to do it *all* on your own, so let me help in the ways that I can." She plucked a small white envelope out of the daisy arrangement and handed it to Emma. "Your admirer left this for you." She winked and went out the door, shutting only the outer screen. Emma heard her footsteps on the stairway, then all was quiet again, except for the thumping of her pulse in her ears.

She nibbled the inside of her lip, turning the small envelope over in her fingers. He had nothing to say that she wanted to hear. Or, in this case, *read.*

"Oh, Emma, honestly. It's just a card." She tore open the envelope and pulled out the flat card.

Chandler is blessed to have such a lovely mother.

Emma's eyes blurred. She looked down at her son to find him looking up at her. "We're both blessed, aren't we, pumpkin? I just figured that a man like Kyle Montgomery wouldn't be able to see that."

She lifted Chandler to her shoulder and readjusted her clothes. Kissing his cheek, she brought her legs up onto the couch and lay back, cradling him securely.

Then she closed her eyes and they both slept.

Chapter Three

By the next morning Emma decided she owed her mother an apology. Hattie Valentine had had six daughters, managing to feed and clothe them all, for the most part single-handedly.

Emma, however, seemed to be completely out of her element with just one baby. Chandler wanted to eat every other hour, which meant she got very little sleep. Sometime in the middle of the night she gave up on the notion of having the baby sleep in his bassinet and just kept him in bed with her. She stacked diapers and wipes on the floor beside them and slept when he slept. Fed him when hungry, changed him when wet.

This was not at all the way it was supposed to go, according to her *Now You Are a Mother!* book which spouted tripe about four-hour schedules and other such nonsense.

By midmorning, her small home looked like a tornado had torn through it, leaving flowers and minute baby T-shirts and receiving blankets behind.

Penny came by, took in the chaos without a blink of surprise and shooed Emma into the bathroom where, she assured her, she'd feel better after a nice long shower.

"As soon as I'm under the water, he'll be hungry,"

Emma had protested tiredly. "I'll shower...oh, I don't know, when he's two years old."

Penny had laughed and scooped Chandler off Emma's lap. "I think I hear a verse of the baby blues somewhere in there." She'd waved toward the bathroom. "Go on now. You need a few minutes for yourself."

Emma wasn't so sure, but she'd gone. She looked at herself in the mirror, grimaced and turned on the shower. A half hour later she emerged to find her apartment tidied up, Chandler sleeping and Penny nowhere in sight.

"Sure," she whispered lovingly over Chandler in the bassinet. "*Now* you sleep."

A creak on the stairs outside told her someone was coming up. Probably Penny. Emma adjusted the strap of her red sundress and smoothed back her wet hair. "You were right," she said as she went to the wood-framed screen door and pushed it open. "I do feel better."

"My sisters always say that flowers make a woman feel better," Kyle Montgomery said smoothly as he reached the top step and smiled at her. He looked dismayingly appealing in pleated khakis, a whiter-than-white collarless shirt and navy jacket. Laugh lines fanned out from his eyes. "Your landlady said you were up and about. You look very nice in red. Fresh as a wild poppy."

Emma flushed. Her hair hung straight and wet to her shoulders, her feet were bare and the poppy-red dress stretched too tightly across her chest. She crossed her arms and moistened her lips. "Thank you for the flowers and card. It was very nice."

A smile flirted with his lips as he looked at her. "May I come in?"

Emma swallowed. "I'm not sure that's a good idea."

"Why not?"

"Because I'll probably end up being rude to you, and being surrounded by beautiful flowers from you when that happens seems like it'd be in poor taste."

"Rude? Ah, Emma, I think you've just been honest. I'm glad you like the flowers, though. I have one sister who insists roses are the only flower worth receiving, but you didn't seem like the rose type to me."

"I'm allergic to them," Emma said shortly. The last man to give her roses had thoroughly betrayed her. She wasn't sure she'd ever disassociate roses from that awful time.

Kyle's eyebrow peaked. "How fortunate I chose otherwise, then." He reached past her through the doorway to the daisies sitting just inside and snapped off a bloom. He lifted his hand, frowning slightly when Emma gave a startled jump.

She clenched her teeth, flushing again when he tucked the short stem of the daisy behind her ear. She swallowed and stepped away from the door, silently allowing him entry.

He walked to the center of the living area, seeming to dominate the space. "How's Chandler?"

Emma shut the screen quietly. "Fine. Sleeping at the moment."

He nodded, glanced at the blank wall opposite the couch. "Why did you get rid of the piano?"

Emma frowned. "How do you know I had a piano?"

He walked over to the spot where her upright had stood for three years. He brushed a leather boot over the permanent indentations the heavy instrument had made in her taupe-colored carpet. "I noticed the marks on the rug earlier. Why, Emma?"

She shrugged. "I'm sure you've already come to your own conclusion."

"You needed the money."

"I had other payments that were more important," she corrected.

"How long have you played?"

"The piano?" *Not long enough.* "Since I was thirteen." She'd been caught sneaking into the church back in Dooley, Tennessee. But instead of hauling her back to her mother with a few strong words, Reverend Harold Chandler had decided Emma could use the piano twice a week in the afternoons after school. They couldn't afford lessons, but Emma had used the music books at the church, and by the time she'd graduated from high school, she'd taught herself enough to earn a modest music scholarship.

She owed a lot to Reverend Chandler.

"I envy you," he said.

She lifted her eyebrows. "Whatever for?"

He shrugged. "I took piano lessons when I was sixteen. Never did get the hang of it. I could play the notes, I guess. Just not...the *music.*"

Oh, she really didn't want to hear anything like that from this man. It bespoke a sensitivity in him she didn't want to acknowledge. It was easier, safer, casting him as the rich man intent on doing a business deal no matter what.

After all, it wasn't as if her one foray into the man-woman arena had been a terrific success. Her judgment had been faulty, her sensibility nonexistent.

Emma nibbled the inside of her lip and sat down on the couch. "Isn't it a workday, Kyle? Shouldn't you be out running your business rather than discussing the finer aspects of being a musician?"

"That's what I like about you, Emma. You get right to the point."

"Which is?"

He sat down on the other end of the couch and stretched his arm along the back. His jacket gaped, exposing more of the shirt he wore beneath.

Emma turned her eyes from the sight of his strong brown throat rising from the open collar.

"This is business for me, Emma. You know that." He looked toward the bassinet situated near the table, presenting Emma with his profile.

It was as perfect as the rest of him. All sharp angles and utterly masculine.

"I was invited to Payton Cummings's dinner party on Sunday evening. I've told him I can't join them because I've other commitments. Family commitments. I'd prefer to back up that statement with some semblance of truth."

His fingertips were inches from her shoulder and she shifted, putting more distance between them. "You've said you have sisters. Make plans with them. It's less of a lie than using Chandler and me."

Kyle shook his head. "Tell me what you need in life, Emma Valentine, and I'll do my damnedest to make it so, if you'll just help me with this. Forget about this *buying* notion you've got in your head and look at it as one favor for another."

"I need my son," she said, exasperated, "but I need no favors from you or any other man." She pushed to her feet, pacing to the bassinet and back again.

"He really did a number on you, didn't he?" Kyle's gaze followed her. "The jerk who was stupid enough to leave you alone and pregnant."

"You know nothing about it."

He nodded thoughtfully. "No, I don't. It's your business entirely. But I can protect you from him."

Emma swallowed. Little did he know she didn't need protection from anyone, least of all the St. James family. They wanted nothing to do with her. Had ensured it. And she didn't need Kyle Montgomery coming in here, smelling like a dream, reminding her how foolish she'd been.

Kyle rose and stepped close to her, bringing with him his addictive scent. He touched her chin with his finger. "I can protect Chandler."

There was no wheedling in his voice. Only the simple utterly confident assurance of a man who'd been around long enough to know his abilities. One who'd been around enough to pinpoint the one thing that would penetrate her defenses.

"Come on, Emma. Help me."

She hesitated. He was so close she could see the darker rim of green around his irises. "Kyle, I—"

"Yoo-hoo, anybody up there?" Footsteps pounded up the stairs outside and Emma blinked, stepping back. She cleared her throat and crossed to the screen door, looking out to see Millie Johnson, her boss at the diner, coming up. "I've brought food," she said when she saw Emma. She lifted the cardboard box that was filled to the brim with foam containers and foil-wrapped packages. "It'll last you a few days, and then I'll replace it with more while I try to talk you into taking more than two weeks off with the baby. You need six weeks, and that's that."

Emma just shook her head. Her boss, her friend, had a heart wider than the Colorado sky. "Come on in, Millie. I'm not sure where I'll put the food, though. Penny's been keeping the fridge stocked, too." She smiled wryly. "Apparently my friends think I'm in danger of starving to death on my own."

"Oh, shush." Millie brushed past her, stopping in surprise at the sight of a man inside. She recovered quickly, though, introducing herself as she strode across to the small kitchen.

Kyle raked his fingers through his hair, squelching an impatient sigh at this latest interruption. He'd been reaching her, dammit. He knew it. He'd seen it in her chocolate-brown eyes. He slid a business card from the inner pocket on his jacket and handed it to Emma. "I can be reached anytime, anywhere, at that number," he said softly. "But I need an answer soon."

She hesitated, obviously indecisive. But then she

reached for the card, her slender fingers carefully avoiding his longer darker ones as she took it from him. "I gave you my answer yesterday."

"Think about it," Kyle suggested. "I'll be in touch if I don't hear from you."

"A threat?"

Her sarcasm didn't faze him. "I have no reason to threaten you, Emma. We can be on the same side. You're completely safe from me." He was making the promise to her as much as to himself, he realized. When she looked up at him with her wide wary eyes, he was reminded of fairy-tale heroines.

Disgusted with the direction of his thoughts, he strode to the door. He'd given up on fairy tales when he was seven. "I'll look forward to hearing from you, Emma." He left then, carrying the image of her studying his card with a sober expression on her lovely unadorned face.

After Millie's brief visit, Emma fixed some lunch for herself and freshened the water for the flowers. Then Chandler awakened and she gathered her courage to give him his first bath. It was a rousing success, and as soon as she finished slipping his wriggling little arms and legs into his lightweight romper, he sighed with his whole little self and went to sleep, perfect as an angel.

Emma sat watching him for long minutes, nearly sitting on her hands to keep from touching him, from disturbing him simply because she wanted to feel his warmth. "My little man," she whispered, then began humming under her breath. Her fingers automatically moved with the music that was vivid and brilliant in her mind, and realizing it, she clasped them in her lap.

It wasn't as if she'd never play again, she reasoned. Every week when she worked with the children's choir at the Benderhoff school, she'd be playing piano. But it wasn't the same as sitting at her own instrument whenever she wanted, playing to her heart's content.

"I'll teach you to play," she promised Chandler softly. Then she frowned as Kyle's words whispered through her mind. He'd learned the notes, but he'd known the true heart of the music wasn't there for him. "You'll feel the music, too, pumpkin. Whether it's piano or something else, we'll share that joy. I know it."

The afternoon was passing when she again heard feet on the steps outside. This time, however, she was expecting visitors, and she went to the door, smiling at the two women coming up. She'd met Taylor Fletcher and Megan Malone at the Buttonwood Baby Clinic when they'd all been taking the same childbirth classes. Except Megan was Megan Macgregor now, thoroughly adored by her new husband, Mac.

Megan had her baby, Tyler, in her arms and led the way up the stairs, while Taylor, enormously pregnant, followed more slowly.

Once they reached the top, Emma held open the door. "We should have met at the diner or something, Taylor. I just didn't think about you having to climb the stairs."

Taylor rolled her eyes and awkwardly settled on the couch, folding her arms across her belly. "Which is worse?" she asked breathlessly. "Me climbing stairs at this stage or you climbing stairs immediately after having a baby?" She looked over at the bassinet. "But you can bring Master Valentine over to see me, if you don't mind, because I think I'm stuck here on the couch for the duration."

Megan settled on the couch, too, resting Tyler on her lap. "Yup. Bring him over here, Emma. Let's compare birthing horror stories and scare Taylor silly."

Taylor snorted softly and Emma shook her head at the two women. She rolled the bassinet toward them, trying to jostle it as little as possible. Then she handed out glasses of lemonade and set a tray of cookies from one of the foil packages of Millie's on the metal footlocker and sat down to catch up with her friends.

"So what's with the floral display?" Taylor finally asked when all the gossip was expended. "It looks like you received flowers from every customer who has ever gone into Mom & Pop's."

"Kyle Montgomery," Emma answered without thinking.

Megan's eyebrows shot up. "As in Kyle Montgomery, head of ChandlerAIR? I read an article recently about him. He's—"

"I know." Emma folded her arms over the edge of the bassinet and gently smoothed Chandler's hair.

"How did you meet him? I thought you were totally off men after what Jeremy St. James did." Taylor tried to sit forward to reach the cookies, but couldn't. Emma leaned over and handed her two.

"I am not *off* men," Emma defended. "I just don't need or want one, that's all."

"Famous last words," Megan quipped.

"Besides," Emma continued, ignoring Megan's comment, "he's not interested in me. Well, not *that* way."

"Oh, now this is sounding *really* interesting," Taylor said lightly. "Come on, Emma, tell me. Then I can live vicariously on the excitement in your life."

"I wouldn't call it exciting to have yet another man try to buy me off."

Both her friends' faces sobered.

"Oh, that's not exactly right," Emma admitted, feeling frustration well up all over again. "He visited me yesterday morning with the most outrageous proposition." She told them the bare bones of Kyle's suggestion. "I told him no, of course."

"No!" Megan stared at her, dismayed. "But Emma, think of what a man like Kyle Montgomery can offer in return for your help."

Taylor was nodding, too.

"It doesn't matter," Emma insisted. "I'll manage just fine with Chandler."

"How?" Taylor asked bluntly. "By selling your television set next? By taking on a *third* job? Emma, you're barely scraping by, and only a week ago you told me your latest fantasy was buying health insurance."

She'd expected her friends' support. She stood up and began pacing. Among the flowers, she fancied that the memory of Kyle's aftershave still lingered. "He's just another rich man thinking he can buy his way through life. I don't want any part of it. It's dishonest."

Megan rose, too, cradling her baby in one arm and catching Emma's hand with her other. "Emma, I know how hard this must be for you. But Chandler is *here*. You have to think about him. What's best for him. Maybe taking this offer is something you should seriously consider."

Emma looked away from her friend's warm hazel eyes. "You agree with her, don't you, Taylor?"

The younger woman nodded. "That's what a good mother does," she murmured. "Thinks of her child first."

Emma felt her eyes burn. Taylor had already decided to give up her child for adoption to a family who could provide for her baby in a way she herself couldn't. She was younger than both Megan and Emma, yet Emma felt that Taylor was quite possibly the bravest woman she'd ever met.

She dashed her hands across her eyes, then propped them on her hips, sniffing hugely. "Shootfire," she said in her best Southern drawl. "This afternoon wasn't supposed to be a weepy wallow. I've told the man no, so that's all there is to it. He's probably findin' himself another young bride as we speak." Then she focused on Megan. "And speaking of brides, how is married life treating *you*, Mrs. Macgregor?"

Megan smiled and said that married life was terrific, but her gaze met Emma's meaningfully. Fortunately, however, she didn't return to the subject of Kyle, and soon Taylor asked Emma if the labor and delivery was really just a matter of "discomfort" as the leaders of the childbirth class kept telling them.

Emma snorted and Megan laughed. Taylor blew out a huge breath and moaned. "That's what I was afraid of." She struggled to her feet to go to the bathroom.

"You're still planning to return to work next week?" Megan asked Emma.

"To Benderhoff," Emma said. "Their summer session begins and I'll be teaching two afternoon classes there." She'd always enjoyed the classes she taught part-time at the private school. But she was willing to teach this session specifically for the money it would bring. Money that would eventually pay the hospital bill. "Millie says that if I set foot in the diner before two weeks are up, she'll shoot me with that shotgun she keeps in the back. If she had her way, I'd take off three times that long."

"What about your fall semester?" Megan asked quietly. "How can you fit in your own classes?"

Emma swallowed, then managed a bright smile she knew didn't fool her friend. "I'm going to take off next semester. It'll be a nice break." She just hoped the one semester didn't stretch into two. Or three. She'd already spent so long working toward her degree that every delay was frustrating. Even this one.

Taylor came out then, pressing her hands to her back. Emma hugged her friends, thanked them for the baby outfits they'd brought for Chandler and watched them carefully descend the steps before climbing into Megan's vehicle.

She stood on the landing for a few minutes, breathing in the crisp clear air. Someone was barbecuing nearby. She could smell the distinctive delectable scent of sizzling steak. A dog barked, and someone was mowing a lawn.

It was a beautiful summer evening. She had her health

and a perfect child. There was no reason to feel the panic welling in her chest. No reason at all.

She went inside and picked up Chandler, rocking him in her arms as she paced her small living room. She didn't look at Kyle's card, which she'd left on the dining table. But she was painfully aware of it sitting there between a bouquet of bright orange daylilies and a yellow balloon that had lost some of its helium and was hovering an inch over the table.

"I love you, pumpkin. I'll never let you down," she pledged, pressing her lips to Chandler's head. He wriggled and Emma chuckled. "Always hungry. Well, food is something I seem to have lots of for you."

Kyle called at precisely seven that evening. Emma's answer hadn't changed, but she was grateful he hadn't shown up in person this time. It was difficult enough re-iterating her "no" over an impersonal telephone line.

He didn't sound unduly disturbed by their brief exchange, which made Emma think even more strongly that he probably had several other women waiting as backups. Kyle Montgomery was the kind of man who had best-case scenarios and worst-case scenarios planned to the nth detail.

While Chandler slept, Emma wrote thank-you notes for the various gifts and cards she'd received, then set about looking through the pile of mail she'd been receiv-ing and ignoring for the past week.

There was a long chatty letter from her mother. All about Emma's sisters—*married* sisters, that was— Emma's nieces and nephews, and Hattie's job at the grocery store in Dooley. There were cards from two of her regular customers at Millie's and a letter from Benderhoff. Emma slit it open, expecting a note about the baby or about the upcoming session.

What she wasn't expecting was the polite missive saying that her services wouldn't be required, after all. She didn't even rate a thank-you for the past two years.

She read it through twice, sure she'd misunderstood. She'd been teaching at Benderhoff steadily. Her work had always been more than satisfactory, or so she'd been told at each review period. Telling herself not to panic, she went into the kitchen and yanked out her telephone directory. She found the home number of Emil Craddock, the headmaster of Benderhoff and dialed it with a shaking finger. They wouldn't do this to her. They couldn't.

But five minutes later she hung up again, knowing that they *had*. She paced. She added numbers in her head. She thought of ways she could get by without the money—the rather good money—she'd earned at Benderhoff.

She finally pulled out her sofa bed, lay down with Chandler beside her and tried to make herself sleep while he slept. But sleep didn't come. All she could remember was growing up in Dooley, getting her clothing secondhand from the rummage sales at church, doing the grocery shopping with her two older sisters, following their mama's list to the letter because they had to pay with food stamps and only certain things were eligible.

At four o'clock in the morning Emma finally climbed out of bed and retrieved the business card from the table. She turned on the light in the kitchen and, heedless of the hour, reached for the phone, dialing hurriedly, before she lost her nerve. It rang only twice. Then Kyle's voice, husky and deep, answered.

She swallowed, but the enormous knot in her throat didn't go away. "Is your offer still on the table?"

"You know it is, Emma."

She drew in a short breath. "Then I accept. I'll pretend to be your wife until your business deal goes through."

"I'll be at your place in a couple of hours."

A tear leaked from the corner of her tightly closed eyes. She was grateful that he didn't express any undue pleasure or satisfaction. That his voice was as steady and sure as ever. "We'll be ready," she said.

Then she hung up and went to pack her clothes and Chandler's stretchy little sleepers and diapers. They were the easy things.

She couldn't help thinking, though, that she was also packing away her honesty. And that wasn't easy at all.

Chapter Four

"This is everything?"

Emma rubbed her hand over Chandler's back. She focused on the suitcases she'd left sitting in the center of her apartment. Kyle was picking them up with ease. "For now," she replied.

He glanced over his shoulder at her, one eyebrow raised. "If there's more, we might as well take them."

"It's just winter clothes and things that won't fit Chandler for months yet." By then, Kyle's need for a wife would be past and she and her son would be back home. Her life would return to normal, and all that would remain to remind her of this time would be the knowledge that she'd had a price, after all.

"If you're sure."

She nodded, even though she wasn't sure of anything, particularly with Kyle standing there with her discount-store suitcases tucked under his arms. They surely did clash with his Rolex watch, she thought.

Chandler squirmed and made a noise, and she pressed her lips to his head, cradling him closely. She stepped out of the way so that Kyle could go out the doorway, then she followed him, picking up Chandler's diaper bag.

"Leave it," Kyle said. "I'll come back for it."

The bag was stuffed to the gills with diapers and wipes and powder and lotion. It shouldn't have weighed a ton, but it felt as if it did. She reluctantly left it sitting on the end table by the daisies and carefully descended the stairs. Kyle had stored the suitcases in the trunk and was waiting by the open passenger door.

Emma looked from his sleek black car to her sturdy orange sedan—ancient and built like a tank. "I should follow you. Then I'll have my car and—"

"It would be better if you left your car here," he said smoothly. "I've got a second vehicle at home that you can use to your heart's content."

Her stomach clenched uncomfortably, and she kept the rest of her suggestion to herself: that she could fit Chandler's bassinet easily into her backseat. He probably figured her old car was too much of an eyesore for the rarefied atmosphere of his neighborhood.

Well, Emma Valentine, you've made your bed... She could almost hear her mother's voice.

"I've already moved Chandler's seat into the backseat of my car. Can you get him into it, or would you like me to?"

"I will." She didn't look at him as he placed his hand on the top of the open door, waiting. But she couldn't help noticing the sprinkling of dark hair on burnished skin, taut tendons and strong, well-groomed hands.

Reaching into the narrow rear of his car was awkward, but she managed to get Chandler into the seat and fasten the harness. He slept through the whole process, but Emma felt positively out of breath by the time she straightened.

Kyle caught her elbow when she swayed. "You okay?"

She nodded and slid herself into the passenger side. A sinfully soft leather seat cradled her like loving arms. She gathered in the trailing hem of her ankle-length broomstick skirt, and Kyle pushed the door closed before heading up the steps again. She heard the slap of her wooden screen door and in moments he reappeared with the diaper bag.

He strode around to the driver's side and set the bag in the back next to Chandler, then slid behind the wheel with an ease Emma couldn't help but envy.

The engine came to life with a low throaty growl, and he backed away from the garage, her apartment, her car and her hold on reality.

She bit her lip, turning her eyes away from the sight. It was a gray dawn, and Penny's house was still dark. She hadn't even told her what she was doing. She'd have to call her. Make some type of explanation.

Kyle shifted gears, and when his hand inadvertently brushed her thigh, Emma jerked. He glanced at her without comment as he drove out of the alley onto the morning-quiet street.

Emma swallowed, the silence in the car weighing her down. She stared out the side window as they passed the diner and headed east. She wasn't surprised. Naturally a man like Kyle would have his home in the wealthier section of town. Eastridge. She'd once had hazy dreams of living in one of the sparkling new homes with a three-car garage and a pool out back. Living in one of the homes as Jeremy's wife.

They drove through the exclusive area. Passed the discreet sign that directed individuals to the outstanding Benderhoff facility. She stifled a sigh and looked over her shoulder at Chandler.

"We'll be there in a few minutes," Kyle said.

Emma nodded, and surreptitiously rubbed her palms down her thighs.

"Baxter will probably have breakfast waiting. I've got to go to the airport for a while. A few hours. But then I'll come home and we can do some shopping."

Who was Baxter? "Shopping?"

"For the nursery. I had a decorator in for most of the house." He turned down an unmarked road, taking them into the rising sun.

Emma looked out the back window at the residential area they'd left behind.

"Something wrong?"

"No. I...well, I assumed you lived in Eastridge," she admitted.

He shook his head and kept driving. And Emma, who had lived in Buttonwood for several years, realized she didn't have a clue where they were. The paved road, only wide enough to accommodate two passing cars, curved and climbed. Then they rounded a sharp outcropping of rocks and shot down again, straight toward a spectacular house that seemed an actual part of the ridge that overlooked Buttonwood.

Kyle pulled up into a drive that was narrow simply because two-thirds of it was being excavated. He parked in front of the house before turning to look at Emma. He hoped she liked it. Only because he wanted her to be comfortable here, he rapidly assured himself. But she was facing out the side window and he couldn't see her reaction, except for the fingertips she drummed silently against her thigh, which was draped with her purple-and-pink skirt. "I realize it's not Eastridge, but do you think it'll do?"

Her fingers went still and she looked at him. "It's big." Then her eyes widened slightly and her cheeks colored. "And...lovely."

He smiled faintly. "Did you expect a circus tent or something?"

"No. No, of course not." Her lips pressed together for a moment. "Who is Baxter?"

"Baxter?" Kyle looked beyond Emma toward the house. How to describe the man. His conscience? His friend? "My housekeeper," he said after a moment. "But he'd say butler. He'll be crazy about Chandler. You'll probably see more of him than me, actually."

Which didn't seem to reassure her any, Kyle thought, noticing the way her fingers started drumming again. "I'm sure he heard us drive up and is probably setting breakfast on the table as we speak." He climbed out of the car and went around to open her door, helping her from the low-slung vehicle. He should have brought the Land Rover. He'd thought it about a dozen times since he'd parked outside her garage apartment.

This family stuff would take some adjusting.

Before she could contort herself into the narrow space to reach the car seat, Kyle reached past her and handed her the diaper bag, then scooped out the baby. He straightened, automatically situating the baby in one arm. Then he closed Emma's car door and settled his free hand at the small of her back, his fingertips tingling at the contact with her soft shirt.

He focused on the white-haired man who'd opened the front door and waited on the porch. Kyle didn't need to look at Baxter's disapproving gaze to know the man didn't like what he, Kyle, was doing. Not with the pretend-family bit, and certainly not with his determination to acquire CCS.

Ignoring Baxter for the moment, he slid the diaper bag from Emma's shoulder and touched her back again, which earned him another wide-eyed look. "Relax. We're not gonna stuff you in an oven and eat you."

"I am relaxed."

He raised a brow, disbelieving. "Let's go inside." He nudged her forward along the narrow stone walkway. It was scheduled to be widened and graded within the next few weeks.

"Bax, this is Emma Valentine and Chandler. Emma, Baxter. Anything you need, he's the man." Kyle eyed him as they approached.

Baxter turned up his nose at Kyle and focused, instead, on the baby in his arms. "There's a handsome boy, with a good solid name. May I?" He lifted Chandler away from Kyle at Emma's nod. He brought his wrinkled aristocratic-looking face close to the baby and cooed.

Kyle caught Emma's eye. "Told you so," he murmured.

"Breakfast is on the patio, sir. Miss Emma." Baxter turned and headed back into the house, still cooing to the baby.

"Does he have grandchildren?"

Kyle shook his head. "No family." Except him. "I think the man was a nanny in a past life, though. Bax, who won't start the day without a starched shirt, tie and crisp black suit, sees a person under two feet tall and goes into coochy-coo mode." The housekeeper also made no bones about his belief that Kyle was throwing away the best years of his life by concentrating so exclusively on his business.

Emma smiled, but she was obviously uneasy. He could see it in her eyes, as well as the arms she'd crossed tightly across her chest.

"If you don't want Bax to take the baby, you can tell him so," Kyle said. "He'll understand."

She uncrossed her arms, only to twist her fingers together. "No, it's okay."

"For a few minutes, anyway," he guessed.

She smiled, a little more easily. "For a few minutes."

"Just like my sister. She didn't want to let her baby out of her sight, either. Come on. Breakfast will be getting cold."

Emma swallowed and stepped into the foyer, then realized her mouth had dropped open and quickly snapped it shut.

The interior of the house wasn't at all like the exterior.

"What do you think?"

He'd had a decorator, she reminded herself. "The windows are fabulous," she said truthfully. They lined the wall ahead of her, giving a beautiful view of Buttonwood beyond the expansive gardens outside the windows.

"I liked them," Kyle said behind her. "Looking out and seeing sky."

Which didn't seem to fit with the coldly beautiful marble, glass and miles of white furnishings any more than those very furnishings fit the nature-blending exterior of the house.

"You mentioned a nursery?" Lord, she hoped the nursery was an empty undecorated room. She could bring some bright cheerful pillows from home. Pin up a quilt on the wall. Something.

"It's upstairs. But let's eat first."

Emma nibbled the inside of her lip, but nodded. She followed him through the wintry house and breathed a sigh of relief when she stepped through French doors that opened onto the garden.

Out there it truly was lovely. Bushes and riotous flowers and lush green grass. Right in the middle of the garden was a lovely glass and verdigris table with matching chairs. The fresh fruit, juices and covered silver serving dishes set on the table looked like something out of a gourmet magazine. Which, of course, made her stomach rumble.

She pressed her palm to her waist, hoping Kyle hadn't heard the distinctive sound. But she suspected by the deepening corner of his mouth that he had.

He pulled out one of the iron chairs for her, then sat across from her, his back to the sharp drop-off. She realized there was an iron fence hidden amid the thick hedges. Beyond that, Buttonwood spread out like a jewel.

She closed her eyes and breathed in the fresh morning air, the flowers, the *green*. They'd no sooner seated themselves, though, when Baxter appeared with a cushioned straight-back chair he insisted Emma use.

She switched from the iron chair to the new one, which was truly comfortable. Then she forgot about the view and the chairs because Kyle sat across from her. Impossibly compelling. Indolent and urbane. Smooth and quietly powerful.

He unsettled her. Pure and simple.

So she focused on Baxter, who'd replaced his severe black suit coat for a baby sling, which held her son cozily against his chest. And Chandler was obviously content as a snug bug, since he slept through the pouring of coffee and juice, the uncovering of a steaming platter of fluffy scrambled eggs and bacon. Baxter asked if she cared for anything else.

"No, thank you, Mr. Baxter. This looks lovely."

He beamed approvingly. "Just Baxter, Miss." He looked at Kyle wordlessly, then returned to the kitchen.

Emma eyed Kyle, but his attention was on the food he was piling onto his plate. The early sunshine glinted off his hair, highlighting deep strands of auburn.

He looked up then, his eyes focusing on her with disturbing intensity. "Emma, stop worrying."

"I wasn't… Yes, I was." And it bothered her that he'd been able to see it. "I can't help it." She picked up her fork, held it suspended over her plate. "My mama says I came out of the womb that way. Worrying."

His eyes crinkled. "And where *is* your mama?"

"Tennessee."

"She's not able to come and see her grandson?"

"Mama's got lots of grandkids." He just kept watching her steadily and Emma found the words coming without volition. "Chandler is just one more, except I didn't have the good grace to get married first like my sisters did."

"She'll feel differently when she holds Chandler in her arms. I can arrange for her to visit if you'd like. The flight would—"

"Mama would never get on an airplane," Emma said hurriedly. Even if Emma had been able to afford the plane ticket for her mother to visit, it would have been wasted. Hattie Valentine traveled by bus or car or not at all. Not even Kyle Montgomery could change that. And her mother definitely wouldn't approve of her middle daughter's latest "shenanigans."

"What about your father?"

"What about him?" She looked straight at him.

He stared right back. "I don't like discussing the man who contributed to my existence, either," he murmured after a moment.

Emma's gaze fell, unable to withstand the intensity in his. Nor the empathy. Then her stomach growled again.

"Eat, Emma."

Cheeks burning, she poked her fork into the eggs and ate.

The nursery, when Kyle eventually led the way upstairs after showing her through the rest of the glacially decorated first floor, was blessedly plain. Emma was also pleased to see that it shared the same panoramic view of the gardens, Buttonwood and the brilliant blue sky. The room had a high ceiling, plain white walls and a warm hardwood floor. Not a piece of marble or chrome in sight.

There was a connecting door to a smaller bedroom beside it, which contained a wide four-poster bed, nightstands and a matching chest of drawers. Emma wanted to sag with relief, but she controlled herself and moved across the squishy carpet to open a closed door. It revealed a spacious walk-in closet.

She looked over at Kyle. His hair seemed darker against the backdrop of the white room. "You kept the decorator from coming upstairs?"

"I can call her back this week if you'd like."

"No!" Emma said hurriedly. "No, I didn't mean that at all. The rooms are just fine the way they are."

"You can pick out what you like for furnishings when we go out later. And whatever you need for the nursery, of course."

"Chandler's bassinet is fine for now," Emma said. "I can bring it over here when I get my car."

"I already said you wouldn't need your car."

"Maybe I want my car. Just because it's not the type of car *your* wife would drive doesn't mean—"

"Hold on there, Emma. The only reason you won't need it is because I've a Land Rover you can use. I don't care if you want to drive a tank or a Ferrari, as long as it's road worthy. But until the work is finished on the drive, there simply isn't room for three vehicles here."

She propped her hands on her hips. "Sugar, I saw the size of the garage off the side of the house. It could handle a fleet of cars."

"Ordinarily that's true. But right now it's got the skeleton of an old Lockheed P38 in it, and that takes up a sight more room than that gunboat you drive. Give me a chance to reorganize things a little, and you'll have your car here with you. Okay?"

She blinked. Nodded. It certainly wasn't the explanation she'd expected. And she actually felt badly for having misjudged him.

"In any case," Kyle went on as if they hadn't had the little sidetrack about cars and garages, "you'll need more for the nursery than a bassinet. Don't you want a rocking chair and—"

"We're not going to be here all that long, anyway, so there's no point in buying a lot of things."

"There's every point." Kyle straightened from his slouch against the wall. "As far as everyone else is concerned, you and Chandler belong here. Naturally I'd provide for my family. What new parents don't go out and buy everything on the planet they can afford for their new child, whether it's necessary or not? I learned that quite well when my sister had her baby."

"For goodness' sake, Kyle. Do you think Mr. Cummings is going to want to snoop around your house to see how well you've equipped your supposed child's nursery?"

"I'm not leaving anything to chance."

She let out a long breath and closed the closet door. "It's a wonder you didn't find a *real* wife, then," she murmured as she opened the next door. A bathroom. A big beautiful bathroom with a big beautiful bathtub that was practically large enough to swim in. It made her forget for a moment the issue about her car. "Oh, my," she breathed.

"So that's what it takes to impress you," Kyle said, coming up beside her. "A big square whirlpool tub."

"Considering my apartment only has a shower about the size of a postage stamp, you're darned tootin' I appreciate a nice tub." She made a soft sound. "Seems kind of naughty to be discussing showers and tubs with a stranger whose house I'm moving into." And since she'd admitted it, it seemed even more inappropriate.

"Mmm. Naughty." He tugged at his ear, smiling faintly. "There's a word I haven't heard in a while."

Emma felt her cheeks heat. She turned on her heel and walked across the room, out into the wide hall and away from him and his intoxicating scent.

There were several rooms off the hallway, and she wondered which one belonged to Kyle. She hoped it was the one on the end, because it was the farthest away. And seeing how just thinking about Kyle and bedrooms made her feel breathless, she figured distance was a safe thing.

Emma, Emma, Emma. What have you gotten yourself into? She tugged on the hem of her hip-length shirt and headed toward the staircase. The banister was gleaming mahogany and the stairs would have been simply beautiful, like something out of *Gone with the*

Wind, if it wasn't for the cold white carpet that flowed over them.

She started down the steps moments before she heard Chandler's demanding cry. Baxter came out of the kitchen, and Emma hurried over to her baby, taking him into her arms with a profound sense of relief. Not that she didn't think Baxter, with his baby sling and all, wasn't quite capable of minding him for a little while. She just preferred to have Chandler with *her.*

"You're hungry aren't you, pumpkin?" She kissed his hand and swayed side to side. She needed to nurse him. Desperately. "I'll just go upstairs now."

Kyle nodded, his eyes on Chandler for a moment. He ran his fingertip over her son's soft cheek, then blinked and stepped back. "Right. I'll be at the office for the next few hours. Bax will help you unpack your things." He strode to the door, scooped up his keys from the table where the diaper bag was and left.

Emma looked at Baxter. "I really can unpack myself," she said in the awkward wake of Kyle's abrupt departure.

"It's no trouble, miss. That's what I'm here for."

"Emma." She moistened her lips. "Please. Call me Emma."

Baxter tilted his white head. "I once knew an Emma," he recalled. "Lovely woman." His eyes twinkled. "I'll let you have some rest with the little one there. I'm sure you need it more than you'll admit. I'll be in the kitchen if you want anything."

"Thank you." He smiled once again and turned away,

walking sedately across the white ocean of carpet toward the kitchen. "Baxter?"

He turned. "Yes, Miss Emma?"

"You know why I'm here, don't you?" It seemed important suddenly that there be *some* honesty, at least.

"Yes. I know."

She rocked Chandler, taking comfort from his warm weight. "You don't approve."

Baxter's aging eyes studied her for a long moment. "Of you, Miss Emma, I approve wholeheartedly. Kyle, now...well, that's another story. He works too hard, that boy. Always putting off the things that are really important. Reminds me of myself actually. I'd like to see him avoid my mistakes." He smiled and Emma marveled at the way it softened his austere demeanor. "And he wouldn't appreciate my discussing it with you. So I believe I'll enjoy telling him all about it." He tilted his head again in that formal way he had and excused himself on Emma's unexpected choked laugh.

Then Chandler started crying again, and Emma hurried up the stairs with him as quickly as her sore body allowed.

She really did look forward to wallowing in that decadently luxurious square tub. "There are some perks to this crazy arrangement," she told the baby as she settled on the bed to nurse him. "That tub is one of them." Then she closed her eyes, leaning her head against the headboard.

And carefully removed Kyle's presence from the daydream she had of wallowing in that lovely big tub.

Chapter Five

Emma slept for a little while with Chandler, then insisted on unpacking her suitcases herself when Baxter clearly expected to do it for her. She ended up settling Chandler in the old man's arms as a consolation, since he seemed genuinely disappointed that she didn't need his help with her clothing.

He was thoroughly happy with the consolation, however, and once the two males left her room, Emma began to suspect that Baxter had gotten exactly what he'd intended to get all along.

She freshened up in the luxurious bathroom, sat on the bed that Baxter had not been dissuaded from making with fresh linens, and started dialing the white-and-gold princess-style telephone that sat on the end table.

Penny assured her that she would keep an eye on Emma's belongings at the apartment. And Emma hung up, feeling hideously guilty for letting her friend gush over how wonderfully romantic the whole thing was with Kyle sweeping her off her feet and all. It was obvious that Penny didn't believe Emma's assertion that she'd be back in her apartment after the month was up.

The call to Millie at the diner was no easier. All Emma could do was tell Millie that she *would* take the six weeks that Millie had said she should have, after all. And in the meantime she was spending some time with a friend.

She called her mother and left a message on the answering machine she'd given Hattie two years ago for Christmas. That was much easier, because all she had to do was leave the phone number at Kyle's home with no explanation at all.

Then she called Megan, who assured Emma that she wouldn't broadcast the real reason Emma was at Kyle's. "You're doing the right thing, Emma," her friend said.

Emma wished she could believe that. As far as she was concerned, however, the "right thing" was not accomplished by telling such a whopper of a lie. She was doing the expedient thing. The financially advantageous thing.

She'd sold a chunk of her honesty for the sake of a hospital bill.

"Miss Emma?"

She set aside the phone and looked up to see Baxter in the doorway.

"Kyle just phoned from his car. He'll be here in a few minutes to take you shopping. I've taken the liberty of making sure the little lad's diaper bag is ready for you."

Emma pushed off the bed and slipped her feet into her sandals, then followed Baxter down the stairs. She nearly looked back to see if they'd left any footprints on that pristine white carpet. "Where is Chandler?"

"In the kitchen. I believe he likes to be right in the center of things." Baxter pointed and sure enough, in the center of the enormous island, Chandler was lying in his springy canvas seat, his eyes wide and alert as he sucked on his fist.

Emma had barely scooped him out of the seat when Kyle arrived. Within minutes they were flying down the road again, this time in the Land Rover Kyle had spoken of.

"We'll drive into Durango," he said. "Okay?"

"Aren't you afraid of running into Mr. Cummings or someone he knows?"

"Durango's not *that* small." He shot her a quick look, then returned his attention to the road. "But you've got a point. We should clear up a few things, just in case."

"Shall we synchronize our watches, too?"

"Geneva time," he said, deadpan.

Despite herself, Emma laughed.

"You've got a nice laugh. You ought to use it more often."

Outside her window the landscape flashed by. "My mama told me I'd never find a husband if I couldn't laugh more ladylike." Her lips quirked with irony. "Guess that doesn't count for pretend husbands."

"Your mother lives in Tennessee, you said."

"Dooley. Population 110."

"Small."

"Well, maybe I exaggerated a little. Dooley's about half the size of Buttonwood. But whereas Buttonwood is a lovely town, Dooley is just…Dooley. A handful of run-down stores, at least a dozen churches and a wealth of people who find nothing more interesting than telling a person that life outside of Dooley simply didn't exist."

"And you thought otherwise. How did your music fit into that?"

She felt his gaze on her hands as if he'd touched her physically, and she realized she'd been absently tapping out the notes of the melody softly crooning from the sound system. And again, his unexpected intuitiveness unsettled her. She moistened her lips and folded her hands. "The only work for a pianist in Dooley is in the bars on Saturday night and the churches on Sunday morning."

"Sinners or saints?"

"Well, the only time one of *those* jobs opened up was when someone died of old age."

"So you ended up in Colorado on the great hunt for musical fulfillment."

She wanted to smile. It would be so easy to like this man. And so very very foolish. Wealthy men whose solution to the challenges of life was to throw money at them. "More or less."

"How many siblings do you have?"

"Five sisters. Two older, three younger."

"Any of them married?"

"All married. What about you? I know you have one sister. The one who had a baby."

"That's Sabrina. She's about your age. Then there's Trevor and Bolt and—"

"Bolt? As in lightning bolt?"

"As in bolting for the door whenever he had to take a bath. If there was a little kid running down the block naked as a jaybird, it was my brother Bolt. His real name is Eugene. Draw your own conclusions."

"I hope he's gotten over that habit," Emma said dryly.

"He says he has." The corners of Kyle's mouth twitched. "But I have my suspicions. The youngest are Felicia and Gillian."

"Are you the oldest?"

"Yes."

"I thought so."

"Why?"

"Just seems to fit." He spoke and people did what he said. Including her.

"I've had a lot of practice at it," he murmured. Then he reached out and with the press of a button, turned up the music. Not enough to disturb Chandler, but definitely enough to signal the end of that particular conversation.

It took her a moment, but then she realized with dismay that she was peculiarly disappointed. She looped her fingers together and looked out the window. Foolish, so foolish. When would she learn her lesson?

She glanced behind her to check on Chandler. He was awake, his eyes wide and inquisitive, and for the moment perfectly content to stare out at the new world around him, even if that new world was the interior of a very well-appointed sport utility vehicle.

"He doing all right back there?"

Emma nodded and faced forward again. Chandler's baby-fresh scent and Kyle's seductive masculine scent combined were heady and unfamiliar, and she rested her head against the seat and silently let out a long breath.

"What about you? Are you feeling all right? Stupid of me not to think you might be uncomfortable riding in the car for any length of time."

The tips of her ears heated. "I'm fine. Lots of extra-strength acetaminophen," she added awkwardly when his gaze rested on her. "Does wonders."

"Mmm."

The silence was broken only by the soft strains of Debussy and the muted rush of wind as they sped along the highway. She drew in the scent of Kyle with every breath she took. "Baxter seems nice," she said somewhat desperately.

"Nice? I guess that might apply on one of his better days," Kyle said dryly. "When he's not being a thorn in my side."

"How long has he been with you?"

"A long time."

Emma thought it was all he planned to divulge. But after a moment he continued. "Bax was a mechanic at the airfield where I learned how to fly when I was fifteen."

Goodness. "I don't know what surprises me more," she admitted after a moment. "The fact that Baxter was a mechanic or the fact that you were learning to fly at such a young age. I just can't picture your Baxter with grease under his nails."

"Trust me. Not only did he get grease under his nails, he was one of the best in the business."

"So how did he end up as your housekeeper?"

"That's a tale you need to ask him about." Kyle smiled. "Bribe him with the offer of holding Chandler. He'll cave in for that, I suspect."

"And you? Did you really learn to fly at just fifteen?"

"Yeah. Chandler, my dad, had me in a cockpit long before he let me behind the wheel of a car."

She could see him in her mind. Young, tall for his age, a little gangly perhaps. But still confident. Probably with a healthy dose of cockiness thrown in. Yet he'd spoken so easily of his father, when earlier he'd seemed to fully understand her unwillingness to discuss hers. She must have misunderstood. For why would he name his business after a man he disliked? "Chandler. Do you actually call him that?"

"Yeah. Lydia is my mom." His jaw hardened, then just as abruptly relaxed. "I went to live with them when I was fifteen. They adopted me when I was seventeen."

She swallowed her curiosity, even though she desperately wanted to ask him about his first fifteen years. But he'd imparted the information in a flat tone that didn't invite questions.

She angled herself slightly in the seat so that she faced him. "I suppose you were flying one of those itty-bitty puddle-jumper kind of planes." Flying was obviously a safe subject.

"A Cessna. We went up the first time and..."

"And...?"

He shrugged. "I liked it better in the air than on the ground," he said smoothly. "And here we are today."

The words definitely weren't the ones he'd been about

to say, Emma was certain of it. "What is it like? Flying? I can't imagine being a teenager and having that control in your hands. Overcoming gravity."

"It's a love affair," he murmured.

"Excuse me?"

"Flying. It's addictive, obsessive, compulsive."

"Sounds rather negative, if you ask me."

"It's also liberating. Exhilarating and profoundly humbling."

He could have been describing the way Emma felt when she sat at a piano and let the music flow from her soul to the keys and back again. Rather than comforting her, though, the striking similarity unsettled her.

She faced forward. "I've only flown once," she said clearly. "It was an enormous airline-jet thing, every seat taken, and the child behind me continually kicked my seat."

"Not an experience you care to repeat."

"No."

"I'll have to take you up myself. You'd feel differently about it."

She imagined sitting in a tiny plane with him and shook her head. "I don't think so."

"You're not afraid, are you?"

Of flying? "No." Of strapping herself into the close confines of a small airplane, with him beside her, starkly masculine, smelling like every female fantasy. "Not interested."

He just smiled faintly.

Emma decided then and there that she really didn't

like the way he seemed to read her mind. Was she so transparent? So obvious?

Just like Jeremy's parents had said?

She looked over at Chandler. *Keep your mind on what's important, Emma Valentine.*

Kyle saw a tangle of emotions flit over Emma's face. He knew how she felt. This wasn't exactly how he spent a lot of time, either, shopping for furniture for a baby's room. *His* baby, as far as appearances went. He took the next exit and parked in the lot outside an upscale furniture store.

"Here?" Emma looked from the long lines of the building to Kyle and back again. "You want to pick out a crib from someplace like this? It'll cost a fortune."

Kyle wasn't sure if he was amused or annoyed. "Are you going to argue your way through every single thing we pick out today?"

Her lips pressed together. Firmly, he supposed. Unfortunately, when she did so, it drew his attention yet again to their soft rosy fullness. And since his curiosity had no business wondering if her lips really were as soft as they looked, he removed himself from temptation.

He got out of the vehicle and went around to the back where he pulled out a spanking-new state-of-the-art stroller. Baxter had arranged it, and now Kyle stared at the contraption and wondered how the hell it worked.

According to Bax, one had only to flip a latch and the whole thing would open up practically on its own. So where was the damn latch?

Emma joined him, touched something near the wheel,

and damned if the gray-and-blue monster didn't unfold as easy as you please.

"Now you know how I felt the other day with the car seat." Emma's tone was sweet as sun-warmed honey. She returned to the passenger side and lifted Chandler out of his seat. Then she tucked him in the stroller with a soft blanket, stowed the diaper bag in the area beneath the carrier portion and wrapped her hands around the padded handle. She looked up at Kyle, waiting.

An intermittent breeze lifted a strand of her hair, and the sunshine turned her rich chocolate-brown eyes a paler coffee color. No less absorbing, no less mysterious.

Focus on the goal. Kyle didn't need to actually form the words. They'd been a part of his life for so long they were a part of him.

Focus on the goal.

It had gotten him where he was. It would get him where he wanted to go. Ultimately into Cummings Courier Service, where he could dismantle, disentangle and destroy. And put the past to rest once and for all.

Right now, however, the goal was the furniture dealer and the plan to fill an empty nursery. So he pocketed his wafer-thin cell phone, locked the vehicle and nodded toward the entrance. "Let's do it, then."

Emma's eyes widened. Color stained her cheeks. He knew, at that moment, that her mind had been following the same path as his.

And it most definitely hadn't been toward the purchase of baby furniture. It had been traveling the darkly seductive path of doing *it*. Which was so far outside the boundaries of their agreement it was nearly criminal.

Emma didn't look at him when they entered the store. A soft-spoken salesperson immediately approached and led them through the store to the infant displays.

Kyle looked quickly, uninterestedly, over the offerings. He'd have been content to let the salesperson write up an order for any one of the room displays. But Emma made her way from one thing to the next, peering at the discreet price tags, running her fingers over spindled cribs, gently setting rocking chairs into motion.

He saw the way she kept looking back at one crib in particular. It wasn't anything like the canopied frilly affair his sister had chosen. In fact, it was nearly austere. The beauty of the crib was in the wood. Rich warm mahogany that reminded him of family heirlooms.

Stuff he really knew nothing about.

He had family, sure. Chandler and Lydia Montgomery had been his parents since the day they'd taken in an angry fifteen-year-old and loved him back to life, even though they'd been busy with the family they already had. Their home had been built for function and simplicity and certainly hadn't run to heirlooms that would be passed down through the generations. No, what the Montgomerys had passed on to their kids had been belief in themselves and one another.

And the home before that? There had been plenty of heirlooms there, but one by one they'd been sold. And the lessons learned in that house were ones that Kyle still struggled against. Despite Chandler and Lydia.

He caught the salesperson's eye. "That crib there."

Her eyes lit up and he could practically see the woman calculating her commission. "Excellent choice, sir."

"Kyle…"

He turned his attention to Emma. "You like it, don't you?"

"Well, yes, it's beautiful. But—"

"The matching bureau and that thing there with the pad on top of it, too." He looped his fingers around Emma's wrist, and the protests he could see forming remained unsaid. "What about the rocking chair?" He looked at Emma.

"Your wife really should try it," the salesperson said quickly. "Sit and rock your baby for a few moments."

"I'm not his—"

"Excellent idea. Honey, go ahead and try it out."

Emma's mouth closed. Kyle was obviously on a roll. She sat in the rocking chair.

The salesperson beamed approvingly and excused herself to begin the paperwork for the order.

"You want to hold Chandler?" Kyle asked.

"He's sleeping." Emma waited until the saleswoman was out of earshot. "Kyle, this is ridiculous," she hissed. "What are you going to do with all this stuff when Chandler and I leave?"

"Send it with you."

Her eyebrows rose. "And just *where* would I put it all? You've seen my apartment."

"Get a bigger place. I'll set you up in Eastridge."

"I don't *want* a bigger place in Eastridge. I like living behind Penny. She's a wonderful landlady and a good friend."

He wasn't even paying attention! Emma pushed awkwardly out of the chair and walked right in front of him, propping her hands on her hips. "Now listen to me, Kyle Montgomery. I agreed to—"

"Shh."

Her lips parted. "I beg—"

"The crib's just fine, honey," he said suddenly, his voice several notches louder than usual. "It'll be pretty as a picture in the nursery. But not as pretty as you." His gaze focused on her and he cupped her cheek with his warm palm. "Smile," he murmured in an undertone.

She smiled blindly. Then caught her breath when he suddenly lowered his head and covered her mouth with his.

She reeled.

Honest to goodness reeled. She had to grab his arms to keep from falling backward onto her foolish foolish head. To keep from running.

He pulled back, his eyes searching. His lips hovered over hers; she could taste his lips, feel his breath. And she wanted it. Wanted him. Wanted all of him.

"Kyle, darling. I *thought* that was you."

Emma scrambled for a coherent thought when Kyle closed his arm around her shoulder and held her close to his side. She couldn't help but lean into him. And she was grateful for his support, because if it had been up to her unsteady legs, she'd have embarrassed herself.

While she was a noodle, Kyle, however, was as tense as a post. She wondered about it even as she wondered who the brittle woman was who'd called out to Kyle as she wended her way around bedroom suites and armoires toward them.

"Winter," he said smoothly. "This is a surprise. Payton said you were in Vail for the summer."

Winter Cummings, Emma realized. The woman whose advances had apparently started this whole charade. She focused a little more steadily on the chic woman.

Ignoring Emma completely, Winter walked right up to Kyle and tried to kiss him on the lips. But he turned his head slightly and Emma watched his expression turn dark for a moment before it cleared. He was once again smoothly urbane as he wiped the smear of red lipstick from his cheek.

"You haven't met my wife, Winter." Kyle's arm tightened around her shoulders. "Honey, this is Payton Cummings's daughter. Winter, this is my wife—" his tone dropped a notch, sounding slightly rough, definitely sexy and completely adoring "—Emma."

Shivers danced down her spine in the most alarming way, but Emma smiled. "How nice to meet you. Kyle has spoken of you."

Winter's smile thinned. "And he's rarely spoken of you. I'm surprised we haven't met before now."

Definitely tense, Emma decided. Kyle was very definitely tense. She looked at him, still feeling off balance by that brief kiss. By the fear that she'd truly wanted him to kiss her again. "I've been a bit busy lately," she said in response to Winter's catty comment as she drew the stroller in front of them with one hand.

Winter peered into the stroller, distaste clouding her sharp features. "A baby. Well, well." She arched a perfectly penciled eyebrow. "Kyle, you secretive man, you. What's its name?"

Emma's jaw clenched.

"*His* name is Chandler," Kyle answered.

"Chandler. Now isn't that just...sweet."

"Why, Winter, that's so nice of you." Emma let the comment flow in dulcet tones. "The name has such meaning to us, since it is Kyle's father's name. Of course we couldn't possibly have named him anything else. I'm sure your mama and daddy felt the same when they named you."

Kyle coughed.

"Oh, Kyle, sugar. I hope you're not catching a cold."

"I'm fine." He looked at her, his eyes amused and seemingly indulgent.

What woman wouldn't melt when an impossibly handsome man looked at her so? Emma dragged her attention away from his intense appeal and back to the other woman. "Winter, are you feeling all right? You look rather ill."

"Actually I am a little tired. I guess I'll have to select a new bedroom suite another day." She fluffed her trendy short black hair. "I'll be sure and tell Daddy that I ran into you and...the little woman."

"You do that," Kyle drawled.

Emma nearly jumped out of her skin when his fingers absently threaded through the ends of her hair. Winter noticed the intimate gesture, too. Which meant that it had been worthwhile.

Winter turned and walked away, her hips swaying.

"Thank you," Kyle said after a moment.

"For what?" Now that Winter was gone, Emma had no reason to lean against his side the way she was. Yet she couldn't seem to make herself move. "Acting like your wife?"

"Yes. You were great. I know Winter is a bi—"

"Bit," Emma cut in quickly. "She is a bit…overwhelming."

"A nice way of putting it." He smiled, satisfied. "And I do thank you."

Emma held her breath as his head lowered to hers. She could feel his breath on her temple, on her cheek. On her lips. Oh, goodness, kissing him was…is…

She swallowed hard and stepped back. "I don't think that's a good idea."

"What?"

"Winter isn't watching us any longer. There's no need to, uh, kiss."

He tilted his head. "Yes. You're right."

"Right." She ran her palms down the sides of her skirt. Cleared her throat. "Right."

The salesperson returned then, all smiles at the plum order she'd received without having to do a lick of work to get it.

Emma didn't even bother to protest when Kyle told the woman to add a nightstand and two lovely lamps. She was too busy reliving the moment when Kyle had brushed his lips over hers. Too busy pretending she didn't want to experience it again, despite her protest.

And too busy ignoring the disturbing knowledge that Kyle had wanted to kiss her, too.

Chapter Six

They made several more stops before heading back to Buttonwood. Emma had to excuse herself occasionally to feed Chandler. She wasn't sure why she felt so self-conscious about breastfeeding with Kyle present, but she did.

Under the circumstances it seemed too intimate. Too personal. So she'd found herself a comfortable spot in the ladies' room of a department store where Kyle had decided they'd needlessly expand Chandler's newborn wardrobe, as well as buy bedding and mobiles and stuffed animals for the nursery; in the ladies' room of the surf-and-turf restaurant where they had lunch; and in the cushy backseat of the Land Rover while Kyle met with a man "about an airplane part."

Emma hadn't quite believed that last, but when they made the return drive to Buttonwood, an enormous greasy-looking thing in a cardboard box was stowed in the back of the vehicle.

Baxter met them at the door with a handful of messages for Kyle, promptly followed with a tsk-tsk for Emma. "Rest for you, miss," he said promptly. "I'll bring you a tray for supper."

Emma glanced at Kyle. He was already focusing on the messages in his hand, walking away. She shifted Chandler. "Thank you, Baxter. That would be very nice."

"Shall I take the little one for a while?"

"I... Yes," she agreed. "I fed him before we drove back, and he's dry for now but—"

"I'll bring him right up to you if he fusses." Baxter delightedly took the baby and waved Emma toward the stairs.

She suddenly felt as if she'd run a marathon. She, whose exercise program before her pregnancy had included regular jogging, weights and cycling, had tuckered herself out completely with one day of shopping.

Baxter had disappeared with Chandler, and Kyle had gone, presumably, to return his calls. He certainly hadn't been tuckered out from the day's activities.

Of course, he hadn't recently had a baby, either.

She looked up the seemingly mile-high flight of stairs and closed her hand over the banister. "One step at a time," she told herself grimly.

From his vantage point in his office, Kyle watched Emma pull herself up the stairs. He didn't often feel like a heel, but he did now. Several times that day he'd felt like a heel. When he'd kissed her, for one. Because he hadn't wanted to stop. When he'd held her pressed against his side because he'd liked, really liked, the feel of one full breast pressed against his ribs.

And when he'd sat across the table from her over lunch and been glad for the cover of the white linen tablecloth as he'd watched her tuck enthusiastically into her meal. He couldn't even remember what they'd eaten. Every time her soft lips had closed over the fork, every time she'd lifted her glass of milk and sipped, every time she'd dabbed the corner of her cloth napkin to her mouth, he'd felt a shaft of heat in his gut.

It was damned inconvenient.

So he'd focused on getting a million tasks done and ended up running the woman ragged.

Even now, even knowing his thoughts were on a road that should definitely be closed, he watched the sway of her hips as she climbed the steps and walked out of sight. He heard the door shut and tortured himself with the vision of her in that big bathtub with nothing but silky water and clinging bubbles covering her creamy skin.

"Sir."

Kyle jerked around, glaring at Bax. The only time his old friend called him "sir" was when he was totally disgusted. Which he didn't need just now. "What?"

Baxter wasn't cowed. "I've prepared a dinner tray for Emma. Perhaps you'd like to take it up to her?"

"If you want to dote on Emma Valentine," Kyle said evenly, "you go right ahead and do it. She deserves all the pampering you can give her. And since you're *preparing trays,* you can bring one in here. I've got work to do."

Baxter, in black suit and narrow tie and spit-shined wing tips, snorted. "Work. Demolition, you mean."

Kyle returned to his desk. He sat down and flipped open a folder of correspondence he'd brought from the office. "I didn't ask for your opinion, Baxter."

Baxter followed him. "Kyle, I understand what you're doing, but it's not going to make you happy."

Kyle scrawled his signature on the letters and deliberately capped his Montblanc pen when he finished. "I don't recall asking for your understanding, either. Is that Chandler I hear?"

Baxter's mouth snapped shut on whatever unsolicited comments he'd been prepared to voice. He turned on his heel and strode out of the room. Within minutes the soft baby cries had ceased.

Which probably meant that Bax had picked up the baby to take to his mama. Which brought thoughts of Emma front and center all over again.

Swearing ripely at himself, at Baxter, at Payton Cummings, Kyle pocketed his cell phone and strode out of his office. Baxter was on the landing, a tray in one hand and Chandler in the other arm. He pointedly ignored Kyle.

Kyle stomped out of the house, taking his frustration and his gnawing hunger for the woman who now lived under his roof.

He'd assured her that their association would be strictly platonic. She was a brand-new mother, for God's sake. The last thing she needed was a workaholic like him changing the rules on her just because he'd developed a craving to bed her.

But when he climbed behind the wheel of his car, he just sat there, unable to push away the memory of the feel of Emma's lips.

"Damn," he muttered. He could go to the office. He *should* go to the office. Unfortunately, for the first time in Kyle's memory, he didn't *want* to. Bax would undoubtedly get a huge laugh out of it if he knew.

Kyle shoved the key into the ignition and drove down the winding road into Buttonwood. Then he ended up driving aimlessly around as the summer evening darkened.

Hunger eventually led him to Mom & Pop's diner. It was brightly lit and welcoming, and judging by the number of people sitting in the booths, it was popular with locals.

Entering it was rather like stepping into a movie out of the fifties. An old-fashioned jukebox belted out tunes, and several customers were drinking malts through long bendable straws. He felt a pair of feminine eyes studying him as soon as he walked through the door and very deliberately headed for the end stool at the counter.

If he'd felt like being sociable, he'd have stayed home and lusted for his pretend wife.

He shoved his hand through his hair and reached for the laminated menu, even though he wasn't particularly hungry. At least not for food.

Millie Johnson, the woman he'd met at Emma's apartment, was working behind the counter, and she flipped over his coffee cup and filled it. "Nice to see you again. Be with you in a minute."

Kyle nodded, but she had already moved off to deliver an order to one of the couples occupying a booth. He picked up the cup and drank.

Millie returned and leaned her hip against the counter. "What can I get for you tonight?"

He liked the woman. Even if he hadn't known how she looked after Emma, he'd have liked her. The expression she bestowed on him was as open and honest as…

well, as Emma's. "I hear from Emma that you make a mean blueberry pie."

"Emma's favorite." Millie nodded. "That it?"

"For now."

She smiled easily and walked over to the display of pastries and pies. Then she took a few more orders, fussed over a very pregnant young woman who walked in the door, and returned in a minute with Kyle's pie. She'd warmed it and topped it with an enormous scoop of vanilla ice cream, which was slowly melting atop the fragrant pie. "Let me know how you like it," she said. Then she topped up his coffee and set off again.

Kyle watched her. She was constantly in motion. The only time she slowed was when she stopped by the pregnant woman and took her order. "Rachel," he heard her say, "you need protein, not a hot fudge sundae. I made fresh chicken potpies today. After that you can have dessert."

The woman, who reminded Kyle a little of Emma because of the brunette hair, laughed, not at all put out by Millie's fussing. "How about I eat the chicken potpie after the sundae?"

The empty stool beside him was suddenly filled with a female who leaned toward him. Very friendly. Kyle ignored her and tucked into his pie. It fairly dissolved on his tongue.

"You don't remember me, do you, Kyle?" The woman beside him pouted lightly. She leaned forward again, bringing a whiff of too-strong perfume. "I'm Jessica. Jessica Wilson. I work in Dennis Reid's office. How are you settling into town?"

"Fine." He picked up his coffee cup.

She wasn't deterred. "I know Buttonwood is small, but the streets don't quite roll up at nine. If you're interested in discovering—"

"I'm...involved with someone," he interrupted.

Her eyebrows rose slightly. "Only involved?" She made a production of looking at his hands. "I don't see a wedding ring."

Wedding rings. Damn. Something so obvious, yet he hadn't even thought of it. It wasn't like him. "Nice meeting you, Jessica," he said absently, looking around the woman to catch Millie's attention. He pushed off the stool and went over to the cash register. "Could you pack up a slice of that pie to go?"

Millie nodded. "You bet. Want a little for later?"

"I thought I'd take a piece home to Emma."

Millie went still for a moment. "You're the friend," she murmured. "The one she's staying with...."

"Excuse me?"

She smiled broadly. "Hang on a second and I'll give you the whole pie."

"That's not nec—" But she was already in action and Kyle closed his mouth.

"You can't stop Millie when she's got an idea in her head."

He realized the pregnant woman, Rachel, was speaking to him. "So I see. You're from the clinic, right?"

She nodded. "Rachel Arquette. And you're Kyle Montgomery. The one responsible for the airlift system we're going to have. Dr. Reid mentioned it to me. It's very generous of you."

Kyle shrugged. "You're a nurse?"

"Guilty as charged. I heard you mention Emma. Valentine?"

"Yes."

Millie returned just then carrying a plain white box.

"Tell her I said hello. The children in peds are looking forward to her coming back again to play piano for them. She and the baby are doing well?"

Aside from being worn-out because of his insensitivity? "They're fine. My housekeeper is doting on them both."

Rachel grinned. "Sounds lovely."

"While you're delivering messages," Millie inserted, "you can tell her to call me. Tomorrow morning. First thing."

"Sure." He pulled out his wallet, but Millie looked at him as if he'd insulted her.

"You're Emma's friend," she said firmly.

"I don't doubt that Emma has lots of friends," he murmured. "And you wouldn't still be in business if you gave away food to all of them."

Millie pushed the pie box into his hands, a smile playing on her lips. "You just deliver the message to phone me, and we'll call it even."

Rachel shook her head, smiling as Millie returned to the kitchen. "Better do as she says."

"I will," Kyle said wryly, and pie in hand, left the diner and walked to his car. His mind was still on wedding rings as he drove out of town and back up the winding road to his house.

He carried the pie into the darkened kitchen. Bax was probably in his room, watching his favorite TV reruns. Kyle cut a chunk of pie, added an uneven scoop of ice cream and carried it upstairs to Emma's room. He tapped on the closed door. Maybe she was already asleep.

"Come in."

His gut tightened as he pushed open the door.

And there she was. Sitting in the middle of the wide bed, her back propped against a stack of pillows and a sheaf of oversize papers spread across her lap. Her hair was damp and curling around her shoulders and her face was scrubbed shiny clean. She looked about eighteen. But the soft yellow nightgown that hung from narrow straps over her shoulders covered a figure that needlessly reminded him that Emma Valentine was most definitely a grown woman. He knew he'd never met a woman whose body shrieked sin and whose lovely face and eyes countered it with such innocence.

"Kyle," she said, those wide innocent eyes expressing her surprise. She set aside the papers. "I thought you were Baxter."

"Disappointed?"

Her cheeks colored and she pushed her hair off her forehead. "Don't be silly."

He started to close the door behind him, then thought better of it. He held up the plate. "A gift."

Her eyebrows rose. "Pie? That looks like—"

"Millie's blueberry pie." He crossed the room and handed it to her. "You were right about it, by the way. Indescribably delicious."

Emma took the plate, carefully avoiding contact with his fingers. "You were at Mom & Pop's?"

"Millie asked me to tell you to call her. Tomorrow first thing."

Her fingers twitched on the plate. "She knows I'm staying here?"

"I didn't tell her in so many words, but she seemed to know. You'd better eat that before the ice cream melts."

Emma obediently took a bite. "Did...did she seem upset?"

"Considering the big smile she gave me? I'd say not."

Emma set the plate on the nightstand. "This isn't going to work," she murmured.

"What?"

"This." She spread her hands. "This charade. All your Mr. Cummings needs to do is walk into the diner where I've worked for a good while now, mention the name Emma, and the truth will get out. Buttonwood isn't exactly overrun with Emmas!"

"Cummings has no reason to go into that diner," Kyle assured her evenly. "He expects me to go to him, not the other way around. Trust me on this, Emma. I know the man's habits. Dropping in at Mom & Pop's isn't one of them. Hell, coming to Buttonwood at all isn't one of them."

"But calling your wife to invite you and her to dinner is."

"What?"

Emma moistened her lips, wishing Kyle would stop

hovering over her. "He called this evening. Probably to speak to you, but when Baxter told him you weren't available, he asked to speak to me. To your wife." She'd actually mistaken his voice for Kyle's for a brief moment when she'd picked up the extension.

She watched a muscle work in Kyle's stubble-shadowed jaw. The man was fantasy fodder when he was all spiffed up and clean-shaven. But looking slightly ragged with a definite five-o'clock shadow, he was positively lethal.

"What did he say?"

"You're making my neck hurt. Can't you sit down?" But he didn't sit in the side chair across from the bed. He sat on the edge of the bed, casually nudging her knees over to make room for himself.

"What did Cummings say?"

Emma swallowed and shifted her knees away from his hard thigh. But she only succeeded in brushing the arm that he'd braced to one side. "Winter duly reported the sighting."

"Figures."

"He called to reiterate his invitation to dinner for Sunday night." She wanted to adjust the square neckline of her nightgown, but resolutely kept her hands folded in her lap. "I didn't know quite what to tell him."

"No, I hope."

She looked at him.

"Emma."

"I'm sorry. I did tell him that I thought this week was still a bit soon after the baby and all. But we're on for three weeks from now."

He rubbed one hand over his face and wrapped his other around her calf. "At least there's that. It was going to happen sooner or later. That's why I needed you."

Emma smiled weakly. But all her attention had become focused on the absent way he held her calf. Her bare calf, since her tentlike nightgown had crept up toward her knees.

"Where's Chandler?" he asked abruptly.

"Sleeping." She pointed to the deep wide drawer that was pulled out of the bureau and sitting on the floor.

"Are you serious? We won't wake him?"

"I think he sleeps better with some noise. Take a look." Emma closed her eyes and drew in a long breath when he got up and walked over to see. She also tugged at the bodice of her nightgown. When Kyle looked back at her, her hands were again folded in her lap.

"Cozy," he said softly. "All the stuff we bought today, and your son sleeps in a drawer."

"Like mother, like child," she quipped.

Kyle moved over to her side once more. Thankfully, however, he didn't sit. "Slept in a drawer a time or two yourself?"

"So I've been told. I don't remember."

He smiled faintly. Rubbed his hand over his jaw.

Emma felt her stomach tighten at the brief silence. She drew her legs up, casually tucking the voluminous folds of her nightgown over her knees, covering even her toes. The fabric was opaque, thank goodness.

"How are you feeling?" His eyes drifted over her. From her covered toes to the top of her damp head. Then his gaze met hers. "Are you, uh, doing okay?"

His unexpected concern, oblique as it was, made her throat constrict. "Mmm-hmm. Fine."

"I didn't mean to run you ragged today."

"You didn't. Much," she tacked on when he just kept looking at her.

"For the rest of the week you can take it easy. Indulge Baxter's yen to pamper you. I've got meetings back to back for the next week that'll keep me out of your pretty hair."

She felt her cheeks heat right up through the tips of her ears. "What about dinner with the Cummingses?"

"What about it?"

"What if I can't...can't carry it off?"

A narrow gleam of green studied her from between dark lashes. "You'll be perfect." He reached out and slowly drew a strand of hair away from her cheek. His touch lingered along her jaw, then her chin. "I knew it when I first saw you."

His hand fell away from her face. "You didn't finish your pie."

Emma looked stupidly at the plate on the nightstand. The ice cream had nearly melted, surrounding the vibrant filling with a pool of cream. "Millie makes her ice cream by hand," she murmured. "There's an ice-cream place right by her, but she makes it by hand."

"You're tired, Emma."

Her eyes burned. She looked down at the sheets of music she'd been studying and started gathering them together. "Yes."

He crouched down beside the bed, stilling her restless hands with his own. "Emma."

She froze. He was close enough that she could see the fine webbing of lines fanning out from his mesmerizing eyes.

"I want to kiss you again," he said.

She swallowed. Moistened her lips.

"But I—" his jaw tilted "—won't if you don't want that, too."

"I—"

From his drawer-bed on the floor, Chandler let out a soft cry.

Kyle looked over his shoulder.

The cry built momentum.

Kyle straightened and retrieved Chandler, drawer and all. He lifted it carefully, then set it on the mattress on the opposite side of Emma. "Your son is watching out for you," he murmured. "Good night."

Emma watched him walk out of the room, pulling the door securely closed behind him. She leaned over the drawer and lifted the baby out of the soft nest they'd made from a dozen folded towels. "I wanted to kiss you, too, Kyle," she whispered softly.

Chapter Seven

Kyle sat straight up in bed, blinking in the darkness. His heart was thundering and sweat beaded on his face. He'd dreamed of Emma. Her kiss. Her touch.

It had been too damn vivid for his peace of mind, and even now his nerve endings crawled with the need to taste her again. He looked at the glowing clock and groaned.

Three a.m.

Then he realized what it was that had wakened him from the dream where Emma had been sending him straight to heaven.

Crying. The baby was crying.

It was an alien sound in his home. He let out a rough breath and fell back against pillows that looked as if they'd done battle. He pressed his arm over his eyes, trying to block out the sound of the baby crying.

An alien sound in this home, but not alien to Kyle. And just as he'd been helpless to stop the crying when he'd been a kid, he was helpless now. Little Annie hadn't wanted her seven-year-old brother to cuddle her. She'd wanted their mother, except their mother, Sally, had been out searching for whatever she hadn't been able to find at home.

Chandler continued crying, little bleats of outrage.

Kyle unconsciously counted his heartbeats in tune with the pulsing cry. Any minute now Emma would tuck the baby against her breast and the little tyke would…

Continue crying.

Kyle shoved back the rumpled sheet and started for the door. Then backtracked to rummage through his closet for the robe he'd gotten last Christmas from Lydia. He pulled it on, thinking that Emma was the first woman he'd ever bothered to put on a robe for.

Looping the slippery silk belt into a knot, he left his bedroom and looked around the doorway of the nursery, but as he'd suspected, Emma hadn't put the baby in the unfurnished room. He continued on to the connecting room. The door was ajar and he pushed it open.

The only light in the room came from the bathroom. He could easily see Emma pacing, though. Wearing her virginal yellow nightgown that left her shoulders bare but otherwise covered her right to her toes. Chandler was a bundle of blanket and cries on her shoulder.

Even though he was already in the room, Kyle knocked softly on the door to keep from startling her. "Emma."

She turned, her hair swinging with the abrupt movement, then settling like heavy silk against her shoulders. "I'm sorry. I'd hoped we wouldn't wake you."

He banished the dream that still hovered, a sight too real, too disturbing, in his mind, and focused on Chandler. "Is he all right?"

"He's dry and fed and—"

"And you're exhausted." He could hear it in her voice. See it in the angle of her shoulders, the bend of her elegant neck as she lowered her head over Chandler. He still felt guilty over his contribution to that exhaustion. What the hell had he been thinking?

He could have given her a dozen catalogs, and she could have chosen what she wanted from the comfort of a soft chair. But he'd had his plan and that was that.

He walked toward her, grimly aware of the wary look she gave him. "Let me give it a try," he murmured.

"I'm sure I can get him settled."

"I'm sure you can, too, sweetness." He simply reached forward and lifted the baby out of her arms. Chandler wasn't as small as his sister's baby was, but still Kyle could hold him within his two palms. He lifted the infant up to his face. Chandler was so surprised his lips parted, but only a squeak emerged.

Kyle couldn't help grinning at the baby. He was so damn cute with his fists scrunched next to his round cheeks. "You're causing a fuss, big guy," he murmured.

Chandler blinked, wide-eyed.

Beside them Emma sighed and sank onto the side of the bed. "Men," she muttered.

Kyle looked at her. He almost suggested that he take the baby out of her room, but decided against it, figuring she wouldn't appreciate the gesture. Her eyes followed him like a hawk as he picked up the path she'd been making when she'd been the one walking the baby.

"I'm sure you didn't have nights like this in mind when you offered me this, ah…"

"When we decided to help each other out?"

She lifted one silky shoulder. "That's a nice way of phrasin' it," she said, her voice thick with exhaustion.

Chandler squirmed, his legs butting Kyle's chest. Kyle changed his hold, carrying him easily in a football-style grip, the baby's chest and head supported by his forearm and palm. Chandler sighed deeply.

"Though you seem pretty adept at handling babies," Emma added after a moment.

Kyle glanced at her. She'd curled her legs up on the bed and was leaning sideways against the pillows she'd mounded against the headboard. Her face was in shadow, but he could feel her eyes watching him closely. "Little brothers and sisters," he reminded.

"And you're the oldest of them all," she murmured.

He smiled faintly. "Yup." Both the family before Sally's death and the family after. Chandler's eyes were closed, his little bow lips parted slightly.

Emma sank a few inches farther into her nest of pillows. One narrow strap of her nightgown slipped off her shoulder and hung loosely over her arm. From his vantage point he could see the upper curve of her breast, and he deliberately paced the other way, removing himself from the tempting sight.

"Why Buttonwood, Kyle?"

He heard the rustle of her nightgown, the shifting of pillows, and despite himself, he looked back at her. She'd looped one arm over a pillow and hugged it to her cheek, her chest.

His body stirred. "Why not? I like Buttonwood. It's not overrun with tourists, but it's not a backward little town, either. The clinic is proof of that." He'd been impressed several years ago with the fine services offered by Buttonwood's clinic. So much so that he'd donated a considerable amount of money to it over the years. It was one of the reasons he'd gone to Dennis Reid in his quest for a wife. He knew the man wouldn't advertise Kyle's personal business.

"That's all? You liked it here?"

Chandler was asleep. Kyle kept walking. "Do you want me to give you some great complicated reason?"

"No," she murmured. "Though you do seem more complicated than that."

There wasn't one thing complicated about him at that moment. He was a man, fully aware of a beautiful young woman lying on a bed only three feet away.

Which meant it really was time for him to get out of this room. He moved next to the bed and carefully reached over Emma to settle Chandler in the drawer that was still on the mattress beside her. "He's asleep."

She caught his arm as he straightened. "Thank you."

He couldn't help himself. He ran his thumb along her satiny cheek, leaned over and pressed his lips to her forehead. "You sleep too, sweetness."

She already was.

"Mama, will you let me get a word in edgewise?" Emma propped her elbows on the kitchen counter and held the phone away from her ear. Her mother's agitated chatter went on and on. Baxter, working at the stove across the kitchen from where she sat, lifted an eyebrow.

Emma put the phone to her ear and tried again. "Mama? If you'd listen to your answering machine like I've asked you to do, you'd know I've been staying with a friend. Calling the sheriff to say I was missing was really unnecessary."

Baxter gave her another brows-lifted look.

Emma sighed and shook her head. "My friend Kyle is—" *handsome, intriguing, sexy* "—a perfect host, and *no*, Mama, we're not living in sin." Her jaw tightened and she wished she'd made the call in her bedroom rather than the kitchen, where she'd found herself spending a lot of her time in the past two weeks since she'd come to stay with Kyle. "How is your job at the grocery?" She changed the subject.

Baxter had turned around, facing the stove again as he put the finishing touches on their lunch. Kyle was at work as usual. His statement that she'd see more of Baxter than of him had proved to be true. There were moments she wondered what on earth she was even doing, living in his arctic-white home. As far as she could tell, her "wifely" presence had been totally unnecessary.

She listened with half an ear to her mother's comments about work, which Hattie peppered liberally with lectures on life, love and the importance of wearing clean underwear.

Emma didn't know whether to laugh or cry. She pressed her fingers to her throbbing temples. "Mama, I've got to go now. Mr. Baxter needs to use the telephone." She shrugged when Baxter looked at her again. "I love you. I'll call you again next week."

She hung up the phone with a clatter. "I cannot believe she did it. She says she called the sheriff back home in Tennessee. Everybody in Buttonwood knows by now that I'm *involved* with Kyle Montgomery to the point of living with him, but does she call the diner to ask for me there? No, she just keeps calling my home number, and when I don't answer after a few days, she jumps to the most ridiculous conclusion. The sheriff! Can you believe it?"

"What's this about the sheriff?"

Emma whirled around on her stool to see Kyle walking into the kitchen. He set his briefcase on the empty stool beside her and tugged at his tie enough to loosen the button at his throat. "You're home."

His eyes crinkled. "You noticed."

She forced her lips into a smile, watching him roll up the cuffs of his wheat-colored shirt. He reached past her for the bowl of fruit on the counter and picked up a cluster of green grapes. Emma dragged her attention from his sinewy forearms and focused blindly on the music score she'd been studying before she'd made her weekly call to her mother. But his scent still beckoned, twining appealingly around her senses.

He popped a grape into his mouth and leaned back against the counter. "What's this about the sheriff?"

"Nothing." Emma closed the score and slid from the high stool. Since that first night when, wearing nothing but a dark silky robe, he'd walked her son to sleep, she'd been careful to keep a good amount of physical distance between them. It hadn't been difficult, really. The man was hardly ever around. And when he was, he'd certainly made no gestures toward picking up where they'd left off. He hadn't entered her room late at night again to help her with Chandler when he was fussy. Hadn't mentioned their kiss nor indicated any wish to repeat it.

She still wasn't sure if she was grateful, relieved or insulted.

She crossed to the oversize refrigerator and opened it, then pulled out a bottle of water simply to fill her hands.

"Miss Emma called her mother," Baxter said blandly.

Emma shot him a dark look, which he blithely ignored.

"Which has what to do with the sheriff?"

"Nothing," Emma said cheerfully. "I'm going to check on Chandler." Carrying the water, she strode out of the kitchen and headed for the staircase.

Thoughtfully munching the juicy grapes, Kyle watched her leave. "Okay, Bax. What gives?"

"I wouldn't know, sir," Baxter flipped a pot of curly pasta into a colander and rinsed it under the faucet.

Kyle snorted. "Nothing goes on in this house that you're unaware of."

"Such as the fact that you've spent all of two hours a day here since Miss Emma and the baby came to stay?"

"I've been busy."

Baxter didn't reply; his disapproval was more than plain in his silence.

"You know, Bax," Kyle said conversationally, "I don't

really have to put up with your attitude. You are an employee."

At that, Baxter laughed, the sound full and unrestrained.

Kyle turned and went after Emma.

He heard her before he saw her. She was singing, her voice low and smooth and rich. He stood in the hallway outside Chandler's nursery and listened.

"Amazing Grace," he realized in the moment before the memory of his mother, his natural mother, singing that very tune sneaked up on him.

She'd often sung to his little brothers and sisters before the accident. Before two-year-old Janice drowned in the big kidney-shaped swimming pool in their backyard. Before his real father had decided marriage and family wasn't for him. After that, Sally hadn't sung anything much at all. Mostly because she'd been too drunk or stoned to remember the words of even the simplest songs.

It had been up to Kyle then to sing to the little kids. Up to Kyle to find some food for them to eat. And his means had been...creative, since Sally had invariably spent any available cash on her habit.

He brushed away the memories as hurriedly as he'd brushed away the memory of little Annie crying that night he'd helped Emma with Chandler.

He never thought about those days. Not anymore. It only distracted him from the one consuming goal in his life. Taking the sum of Payton Cummings's life's work—his courier service—and erasing its existence from the planet.

Emma was standing in the middle of the room, her long pink skirt swaying as she rocked Chandler and sang. He frowned, wondering when she'd transformed the high-ceilinged room into a cozy colorful haven.

The crib and other furniture they'd chosen that day had been delivered and filled up some of the space in the large room. But it was the yellow-and-blue hanging on the wall above the crib that added some real personality. That, plus the soft matching rugs covering the wood floor.

He looked along the hallway. Pristine white. Glass. Marble. And back into the nursery. Lots of soft colors, warm wood. And Emma and Chandler there in the center of it.

She turned, her brown eyes growing wide when she saw him. Her soft singing was cut off. "I didn't know you were standing there."

He felt strangely reluctant to enter the room. So, of course, that meant he had to. If only to prove he could.

He wandered around, setting the rocking chair into motion when he passed it, picking up a stuffed bear dressed like a jockey in blue-and-yellow silks.

"Kyle? Are you okay?"

He set down the bear. "Fine. How's your mother? And what's this about the sheriff?"

"Mama's fine. Overreacting as usual."

She briefly explained, but Kyle figured there was a lot of detail she left out. He also figured pursuing it would only upset her.

"What are you doing home this afternoon, any-way?"

"Doesn't Chandler have a checkup this afternoon at the Buttonwood Baby Clinic?"

"Well, yes. But how—"

"I saw your note on the calendar by the phone in the kitchen. I thought I'd drive you. Unless you don't want me to."

"No, no, of course not. I'm just…surprised."

"Why?"

Her soft lips curved and he saw both curiosity and wariness in her expressive eyes. "You're not exactly the kind of guy who does the pediatrician thing, sugar."

"Meaning?"

She eyed him. Firmed her lips and sat in the rocking chair, settling Chandler across her thighs. "Your ease with Chandler is admirable. But playing the dad isn't necessary, you know. Our deal was for me to play your wife for Mr. Cummings's sake, that's all."

"You don't want me to take you and Chandler?"

"I didn't say that."

"Then what exactly did you say, Emma?"

She moistened her lips, pushed her narrow elegant foot against the floor to make the chair rock slightly. "Just that you don't need to feel obligated to—"

"Obligated?" He smiled faintly. "Emma, honey, you do have one helluva way of making a man feel like a crumb."

"Don't be silly. I was merely—"

"Putting me in my place."

Her mouth opened. Closed. She rocked for a moment.

"People in Buttonwood are talking," she finally said. "About me living with you."

"I'm sorry."

She waved one hand. "I expected something like this when I agreed to this insane plan of yours. But, Kyle, it'll only be worse if you take us to our appointment with Dr. Parker at the clinic. Whatever gossip doesn't get traded around the corridors there will be bandied about over pie and coffee at Mom & Pop's for the next two weeks. I don't see any need to add fuel to the fire."

There was nothing wrong with her reasoning. Yet her reasoning had nothing to do with his unrelenting decision to accompany her that afternoon. "Well, as it happens, there's something else we need to take care of at some point, so this afternoon is as good as any since my schedule is already free."

"What do we need to take care of?"

"Wedding rings."

Chapter Eight

*W*edding rings.

The pronouncement seemed to echo around the room.

Emma folded her hands together. Protectively, he suspected. Her lashes fell, hiding her eyes from his. "I... see."

"You don't have to wear it until Sunday when we see Payton and his wife."

She was nodding, though. "Couldn't you just, ah, pick something out?"

"I can. But I don't know your ring size."

She moistened her lips, still not looking at him. "Size five," she murmured. Then she stood up, carefully settling the now sleeping Chandler back in his crib.

She headed for the door, but Kyle closed his hand over her arm as she passed him. "Emma? What's wrong?"

She shook her head, her lustrous brown hair shading her face. "Why, not one single little thing."

He knew her well enough now to know that when she fell into that drawling Southern mode, he'd better tread carefully. He settled his hands on her shoulders, inexorably turning her to face him.

She gave a little shake of her head and looked up at

him, her expression closed. "Baxter is probably waiting lunch for us."

"Baxter will forgive us." He touched her satiny chin with his fingertip, lifting her face to his gaze. "What is it?"

She could withstand Kyle in his smoothly urbane CEO mode. She could withstand him in his steamroller get-the-job-done mode. But she couldn't withstand him when his emerald eyes looked at her with such befuddled masculine concern. And she couldn't withstand the fact that he stood so close to her she felt wrapped in his scent, his warmth.

Her eyes burned. "It's nothing. Really, Kyle. Just forget it."

"Too late, honey."

"You don't need to call me that."

His eyebrows drew together. "What? Honey? That's what you're like though, Emma. Rich and smooth with a taste that sweetly lingers."

His gaze on her lips might as well have been a caress for the effect it had on her. An effect that was neither safe nor wise. "The last time I thought about wearing a wedding ring," she said, pushing the words out, "was when I was involved with Chandler's...father." As she'd intended, an unmistakable curtain came down over Kyle's intense gaze. Even the hands on her shoulders seemed suddenly less intimate.

"I see," he said smoothly.

Emma bit the inside of her cheek. She'd only told the truth, but it hadn't been the entire truth. And that bothered her greatly. Once a person sold a piece of her honesty, it seemed as if it became easier and easier to prevaricate.

"All right, I'll take care of it," he said, patting her shoulder and dropping his hands.

Emma felt chilled. "Thank you."

He angled his head, gestured to the doorway calmly, as if the moment had never been. "Lunch."

She wasn't the least bit hungry, but she preceded him downstairs. Once again Baxter had set the meal on the lovely table in the garden. She'd eaten lunch out there almost every day. Except this was the first time Kyle had joined her since that first day.

The sun was warm on her shoulders and the sweet scent of flowers surrounded them. Kyle was his typically smooth self.

Just the way she expected, and she felt a good portion of her stress drain away. She was only a woman and he was only her...employer, for lack of a better word.

As he had that first morning, Kyle took the seat with his back to the drop-off. Once Baxter had served their cold pasta salad and fresh rolls and returned to the house, she finally gave in to her curiosity. "Don't you like the view?"

"I bought this place for the view. And the size of the garage. It held the *Lightning* without requiring any modifications."

The *Lightning,* she knew, referred to the treasured Lockheed P38 aircraft he was restoring. She hadn't actually seen the thing herself, but Baxter had told her a little about it. About how Kyle had transported the old war plane here, and that the weight of the truck and the plane had put the kibosh on the winding drive, which he was still awaiting a crew to come in and replace. Which, incidentally, meant there still wasn't room for her big orange car.

"But you don't look at the view," Emma pointed out, pushing her salad around with her fork.

He looked over his shoulder, then back at her. "There. Satisfied?" When he wasn't focusing completely on her, he was focusing completely on consuming the meal before him.

"Baxter is right," Emma decided aloud, watching the noonday sunshine glint off his hair. "You really do work too hard. Do you ever truly relax?"

A faint smile lifted the corners of his mouth. "Of course."

"When?"

"I'm not exactly poring over flight routes and FAA regs right now, Emma."

"And you did loosen your tie," she added dryly.

"And I came home this afternoon when the conference call I had scheduled was canceled."

"So if it hadn't been canceled, you wouldn't have decided you needed to accompany Chandler and me to the pediatrician?"

His eyes crinkled with amusement. "Is that one of those female questions I can't answer without putting my foot in my mouth?"

Emma laughed, liking him immensely at that moment. "You don't have to answer if you'll do me one favor. Trade seats with me."

He lifted his eyebrows. "What for?"

"You're an adventurer," she said lightly. "Think of it as a new adventure."

He reached over and pressed his palm to her forehead. "No fever."

Emma stood up, gathering her plate with hands that trembled slightly. She hadn't expected that touch. It was one thing when she was expecting it. She could brace herself, prepare herself for it.

"Why on earth would you call me an adventurer?"

She walked around and stood behind him, tapping her bare toes with exaggerated impatience.

"You're a pilot for one thing," she said as he finally shoved his plate around to the other side of the table. "A successful businessman in a rather atypical business. Moving your business to this area from a tried-and-true location. That all seems adventuresome to me. And of course, there's that babe-magnet you race around in."

She took his seat, smiling. "There. What do you think?"

Kyle looked across at her. The spectacular view behind her shoulders was nothing compared to the view of her. In the past two weeks, she'd regained an incredible amount of energy. She fairly radiated health and vitality, and he couldn't be within arm's reach of her without finding himself beating back the urge to taste her lips again. To press every inch of her creamy body to his.

She was waiting for a response.

"I think the view is way too distracting for my peace of mind," he said truthfully.

Her brows drew together. "You're the type of executive who faces his desk away from the window, or the doorway, or the hallway, I'll bet. So you can focus exclusively on your work."

"And you look at the world around you and see music in every single dust mote."

"Well, sugar, no wonder our marriage is so successful." She let the words flow lazily.

He was hard. She'd spoken in the tone that fairly oozed hot lazy afternoons and tangled sheets, and that was all it took. Dammit.

He reached for his glass of iced tea and chugged it.

"You all right?" She moved his untouched glass of ice water toward him. "Did you swallow wrong? I don't need to do the Heimlich maneuver on you or something, do I?"

Kyle wanted to laugh. "Or something," he muttered dryly. "I'm fine. Just hot."

She smiled. "It is warm out here in the sunshine." She pushed her nearly untouched plate out of the way and rested her arms on the table, her fingers linked together. Her wavy hair brushed over her lightly tanned shoulders as she turned her head to look back at the view she'd just traded away.

Thanks to Baxter's relentless updates, Kyle knew that Emma spent quite a lot of her time working in the overgrown garden and taking Chandler for daily walks up and down the winding road leading to the house. And the lighter streaks of brown threading through her shiny hair and the golden cast to her skin bore out Baxter's stories.

"I think the heat feels marvelous, though," she was

saying. "It's days like this that I dream about during the winter when I can't seem to get warm enough."

Kyle dragged his eyes from the enticing shadows at the scooped neckline of her sleeveless vest. He'd always considered himself more of a leg man, but Emma's curves were seriously hindering his sanity. Thank God he hadn't seen any more of her perfect legs than he had.

"Sir."

His attention was jerked to Baxter, who was eyeing him knowingly. Who needed a conscience when Baxter was right at hand? "Yes?"

"There's a call for you."

"Who is it?"

"Your father."

Emma saw Kyle's quick frown. He tossed his napkin onto the table and strode inside.

"Not hungry, Miss Emma?"

"It's delicious, Baxter," Emma assured him. "I guess I'm just a little nervous about this afternoon. Taking Chandler to the doctor and all."

"Mmm." Baxter began collecting plates.

Emma rose to help him. He'd finally given up on telling her he didn't require her help with the household tasks. "Mmm," she said, imitating his tone impeccably. "What, exactly, is that supposed to mean?" She followed him into the house and set her load on the kitchen counter.

"I didn't notice any particular nervousness about the appointment earlier today," he said smoothly.

She propped her hands on her hips. "I swear, Baxter,

you beat around a bush better than anybody I know. You sure you're not from the South?"

"Buffalo, New York, I'm afraid."

Emma waited a moment longer, then tossed up her hands. "Baxter, I'm warning you—you'd better stop being so cryptic around me or I'll decide that Chandler really doesn't need to spend those two hours every morning with you."

Baxter looked horrified. "Miss Emma, I—"

She laughed lightly and kissed his aristocratic cheek. "Relax, Baxter. I'm just teasing you."

He relaxed. "Dirty pool," he declared.

"You betcha." She headed out of the kitchen, looking over her shoulder for a moment at the housekeeper. "Just like you do with Kyle," she said pointedly. Then she had the pleasure of hearing Baxter's laughter follow her as she went upstairs to freshen up before she took Chandler into town for his appointment.

She was standing in front of the wide bathroom mirror pulling her hair back into a ponytail when she realized she wasn't alone.

Her eyes met Kyle's briefly in the mirror, and she lowered her gaze, quickly finishing with her hair. "How's your father?"

"Fine."

Emma squared the handle of the brush with the matching comb, braced herself mentally and turned to face him. She'd already put on her shoes, and the small bit of heel brought her eyes a little closer to the level of his shoulders, but he still seemed tall and broad and...

In her way. She focused on the loosened silk tie at

his strong throat. She felt like a yo-yo around him. One minute comforted by his presence, the next trying not to tremble because of the shivers he set off down her back with one glance. She moistened her lips. "What is it?"

"Winter has struck again."

Winter. Winter who'd kissed him as if she'd done it many times before. But, she reminded herself, Kyle hadn't exactly encouraged her that day in the furniture store. "Winter Cummings?"

"Apparently she goes to the same fitness center as a friend of one of my sisters."

"Oh, dear."

"When the story reached her, Felicia was smart enough not to let on that her big brother certainly *wasn't* married with a new baby, but she didn't waste any time getting on the horn to the folks." He didn't betray his irritation by so much as a twitch of a muscle, but Emma could tell he was rigid with it. "As a result, Chandler said he and Lydia decided to cut short the cruise I sent them on and come to visit."

"Your parents are coming?" The thought sent horror coursing through her and she pressed a nervous hand to her chest. "Here?"

"I talked him out of it for now."

Emma let out a relieved breath. "Thank goodness. I mean there is a limit to how much playacting I can do."

"You don't think you could fool my folks?"

Her nerves prickled. "Well, of course not. You wouldn't want to, right? And—and there'd be no need to. You'd just tell them how you're buying Mr. Cummings's company and—"

"No."

She blinked. "Excuse me?"

"My parents don't know. And they're not going to know."

"Why not?"

His lips compressed. "It's complicated."

And none of my business, Emma finished silently. She suddenly felt awkward, ridiculous, standing there, hemmed in the luxurious bathroom. She was only the hired wife. So it was ridiculous to feel hurt.

But she was. And no amount of pretending would make it otherwise.

"Well, I'm sure you know best." She stepped forward, lightly pushing her hands against him to move him out of the way.

Except he didn't move. Not out of her way. He raised his hand and captured both her wrists, holding them captive against his wheat-colored linen shirt. Captive against the hard chest beneath, warm and strong and pulsing with the heavy beat of his heart.

Emma focused desperately on their hands. "Kyle—"

"I think we could fool my folks," he murmured.

Her cheeks heated. "As you said, there's no need."

"No, actually. You said that."

"Well…regardless, it's a moot point. The situation—" his thumb rubbed slowly over the sensitive flesh of her inner wrist, sending her pulse skittering "—isn't going to, um, occur." She tugged weakly at her hands, but he still held her fast. Drew her closer. "Kyle—"

"We've got a problem, Emma."

"Of course we do. We're livin' a lie."

"I thought if I ignored it, I could make it go away. Pretend it didn't exist. Stupid. I usually know better."

She swallowed. She couldn't pretend she didn't know where he was going with this. That she had such an effect on him was something she'd have to take out and examine at another time. Right now she was having enough difficulty not letting her body soften against his. Not pressing herself against him and—

She cut off the tempting utterly foolish thought. He was a wealthy man who truly believed that every situation could be solved with money. "You said..." Her throat tightened around the words. "You promised me that things would, ah—" she broke off when he lifted her hand and pressed his lips to her inner wrist.

Her head swam. Good gravy, didn't she ever learn her lesson?

She yanked her hand free, scrambling inelegantly back until she thumped her rear against the marble vanity. "Platonic," she blurted, her entire body raging with heat. "You promised."

A muscle twitched in his jaw. "Yes, I did." He raised one hand, wrapping it around the doorjamb above his head. "I—"

"Just because I've obviously...been with one man, seeing as the proof is sleepin' in the nursery, that doesn't mean I'm going to hop into bed with you, even if you are catnip to a girl like me. So if that's what you've had in mind, you can forget this whole crazy idea right this instant. I may be foolish, but I'm not easy."

"You sure in hell aren't," he agreed. "I never once implied you were promiscuous."

Embarrassed, annoyed, and still shaking because she couldn't recall ever wanting to be with Jeremy St. James quite as badly as she wanted to feel Kyle's body against hers, Emma crossed her arms tightly across her chest. "If you want some good lovin', I'm sure Winter Cummings would be happy to accommodate you again," she drawled, desperate to put some distance between them. Not physical distance, either. Though that wouldn't hurt any.

His eyes narrowed and he dropped his arm from the doorway. "Again?"

"I could tell that day in the furniture store that you and she have...been together." Regardless of what he'd led the other woman to believe about his marital status.

"You think Winter and I have been intimate?"

She forced a casual shrug. "I say easy, you say promiscuous. I say together, you say intimate. Sugar, even if I was inclined to..." She unfolded her arms long enough to wave a vague hand. "Well, I am the black sheep of my Tennessee family. I'd know better than to set my sights on a country-club type like you who probably doesn't even own a pair of blue jeans."

She thought for a moment she'd gone too far. His green eyes turned to chips of stone and his lips compressed. Her stomach fluttered, but not with fear.

Then his lips softened and his rigid stance eased.

The flutters gained speed.

He came toward her, his movements lazy and screaming, "Dangerous man approaching." She took a hasty step back, but the marble vanity wasn't budging.

One corner of his mouth curled. "For a black sheep you look a mite nervous, honey."

She unfolded her arms and pressed her hands to either side of her, tilting her head back bravely. Even when he stepped right up to her, invading her personal space and encompassing her with his sensual scent.

"You're a babe in the woods in comparison to a man like me," he murmured. "And your ridiculous notion about Winter and me aside, I do like the way you cut to the chase." Between his dark lashes, his narrowed eyes held a primitive gleam. "I want you. In my arms. In my bed. Under me. Over me."

He ran his thumb along her jaw and all her bravado died a hasty ignominious death. She trembled, knowing that at that particular moment nothing could prevent what he described so simply, so devastatingly. Not even the fact that Chandler wasn't yet a month old.

Then his hand dropped and he stepped away. Emma blinked. The dangerously prowling male had been replaced with the dangerously smooth male.

"But I like you," he said quietly, "so I won't do that to you. Just don't poke that sleeping dragon too hard, Emma. When he awakens, it's not easy to get him back to sleep."

Chapter Nine

Emma endured the drive to Buttonwood in silence. If asked, she wasn't sure she could put a name to what had transpired between Kyle and her in the luxurious bathroom. All she knew was that somehow something had changed.

She'd been so certain she had Kyle pegged. Yet he kept popping out the sides of the tidy box that her mind, her sense of security, had fitted him in.

And the fact that she'd had such preconceived beliefs about a man she'd met less than a month earlier horrified her. Heaven knew how many occasions she'd chafed at the opinions people formed about her without ever actually knowing her.

One more welfare kid of Hattie Valentine's. The teenager who never quite fit in because she doodled with Handel and Rachmaninoff when her classmates were listening to Foreigner or Billy Ray Cyrus, sneaking their daddy's smokes and joyriding on Friday nights.

The cheap little Southerner who'd tried to trap golden boy Jeremy St. James into marriage by getting in the family way.

None of which was really *who* she was any more than she could be certain silk ties, gold watches and alligator boots were who Kyle was.

Life was just too confusing sometimes.

When they drove by Mom & Pop's diner, Emma stifled a sigh. She missed the familiar. Missed her days, long as they'd often been, that she'd spent serving up coffee and pie and chicken fried steak to her regulars. Many who came from the complex across the street. Goodness knew Millie's food was ten times better than anything served up over there in the cafeteria.

Kyle parked and Emma surreptitiously watched him round the vehicle to open her door.

"Do you want to get Chandler or shall I?" His voice was perfectly ordinary. As if nothing had happened between them at all.

As if she hadn't stood beside him in her bathroom and felt the waves of desire emanating from him.

"Maybe you could get the stroller," she suggested faintly.

He nodded and went to the rear of the Land Rover to pull out the stroller. Emma deftly unfastened Chandler, then turned to place him in the stroller when Kyle brought it up next to her. He slipped the strap of the diaper bag from her shoulder and looped it a few times through his fist, then walked with her toward the clinic.

They could have been any ordinary couple, taking their new baby in for a checkup. But once again appearances were deceiving.

Kyle stayed at her side right through the brief examination that set Chandler into an outraged crying fit from start to finish. Emma felt like crying herself by the time they were finished.

She cradled Chandler to her shoulder, trying to comfort him as Dr. Parker made some final notes on Chandler's chart. Kyle stood near the closed door, one shoulder leaning against the wall, decorated in cheerful blue and red. One hand was pushed in the pocket of his perfectly pleated trousers, and she would have thought he was as calm as Donald Parker was in the face of Chandler's outrage. But she could see the muscle jump in Kyle's jaw.

"Good set of lungs there."

Kyle gritted his teeth when Dr. Parker grinned and patted Chandler's back, his hand touching Emma's slender one. He suddenly straightened from the wall and settled *his* hand on Emma's shoulder. He'd had enough of Parker's none-too-subtle friendly overtures toward Emma. "Are we finished here?"

Dr. Parker's brown eyes studied Kyle for a moment, seeming to take his measure. Then he clicked his pen, pocketed it in the front pocket of his white lab coat and folded up the baby's medical file. "All set," he said easily. "Emma, give me a call if you need me, but that little boy of yours is in great shape. And in great hands."

Kyle knew how Emma worried about every little hiccup of Chandler's, so he told himself it was reasonable that her shoulders would relax at the doctor's assurance. But he still didn't like the way the other man was looking at Emma. He pulled open the door to the examining room, grabbed the diaper bag and ushered Emma and Chandler out into the corridor.

He headed straight for the appointment desk so he

could make arrangements for the bill and they could get out of there.

"Kyle." Emma pulled back. "Where's the fire?"

He slowed his steps, realized his fingers were too damn comfortable cupping the silky curve of her shoulder and dropped his hand. "There's no reason to hang around, is there?"

Her eyes didn't meet his. "There's no reason to race out of here like the devil is at our heels, either."

He handed the nurse behind the desk his business card. "Send the bill there," he told her, then turned to face Emma. "You like that guy coming on to you?" he asked softly.

She looked at him then. Her lips parted. "Who?"

"Donald Parker."

Emma's eyebrows skyrocketed. "You must be joking. He wasn't—"

"He was."

Aware of the attention they were garnering, he put his hand on Emma's arm and escorted her through the waiting room where the stroller was. He dumped the enormous diaper bag into the stroller and pushed it one-handed toward the exit.

Emma waited until they were in the main lobby. "Just because Dr. Parker is friendly doesn't mean he has designs on me," she said stiffly. "Good heavens, the man has nurses tripping over themselves to have a chance at him."

"He wasn't thinking of nurses when he was looking at you," Kyle assured her. "Trust me, honey, I know where his mind was."

"You're being ridiculous. He is a professional! He wouldn't—"

"He's a man."

Her soft lips compressed. Color ran high in her cheeks. "A person might think you're feelin' jealous, with all the fuss you're causing."

"You're supposed to be my blushing wife," he reminded softly. "The last thing I need is word getting out that my *wife* is seeing Dr. Lothario."

Every drop of color drained from her face. She moved the diaper bag and settled the baby in the stroller. And without a word, she strode out of the building, silent pain shrieking from her with every swish of her skirt around her ankles.

Dammit to hell.

He started after her.

"Kyle? Kyle Montgomery?"

He looked at the middle-aged woman who'd entered the building only moments after Emma had exited. "Helen," he greeted, hiding his consternation as he recognized Mrs. Payton Cummings. "What brings you here?" And how the hell had he not known she frequented the clinic?

"A friend of mine works here," she said, smiling pleasantly. "Payton and I are looking forward to having you and your wife join us on Sunday. Is she here? Winter tells me you two have recently had a child."

"I'm joining her shortly," he said not untruthfully.

She tilted her stylish salt-and-pepper head. "I feel so silly that we were unaware you were married."

Kyle's nerves tightened. "Emma prefers not to get

involved with the business." He realized that could be taken in a not entirely flattering way. "She's working toward her degree in music," he added.

Helen's blue eyes softened. "I do find it lovely when a man can be proud of his wife's accomplishments even when they aren't mirrors of his own." She clasped her hands together over her purse. "How long have you been married?"

Kyle tucked his clenched hand in his pocket. "Not quite a year."

"Newlyweds." She sighed happily. "You *must* bring your wedding photos on Sunday," she declared. "I simply adore looking at wedding photos." Her lips pursed. "Since Winter shows no signs of wanting to walk down the aisle anytime soon, I have to have somebody's wedding memories to pore over."

She glanced at her watch, completely unaware of the pillar of stone Kyle had turned into. "I've got to run." She gave Kyle's arm a motherly pat. "Until Sunday. And don't forget those photographs."

Kyle watched her walk toward the elevators. Managed to smile faintly and sketch a return wave before the elevator doors shut and carried her safely out of sight.

He raked his fingers through his hair and headed out into the bright sunshine. The delay had been only minutes, but Emma had been moving, fast and furious.

He didn't blame her.

But he did have a good idea of where she'd gone.

He headed down the street to Mom & Pop's.

* * *

Emma was breathless by the time she pushed the stroller through the door of the diner. Millie, in her customary position behind the counter, spotted Emma right away. "You brought the baby!" she cried, delighted.

She set down the coffee carafe and hustled around the counter, giving Emma a quick hug before leaning over the stroller. "Oh, please tell me I can hold him."

Dear Millie. So familiar, so wonderful. Emma felt her eyes sting and nodded. "Sure."

Millie's eyes lingered on Emma for a moment, then she turned her attention back to Chandler. He'd stopped crying as soon as she'd tucked him into the stroller and made her mad dash for the diner, and now he was bright-eyed and positively charming as Millie picked him up and carried him around to the regular customers, as proud as any grandmother.

Prouder, Emma corrected silently. Goodness knew her own mother had been less than pleased with Emma's pregnancy. As Millie showed off her little "sweet pea," as she called Chandler, Emma folded up the stroller and set it out of the way of the door, then headed toward one of the empty booths. The lunch rush had passed, and about half the diner was occupied.

She'd just slid into the booth when two women stopped next to the table. Emma looked up, squelching a sigh. "Hello, Flo. Blanch. How are you today?" Florence Harris and Blanch Hastings had good hearts, she knew. But she didn't think there were any two women in Buttonwood who knew more about other people's business than they did. And the ladies, now in their sixties, seemed to take great pleasure in making sure everyone knew their opinions, too.

They slid into the bench opposite Emma. "Is it true?"

Hidden under cover of the table, Emma clasped her hands tightly. "Is what true?"

"That you're living with that man," Flo said, her hair practically bobbing with her agitation. "Blanch told me, but I said right back to her, 'Blanch, that can't possibly be so.'"

"That's right," Blanch agreed. "She said that."

"Since we all know you were crazy in love with that law student last summer, I just assured Blanch that you wouldn't go from the frying pan into the fire."

Emma's mouth parted, ready to respond. Somehow. Some way. But Blanch hadn't finished.

"I hear *he* wants our little airport to be the next Denver Stapleton." Blanch leaned over the table toward Emma. "Is it true he donated all that money to the clinic? That his sheets are silk and he has caviar for breakfast in his fancy house up on the mountain?"

Flo tsked. "Oh, Blanch, don't be ridiculous." She focused her intense gaze on Emma. "You're too innocent for your own good, Emma dear. If your mother was here, she'd surely counsel you not to become involved like this with another man so soon after…well, after that unfortunate business last summer."

Emma flushed. She looked over at Millie, hoping for rescue, but Millie was busy introducing Chandler to one customer while she served up chicken soup to another.

"A man won't buy the cow if he can get the cream for free," Blanch said.

Kyle's insults were easier to take than these busy-bodies' counsel, no matter how well intentioned. But if she said anything to the two women, anything at all, Emma knew her words would make it through the town's gossip mill faster than a three-eyed rat running through a cheese factory.

"Oh, dear me!" Blanch exclaimed. "That's him, isn't it?"

"Handsome one," Flo added.

Emma swallowed, deliberately keeping herself from looking toward the door. She didn't need the ladies' comments to know that Kyle had entered the diner. She could *sense* him. Her nerves tightened and the hair at her nape prickled.

"He's coming over here!" Blanch squeaked.

"Good afternoon, ladies," Kyle said smoothly.

Flo sniffed, her eyes raking Kyle. "Taking advantage of an innocent young woman," she muttered. Then her eyes flashed on Emma. "And you, Emma Valentine. It's no wonder Emil Craddock had to let you go from your teaching position at Benderhoff. What kind of example are you setting for those impressionable children, openly living the way you are with a man? A newcomer to Buttonwood, furthermore."

Emma wanted very badly to tell the woman that Emil Craddock had canned her *before* she'd taken her sinful ways up the mountain to live in Kyle Montgomery's fancy house.

"Emma doesn't need to work at Benderhoff," Kyle

said smoothly, sliding into the booth beside Emma. His hip burned against hers, but he closed his arm around her shoulders before she could slide farther over. "Now that she's my wife, she can concentrate on finishing her degree."

Emma's eyes flew to his. He was smiling at her, his green eyes hard. He dropped a light kiss on her numb lips, then casually looked across the table to see the reaction his statement had caused the two women.

They were staring, their jaws slack.

And Emma realized with dismay that *everyone* in the diner was staring at them. Kyle brushed his fingers over her cheek. "Did you want to have some blueberry pie before we drive home?"

Emma couldn't have swallowed food right then if her life depended on it. Not even Millie's pie. "No," she managed to say. "I'm ready to go." She was glad no one looked at her ringless hand. She wouldn't have thought about it except for Kyle's earlier comments.

He smiled indulgently. "You'll excuse us, ladies, won't you? I don't like Emma to overtire herself."

At any other time Emma might have enjoyed the speechlessness of Flo and Blanch. She let Kyle take her hand and help her from the booth, then tried not to stare too hard when Kyle retrieved Chandler from Millie. Her boss caught her in a hug before she could unfold the stroller.

Conversations had returned to normal in the busy diner, thank heaven, and so Emma was reasonably certain Millie's "We're going to talk, young lady" wasn't overheard.

Kyle settled Chandler in the stroller, then took Emma's cold hand and ushered her out of the diner. She waited until they were across the street and hidden by the cars in the parking lot before yanking her hand out of Kyle's grasp. She'd been such a fool to agree to his insane plan.

"Nothin' good ever comes from a lie," she muttered, stalking to the passenger door of the Land Rover.

Kyle set the brake on the stroller and caught her shoulders in his hands, turning her inexorably toward him.

She hated the knowledge that, as hurt and angry as she was, she still couldn't help noticing his powerful forearms, revealed by the rolled cuffs of his wheat-colored shirt, or the hollow at the base of his throat, exposed by the two buttons he'd unfastened. "What is it, Kyle?" Her throat felt raw. "You want to lecture me some more to make sure I don't embarrass you by acting like an improper wife? Boy, imagine their surprise if they *really* knew the truth."

"Stop."

"Why?" Her laugh was brittle. "I should've known better, of course. You're cut from the same privileged cloth as Jeremy. And he'd wanted my body, too, just like you. But I wasn't good enough for anything more. I didn't carry the right pedigree and I might damage the family name with my scarlet behavior."

"I shouldn't have said what I did about Parker," Kyle said, his voice rough. "But I want you to stop talking about yourself that way. That is *not* what this is about at all."

"Oh, really? I just imagined that you accused me of being unfaithful?" Her lips twisted. "So ironic, of course, considering there's nothing between us for me to be unfaithful to."

"That's the problem, sweetness, there *is* something between us and you know it as well as I do. The very thing that makes you so perfect to be my wife is the very thing that is sending us both around the bend."

"I'm an adult," she said tightly. "I think I can control myself from throwing myself at you or Dr. Parker or any other man who looks my way."

"Dammit, Emma, that's not it, either." He propped his hands on his lean hips, bowing his head for a moment. "I'm not sure I can control myself," he finally said. "I told you earlier today how I felt. And I meant what I said, Emma. You're safe from me." He shook his head. "But I didn't like the way Parker looked at you. Pure and simple. 'Cause he looked at you the way *I* look at you. Like a woman he wants."

She swallowed past the knot in her throat. "He may want," she said thickly, "but that doesn't mean he's going to *get*. You *hurt* me," she admitted flatly.

"I didn't mean to, Emma. I'm just… Damn. I'm not good at this sort of thing."

"Pretending to be married?"

"Letting someone into my life."

Her lips parted. She moistened them. "Then we have no problem at all," she countered. "Because you didn't let me into your life. You hired me to play a role."

He slammed his hand against the hood of the Land Rover and Emma gasped. "You know what I wish? I wish I'd married you for real," he growled in a low voice. "Because then I wouldn't have the conscience that was drilled into me by Chandler and Lydia Montgomery to contend with. I'd have you in my bed, even if we couldn't *really* be together quite yet because of the baby. There are dozens of ways to make love, sweetness, and I'd make sure we devoted plenty of time to discovering each and every one of them."

Emma dragged her eyes from the dent he'd left in his vehicle, his words ringing in her ears. "What you want more than anything," she corrected, "is to complete your deal with Mr. Cummings, and if it wasn't for that, you and I wouldn't be having this conversation at all. You wouldn't have looked twice at a woman like me."

He shook his head again. "We've got to do something about this self-image thing of yours, Emma." A car drove slowly past. Then stopped and backed up.

An elegantly coiffed woman rolled down her window, a smile on her face. "Kyle. Is this your lovely wife?"

Kyle clamped his hand around Emma's wrist and drew her toward the idling car. "Yes. Emma, this is Helen Cummings. We ran into each other while you were at the diner."

Emma thought she managed a smile. She wasn't sure. But Helen Cummings was smiling wide enough for both of them. "It's such a delight to meet you, Emma," Helen said. "I know we'll have a lovely time this weekend when you and Kyle come up to see us. Payton thinks so highly of Kyle." She laughed lightly. "I made Kyle promise to bring your wedding photos."

"But—" Kyle's arm about her shoulders tightened warningly.

"I won't forget," he assured her smoothly. "You drive carefully."

With a wave Helen took off.

Emma leaned back against the sun-warmed car. "I'm not up to this," she said, feeling frantic at the way her life was snowballing out of control. She looked up at Kyle. "Wedding photos? You couldn't have told her that we eloped or something?"

He made a rough sound. "She caught me off guard," he said. "Had I not been thinking how satisfying it would be to wrap my hands around Donald Parker's throat, I might have been thinking a little faster on my feet."

Emma sighed. She was exhausted. Physically. Emotionally.

And it didn't help that nothing had really been resolved. "I won't sleep with you, Kyle." She stared down at her twisting hands. She didn't even like acknowledging the fact that she wanted to. She looked over at Chandler, content in his stroller. "I don't regret my son. But I won't be so unwise with my heart ever again. Not even with you."

She only wished she could be certain she could live up to her words.

Chapter Ten

"Kyle said he'll meet you at the airport, Miss Emma."

Emma nodded and finished fastening Chandler's fresh diaper. "Thank you, Baxter."

"Are you sure you don't want to leave the lad with me while you go to Denver?"

Emma smiled gently. "I'm not ready to leave him overnight. But I promise you'll have first dibs when I am."

Baxter smiled. "Good enough, Miss Emma."

He followed her down the white stairs. It was Friday morning, and Kyle was flying them to Denver to take care of the little problem of a wedding photo album.

Emma had barely been able to sleep the night before, wondering just exactly how Kyle thought he was going to "take care" of anything. All he'd told her was to be ready for an overnight stay.

Since their encounter with Helen Cummings outside the clinic, they'd both gone out of their way to avoid being alone with each other.

Kyle had an easy solution for that, of course. He left for the office well before dawn and didn't return until well after dark, just as he'd done since they'd entered into their unorthodox arrangement.

Emma didn't think so highly of her own appeal that she considered Kyle's long hours to be an avoidance tactic. He was simply an extremely busy man—the head of a thriving company and one of the state's major employers, so she'd discovered when she'd made it a point to learn more about her "husband." She'd also found out that he'd been accurate when he said he kept his private life private. Nowhere had she found anything that concretely said he did or didn't have a family. Immediate, adoptive, birth or otherwise.

Since Kyle had been scarce, Emma had spent a good portion of her time wondering what on earth she had in her wardrobe that wouldn't appear inappropriate in wedding photos. She'd finally settled on an off-white blazer that she fancied up with a sheer ivory scarf tucked in along the collarless neckline. The scarf also conveniently disguised the fact that the jacket, which buttoned past her hips, displayed a bit too much cleavage for comfort. With it, she wore an ankle-length skirt with minuscule pleats.

Though she felt as if she looked like she was ready to attend Easter worship, Baxter had assured her that she looked "quite lovely." She could've kissed him for his sweetness, because he'd known she was nervous as a cat.

When they arrived at the airport, entering a key-accessed lot behind some buildings, Emma felt like a wreck. Kyle's car was parked under a shade structure.

Then the man himself walked out of a rear door of the building, writing on a clipboard. He handed the clipboard to the man beside him, then strode toward the Land Rover.

She felt dizzy. She simply couldn't forget Kyle's saying he wanted to make love to her. It was always there with them. Like a physical presence.

Kyle reached the vehicle and opened her door. "Thanks for driving them out here, Bax," he greeted. His attention rapidly switched to Emma and he helped her from the vehicle. "It's been a hectic morning," he murmured. "You look very nice. But a bit pale. Afraid to go up with me?"

She smiled shakily. If he wanted to attribute her pallor to fear of flying, that was okay with her.

Baxter handed over Chandler with a sigh. "You're sure you're not ready for a vacation from the baby yet?"

Emma had to laugh. "Quite sure, Baxter."

Kyle pulled her overnight case and the diaper bag from the vehicle. "We'll be back tomorrow," he told Baxter, then placed a hand at Emma's back and ushered her into the building.

Emma barely gained the impression of busy offices, clacking printers and chatter as Kyle hustled her through the building and out the other side toward a sleek airplane that looked nothing like the two-seater she expected.

A svelte young woman with a perfect smile and showgirl legs greeted them when they reached the top of the rolling staircase. "Good morning, Mr. Montgomery." She smiled, blindingly white, at Emma. "Everything is ready for your flight."

Kyle nodded, accepting the woman's deferential manner as his due. "Thank you, Jennifer." He followed Emma into the plane, gesturing vaguely to the oversize seats. "Take your pick, honey. Ah, Jennifer?"

The flight attendant pulled out a safety seat for Chandler, which she strapped into one of the seats. Satisfied, Kyle nodded. "We'll be on the ground for a few minutes yet, Emma. If you need anything, Jennifer will see to your needs."

Emma nodded, wondering just what Jennifer thought of Kyle's passengers. She sat in the decadently comfortable leather seat facing Chandler's safety seat and leaned forward to fasten him in. Across the aisle was a long equally comfortable-looking couch.

It was silly to wish that Kyle would sit with her. But when he went through the narrow door to the cockpit and shut it securely behind him, she wished just that.

She sighed deeply, running her palms over the armrests. Jennifer moved about the cabin doing whatever it was she did.

"Mrs. Montgomery, we'll be departing momentarily."

Emma jerked her face from the window she'd been peering through. "Ah, thank you."

"You'll need to fasten your safety belt," Jennifer said gently.

"Oh." She glanced down. "Of course. I'm sorry." Then she felt her cheeks heat.

Jennifer's sleek smile suddenly took on an impish cast. "It's pretty fancy digs, isn't it?"

Emma chuckled, feeling rather uneven. She wondered what it would feel like if she really *were* Mrs. Montgomery.

The plane shuddered ever so slightly, and Emma quickly fumbled her safety belt into place. She looked over at Jennifer who sat on the end of the long couch, the picture of calm.

Emma wished she felt the same. The plane moved. She leaned forward to check on Chandler. He was working contentedly at his pacifier and Emma rested her head against the seat back and stared out the window. The takeoff was smooth as glass, and Emma finally relaxed. The landscape far below looked like a patchwork quilt.

"Chandler seems to like flying."

Emma looked up to see Kyle standing beside her seat. "Good gravy, who's flying this thing?"

"My very capable copilot. Want something to drink?"

Jennifer undid her safety belt and disappeared into a little nook near the open cockpit door.

Kyle noticed the direction of Emma's craned neck. "Want to see the action up front?"

"Well, yes, actually," she admitted.

He grinned, looking impossibly sexy despite his conservative gray suit. With an easy motion he unfastened her safety belt and pulled her to her feet, holding her hand as he led her to the cockpit door. It was remarkably small inside, filled with control panels and computerized-looking buttons versus the levers and knobs her mind had hazily envisioned. Kyle introduced her to his copilot, Mark Houseman, who tipped his cap and greeted her as Jennifer had done. As Mrs. Montgomery.

Kyle nudged her to the captain's seat, but Emma dug in her heels. "I couldn't. What if I bumped something?"

"There's that worrier in you coming out again."

"That's right," she agreed, and scooted past him back to her seat. Kyle joined her, accepting the steaming cup of aromatic fragrant coffee Jennifer served him in a sturdy mug—very different from the fine china that Baxter used at the house.

Emma realized that Kyle's hands looked just as comfortable wrapped around delicate English china as they did the plain white mug with the ChandlerAIR logo emblazoned on its side. Suddenly Jennifer appeared with an elegant breakfast. Frosty orange juice was in a slender crystal tumbler, and the tray holding dewy-fresh fruit and tiny pastries, which Jennifer placed on a fold-down tray near Emma's knee, was gleaming silver.

Emma couldn't resist the ripe strawberries, and she reached over and selected one, savoring its succulent sweetness. "Do all your passengers receive such five-star treatment? I imagine folks who charter this baby pay through the nose."

"This baby isn't chartered out." He leaned past her and lifted a cluster of grapes from the tray, offering it to her first. "It's mine."

She rolled the plump green grape between her fingers. "Mine as in the company's? Or mine as in mine and you can't have it?"

Kyle chuckled. "Mine as in I share it on occasion

when the need arises. But yes, mine as in I don't have to share it if I don't want to."

Emma let out a long breath. "You know, Kyle, one minute I actually let myself think you're just a regular guy, but then, this—" she waved her hand, indicating the luxuriously appointed plane "—reminds me that you're anything but ordinary. This is crazy."

"Crazy or not, we're committed to it."

"I just wish—"

Kyle touched her arm when she broke off. "Wish what?"

She shrugged, searching for the right words. "That all this wasn't necessary," she said softly. "Aside from encountering Helen Cummings, the past few weeks have been basically uneventful. I guess I let it lull me into forgetting just what we are doing." She shifted again, focusing on Chandler across from her. Watching her son was a darn sight safer than watching Kyle. "One lie leads to another, and another, each one bigger than the last."

"Do you want to turn around and go home?"

She made a face. "Right."

"I'm serious, Emma."

His voice, quiet as a sigh, was certainly serious enough. She looked at him, searching his face. "What about the Cummingses?"

"I'll figure out some plausible explanation. Tell them that you decided our brief marriage was a mistake when you found yourself married to a workaholic who put his company ahead of his family. Considering my life, it would be fairly close to the truth."

She stared at him. "You'd really turn around."

"Yes." He grimaced. "I don't want to, but I would. It's up to you, Emma. If this really is something you can't bring yourself to do, say the word. We'll turn around for Buttonwood right now."

Her chest felt tight. She had agreed to his proposition because of the financial benefit. And now she was being offered an out. She could stop it all with one simple statement. She and Chandler would go back to her cozy apartment over Penny's garage. She'd go back to work at Mom & Pop's, and while she worked, Chandler would be safely tucked in a playpen in the back office. The gossip would be ripe around Buttonwood, but it would eventually die. It always did.

One statement. A string of words that would return her and Chandler to their normal life, as if the past few weeks had never happened. As if Kyle had never been in her hospital room that first morning.

She looked down at her hands, frowning at the grape she'd squished between her fingers. Kyle slipped one of the linen napkins free from the tray and calmly wiped her fingers clean.

Except her life wasn't the same. Because she'd met Kyle Montgomery and realized she was still capable of being moved by a man, despite what Jeremy had done last summer. Not just any man, either. This man.

For that alone she knew she wouldn't back out. "No," she said softly. "We needn't turn around."

He set aside the napkin. Wrapped his hands around hers and lifted them to kiss her fingertips. "Thank you."

Jennifer stepped up to them, her expression indulgent. "Excuse me, sir. Mark says we're on the final leg."

Kyle rose. His gaze lingered on Emma. "It'll all work out, Emma. I promise you that. I don't make promises anymore I can't keep."

She nodded. He'd meant to be reassuring, she was sure. Yet she couldn't help wondering when, in his lifetime, Kyle had ever made promises he *hadn't* been able to keep.

The landing unnerved Emma only half as much as the takeoff. But it seemed that the moment the wheels of the sleek jet touched ground, every single person went into high gear. Before she knew it Kyle was holding Chandler, waiting while she climbed into the back of a long, *long,* black limousine.

Then he handed the baby to her before climbing in himself. He watched her for a moment, a faint smile playing about his lips. "You haven't ridden in a limo before?"

Emma closed her slack mouth and quickly fastened Chandler into the safety seat that was waiting inside the vehicle. But when she sat back in her seat, she realized that, for all the limo's spaciousness, Kyle still seemed a little too close for easy breath. "My drooling gave me away, I suppose."

His eyes crinkled. "It was the 'good gravy' you murmured when the driver pulled up at the plane that gave you away, I'm afraid."

Emma felt her cheeks heat. She crossed her ankles, determined not to embarrass herself any more than necessary. But she couldn't keep her eyes from roving over the luxurious interior, from the small gleaming wood bar, to the black screen of a small television, to the electronic gadgetry that controlled who knew what. "I suppose traveling this way must be very mundane for you."

He lifted one eyebrow. "I think I sense an insult in there somewhere." Yet he didn't seem the least bit offended. "Using the limo is often expedient. I can work rather than waste valuable time driving."

Emma automatically glanced at the briefcase by his feet. She'd come to realize over the past several weeks that he was rarely without it.

"In truth, I prefer to drive when I can," he finished.

"But then only if you can't fly," she said.

"You got it."

His sudden grin caught her unprepared. She was faintly aware of soft music coming from the sound system. Could barely discern the motion of the car as it built speed, leaving the airport behind. Kyle's teeth weren't quite perfect, she realized dimly. He had a minuscule chip in a front lower tooth. "You don't have caps," she said stupidly.

His eyebrows drew together. "Caps?"

She pressed her hands to her cheeks, mortified. "Never mind." She longed to open a window, to feel the rush of air on her hot cheeks. But she wasn't even sure this thing they were riding in had windows that opened.

Kyle chuckled. "You make me laugh, Emma."

She blew out a noisy breath. "Sure. Rub it in."

His smile took on a devilish cast. "Be careful, sweetness. I might think that was an invitation."

She blinked. Then turned to face front, her whole body flushing. "And wouldn't you have a heart attack," the leading words came out without volition, "if it was."

Kyle managed to keep his smile in place. "I think we both know the fallacy of that, sweetness."

He saw her swallow hard. And he found himself wishing that no man had ever tasted that long elegant neck. His fingers slowly curled into a fist on his thigh. He'd had his secretary, Amelia, arrange the limo because he'd thought Emma would get a kick out of it. And because he could use the time to take care of some of the work he'd brought along.

He hadn't expected to sit beside Emma and think about the heavily tinted windows that afforded them tempting privacy. Or the depth of the leather seats that would accommodate them both if he should happen to pull her over to him and—

"Where's the photography studio where we're having the pictures taken?"

He shifted in the seat, reaching over to adjust the air-conditioning. "We're not going to a studio," he said. "Arrangements have been made for us at the Crest."

He was aware of the surprised look she gave him. Extraordinarily aware of the way she turned toward him, young and vibrant and so open with her emotions it was almost painful.

"The Crest is a five-star hotel."

"Gotta sleep somewhere," he said dismissively.

Her big brown eyes widened even more.

"We'll have a two-bedroom suite," he said evenly. "A nanny will be there to help with Chandler while we say cheese for the camera. And she won't remove him from your eyesight unless you want her to. The photographer will be set up for us in the gardens."

"Won't someone see us? I mean, that was the point of going as far away as Denver to get this done, wasn't it?"

"Partly. Mostly we came to Denver, though, because the photographer I wanted couldn't make it down to Buttonwood with his schedule right now." He decided he might as well tell her now, because she was going to find out soon enough. "The photographer is one of my brothers."

She smiled, her eyes sparkling with pleasure that she would probably try to hide if she knew it was there. "How nice. Why didn't you tell me? Which brother?"

He wished he could be as certain as she that it would be nice. But at least he could be assured that news of this particular wedding shoot wouldn't make the society page. "Actually, I haven't told you about him. His name is Jake. He can be difficult," Kyle felt compelled to warn.

"Is he a lot younger than you?"

"A few years." He saw the consternation in her eyes. "Three years," he provided. "He's thirty-six. So now you know the dirty truth. I'm looking at forty this year."

"The sight doesn't look too bad to me."

And when she looked at him from beneath her silky lashes the way she was doing now, he felt as randy as a seventeen-year-old gazing at the woman of his fantasies. He shook his head, smiling wryly, and swung his gaze to the window. The limo was just pulling up the tree-lined drive that led to the entrance of the exclusive resort. He swallowed the unease that rose in him.

He wasn't used to being so distracted by anyone or anything. Yet when he was with Emma, he was finding it increasingly difficult to remember the reason she was in his life in the first place. And finding it difficult to concentrate on the goals that had been driving him for longer than he could remember.

The car halted smoothly in front of the entrance. The chauffeur got out and opened the door for them, his expression bland while Emma climbed from the vehicle, holding Chandler against her shoulder. The long hem of her skirt dragged behind her on the carpet of the limo and Kyle felt anything but bland as one curvy calf was exposed.

He knew he had a bad case when he actually held his breath to see if Emma's skirt climbed an inch or two higher to expose the rounded curve of knee, sleek and smooth in her nylons with the pearly shine. He swallowed an oath and focused on the concierge who greeted them.

Kyle listened to the man with half an ear as he snagged the diaper bag from the bellman before it could be taken away with their other few pieces. Emma was doing her level best, he could tell, not to gawk. He found her wide-eyed fascination as they were escorted through the grand old lobby far more charming than the concierge's obsequious commentary about the hotel's amenities.

They'd reached their suite on the top floor when Kyle had finally had enough. He took the room key from the concierge and eyed him silently. Fortunately the man was quick on the uptake and excused himself without delay.

Beside her Kyle unlocked the door and pushed it open. Yet Emma couldn't quite make her feet take that step across the threshold. She pressed her lips to Chandler's head, nervously patting his back.

Then let out a gasp when Kyle swung her up into her arms, Chandler and all. "Kyle, what on earth—"

"I'm carrying you over the threshold." And suited action to his words.

But rather than setting her on her feet inside the suite, he carried her through the entry, which smelled of the enormous bouquet of fresh summer flowers, and into the living area of the suite. And when she saw the beautiful grand piano standing in front of the sparkling bay window, she couldn't help sighing with delight.

"I thought you'd like it," he murmured, and carried her right over to the magnificent instrument before letting her feet find the floor. He eased Chandler out of her arms, and Emma drew her fingers along the spotless black finish.

Then she turned around only to find Kyle looking down at Chandler with an expression she couldn't quite define. Yearning, maybe.

She wanted to sit at the piano and open the lid and just let her fingers rest on the keys. She wanted to watch

Kyle hold her son just the way he was doing. Capably. With a hint of awe shaking his confident green gaze.

What she needed to do, however, was use the bathroom. So she excused herself, going into the bedroom that Kyle pointed toward, distracting herself for a moment with the sight of the enormous king-size bed. She shook her head at the thoughts the bed inspired. "No way, Emma."

When she reentered the living area, a uniformed maid was rolling a plastic-sheeted rack into the room, and another rosy-cheeked woman was cuddling Chandler.

Once the rolling cart was situated in the center of the room, the maid departed. Emma looked from the cart, which was nearly as tall as Kyle, to the strange person holding Chandler.

"Honey, this is Mrs. Schneider. She comes highly recommended by my sister, Sabrina."

Emma felt herself relax a little. Surely Kyle's sister's judgment was sound when it came to entrusting one's child to someone else.

"He's a beautiful boy," Mrs. Schneider said comfortably. "But a wet one, I'm afraid. So I'll just get that taken care of."

"He'll be fine," Kyle said for Emma's ears alone when the older woman took the diaper bag and went into the bedroom Emma and Chandler would use. "You need to look through the gowns and see if there's anything you like. Because if there isn't, it'll take an hour or so for the bridal shop to send over another selection. I guessed about the size, so if they're wrong, you can blame me."

Emma's mouth ran dry as his words penetrated. She crossed to the cart and pulled away the thick black plastic to reveal a sturdy metal garment rack loaded with wedding gowns. "Oh…my…goodness." They ran the gamut from slinky and sophisticated, to heavily beaded and elaborate, to puffy and ruffled. Her hands trembled as she nudged the hangers, and she quickly dropped her hands before Kyle could notice. "Well. This is unexpected."

"They're wedding photos, honey. What did you expect?"

She shook her head, thinking of the hours she'd spent dithering over what to wear. She knew she looked presentable. But these gowns—elaborate, expensive, impossibly beautiful—made her feel as if she was wearing sackcloth.

"You look fine just the way you are. If you prefer to wear your own clothes, say so. I'll wear a suit, instead of my tux. It'll work."

"Don't do that. Don't read my mind."

He pushed his hand into his pocket. "Emma, I'm only trying to get this done without—" He broke off, looking down for a moment. "Without reminding you of the jerk," he finished flatly.

It took a moment. A long telling moment, which she'd have to examine later when her thought processes weren't muddled by Kyle's nearness. He was talking about Jeremy. He'd been thinking about the man even though Emma hadn't given him a thought at all.

It was positively liberating.

She turned to the array of gowns. There was really

only one that truly tempted her. She pushed the gowns on either side of it away and pulled it from the rack, carefully easing the long skirt free from the others.

It had tiny cap sleeves, a simple scoop neck and a triple row of narrow satin ribbon circling the waist. But the skirt was like a bell-shaped cloud. She loved it on sight.

It would probably be too tight. Too long. Too something. But it was the only one she wanted to try.

She draped it carefully over her arm and turned to face Kyle. "You really brought a tux?"

He nodded once.

"Well, then, sugar, I guess you'd better go get yourself all prettied up. Because it's bad luck to see the bride in her gown before the camera flashes."

Kyle's smile was slow and sexy as sin.

And Emma's heart rolled over.

Chapter Eleven

Two hours later Kyle was pacing in the elaborate gardens the Crest laid claim to when his brother finally deigned to saunter into sight. He had a leather bag that Kyle hoped contained photographic equipment hanging from one shoulder.

Jake caught sight of him and pushed his aviator glasses down his nose to look over the rims. "Now, don't you look purty in your penguin suit."

Kyle's lips tightened. "You're late."

His brother shrugged. "Fire me." He dumped his bag on the end of a linen-draped table complete with champagne glasses and wedding cake. "Oh, that's right." Jake's mouth twisted. "You can't fire me, 'cause I'm doing you a favor."

The damnable thing was his brother was right. "Are you drunk?" Kyle demanded bluntly. Jake's eyes hadn't looked particularly bloodshot, but that didn't necessarily mean anything. Not when it came to Jake.

"If I am," his brother replied silkily, "I can still click the shutter. So where's the bride? I'll have to be sure to use filters so the dollar signs that're probably in her eyes don't show in these fool photos."

Kyle's hand curled into a fist. "You'll be nice to Emma, Jake, or I swear I'll…"

Jake shrugged out of his leather bomber jacket and dropped it carelessly on the grass. "Ground me? Cut off my allowance?" He flipped open the bag. "Don't bother. I'd just sneak out my window at night and steal some car radios to fence for money." He pulled a camera out of the bag, his smile humorless. "Oh, wait. That was you who did that stuff."

Kyle hated the reminder, even though the words were essentially true. He reminded himself that he'd come a long way from that kid and spoke calmly. "Emma hasn't done anything to deserve your disdain, Jake. So I'd appreciate it if you'd—" He sensed movement behind him. He turned and there she stood, all in white. She was...

"Exquisite," Jake said beside him.

Yes. Exquisite. More than pretty. More than striking. More than beautiful. And she took his breath away. There was nothing fancy about the dress she'd chosen. In fact, it was strikingly simple. And utterly feminine.

He barely noticed Mrs. Schneider bringing up the rear with Chandler in her arms. He had eyes only for the entrancing creature before him.

Jake stepped forward, his smile pure wolf, and Kyle felt his gut knot. Since the death of Jake's wife five years earlier, his brother had been going out of his way to live hard, fast and furious. He was the last kind of man Emma should be exposed to.

He brushed smoothly past his brother and took Emma's hands in his. "This is Jake," he said curtly, giving his brother a hard look.

Emma wasn't sure she could find her tongue, having

swallowed it at first sight of Kyle dressed in an inky-black classic tux, tailored perfectly to his wide-shouldered narrow-hipped physique. The blinding white shirt he wore made his chestnut hair look darker and his eyes even more strikingly emerald.

But good manners reared their muddled head, and she looked away from Kyle to his brother. And blinked. She immediately realized that this brother was related to Kyle by blood rather than adoption. The similarity between them was marked. But while Kyle was the epitome of strength and sophistication, Jake seemed to embody a rough earthiness. She wondered if there were more siblings Kyle hadn't mentioned.

Jake had pushed his sunglasses down his nose and was running his gaze over her from head to toe, a smile curling about his lips—lips that screamed sex and sin. She looked back at him, smiling faintly, too. Oh, he was a wild one, she was sure. And as far as she was concerned, harmless in comparison to his intense brother.

"Do I get to kiss the bride?" he asked in a husky low tone.

She tilted her head, hoping the bright sunlight didn't wilt the curls she'd coaxed into her hair before they were done with the picture-taking. "Why, of course you do." She felt Kyle stiffen beside her as she pulled her hands from his and lifted her full skirt to cross to Jake. She reached up, took his head between her hands and tugged it down to hers, then chastely tilted her cheek to him and stifled a laugh when she heard his muttered oath. But Jake kissed her cheek lightly and when Emma slid a look into his green eyes, she saw laughter there.

Then Jake looked over her head at his brother and slid his glasses back up into place. "I've got two hours to spare here, Kyle," he said abruptly, "if I'm going to be able to digitize the photos and integrate wedding guests on the computer. So let's get the show on the road."

The muscle in Kyle's jaw jumped, and Emma looked from one man to the other. Too much conflict there, she thought. She walked over to stand by Kyle and slipped her hand into his. "You can really add in people on the photographs to make it look like we had guests?" she asked Jake.

Jake nodded, his lips quirking. "We could do the whole thing without PJ there, if we put our minds to it."

Emma glanced up at Kyle. "PJ?"

He grimaced. "Forget it."

Mrs. Schneider had settled herself and Chandler off to one side under the shade of a lovely old tree. She was already burying her nose in the book she carried even as she slowly moved the carriage she'd produced back and forth. Emma had fed Chandler before dressing in the gown that had miraculously fit perfectly, and she figured he'd be quite content for the next several hours.

"At least Jake doesn't have to fabricate the wedding cake like he does guests," she murmured to Kyle. "Talk about attending to detail." She jiggled their linked hands, leaning toward him so that only he would hear. "Relax, sugar, or instead of looking like the happy bridegroom, you're going to look like you've got a shotgun pointed at your back."

Jake, apparently finished with setting out his equipment, looked up then. He'd discarded his sunglasses, and his eyes were narrowed in thought as he studied the garden setting. "Emma, love, let's get a few shots of you by the stone bench there. Do you have a veil?"

She nodded and pulled it out of the carriage where she'd stashed it, then gently shook out the long delicate tulle.

"Just hold it in your hands and look at it," he said shortly. Emma did what he requested. She tilted her chin when he said and lifted the veil when he suggested she do that so the breeze could drift through the glistening fabric.

She took the bouquet of exotic white orchids and tried to think virginal thoughts even though the sight of Kyle waiting on the sidelines sent her mind along another much more dangerous track.

The only sounds in the garden came from Mrs. Schneider, who was humming a soft lullaby to Chandler, and the whirring noise of Jake's camera.

After a long while Jake gestured for Kyle to join her. She leaned her head back against Kyle's hard chest when she was told to do so. She looked up at him when Jake said to. She even propped her satin pump on the stone bench and lifted the long skirt of her gown to reveal the lacy garter belt around her leg just above her knee.

Jake wanted Kyle to kneel at her feet and pull the garter from her knee, but Kyle hesitated, his expression unreadable. Emma put her foot back on the grass. "I need a break," she announced. She was reluctant about all this, but Kyle seemed even more so.

Kyle nodded, his lips tight. Jake shrugged and wandered over to look down at Chandler in the carriage. Emma dashed a stray curl away from her cheek and tugged Kyle down on the stone bench beside her.

"Your brother seems nice," she said after a moment.

He gave a disbelieving snort. "He detests me."

Emma turned toward Kyle, the flowing folds of her gown settling over his gleaming black boots. The man wore a tux straight out of a fashion magazine, but on his feet he wore cowboy boots. Dress boots, but boots nonetheless. "I'm sure he doesn't," she countered softly. There was a lot of strain between the two men, but Emma could honestly say she didn't believe true dislike to be part of it. "But why do you think he does?"

His lips compressed. "Well, honey, it's not a particularly pretty story. And it goes so far back I'm not sure I can even remember it all, anyway."

"Talk about a whopper," Emma murmured. But she smiled gently. "I know all about the good and bad of families. If you don't want to talk about it, I understand. Though I don't see why you never mentioned you had a natural brother."

Kyle glanced over at Jake. "More than only a brother. I couldn't keep our family together despite my promise that I would," he said after a moment. "Jake blames me."

Emma frowned. "You said you were adopted by Chandler and Lydia when you were just a teenager."

"Yes."

"But they didn't take Jake?"

Kyle shook his head. "We went into the foster-care system when my natural mother died," he said flatly. "I was twelve, Jake, nine. Trace was only seven and little Annie was five." He rose, tucked his hand in one pocket. "The state separated us. It took me years to find everyone again."

Emma stood, also, her heart breaking for a young Kyle who'd tried to keep his family together despite the realities working against him. "That's hardly your fault, Kyle. You were a child."

He shrugged. "Like I said, it's an old unattractive story." Again he glanced at Jake. "Let's get this wrapped up." He raised his voice enough for his brother to hear.

Jake nodded and sauntered back toward them. "If I recall from my misguided past, you ought to have some ceremony shots. Don't suppose there's a minister around. It'd save me some time later."

"No," Kyle said, "but give me a few minutes, and I'll take care of it." He touched Emma's elbow gently, then strode alone down the winding path toward the hotel.

Emma gathered up her skirts and headed over to Chandler, who wasn't the least bit impressed with her fancy dress. He far preferred sucking on his fist. Emma started to tuck the veil back in the storage area under the carriage, but Jake stopped her. "You'd be wearing the veil during the ceremony," he said.

She nodded. He was right. She wandered over to the bedecked table. The wedding cake was three tiers, all in white with elegant curls and ruffles of icing.

Jake came up beside her, stuck his finger into the icing at the base of the rear of the cake.

"You're plain wicked, aren't you," Emma said mildly.

He licked his finger, then wiped it on his worn-white blue jeans. "If Kyle is the virtuous one, then I'm the sinner," he agreed blandly. "You don't have a clue what you've gotten yourself into, do you?"

Emma looked up at the man who was so like Kyle, yet so unlike him. "Considering the tension that even an infant could detect between the two of you, I'm quite sure you don't have a clue what I've gotten myself into, either."

His eyes narrowed. Then a slow smile stretched across his mobile mouth. "Touché." But his smile died when he turned and looked at the wedding cake. "My wife would've liked this cake," he murmured.

"You're married?" She was surprised.

He slowly shook his head. "Not anymore." He abruptly turned to dig in his big battered bag.

Kyle returned with the concierge in tow. He'd even brought a Bible, and Emma swallowed the protest that immediately rose in her throat. She let Mrs. Schneider fit the veil with its minuscule Juliet cap into place on her head. Then Jake gestured them into position, with the concierge acting as the officiant, open Bible in his hands. Emma set aside the bouquet, deliberately breathing past the breathlessness that rose in her when Kyle folded his hands around hers.

"We don't have rings." As far as she knew, Kyle hadn't done anything about that situation since their one conversation about them. Frankly she was grateful. It was one less falsehood she would have to tell on film.

Jake sighed and stepped forward, pulling a long chain out from beneath his loose black jersey. Emma barely saw the glint of diamonds and gold before Kyle lifted his hand, stopping them all. Then Jake's rings disappeared once more underneath his shirt.

Kyle reached into his pocket and pulled out two bands, one plain gold and the other glittering with a row of diamonds, opening his palm for her to see them. "I didn't forget," he said in a low voice. "But I also didn't forget your reason for not wanting to pick them out yourself."

Emma's heart pounded in her breast. How could she tell him that she hadn't been as wary of choosing wedding rings because of Jeremy as she'd been of choosing them with *him?* She plucked the larger band off his palm, curled it in her damp palm and stuck out her left hand. "Slide that little shackle into place, sugar," she drawled lightly, and pretended her hand wasn't really trembling.

Jake's camera whirred as Kyle slid the ring over her knuckle and into place on her ring finger. The band felt disturbingly comfortable on her finger. And it wasn't because she'd spent all last summer imagining Jeremy St. James's wedding band there, either. Then Emma returned the gesture, pushing Kyle's ring onto his finger.

Finally Jake lowered his camera, and Emma started

to breathe easier. But he simply reloaded film and lifted it once again. "Okay, kids," he muttered. "Pucker up."

Kyle grimaced. "Dammit, Jake…"

Emma closed her hands on his forearms to keep him from saying something to his brother. "Your enthusiasm is dampening, darlin'." She smiled, even though she felt a little like kicking Jake herself.

Chandler suddenly sent up a squawk.

It seemed to jolt Kyle into action. He ran his thumb along her jaw, and just that easily, Emma blocked out the sound of Jake's camera, the way he was constantly moving around them, searching for the perfect angle, the perfect light. She forgot the concierge, who was probably damned for eternity for playing a man of the cloth in this charade.

She forgot everything but the bubble surrounding her and Kyle. Her fingertips flexed against his arms. She swallowed, her eyes falling to his lips, rising to meet his eyes. Then her lids were too heavy, and they fell as his mouth covered hers.

Indescribable pleasure sighed through her. Their lips separated for a moment and Emma heard him inhale sharply. His hands cradled her face. She slowly opened her eyes to find his gaze, hot and searching. "Kyle," she murmured, lifting her hand to touch the gleaming hair that had tumbled onto his forehead. She slowly combed through the thick strands with her fingers.

She thought she heard him say, "I'm sorry," in the moment before he lowered his head once again. It was like being consumed by fire. Her head fell back and she felt his hand slide along her spine, pulling her against him.

Just where she wanted to be, she realized dimly. Her lips parted and she tasted him fully. A soft moan rose in her throat and she wrapped her arms around his shoulders, wanting to be closer, closer—

"Well. I think that pretty well melted my film," a voice said from somewhere.

Emma swayed weakly when Kyle lifted his head. He cupped her neck in his warm palm and pressed her head gently against his chest. "Dammit, Jake," he growled.

Embarrassment came swift and hard.

She pushed out of Kyle's arms and brushed her palms down the flowing skirt of her wedding gown. Avoiding Jake, who was probably smirking, anyway, she quickly crossed to Chandler and swept him out of the carriage. He wriggled his legs and settled happily in her arms.

Reining in his irritation with his brother, Kyle thanked the concierge for his assistance. He knew the man wouldn't utter a peep about what he'd seen and done here, not with the exorbitant tip he received.

Jake switched cameras and snapped some random shots before pulling out a heavy silver pocket watch from his jeans pocket. "I've got ten minutes to clear outta here, bud," he said.

Emma must have heard him, because she surrendered the baby to Mrs. Schneider and joined Kyle by the cake. She pulled off her veil and left it sitting on the end of the table out of range of the camera, then picked up one of the crystal flutes. Kyle pulled the bottle from the ice and removed the cap from the sparkling cider.

"Turning teetotaler in your old age?"

Kyle ignored Jake's mocking question and poured the sparkling golden liquid into their two flutes, then shoved the bottle back into the silver ice bucket. He picked up his flute and gently touched it to hers.

Emma smiled brilliantly, but he could see the confusion in her dark eyes.

He couldn't blame her. He was feeling a good measure of confusion himself, and he knew the reason for the undercurrents running between him and Jake. He also knew that, right or wrong, he wanted to make love to Emma.

It didn't bother him to know that Jake knew it, too. But he did feel for Emma, who was clearly unnerved by it all.

They drank the sparkling cider while Jake burned up more film. Then Emma turned to the cake and picked up the beribboned knife. When Kyle closed his hand over hers, he could feel her hand trembling. But her wide vivacious smile didn't dim a watt, and he found himself mentally applauding her.

They cut a small piece of the very real cake, and when he lifted the morsel to her mouth for her to eat, she hesitated, looking away from him. But not soon enough to hide the telltale glisten. Her throat worked for a moment, then she opened her mouth and delicately took the cake from his fingers. Her lips brushed his fingertips before she took a step back, swallowing.

His fingers tingled from that brief touch of her lips, and he stared at the bits of creamy frosting that clung to his thumb and forefinger. She was near tears and Kyle hated it. He hated having gone so far in his strategy against Cummings that he was hurting a young woman who deserved nothing of the sort.

He hated that, even knowing he was hurting her, he couldn't stop the forward momentum of the plan he'd set in motion.

She was probably thinking about the wedding she *didn't* have with the jerk who'd left her alone and pregnant. Just because Emma responded physically to Kyle didn't mean that her heart didn't still belong to that other guy.

He grabbed one of the linen napkins and wiped his fingers clean. If Emma still loved Jeremy-the-jerk, it was no business of his.

"Kyle? Don't you want your piece?"

He looked up to see Emma holding a small wedge of cake. *A piece of your heart.* The thought came out of nowhere. Unwanted. Unbidden.

He tossed down the napkin. "I think we've got enough photos by now," he said abruptly.

She didn't flinch. Didn't move. Just stood there, impossibly desirable, her slender fingers holding a morsel of cake. Everything was silent, as if the world was holding his breath.

Kyle realized he actually was. He released it just as a peal of laughter from somewhere else in the gardens drifted toward them on the breeze.

Her long lashes swept down suddenly, and she turned toward the table, accidentally dropping the piece of cake into her champagne flute, in which a couple of inches of sparkling liquid still remained.

Just then, he felt about as appealing as that soggy piece of cake with cider bubbling and biting into it. Emma reached for a napkin, her movements uncharacteristically abrupt.

Dammit. He hadn't spent as much time feeling like an inept fool since Dennis Reid had opened Emma's hospital-room door. "Emma..."

She dropped the napkin on the table and walked away, her full skirt rustling. The sound was somehow just as accusing as the straight rigid line of her back. She stopped briefly to sweep Chandler up into her arms, and her actions seemed to scream at him not to follow her as she hurried along the winding path toward the hotel. It would be prudent to let her go, he knew.

Jake was packing up his equipment with his usual rapid thoroughness. Mrs. Schneider was brushing her palms down her clothes. Neither one seemed the least bit concerned that Emma had practically run away from their particular wedge of garden.

Kyle, on the other hand, was all too aware of it.

He yanked at the narrow bow tie strangling him and strode after her.

Chapter Twelve

Emma's flight through the luxurious lobby was interrupted by the concierge. Perhaps he thought a bride practically running through his lobby while carrying an infant was someone he needed to immediately tend. Perhaps Kyle had greased his palm so thoroughly that any sight of Kyle's party guaranteed instant personal service.

Perhaps, and more likely, she looked just this side of insane as she raced past his desk, and the safest course of action for the concierge was to make sure she made it to the suite without delay.

Whatever the man's reasons, Emma was grateful that he only handed her a key card, escorted her to the elevator and punched the floor button for her.

Once she slammed the door of the suite behind her, however, she wished she was anywhere else than this space that she was expected to share with Kyle, no matter how platonically.

She clutched her full skirt in one hand and collapsed on one of the couches.

What a fool she was.

The gardens had been lovely with color. The wedding cake looking like something out of a magazine. And Kyle...

She was such a fool. How could she let herself get so carried away as they toasted each other with the sparkling cider? As they cut the cake?

How could she let the lines of reality and pretense blur so completely that she'd actually been living a moment that hadn't existed except in her mind?

Chandler fussed. Probably didn't like being clutched like a lifeline. She quickly wiped the tears from her eyes and took the baby into the bedroom. Once in the portable crib with his favorite blanket, he snuggled down like an angel and slept.

If only she could press her cheek to a pillow and sleep away all that was wrong. Too agitated to remain in the bedroom with Chandler, she went out into the living area. The piano drew her like a magnet and the gown swished around her feet when she perched sideways on the bench.

Her eyes burned as she stared down at the gown. The style hadn't been particularly formal, but she'd still let herself feel like Cinderella at the ball.

Except her Prince Charming didn't come calling with glass slipper in hand and words of love and forever on his lips. He flew a plane and worked too hard and believed that the end justified the means.

She bent forward, propping her forehead in her hands. A hot tear burned its way down from her tightly closed eyes. "I knew he was trouble," she muttered. "But did I pay attention? No, of course not. That would've been too smart. Too sensible."

She wiped her cheeks and lifted her head. She couldn't even be angry with Kyle. For what had *he* done? Been generous with his home? Offered security for Chandler that she could've spent years trying and failing to achieve? Shown her that she wasn't dead inside, the way she'd thought, after being betrayed by Jeremy and the rest of the St. James family?

She sniffed and swung around on the piano bench, automatically lifting the lid. She stroked the surface of the keys with her fingertips.

When had she begun falling for him?

Had it been when he'd brought her warm blueberry pie with ice cream melting all over it? When he'd walked Chandler to sleep that one night?

Perhaps it had been the day he'd shocked Flo and Blanche by telling them she was his wife.

Or maybe it had been that very first day. When he'd looked at her with his mesmerizing green eyes and said he was looking for a wife.

It didn't matter when. It just was. And if she'd been unsuitable for the St. James family, she was *really* unsuitable for the position of Mrs. Kyle Montgomery.

Taking a shuddering breath, she found the only solace there was just then. Playing the piano.

Kyle heard the haunting notes as soon as he opened the door to the suite. The sight of Emma, her head bent over the piano as she drew a painfully bittersweet tune from the instrument, was unobstructed from where he stood.

He closed the door quietly, but it wouldn't have mattered if he'd made more noise. She was lost in the music.

He could see it in the angle of her head, in the vulnerable curve of her neck. In the fingers that seemed to
become part of the piano, making it a part of herself.

God, did she weep inside the way the music wept?

He crossed the room. "Emma."

Her shoulders stiffened and she pulled her hands off
the keys as if she'd been caught with her fingers in the
cookie jar. She pressed her hands to her lap until they
disappeared among the fluffy white stuff of her wedding
gown. "Has your brother gone?"

"Probably." Kyle didn't want to talk about Jake.

"What does he do?" she asked after a moment.

"Keeps everyone and everything at a comfortable
distance."

"He's like you, then."

Kyle frowned, but couldn't quite deny it. "Perhaps."
He pressed his thumb against the underside of the unfamiliar gold band he wore. "Tell me about Chandler's
father."

He heard her audible intake of breath. "What for?"

He waited a few moments before responding. He
didn't want to make yet another false step. Blunder more
than he already had. He didn't want to be the reason she
played such sad notes on the piano.

He didn't want the memory of an old love to be the
reason, either.

"You were in love with him."

She slowly replaced the lid over the keys, and his
body tightened at the way her fingers lingered over the
gleaming black finish. "I thought so," she admitted after
a moment.

"Where did it go wrong?"

Her lips twisted. "He didn't love me."

Kyle found that hard to believe. "He said that?"

"He didn't have to. He already had a fiancée. Who wasn't yours truly. That made it pretty clear."

If he'd only heard her dry tone, he might have believed that her heart hadn't been wounded by the jerk's actions. But he saw her face. Saw the wounds that hadn't yet healed. "His being engaged to someone else doesn't necessarily mean he didn't love you." Kyle made himself say the words, for they were true even if he found them unpalatable.

"Well, it's all water under the bridge now. Last I heard, the wedding is expected to be the summer's society event for Colorado Springs."

"He comes from money," Kyle murmured.

She nodded, her palm slowly caressing the surface of the piano.

"And his family didn't approve of the music student for a wife."

Emma stiffened, looking up at him with surprise. Then her soft mouth turned down at the corners, and her cheeks flushed. "I guess it's not a particularly original story. But I suspect it was my Tennessee background they found particularly embarrassing. Goodness knows they spent enough time investigating what they termed my welfare roots."

"It's their embarrassment, Emma. Not yours. You didn't do anything wrong."

She pressed her palms flat on the curved keyboard cover. "Are you so sure?"

Her voice was low and he could barely hear the question. "Yes," he said quietly. "I am sure."

She was silent for a moment. Then she looked at him, her eyes dark and so full of emotion that his gut ached. She moistened her lips. "Thank you."

Their eyes held for a moment that stretched a little too long for comfort. Kyle's comfort, anyway. "I'm hungry," he announced abruptly. "Think you can trust Mrs. Schneider long enough with Chandler to join me for dinner?"

"Oh, I don't… Is she still here?"

Kyle was glad she hadn't completed her immediate objection. "I arranged lodging for her here, too." He hadn't allowed for a single thing to interfere with his plans to get their wedding album under way. "We can have dinner right here at the Crest. There are a couple of restaurants." He held out his hands, palms up. "It's been a long day, Emma, and we might as well have a nice dinner. What do you say?"

"I'll need to change first."

"Take as long as you need." He smiled slightly. "I'm starving, but I guess I can wait a little longer."

"Ah, no—" her cheeks went pink "—that's not what I meant." She rose, smoothing her graceful hands down the folds of her sweeping dress. "The gown," she said. "I, well, I can't reach the buttons. Mrs. Schneider helped me earlier." She turned, showing him her back and the long line of tiny round pearls that ran from the base of her neck to below her hips.

He curled his fingers. "I'll get Mrs. Schneider."

"Oh." She didn't look at him. "Actually, if you could

just, ah, undo the top few, I can get changed while you make sure she can watch Chandler. It'll save a little time, since you said you were really hungry."

"Starving," he murmured. He uncurled his fists and stood, walking up behind her, nudging his boots under the folds of the gown so he didn't damage the fabric. He smoothed her shiny hair away from the nape of her neck, exposing the top buttons.

She reached up and held her curls out of his way.

Kyle's jaw tightened and he reached for the first button. His pulse roared in his ears and his fingers felt too big and clumsy as he tried to slip the round little button through the narrow loop.

"There's a hook at the top," she said.

He looked. Unfastened it and then managed to unfasten the top one. And the second. And the third. Her skin was pale and smooth as dairy cream. The fourth. The fifth. Her shoulder blade where a tiny mole taunted him, sassy and sexy as hell. The sixth. The lacy edge of a corset-looking thing. The seventh. Eighth.

The little cap sleeves slid forward from her slender shoulders, and Emma lifted her hands to hold the gown against her breasts.

He drew in a long breath. More buttons. Her corset was clearly visible now, hugging her slender back. Her narrow waist. The seductive flare of hip. He worked free another button, his knuckles grazing the slick fabric that molded her skin. He went still for an agonizing moment. Then moved his hands from temptation and stepped away. "There're still some buttons left, but it looks like you can—"

"Yes," she said quickly, turning, holding the dress up, avoiding his eyes. "It's fine, Kyle. Thank you." With her free hand, she gathered up a fist of skirt and headed for her bedroom.

Close the door, Emma, he commanded silently.

She looked back at him as if she'd heard his thoughts. She let go of her skirt and slowly closed the door, hiding her creamy skin and satin-clad curves from view.

Kyle blew out a long breath and yanked at the studs on his shirt.

"Kyle?" Emma peeked at him from behind the door, but he could see her bare shoulder.

Torturing himself wondering what else was bare, he shoved his hands into his pockets. "Yes?"

"I should probably wear the outfit I came in rather than jeans, right?"

Jeans. Snug ones that hugged her hips and outlined her legs. Which Baxter had delighted in describing a time or two, but which Kyle had not had the pleasure to witness himself. He'd been too busy at ChandlerAIR. Too busy with finding one reason after another to stay away from his house.

Or the classy number she'd worn on the plane. Either one was fine with him.

Nothing at all was fine with him.

"The skirt and jacket," he suggested gruffly. "That'll be more than fine for the dining room."

She nodded and softly closed the door.

Kyle raked his fingers through his hair. He couldn't believe he'd been stupid enough to think he could keep things strictly business where Emma was concerned.

* * *

Subdued lighting, soft music, lowered voices. Linen tablecloths, heavy silver and gleaming crystal. That was Emma's hazy impression of the dining room at the Crest. Despite the fact that it was summer, a fire flickered in an enormous stone fireplace across the room. Yet it didn't seem to add undue heat.

Every table was placed for optimum privacy, and the waiters anticipated the needs of their patrons almost before the diners were aware of any.

What Emma was most conscious of, however, was not the elegant décor, the intimate atmosphere, the impeccable service or the perfectly prepared meal. It was the man seated across from her. The man who'd turned her world on end from the moment he'd entered her hospital room that fateful day.

The man who had turned the simple task of undoing a few buttons into a wholly sensual experience, which still had her nerve endings jangling.

"How's the dessert?"

She looked down at the fluffy concoction of cream and kiwi and ten other things that the waiter had described but that Emma couldn't recall. "Delicious." She set down her dessert fork, though. "But I'm afraid if I eat another bite, I'll burst a seam."

His eyes crinkled. "That might be an interesting sight."

Emma smiled and shook her head. It was safer looking around at the other diners than at him, so she did. "Have you been here before?"

"Once."

"With a beautiful sophisticated woman on your arm, no doubt," she said lightly.

His lips twitched. "I'm sure my sister Sabrina would appreciate the description. I brought her here for her twenty-fifth birthday."

Emma absently rotated the stem of her water goblet between her thumb and forefinger. "She lives in Denver, too?"

"Yes. So do Bolt and Trev and Felicia when she's not traveling around the state. Gillian is in Europe with her ballet company."

"My goodness. How exciting."

"Grueling, actually. At least that's what she said in her last letter."

Emma propped her elbow on the table and rested her chin in her palm, looking right at him, because no matter how hard she tried, she couldn't help it. Her gaze just naturally wanted to rest on him. "You keep up with them all, don't you? I admire that. The perfect big brother."

His lips twisted. "Jake would disagree."

"You said you've reconnected with your other birth brothers and sisters?"

He nodded.

"And they all know one another, as well? Your birth family and your adoptive family?"

"No. Let's dance."

Emma blinked, sitting up straighter. Looked beyond his shoulder to the small dance floor where a few couples were lazily circling in time to the strains of a lone guitar. What an appealing idea. But she knew that the idea of holding her in his arms wasn't what prompted his abrupt suggestion.

"You know, Kyle," she said softly, "sometimes talking about the past helps put it to rest."

"And sometimes, Emma, talking about the past leads only to *un*rest."

"In other words, don't ask you why Jake called you PJ?"

He looked at her, then shook his head and smiled wryly. "Yeah."

She smiled, too. It was hard not to when he was this way. Relaxed—at least as relaxed as she'd seen him, his remarkable eyes glinting with humor. "If you have brothers and sisters living right here in Denver, why are you staying at the Crest? Having dinner with me? Don't you want to see them while you're in town?"

"I'd just as soon they not get too big a whiff of what I'm doing."

"Having fake wedding photos created, pretending to be married, you mean?" She pulled her elbow from the table and folded her hands in her lap. "You don't want to lie to your family, but it's okay to lie to Mr. Cummings. To my friends in Buttonwood."

"Emma."

Sharp disappointment was coursing through her, and no matter how badly she'd like to be sophisticated and capable, she couldn't. "That's not an accurate take on the situation?"

"I don't want the rest of my family to know what I'm doing because word would get back to my adoptive parents about the deal with Cummings."

"So?"

"So they'd try to stop me. And I won't be stopped. Not about this. Not when I'm so close."

"But why? You said yourself that it's good business sense for ChandlerAIR. And if Mr. Cummings wants the deal, as well, what could your parents possibly object to?" If he could only explain it to her so she'd understand, then perhaps she could justify her foolish fascination for him.

Kyle just shook his head, then subtly motioned for the check. Emma sat back, sighing. So much for the lovely dinner they'd just shared. All because she couldn't keep her tongue under control. She looked at the dance floor, wishing she'd had the nerve to dance with him when he'd suggested it. "You're a complicated man." She'd thought as much before.

The waiter appeared silently beside Kyle, then disappeared just as silently after Kyle had scrawled his name on the check. Kyle looked at Emma, one brow raised slightly. "Not really. I have a goal and I don't want any more hitches in the plan to achieve it than necessary."

"And my pretending to be your wife is all part of the plan."

"Essentially." He rose and held out his hand to her. "Except you've thrown a few unexpected hairpin turns in the road."

Emma looked at his hand. Long blunt fingers. Wide square palm. He had hard little pads of callus that she wouldn't have expected from a man who was the employer rather than the laborer. "Hairpin turns? I can't imagine what you mean."

He wrapped those long blunt fingers around her wrist and pulled her to her feet. "You know, sweetness," he murmured. "You know damned good and well what I mean. You have a tiny little mole on your shoulder blade," he said for her ears alone.

"I know." She tugged her hand from his. "Chandler is probably hungry by now."

"Right here," he continued, as if she hadn't spoken. They walked through the quiet lobby toward the elevator and he pressed his palm against her shoulder blade. It seemed to burn right through her jacket to her flesh. "I'm going to be thinking about that tempting little spot for the rest of my days. Wondering if your skin is as soft as it is creamy. If it's as sweet as the honey that flows in your voice."

And now she'd be thinking about his lips on her shoulder blade, too.

But nothing had changed between them. Not really. He might be able to send her from amusement to hurt to heaven within the blink of an eye. But Kyle still believed the end justified the means. And he'd made his priorities perfectly clear. His business came first with him.

It always would.

Chapter Thirteen

Chandler was crying.

It was nearly two in the morning, and Kyle was still sprawled on the couch in the living area of the suite, where he'd been since Emma had gone to bed hours earlier. Still staring at the television screen.

He didn't want to listen to the television any more than he wanted to listen to the voice inside him that kept insisting he was heading down the wrong path.

He picked up the tumbler of scotch he'd been nursing since midnight and stared into the liquid. He wasn't much of a drinker. The booze only reminded him of his first mother, Sally, and as such had about as much appeal as swallowing glass shards.

Chandler continued crying.

It would be risky to go into Emma's bedroom, though. Particularly after the day they'd had. His resistance was shot to hell. Emma was still recovering from the jerk. It was a combination that spelled disaster.

He could too easily take advantage of Emma's generous spirit. God, he already was. Using her need to provide for her son in order to obtain her help in closing the deal on CCS. Kyle didn't want to hurt her even more. He couldn't give Emma what she deserved any more than the jerk had.

Families and forever were for the young and idealistic. Kyle was neither. He was thirty-nine and a little too jaded and a lot too committed to his work to even think about starting out on that life course.

Yet still he wanted Emma. Wanted to run his fingers along her lovely cheek. Wanted to see her shiny dark hair spread across his white pillowcase. Wanted to draw her floaty feminine skirt slowly up from her ankles, over her curvy calves and above her knees...

With an oath Kyle set the glass on the cocktail table. Thinking that way would only ensure he'd spend the rest of the night as sleepless as he was now.

Chandler's crying had grown more fretful. He rose and crossed to Emma's closed door. Pressed his palm against the wood and told himself he wasn't going in there.

He could hear Chandler's pitiful wails. Hiccuping, brokenhearted.

Suddenly the door opened right beneath his hand, and Emma stood there, Chandler pressed to her shoulder. She gasped, backing up a step. "Kyle."

Her eyes were dark and worried. "What's wrong?" he asked.

"I think he's sick," she said miserably. "He feels hot and he...he won't nurse, and I know he must be hungry."

Kyle reached out and cupped his hand around Chandler's head. His neck was warm, but then, weren't most babies' squirmy little bodies warm? He held out his other hand and took the baby from her. "Are you sure he's hungry? Maybe he just doesn't like the unfamiliar surroundings."

He looked at Emma, who nibbled her lip and glanced away from him. She waved her hand vaguely. "I just know."

Kyle lifted a brow. "This is one of those mother-child nonverbal things?"

She flushed. Pressed her fingertips to the hollow in her throat. "My milk," she whispered. "I..."

Kyle couldn't help it. He was a slug, but he was a male slug. He looked at her breasts, pushing against the oversize tomato-red nightshirt that hung off one slender shoulder and fell past her knees. He turned away, striding to the telephone. Chandler *did* feel warm.

"What are you doing?"

"Calling the concierge. He can round up a doctor to come and check on Chandler."

She followed him, her arms folded protectively across her chest. To ease her need to nurse or to hide from his eyes? He almost told her not to bother. She could wear stinking wet burlap and he'd still feel compelled to look.

"They can really do that?" She looked relieved and surprised all at once and Kyle nodded, impulsively putting his hand behind her neck. The kiss he pressed to her forehead was for him as much as for her, he realized. "Thank you. I'm sure it's probably nothing, but..."

"You'll feel better knowing for sure."

She brushed her hair away from her face. "Yes."

Kyle's gut tightened. Her eyes darkened. The moment lengthened.

Then she deliberately moved away, putting the width of a couch between them. "I guess you're mighty used to figuring a woman's mind." Her drawl was smooth.

"Just yours, honey."

She rolled her eyes and turned toward the piano, and he let it pass. What good would it do to let her know how easily she'd gotten under his skin? How her feelings were transmitted so easily to him?

Chandler seized that moment to tangle his little fingers in the hair on Kyle's chest, and Kyle gingerly removed the baby's grip. At least he'd stopped crying so hard, only shuddering now and then with a sad little sob. "I get the message," he murmured. "Protecting your mama again."

He picked up the phone and dialed. Within minutes he was assured that a physician was on his way. He hung up and turned to see Emma sitting sideways on the piano bench. She'd drawn up her knees and pulled the stretchy shirt over her knees until all he could see were the pink tips of her toes. "Play if it'll make you feel better," he suggested.

She looked at the instrument beside her. "I'd be afraid of disturbing one of the other guests," she murmured. "It's awfully late." Her gaze followed him as he slowly walked Chandler around the suite. "Kyle?" She hesitated for a moment, then decided to ask. "Why haven't you ever married? Had kids of your own?" She suddenly frowned. "Or have you been? I mean, I just assumed—"

"Never had time." He cut off her flustered words.

"You're a natural with kids. Look at Chandler. He's

practically asleep again, and it's because of you." Her face went pink. "I know it's none of my business."

Sure enough. The baby's eyes were closed, the picture of innocence. "When I was younger," he found himself admitting, "I always said that marriage and kids could come later. That I wanted to get the business fully established before I concentrated on my personal life."

"Sugar, I don't know how you define *established,* but it looks to me like ChandlerAIR's pretty well grown-up."

He smiled faintly. "Yeah. I guess the real reason I kept putting off having a family of my own was that I didn't want to be the miserable failure at it that my father was. My birth father," he elaborated. And admitting it seemed ridiculously simple.

Because she was a good listener? Because she had her own share of demons to struggle with? Or just because she had a voice like warm honey and melting brown eyes a man could get lost in?

"Jake had a twin," he found himself telling her. "Janice. She drowned in our swimming pool when she was two. I think my...father blamed my mother."

"Oh, Kyle. How terrible for your family. Your mother must have been devastated."

"If she was, she kept it buried under pills and booze." He wished he'd kept the bitter words unsaid when Emma's eyes suddenly glistened. "She held it together for a while," he allowed. "Eventually, though, the old man decided the family he had left wasn't worth his time, and he took off a few years after the accident. She pretty well fell apart after that."

"My daddy left, too," she murmured. Then smiled sadly. "Stinks, doesn't it?"

Amusement, faint though it was, where there had only been bitterness whenever he thought of his father, rolled through him. "Yeah," he agreed. "It stinks."

"You wouldn't do that to your family."

"How do you know?"

She gazed at him. "I just do. Look at the way you found your sister and brothers when you were separated after your mama died. And the way you talk about Sabrina and your adoptive family now." She pushed her feet out from under the nightshirt and stood. "But don't worry, Kyle. I won't tell anyone that under that power suit and tie of yours resides a closet family man. Your secret is safe."

The knock on the door precluded his having to respond. Which was just as well, because if she knew the thoughts swirling in his head whenever he looked at her, she wouldn't be worrying about the safety of his secrets. She'd be worrying about how to fend off a man whose good intentions had been eroded under the onslaught of the desire she aroused in him.

Emma hurried to the door and flung it open, reminding Kyle forcibly that she was entirely too trusting. But it was the doctor, and after handing over her business card, the woman quickly examined Chandler. Being wakened, however, pleased the baby not at all and within minutes, he let everyone within earshot know it.

Emma sat on the couch beside the doctor, trying to comfort Chandler. She recounted the past few days, trying to explain his fussiness, but felt helpless to come up with a real reason. The doctor listened, nodding. "I imagine this is a reaction to the inoculation you mentioned. Babies sometimes experience discomfort after receiving vaccines."

"Discomfort," Emma muttered. "There's that word again. I didn't even think of that."

The doctor smiled sympathetically as she wrote on a pad. Then she tore off the scrawled instructions and handed them, along with a small bottle of infant acetaminophen, to Emma. "If he's not feeling his usual self by tomorrow, give your regular pediatrician a call. But truly, I think your son will be fine very soon. And if he doesn't want to take the breast, express as you need to so that you're not uncomfortable and keep it in the fridge. He'll probably make up for his lack of hunger with a vengeance later."

Emma gathered Chandler against her shoulder, feeling her cheeks heat because Kyle was standing right there and had heard every word. It was juvenile, she knew. And if he were anybody else, she wouldn't feel so conscious of the very natural functions of her body.

She just couldn't help it. The thoughts she had of Kyle were not *remotely* maternal. With each passing minute in his presence she only became more aware of her femininity. So acting blasé about breast feeding with him so close by, his white shirt hanging, unbuttoned and sexily rumpled to expose a chest that was most definitely male, most definitely mature and most definitely the finest chest she'd ever seen, was simply beyond her ability.

She realized the doctor was at the door, and Emma

flushed even more as she rose to thank the woman for coming at such an hour.

Then she turned to face Kyle. Kyle who didn't have on his regulation tie, whose sharply carved jaw was blurred with a sexy shadow of whiskers, and whose rigid abdomen drew her traitorous attention like a magnet. Kyle, whose words about exploring the small mole on her shoulder blade had been tormenting her since he'd delivered them.

She snatched up the bottle of pain reliever the doctor had left. "Thank you for getting the doctor. I appreciate it."

"I wanted to make sure he was fine, too."

"I believe you." As far as she could tell, he hadn't been dishonest about a single thing.

Except pretending that they were wed.

She stifled a sigh and held up the little bottle. "Well, I guess we'll go back to bed. I'm sorry we woke you."

"You didn't." He shoved one hand through his hair and sat on the couch, picking up the drink that was still sitting there. He propped one boot on the edge of the cocktail table and leaned back, resting the squat glass on his hard bare stomach. He dropped his head against the couch and closed his eyes. "Go to bed, Emma."

She curled her bare toes into the plush carpet, wanting to say something more, but not knowing what.

Stifling a sigh, she carried Chandler into the bedroom. Then she coaxed a few drops of sticky red liquid into his mouth and settled him in the portable crib the hotel had provided where he miraculously closed his eyes with a little sigh and went to sleep.

Emma wearily climbed back into the enormous lonely bed and tucked a pillow under her cheek. But sleep didn't come to her the way it had to Chandler.

She turned onto her other side, looking at the faint line of light at the bottom edge of the closed bedroom door. She didn't know how long she lay there, waiting for that light to go out. For the sound of another door closing. Anything to indicate that Kyle had gone to bed.

Nothing. The light remained.

She pressed an arm over her eyes, but she couldn't blot out the vision of him, sprawled on the couch, a tumbler of amber liquid propped on his stomach.

She pushed herself up on her elbows, staring at the door. Beside the bed, she could hear the soft cadence of Chandler's breath. In her head, she could hear the thump of her own heartbeat.

She blew out a long breath. Pushed back the blankets and climbed out of bed. Kyle looked up from his position on the couch when she opened the door.

"Chandler?"

Emma shook her head, quietly closing the door behind her before walking toward the couch. "He's sleeping, thank goodness." Her nerve took her as far as the arm of the couch and she lowered her hip onto it, self-consciously smoothing the nightshirt over her knees.

"So why aren't you sleeping, too?"

She lifted one shoulder. "You aren't."

He smiled, but it was grim. Either he'd refilled the tumbler he still held or he hadn't had so much as a sip.

"Why *aren't* you?" She slipped from the arm to the

couch, curling her legs up on the cushion beside her. "Sleeping, that is."

He looked at her and heat swirled through her chest just that quickly. That easily.

That frighteningly.

He sighed, took a grimacing sip of his drink before setting it down and stole her breath when he wrapped one warm hand around her ankle. "Talk to me, Emma." His voice was low. Husky. Made her skin tingle. Or maybe that was because of the thumb he was rubbing back and forth over the sensitive spot behind her ankle.

"About what?" she asked.

He shook his head slightly. "Doesn't matter. Anything." A slice of sharp green looked her way, then he closed his eyes and dropped his head against the cushion. "Talk to me, honey, or we're gonna get into trouble here, no matter what kind of intentions we've got."

Emma swallowed, unable to find words. But Kyle's warm hand slid up her calf, nudged beneath the baggy hem of her nightshirt and cupped her knee. Her lips parted. The only word she could form was his name, which emerged like a squeak. She moistened her lips, agonizingly aware of Kyle's fingers slowly caressing her knee. "Is Jake usually a wedding photographer?" she asked desperately.

"No. He was a photojournalist."

"Was?"

"Before his wife died. Were you a virgin when you met the jerk?"

Emma blinked. The nightshirt crept up to her knee as Kyle's fingertips brushed the outer curve of her thigh.

"I...yes." Her eyes closed for a moment and she let out a long shaky breath. "Not that it's any of your business," she felt compelled to add.

"First time I slept with a girl I was fourteen. She was nineteen. She rented a room in one of the foster homes I'd been stuck with. I didn't get to stay there long, needless to say."

"Were there a lot of foster homes?"

He smiled faintly. "That's all you have to ask? Nothing more about my sexual precociousness?"

She pressed her hand over his. Separated only by the material of her shirt, but keeping his long fingers from creeping any higher. He was halfway up her thigh. Much farther and she was going to go out of her mind. "Were there?"

"Five."

"What about Jake and...Trace, right? And little Annie. Where did they go? Wasn't there any attempt to keep you all together?"

"I was one step from being a juvenile delinquent," he said evenly. "We were deliberately separated so that I couldn't continue being a bad influence on them. Annie was younger. She was adopted almost immediately, but the family moved around a lot. Trace lucked out a bit, too. He ended up in a group home in Wyoming on some children's ranch. He's still there. Helps run the place now. Jake...well, you've met him."

"I can't see you as a juvenile delinquent."

His lips twisted. "Doesn't fit with the suit?"

"Doesn't fit with your...oh, code, I guess. You're too ethical."

"Considering how you feel about our make-believe marriage, I'm surprised you credit me with ethics at all. But ethics didn't buy food for my sister and brothers. And the car radios I got busted for stealing did."

"My mother never had money, either."

"Sally had money," Kyle said. "She just blew it on other things."

From the bits and pieces Kyle had imparted, Emma could just imagine what those other things had been, and her heart broke for that long-ago family that had borne more than its share of tragedy. It surprised her not at all that Kyle had turned to whatever means he'd felt he needed to in order to provide for his brothers and sister. "Why wasn't some attempt made by the authorities to find your father when your mama died?"

"There was." With the ease of long practice, Kyle kept the dark anger inside him from rearing its head. "He didn't want us before Sally died. He didn't want us after."

Emma shifted on the couch beside him, leaning toward him. Soft and warm. Strong and healthy. "But then you and the Montgomerys found one another. You moved on. And look at you now. Successful. Respected. You've put the bad stuff behind you."

Her earnestness moved him more than he wanted to acknowledge. "I'll bet your personal motto is that one about life giving you lemons, so you make lemonade."

"What if it is? It's yours, too, even if you haven't realized it."

He nearly laughed. "Honey, trust me. That isn't my motto."

"A rose is a rose," she insisted, pushing one hand through her hair, tucking it behind her ear. "Your home life with your first family was less than ideal, but you didn't cut yourself off from them. You reconnected with them when you had an opportunity to. And now you employ hundreds of people at ChandlerAIR, employees whose loyalty you have because of your progressive employee relations. Gracious, you've won business awards and all sorts of things, even."

He raised an eyebrow.

"I've been reading up on you," she said, then blushed. "I mean on ChandlerAIR, of course."

"I liked the first version better."

She pressed her lips together for a moment. "Anyway, I…"

He waited. "You…?"

"Forgot what I was going to say," she whispered.

He felt her gaze on his lips, and the simmering heat inside him instantly shot to full boil. "Emma."

She sucked in her lower lip for a moment, leaving it with a glisten that cranked up the flame inside him even more. He slipped his hands easily around her waist and pulled her right across his lap, anchoring her hips shockingly against his. "Talking isn't working anymore," he said, and swallowed her gasp with his lips.

Don't ever stop.

The plea ran silently through Emma's whirling mind. Kyle's hands burned through her nightshirt, and she curled her fingers against his shoulders.

His kiss devoured. Teased. Seduced. And his hands, oh, his hands shaped her back. Drifted along her spine, making her shiver, arch against him. Wish frantically that there wasn't so much fabric separating them.

Don't ever stop.

An involuntary moan rose in her throat when he lifted his mouth from hers. There was no hesitation in his heavy-lidded gaze. He curled his fingers in the bunched hem of her nightshirt. Yet Emma knew she could halt this heavenly madness now.

She caught the tip of her tongue between her teeth and raised herself ever so slightly onto her knees. The nightshirt slid upward. Cool air. Then heat when his hands followed the upward ascent of the material. Her breath shuddered through her. Her pulse deafened her.

She slowly lifted her arms. Up. Off.

His long fingers captured her wrists, gently anchoring them at her sides, and his eyes burned over her, making her flesh tighten. She wished with the one brain cell that was still functioning that she was wearing more seductive panties than her plain white cotton. "Kyle."

"Shh." His warm palms slid over her hips, running along the hem of her unimaginative panties with such thoroughness that she forgot what was wrong with them in the first place. She forgot everything except him when his palms glided along her back, cradling her weight as he slowly lowered his head to one aching peak. "You're beautiful," he murmured, then touched his tongue to her.

She sucked in her breath, her very soul quaking. One tiny little touch, exquisite in its deliberate goal. She caught her hands in his thick chestnut hair and tugged, blindly pressing her lips to his. Mindlessly fitting her soft curves against him.

She opened her mouth to him, pushed her hands beneath the sides of his shirt and reveled in the feel of hard bunching muscle sprinkled with intriguing swirls of hair. But even that wasn't enough, and she tugged the fine fabric off his shoulders. He released her long enough to yank his arms out of the rolled-up sleeves. Emma trembled wildly, sinking her teeth into her lower lip as their frenzy was suspended for a taut moment.

Kyle closed his hands over her shoulders. Slowly drew them along the sides of her breasts. Down her rib cage. Her hips. She opened her mouth for breath. "Don't ever stop," she whispered.

A muscle worked in his jaw. Then he put his hands high on her thighs and pulled her tightly against him. Her head fell weakly forward to his shoulder and she sank helplessly against him as convulsions swept through her with lightning speed.

"Ah, sweetness," he breathed against her forehead, his hands on her hips guiding, urging.

Holding her safe when she finally stopped quaking and could only cling to him, heart racing, eyes burning.

His fingers threaded through her hair, and he looked into her face. "You're beautiful," he said softly, thumbing away a tear from her cheek. "I've never wanted a woman more than I want you right now."

She simply had no words. She pressed her lips to his. And held on, when he pushed them both from the couch and carried her into his bedroom.

He settled her in the middle of the bed, and Emma drank in the sight of him, standing there so masculine. So sure. He was more than beautiful, she thought faintly. She knew a man could be handsome on the outside and empty on the inside. But Kyle wasn't like that.

He was determined and responsible and, despite the marriage charade they were playing, honorable to the core.

She pushed up on one arm and reached for him. But he caught her hands and shook his head. "I don't have anything with me," he said evenly.

She blinked. Then realized. Her mouth rounded in a silent *Oh*.

He smiled slightly. "Your disappointment flatters me." He let go of her hand and sat on the bed, leaning over to yank off his boots and socks. Then he stretched out beside her, sliding away her panties in one sure stroke. She stilled his hands. "Kyle, I want to, but...but we can't."

His smile was slow, decidedly wicked and filled with promise. "There're dozens of ways, Emma," he reminded her.

Emma's heart seemed to stutter. He smoothed his palms along her thighs. "Mercy," she said.

He chuckled softly and drew his fingertips enticingly along her knees, parting them ever so sweetly. "Did I ever tell you that I've got a thing for your knees?"

Emma couldn't answer to save her soul. She was too busy climbing to the stars.

Chapter Fourteen

"Stop fidgeting."

"I'm not." Emma let her hands fall to her sides to prove it. But not two seconds passed before she touched the locket at her throat to make sure she'd fastened the necklace correctly.

Kyle shut the car door and caught her hand in his. "You are."

She sighed and shifted on the sidewalk. "I don't want to mess this up for you," she admitted. They were two minutes away from entering the Cummingses' home. In Kyle's hand was the photo album, delivered by courier to his place that very morning.

Jake had done his job well. The photographs showed a beautiful wedding, a beautiful setting, laughing, smiling guests and a bride and groom who appeared to be totally in love.

In Emma's case that last was all too true.

"Are you sure Baxter doesn't mind keeping Chandler for us while we're gone?"

Kyle lifted a brow. "Emma."

She shrugged, knowing how ridiculous the question

had been. She couldn't help it. She was as nervous as a cat. "I'm not a good actress," she reminded him.

"Relax. You're not going to be put on a witness stand. Look at all the cars lining the street here. There's probably two dozen people in that house."

Emma nodded. "I know that. I just…well, sugar, you're tense, too." His hands were tight on the thick album and a muscle jumped in his jaw. She could handle her own nervousness. But knowing that Kyle wasn't entirely certain about the evening completely unnerved her. "We should have come up with some excuse to cancel."

"There's no time to cancel," he said. "The final contracts to acquire CCS are ready. Cummings just needs to sign on the dotted line."

Emma shouldn't have been surprised. It was the whole point of this make-believe marriage. But the dagger-sharp pang of dismay she felt at the news was all too real. Once the deal was done, her presence in Kyle's life would no longer be necessary. She swallowed past the lump in her throat. "You must be happy about that."

"Yes."

He didn't look happy. He looked…tense. There was simply no other word for it.

"Is there any chance that Mr. Cummings might back out?"

"There's always a chance. It's unlikely, though."

"And after the dotted line is signed, then what?"

"Then I'll have everything I want," he murmured.

Emma looked down at her hands. Of course. Kyle had never made any bones about the priorities in his life. And ChandlerAIR was the number-one priority. She took a breath and let it out, turning to face the Cummingses' pillared house. "Baxter told me he'd been married," she said as they started walking toward it. "Back when he was a mechanic."

"So you asked him about that."

"This morning." She stared blindly at the neatly groomed shrubbery lining the walk. "He says he put his career before his wife, and when she left him, he took it badly. Started drinking too much. Nearly caused a terrible plane accident because of it."

"He never drank again, never worked on a plane again and never forgave himself for losing his wife and the family he'd wanted to have with her," Kyle finished.

"So he made you his family, instead," Emma said. "He thinks you're making the same mistakes he did."

"It would be nice if Bax would keep his opinions to himself once in a while."

Their feet halted at the foot of the wide steps leading up to the wide door. She looked at him. "I think the situations are completely different."

"You do."

"Yes. Although I agree with him that you work much too hard."

"Better this young man working hard than me," a voice greeted from the top of the stairs.

Emma swallowed nervously and looked up at the open doorway. An older man stood there, tall and distinguished-looking. Kyle settled his hand at the small of her back and they went up the stairs.

"Payton," Kyle greeted blandly. "This is Emma."

The man's eyes crinkled with his smile. "You're as lovely as I expected," he said gallantly. "Helen and I are delighted you and Kyle can join us this evening."

Emma started to relax. The older man was simply too gracious not to respond to. "Thank you for having us," she said, glancing at Kyle as Payton ushered them into the spacious home. He was smiling, too, but it didn't come close to reaching his eyes.

Kyle realized Emma was looking at him in concern. He deliberately relaxed his shoulders and smiled. But he knew she wasn't fooled.

Fortunately, however, Helen Cummings joined them and the rounds of introductions began. The older woman eventually slipped her arm through Emma's as if they were old friends and happily spied the photo album Kyle held. The women wandered away, leaving Kyle with Payton and several of the older man's golfing buddies.

Kyle responded with half his attention while they discussed the merits of various golf courses. He noticed that Payton's stepdaughter was also there. Winter made a beeline for Emma and her mother, who was smiling as she pored over the pictures.

Kyle nearly went over to rescue Emma. But when Winter left the group after a few minutes, her expression sulky, he realized that his lovely Emma needed no rescuing. Not this time.

He pushed one hand into his pocket and watched

Emma. She wore a red dress that ended just above her exquisite knees. The square neckline and crisp linen followed her lovely figure closely, but was by no means tawdry. She looked impossibly beautiful and utterly confident.

"Makes a man proud to have such a lovely wife."

Kyle realized that everyone but Payton had scattered. "Yes."

"Helen told me she ran into you at the Buttonwood Baby Clinic. She's impressed with your devotion to your family. You know I like that in a man."

Inside his pocket Kyle's hand curled into a fist. "Yes."

The older man studied him for a long moment, his hazel eyes thoughtful. "We will meet tomorrow," he finally said. "Get this paperwork signed and done with. I've spent all my life making Cummings Courier Service what it is today." He looked over at Winter, who was pouring herself a drink at the marble bar in the corner of the elegant living room. "I wish I'd had sons to pass it on to, but since I haven't, I'm glad to be handing CCS over to you. To a person who'll respect my life's work."

Kyle's gut churned. But his smile was smooth as butter. He looked the older man right in the eye, inwardly cursing everything that Payton Cummings was. Including the company that would soon be his to do with as he saw fit.

"Darling, dinner is ready in the dining room," Helen said as she glided toward them, Emma in tow.

Kyle slid his arm around Emma's shoulders and

smiled blandly as they followed the older couple into the dining room, where all the guests were chatting and laughing and finding seats at the long elegant table.

He and Emma were placed at one end, right beside Payton, who was at the head. Now that the moment was here, Kyle wasn't sure he could actually stomach so much as a bite. But hidden by the white damask tablecloth, Emma's hand covered his, and Kyle managed to get through the interminable meal without revealing how much he hated the man who sat at the head of the table.

"Kyle. What's wrong?"

Kyle didn't look up from the grease he was wiping from his fingers. When they'd arrived home from their evening with Payton and Helen Cummings, he'd been grateful that Emma had been immediately busy with Chandler. He'd changed clothes and headed out to the garage and the *Lightning,* assuming that Emma would simply go to bed, seeing how late it was.

Instead, she stood in the doorway, looking at him with concern and determination in her eyes.

"Just keyed up," he said truthfully.

She eyed him skeptically. Then she padded down the concrete steps and crossed the barn of a garage, ducking under the wing of the partially restored plane.

"You should have on shoes," Kyle muttered, seeing her bare feet.

"It's perfectly clean," she countered. "I think a person could eat off the concrete in here. Does Baxter wash it down weekly? Oh, my goodness, you *do* own a pair of jeans."

Kyle smiled faintly. "Don't have a heart attack."

"Sugar, I just might. You look real fine in those blue jeans. I think you ought to go for this look more often. Greasy white T-shirt. Very old blue jeans. You could give the cover of *Colorado Business Weekly* a whole new look."

Kyle shook his head and tossed down the rag he'd been using. He nudged Emma back toward the door. "You should be sleeping."

"So should you." She wrapped her arms around her waist and her yellow nightgown drifted around her toes. "Tomorrow's the big day. Dotted-line day."

"Yes." She wasn't leaving, so Kyle took her hand and pulled her out the door and across the moonlit flagstone walk toward the house. The night was clear and warm and utterly silent.

"I guess I should start packing, then."

He stopped. "What?"

She pulled her hand from his and tucked her glossy hair behind her ear. "Once your business deal is done, you won't have need for a wife anymore."

"You're in a rush, then, to get back to your little apartment?"

Her lips parted. Compressed. "I…well…that was the agreement, wasn't it?"

He couldn't deny it. "I think you should stay for a while longer," he said. "Just in case."

Her eyebrows rose. "In case of what?"

"Who knows?" He pushed his hands into his pockets to keep from reaching for her. Their night together in Denver had been exquisite torture. But here, in his house, he knew he would not have the absolute concrete reason to keep their lovemaking from reaching its full conclusion. Not with the box of condoms Baxter had mockingly placed in his nightstand drawer. "There's no need for you to rush back to your apartment," he said. "You're comfortable here, aren't you? Consider it a vacation of sorts. Or an act of mercy. Because you know that Bax will be brokenhearted when you leave."

"Baxter," she murmured so softly he barely heard. Her shoulders moved in a great sigh, then she looked up at him. Her hair slid over her moon-gilded shoulders and her eyes glistened like dark pools. "I'll think about it."

He nodded. He wasn't comfortable at all with the knots in his stomach at the notion of her leaving. But knew that as soon as the deal was done, as soon as his long-sought goal was achieved, his knots would ease. He turned and walked into the kitchen, flipping on the overhead light and holding open the door for her to precede him.

"I liked Helen and Payton," she said as she passed him. "They're very genuine, I think. I feel badly about our pretense."

"You always did," he said. "From the get-go you didn't like the deception."

She leaned back against the butcher block in the center of the room, her hands curled around the thick edge on either side of her. "Yet you felt it was necessary." She eyed him. "Why is that, Kyle? I know all your explanations already. But it just doesn't fit somehow."

"You're imagining things." He prowled over to the refrigerator and pulled out a beer.

"Am I?" Her gaze followed him. "Do you know that you didn't smile once this evening?"

"Yes, I did."

She shook her head. "Not really. Your mouth moved certainly. But when you smile, Kyle, really smile, your eyes show it, too." She pushed away from the island and walked over to him. She lifted her hand and smoothed her fingertip along his temple. "It shows here," she murmured. "You were not happy to be there. I was nervous about making some silly blunder, but you…sugar, you were not happy." She lowered her hand, her fingertips resting on her collarbone, and he realized she wasn't quite as certain as her words would have him believe. "I can't help but wonder why."

"I've been waiting a long time for this opportunity."

"Which should make you happy, then. Your plans for CCS and ChandlerAIR are coming to fruition. Payton is delighted you'll be keeping his company intact, moving ahead with—"

"I'm not."

Her words halted.

"I'm going to take it apart piece by piece and enjoy every single moment of it," he said deliberately.

"You mean because the company will really be part of ChandlerAIR now?"

"No."

She frowned. "I don't think I understand."

"When I'm finished with CCS, there will be nothing left of it to even remember."

"Why?"

"It doesn't matter."

Emma couldn't prevent an impatient huff. "Of course it matters. It concerns you, Kyle. Everything about you matters to me." She closed her mouth on a snap, feeling her cheeks flame. "This isn't like you."

"It is exactly like me," he said roughly. "This is what I do, Emma. It's business."

"No," she said. "There's something more to it. You're a builder, Kyle. An achiever. Why would you acquire CCS just to tear it down? That's not what you said you wanted it for when we first met."

"I lied."

She swallowed, nearly falling back a step. "Despite the fact that I'm wearing this ring of yours—" she raised her left hand until the diamonds on the wedding band glittered in the bright overhead light "—I don't believe you make a habit of deception any more than I do."

"You'd be wrong, then," he said, his voice flat. "Don't credit me with any finer motives, Emma. They don't exist. I will obliterate CCS, because it will be mine to do with as I choose."

She shook her head. "This is wrong, Kyle. You know it inside. That's why you're so… Oh, *tormented* is the word that fits, I think. The man I've come to know is not a man who can blithely obliterate another man's life's work!"

Kyle slammed his unopened beer bottle down on the butcher-block island. "He's not just another man," Kyle said, gritting his teeth. "Payton Cummings is my father."

Emma's mouth parted. She backed blindly toward the kitchen table and pulled out a chair, sinking weakly onto it. "Your father?" she whispered. "Your...birth father?"

"The man who claimed at dinner tonight that he had no sons to whom he could rightfully pass on his company." Kyle's expression was tight. "Ironic, isn't it?"

She pressed her fingers to her mouth. "He really doesn't suspect? Doesn't know you?"

"Kyle Montgomery, CEO of ChandlerAIR, is a far cry from the seven-year-old son who begged his father not to leave."

"There must be some mistake. He was so...nice."

"He's a bastard who left me and my brothers and sisters in the care of a woman who couldn't find her way out of a pill bottle. A man who didn't contribute one bloody dollar to our support, and, my sweet Emma, I assure you he had plenty of it to go around. When Sally died and the state tried to find him, the social worker learned that he'd legally relinquished his parental rights to us. He didn't want us. And now he's got the almighty gall to pick and choose who he does business with on the basis of their fine upstanding family values!"

Emma's eyes burned. "PJ. Payton what? Junior?"

"Payton Kyle Cummings, Jr.," he said. "CCS *will* be mine. And I *will* do with it what I choose."

"You're going to tell him after the fact, aren't you?"

His jaw clenched.

"You think that will finally put the past to rest."

"I know it will. Don't bother giving me reasons to the contrary."

"I wasn't going to." She dashed her fingers across her cheek and rose. She walked up to him and placed her hands around his corded neck. "You have to do what you feel you must." She rose onto her toes and pressed her lips gently to his.

His hands came around her waist. "What's that for?"

She swallowed. Thought about the feelings she'd had for Jeremy St. James. He'd said he'd loved her. Had taken her virginity and her heart and given back nothing.

Yet she didn't even hate him for it. Not anymore.

She had Chandler because of Jeremy. She'd met Kyle because of Jeremy.

And the feelings that filled her entire soul for Kyle made everything pale in comparison.

"Because I love you," she said softly, then smiled faintly when he just stared at her, his green eyes searching. "And I know you don't love me, so stop thinking of a way to let me down gently."

"I have nothing to offer you, Emma. I could provide every material comfort, but you'd still be with a man who only knows how to work. Baxter's belief would be all too true. And I don't want to hurt you that way."

Aching sadness welled in her chest. "I told you not to let me down gently."

He sighed and tugged her against him. "I don't know what else to do."

She pressed her forehead against his shoulder. Felt his heart beating beneath her cheek. She closed her eyes tightly, willing the tears away for now. He didn't need them. She didn't want them. "Take me to bed, Kyle."

He pulled back an inch. Lifted her chin with his thumb until their eyes met. "Emma."

"I don't want your reasons why we shouldn't any more than you want my reasons why you shouldn't continue with your plan for your father's company. I just want to make love with you, Kyle." Her heart raced as she pressed his palm against her breast. "Don't you want that, too?"

He lowered his forehead to hers. "You know I do."

"Then take me to bed," she whispered.

Kyle hesitated and her heart quailed. But he swept her up into his arms and carried her out of the kitchen, stopping long enough only to snap off the overhead light.

He carried her up that wide sweeping staircase, and she didn't care at all that the carpet was arctic white. She only cared that she was in his arms. And for this night, at least, he was hers.

Behind the closed door of his bedroom, Kyle set Emma on her feet beside his bed. He tossed back the blankets and Emma moved around behind him, wrapping her arms around his waist, pressing her cheek against his strong back.

She tugged up the bottom of his T-shirt and flattened her palms against his abdomen. Then she found the button at his waist and popped it loose. "I mentioned that I liked you in jeans, didn't I?"

Kyle stood, still as stone as her fingers found the next button on his strained fly. "Yes."

"Mmm." She drew in a breath and he felt every luscious curve against his back. "Well, sugar, I like you even more out of them." Her voice was pure sweetness. Pure invitation. She tugged and two more buttons popped free. Then her fingers were tormenting him even more.

He turned and dragged her nightgown up her hips and off. It was still fluttering to the floor when the rest of his clothes joined them and he dragged her down onto his bed.

Her legs were satin smooth. Her breasts creamy and thrusting against his lips. And her hands were busy driving him to the edge of sanity. He swore under his breath and caught her wrists in his, pressing them above her head where they couldn't do more damage before he was prepared. And then he looked at her. Really looked at her.

Her lips, glistening pink. Her beautiful body. Her hands that rested above her head, palms up. Totally vulnerable. Totally his. But it was her eyes that ensnared him. Dark. Shimmering with emotion.

His heart ached, because the emotion in her eyes felt

like a weeping kiss goodbye. "I don't want to hurt you." He meant more than the physical.

She didn't waver. "You won't," she promised. She drew up her knee, brushing it along his hip.

His control snapped and he reached for the nightstand drawer.

When he made her his, Kyle knew that no woman would ever come close to moving him as deeply as Emma.

And when he awoke in the morning, hours later than his usual five o'clock, he knew without having to get up and look that she was gone.

Her wedding ring sat on the nightstand beside the bed.

Chapter Fifteen

"I hear this is the best place for a guy to get a cup of coffee."

Emma turned, her heart stuttering. But rather than Kyle standing on the other side of the counter, it was Jake. She tucked her order pad in the pocket of her Mom & Pop's apron and reached for the coffee carafe, pouring a cup, which she slid in front of him. "Why are you here, Jake?"

It had been two weeks since Emma took Chandler and left Kyle's home. Even the rampant speculation about her and Kyle had begun to die.

During that time, she hadn't heard anything from him directly. Despite her desire to leave his home with nothing more than what she'd taken to it, she'd found her apartment filled to the gills with the nursery furniture that had been delivered that first week at Kyle's.

If that wasn't enough, the baby grand piano that had arrived shortly afterward meant she couldn't even unfold her sofa bed at night.

She knew she had to send it all back. She'd gone into her arrangement with Kyle to cover her debt to the hospital. To provide some measure of security for her son. Now that the arrangement was over, she wanted none of those things. She only wanted Kyle's heart.

It was the one thing she wasn't sure he realized he even possessed. He'd convinced himself that all he cared about was ChandlerAIR. And avenging the past by tearing apart the company founded by his birth father.

She looked across the counter at Kyle's brother, waiting for an answer. He tucked his sunglasses into the neck of his black T-shirt and slid a manila envelope on the counter toward her. "That's for you."

"What is it?"

"Look and see."

There was no hint in his eyes. Only a similarity in shape and color to Kyle's that made her hurt inside. She picked up the envelope and opened it. Two eight-by-ten photos slid out. Emma holding Chandler that day in the gardens at the Crest. And Kyle, impossibly handsome in his severe black tuxedo. A breeze had caught his hair, and he was focusing on something out of the camera's range.

She swallowed and slid the photos back into the envelope. "Thank you. Have you, um, seen Kyle?"

"Nope."

It was midmorning and the diner wasn't busy. Emma leaned against the counter. "You plan to, though."

He pursed his lips. "Can't say I do."

She touched the envelope. "You could've mailed these. You're in Buttonwood because you want to see your brother."

"What's he doing these days?"

She folded her arms. "I wouldn't know. I haven't seen him in nearly two weeks."

"You love him."

She didn't flinch. "Yes."

"So why aren't you together?"

"Ask him."

He shook his head. "My brother has moved on with his life quite well. He doesn't need people from the past dragging him down."

"For intelligent men, you two behave incredibly stupidly. I'd like to thump you both upside the head."

Jake set down his coffee cup, his eyebrows raising.

"Why do you think Kyle tracked down you and Trace and Annie?"

"He told you about us?"

"Yes, he did. He takes his family ties very seriously. Both the old ones and the new ones. Even if he doesn't want to acknowledge it." Emma touched his hand briefly. "He worries about all of you."

She glanced up automatically when the bell over the door tinkled. And felt the blood drain from her face at the sight of Jeremy St. James, standing there all tanned skin and golden hair and gleaming teeth.

She was vaguely aware of Jake turning around to see who'd entered. Heard Millie, dear Millie, swear under her breath and march across the diner, saying loudly and ridiculously that the diner was closed just now.

Everybody knew that Millie's place was open every day. Rain or shine.

Jeremy simply stepped around Millie and approached the counter. "Hello, Emma."

The shock was fading quickly. Emma pressed her palms to the counter. "What do you want, Jeremy?"

He glanced around. The few customers who were present were all watching avidly.

"Perhaps we could discuss this more privately?"

"We have nothing to discuss."

"The baby," he said stiffly.

She widened her eyes. "What baby? If you're referring to my son, I believe we both know where we stand on that issue." She was giddily grateful that she'd left Chandler with Penny that morning rather than bringing him into the diner with her.

"It's a boy." There was a strange satisfaction in Jeremy's voice that sent a wave of unease through Emma.

"Go away, Jeremy."

He looked at Jake, who was listening unabashedly. "This is a private matter," he said, his tone dismissive.

Emma wondered what on earth she'd ever seen in the man. "Then you shouldn't bring it up in the middle of a diner," Jake said easily. "Emma, love, you want me to get rid of the jerk?"

The jerk. Tears stung her eyes because it was the term Kyle had always used. "He's not worth it," she said thickly. "Excuse me."

She rushed past Millie and went into the kitchen. Scrubbed furiously at her cheeks.

Millie followed her. "That little…snot," she said furiously. "Coming in here, making you cry."

Emma laughed brokenly and hugged her friend. "I'm not crying because of him," she assured. "But if you don't mind, I think I'll take my lunch break now. Just until he gives up on whatever he wants and leaves."

Millie was nodding, walking with Emma to the rear entrance. "If he's not gone in an hour, I'll call Sheriff Wright and have him removed."

"The St. James family would love that," Emma murmured. "I'll be back before the lunch rush," she promised, and slipped out the back door.

Walking quickly, she crossed the street and headed toward the park. Rachel Arquette was sitting on one of the benches, her hands folded over the enormous swell of her pregnant tummy. "Getting closer?" Emma asked, smiling sympathetically.

Rachel nodded and pushed awkwardly to her feet. She tugged at her nurse's uniform, smoothing the maternity top over herself. "What's the lunch special at Mom & Pop's?"

"Chicken potpie or meat loaf."

"Sounds good."

"Which?"

"Both." Rachel laughed and headed back toward the clinic. "Make sure Millie saves plenty for me when I take my lunch break in a few hours."

Emma watched Rachel for a moment. She wondered if it was any easier for Rachel than it had been for her, being single and pregnant. But while everybody in town concluded that Jeremy had been the father of Emma's baby, conjecture had been ripe over who'd fathered Rachel's.

She took the bench vacated by Rachel and gazed at the pretty flowers lining the walking path. The sun was warm and she slowly relaxed, closing her eyes. The flowers were nowhere near as riotous as the ones in the garden at Kyle's home. But for a little while she pictured herself back in that colorful retreat.

How she missed Kyle! Missed the way he'd grab a bunch of grapes and absently pop a few into his mouth. Missed the way his eyes crinkled when he smiled and missed the way he held Chandler.

Why was it that Jeremy's unexpected presence made her feel that loss so much more acutely?

"Is this seat taken?"

Her eyes flew open and she pressed her hand to her heart. "Gracious."

Payton Cummings smiled down at her. "Didn't mean to scare the wits out of you, my dear."

Emma rose. "I'm surprised to see you," she admitted. "How are you?" For a man whose company had been bought and parceled into nothing, he seemed surprisingly content. Now that she knew who he was, she wondered why everyone on the planet couldn't see the resemblance between him and Kyle. Except for the eyes and Kyle's darker hair, the men were very similar.

"Fine. I brought Helen into town to visit with her friend who works at the clinic. I thought I recognized you walking over here." He nodded at her apron, which had the Mom & Pop's logo plastered across it. "Taking a break?"

Emma nodded. She wasn't sure what to say. Wondered what Payton knew and didn't know.

"How is your son?"

"Fine. Just fine. Growing very fast."

"Just wait," he said easily. "Soon he'll be wanting the keys to your car. I'd like to see Kyle's face that day. If you two have a girl, it'll be even worse on that boy."

Emma's smile stiffened. He didn't know. He couldn't. Because if he did, he wouldn't be standing here visiting with her as if there was nothing on earth he'd rather be doing. She looked over her shoulder and could see the front of the diner. It was entirely possible that Jake was still there.

Payton sat down on the bench and let out an appreciative sigh. "Helen was right about all work making Payton a dull boy. The best thing I've done in a long time was to sell CCS to Kyle. It was the only thing in my life for a long while until I met Helen and Winter. But a man needs more than his work."

Emma wondered if Kyle would be Payton's age before he realized that, too. She pushed her hands in the patch pockets of her apron. "Your wife said you were in New Mexico for a while."

He nodded. "I went there after my first marriage broke up." He frowned, staring into the flowers near his feet. "It was an unpleasant situation," he explained. Then his expression cleared and he smiled at her. "And one of the reasons I'm so particular about the people with whom I do business. Kyle is an admirable man. He already knows the things it took me a lifetime to learn. And he's a lucky man to have a lovely woman like you at his side."

Emma felt ill. "Mr. Cummings. Payton. I—"

The squeal of tires shattered the quiet morning. They both looked over to see a low-slung black car pulling up in front of the diner. Kyle climbed out.

"Good gravy," Emma said faintly, her eyes following Kyle as he rounded the car and disappeared into the diner. Jake, Jeremy, Payton and Kyle, all in one day. This was a recipe for disaster.

"Looks like your husband is in a hurry to see you." Payton rose and closed his hand around her elbow. "Shall we?"

Emma swallowed and nodded, since there really was no alternative. They walked out of the park and crossed the street, Emma's stomach tightening with every step. Kyle had no idea that Payton was here. She wished there was some way to prepare him.

But there wasn't. And in bare minutes Payton was following her through the front door of the diner.

Emma's eyes immediately focused on Kyle, who was standing at the counter beside Jake. He held the two photos from the envelope in his hand.

Emma fiddled with her apron, not knowing what to say. Jake, however, said it all.

"Well, well," he said in a goading voice. "Look who's here, PJ."

Beside her, Payton went still. Emma glanced at

him, then hurried across to Kyle. The muscle in his jaw twitched, and she put both her hands around his arm. Reveled in the presence of him. The strength. The scent. The sight.

"What are you doing here, Kyle?"

"Millie called me. She said the jerk was here bothering you."

Emma looked over at her boss, who merely shrugged. So much for calling Sheriff Wright. Emma wasn't surprised, though. Millie had made it perfectly obvious that she thought Kyle was Emma's very own Prince Charming and that it was just a matter of time before Emma was living in that house up on the ridge for real.

Emma wished she had Millie's faith. But there was more at work here than Emma's overflowing love for the man standing so tensely beside her. She didn't know what had happened about the CCS deal. All she knew was that Kyle felt like a coiled cobra beside her, and Payton was staring at the two brothers like he was seeing ghosts.

"PJ," he murmured. "And Jacob. My God." He fumbled with a chair, wrapping one hand around the back of it for support. "How can this be?"

Desperately torn, Emma looked up at Kyle. But his lips were tight and Jake looked no better. Payton looked ashen.

"Why didn't you tell me?" he asked. "Why, PJ?"

"My name is Kyle. Kyle Montgomery. There hasn't been a PJ Cummings since the day you walked out of our house and forgot we existed."

Payton shook his head, rubbing his shoulder with one hand. "No. No, son, it wasn't like that."

"I am not your son."

Payton frowned, his pain clear for all to see.

"I, on the other hand, am your son," Jake said bitterly. "But I still hate your guts for abandoning us the way you did."

Emma looked from one man to the next. She understood Kyle's and Jake's feelings. But couldn't they see that Payton was suffering, too? She pressed her cheek against Kyle's shoulder, murmuring his name. He was unmoving.

She couldn't stand it. Payton looked as if he was ready to collapse. She let go of Kyle's arm and started for the older man.

She didn't reach him in time. With a grimace and a long low moan, he collapsed.

Emma cried out, rushing to the man. She couldn't find a pulse and she gently rolled him onto his back. "Millie!"

Millie was already heading to the phone. "Across the street from dozens of doctors and nurses," she fretted, "and not one of them in here when we need 'em."

Emma leaned over Kyle's father, but he wasn't breathing. Heart racing, she started CPR. Then nearly jumped out of her skin when Kyle crouched beside her. Her eyes met his and he grimly took over pressing his folded fist over his father's heart while Emma counted beats, then put her mouth over Payton's, breathing air into his lungs.

She knew it hadn't been long at all before the bell over the door jangled and the room was filled with medical personnel. But it felt like an eternity.

She moved gratefully aside when a doctor took her place. She pressed her fingertips to her forehead and backed out of the way, tugging Kyle to move, as well.

"That's Colt Rollins," she told him when he finally moved. "He's a wonderful doctor." She remembered the man from his time at the clinic. He'd been the one to confirm her pregnancy. But shortly after, Emma had heard that he'd left for a position in New Mexico.

Emma pushed Kyle toward an empty booth. "Sit down," she said softly. "Payton will be all right. Dr. Rollins will see to it."

Even Jake looked shaken. He walked up beside them, closing his hand over Kyle's shoulder.

Kyle tugged his tie loose and pulled Emma against him. She went willingly. She rested her hand atop Jake's and the three of them watched while Colt and two other doctors worked over Payton.

"Oh, my Lord," Emma said. "Helen Cummings is visiting her friend at the clinic. We have to find her. Tell her."

Jake started toward the door. "I'll find her."

"Does he know who she is?" Emma asked Kyle.

"Yes."

Emma's eyes followed Jake as he walked out the door. Then Rachel and another nurse caught Emma's attention as they arrived with a rolling stretcher, Rachel huffing and puffing and pressing one hand to her side.

Emma glanced at Millie, who took one look at Rachel and shook her head, pointing to a chair. "You've got no business rushing around like this in your condition, missy. Now sit down."

Rachel, who did indeed look pale, sat. The doctors strapped Payton onto the stretcher and rolled it toward the door. Emma watched as Colt did a double take when he saw Rachel sitting there. He looked at Payton, who was already being borne to the emergency room just across the way.

Rachel pushed to her feet. "I didn't realize you were back," she said to Colt, who was staring at her pregnant belly as if he'd never seen one before. Then he grasped her wrist and pulled her outside.

With Payton, Rachel and Colt all gone from the diner, Emma crouched in front of Kyle, her attention on him. "Are you okay? We could go to the emergency room and wait with Helen and Jake."

"I've hated Payton Cummings nearly as long as I can remember."

Emma didn't know what to say.

"But I realize that I don't want him to die." He scrubbed his hand down his face, then folded her hands in his. His green eyes focused on her face. "Are you okay?"

She nodded. "I'm worried about Payton and Helen." She pressed her cheek to his hand. "And you."

"That's not what I meant."

She raised her brows.

"The jerk," he said abruptly. "Jeremy. Millie called

me to tell me he was here. He's not good enough for you, Emma. I thought for a while that, if you really loved him, I could stand it."

Emma shook her head and pushed to her feet, tugging at his hands until he stood, also. "He's gone," she said dismissively. "And the only man I love is you. Let's go across the street."

He didn't move. He was like an anchor, drawing Emma back toward him. "Why?"

"So we can see how Payton is, of course. The doctors here are wonderful, so I don't want you automatically assuming the worst."

"I thought you were the one who came out of the womb worrying." He pulled her into his arms, kissing her silent.

Emma could do nothing but respond. But her cheeks heated when she finally came back down off her tiptoes and realized that Millie was watching them, a wide smile on her face. She looked away, out the windows toward the clinic. Colt and Rachel were standing just outside. They appeared to be in fierce conversation.

Emma unwrapped her apron and left it behind the counter to Millie's easy assurance that she'd manage the lunch rush just fine. "There's so much adrenaline pumping through my system," she said, "it'll keep me going until three o'clock at least."

Emma retrieved her purse and the photos Jake had delivered. "Thanks, Millie."

Her boss shooed her and Kyle out the door.

Kyle tucked her hand in his and they crossed the street.

Jake had obviously found Helen Cummings, because the two were sitting side by side in the small emergency waiting room. Helen jumped up at their entrance, her face worried. "Kyle. Please. They haven't told me anything. Won't you see what you can find out?"

He sighed, gently nudging her back into a seat. "Looked like a heart attack."

Helen covered her mouth with a shaking hand. Emma sat down beside her and put her arm around her, comforting. "Kyle will see what he can learn," she assured her softly.

He nodded. Pulled loose his tie another inch and turned toward the desk where a nurse was talking on the phone. But he didn't have to wait long, because Dennis Reid strode into the waiting room. He stopped to speak to Kyle, then turned to Helen. "Payton is stable for now," he said, and they all sighed with relief. "He's conscious and demanding to see the whole lot of you. But I think you're enough for now, Helen. For the next day or two at least."

He waited for Helen to stand, then escorted her through the doors leading out of the waiting room.

"Guess it's safe to go now," Jake said.

Emma held her breath, looking from one brother to the other.

"There's room at the house," Kyle said, "if you want to hang around awhile."

Emma's shoulders relaxed.

But Jake shook his head. "Maybe next time." He smiled faintly. "I'll do some shots at Chandler's baptism," he offered.

Emma knew Jake was only being sweet. He could have no idea how his genuine offer pained her. But Kyle was nodding and shook his brother's hand briefly. "That'd be great," he said.

Jake leaned over and kissed her cheek. "Forgot to tell you," he said when he straightened. "I might bring a date next time." He smiled crookedly. "You'd both like her." He sketched a wave and strode through the sliding doors of the emergency room.

Leaving just Kyle and Emma.

Her eyes burned. "I should get back to the diner," she said after a moment. "Despite Millie's optimism, she *will* need help with the lunch rush." Realizing she'd brought the photos with her, she pulled out the photo of him and handed it to him. "Do you want it?"

"Not that one. I want the photo of my wife."

"Your pretend wife," she corrected. But she handed him the envelope that still contained the photo of her and Chandler. She was glad he didn't want the photo of himself, actually. She could frame it and keep it always. "Will you keep me posted on Payton's progress?"

Kyle nodded, his expression unreadable.

Emma picked up her purse, clutching it and the photo like a lifeline. "Well, everything is out in the open now," she said. "I hope you give Payton a chance to explain his side of things, Kyle. He admires you greatly, and he had no idea who you really were."

He didn't answer. Not that Emma had expected otherwise. "Give Baxter my best," she said brightly. "And, um, take care of yourself. Don't work too hard." Her voice wavered. She reached up and kissed his lean cheek, then hurried out of the emergency room.

Tears clogged her throat as she jogged across the street toward the diner. Millie took one look at her and told her to go home.

Emma gladly went, cradling Kyle's picture to her breast.

Chapter Sixteen

The moment Kyle got out of his car, he heard the music. He shut the car door softly and stared up the narrow flight of stairs to Emma's apartment.

She was playing the piano. And it was as soul-wrenching as it had been that night in Denver.

He climbed the stairs. Grimaced when he found the wooden screen door unlatched. But that didn't keep him from taking advantage of the unsecured door, and he quietly stepped inside. The apartment was stuffed with furniture from stem to stern.

The piano stood where her round dining table had once stood and was now nowhere in sight. Emma's back was to him as she sat at the piano and let her fingers drift hauntingly over the keys. Beside her on the floor Chandler kicked his legs, making his canvas seat bounce.

Kyle crossed the room, leaving the thick binder he'd brought with him on the couch before stepping around the crib and changing table. He crouched down beside the baby and tickled his chin. And grinned when Chandler's mouth parted happily. The baby jerked his feet even more enthusiastically.

Emma closed the piano, not surprised to see Kyle. She'd been aware of him the moment he'd entered the apartment. He'd obviously gone home since she'd seen him earlier, because he'd changed into those ridiculously sexy jeans and a soft blue-and-red polo shirt. "I called to check on Payton," she said. "He answered the phone in his room himself. I was surprised. But he sounded good."

"Colt Rollins ran tests. All in all they consider it a mild attack. No permanent damage to his heart."

"I'm glad." Her apartment was too close for words. First with the furniture, then, more disturbingly, with him. In the diner and even at the emergency room, things had moved so quickly, so frantically, there'd been no time for awkwardness.

But now, oh, now there was plenty of time. She stood and brushed her palms down the sides of her denim shorts as she scooted the piano bench in with her knee. "Would you like something to drink? Iced tea or...?"

He straightened. "No." He picked up the photo that Emma had placed on the top of the piano. "Jake sees a lot through that camera of his," he murmured. "He always did." He set the photo back on the piano. "I know the exact moment he took that photo. I was looking at you and Chandler. Jake must have looked, too. Because the second one he took showed exactly what I was seeing."

Emma started to sit on the arm of her couch, but stopped when his intense eyes focused on her.

"It's as if he could see inside my head with that one photo," he said. "There you were. Beautiful in white. The loving mother. Everything I ever dreamed a woman could be, but didn't really believe existed."

Emma swallowed. "Kyle—"

"Let me finish."

She sat on the arm of the couch because her knees were simply too shaky to hold her up. "Finish away, sugar."

He smiled faintly. "Not only did she exist, but she wore my ring. At least for appearances' sake. And at times she seemed to know me better than I knew myself. I am a builder, Emma. Just like you said. Not with wood or metal, maybe." He scooted out the footlocker and sat on it, his hands resting on his thighs.

It reminded her of the first day she'd met him when he came to her hospital room. Except this time he wore faded jeans and scuffed athletic shoes instead of a dress shirt and perfectly tailored trousers. But he still smelled like a fantasy come true. Except Emma knew that Kyle Montgomery was no fantasy.

He was a flesh-and-blood man, who'd overcome pain and loss and disillusionment to make a success of himself.

"I decided not to dismantle CCS," he said quietly.

Relief swept through her. "I'm glad. For you and for Payton."

"Jake and Trace and Annie, too," he added. "I'm making sure they've got equal interests in CCS. Everybody benefits." He was silent for a moment. Reached across the space between them and captured her hands in his. "He says he didn't know."

Emma didn't need to ask who *he* was.

"Not about Sally's death. Not about the booze or the drugs. He left because she blamed him for Janice's accident. Says he thought she would finally move on if he wasn't around constantly reminding her of the drowning."

"Do you believe him?"

"I don't know. I've spent a lot of years believing otherwise." He sighed. "But it was a belief I formed from what I knew as a kid. What Sally told us. God knows she wasn't the most reliable of sources. Payton says he kept paying child support into Sally's account, but that one day when I'd have been around eighteen his payments came back because the account had been closed. When he looked into it, he came up against a brick wall. We'd been gone for several years. PJ Cummings didn't exist. Jake and Trace and Annie were in other states.

"When I learned that Payton was back in Colorado, I knew I wanted his company, one way or the other. Chandler and Lydia would have known right off what I was up to, which is why I sent them on a cruise until it was over."

"You wouldn't have wanted to disappoint them," Emma surmised.

"Once you meet them—" Kyle grinned "—you'll know what I mean. Chandler wouldn't have been disappointed. He'd just have gone to Payton himself and demanded to know what the hell he'd been doing when his oldest son was stealing car radios to pay for food for his little brothers and sister. He's an up-front kind of guy."

Emma was happy to hear it all. She truly was. But sitting there listening to Kyle talk as if she'd actually meet the rest of his family was too painful. She got to her feet. "I'm thirsty," she said. "Are you sure you wouldn't like something?"

He rose, too. "Emma, sweetness, I'm not here for iced tea."

She closed her eyes for a moment. "Then what are you here for, Kyle?"

Emma frowned with dismay when she heard footsteps pounding up the outside stairs. She pushed a hand through her hair and turned toward the door. It was probably Penny or Millie.

It was Jeremy St. James.

Emma stared at him through the screen door. She felt only irritation at his unwelcome interruption yet again. "Go away."

He pulled open the unlatched door and stepped inside. "Emma... Good grief," he stopped short at the sight of all the furniture packed into her small space. Then the corner of his lip curled distastefully when he saw Kyle. "I guess I can see what you did with the money," he said, turning his attention back to Emma. "Your tastes are more expensive than I'd have thought, darling. Here I gave you dozens of roses and it seems that furniture would have been more to your liking. Oh, that's the baby over there, I suppose."

Emma stepped into his path when he started to cross the room. "You have no right to be here, Jeremy. Or is your memory so short you can't remember that?"

"Things are different now," Jeremy said confidently. "I'm married."

"Congratulations. I'm sure you both deserve each other," Emma said. She would be forever grateful that she hadn't become Jeremy's wife. She'd rather have the brief time she'd had with Kyle than a lifetime with the weak Jeremy St. James.

"We've decided," Jeremy said, "that we'd like to raise the baby ourselves."

Emma sensed Kyle coming up behind her. She was grateful for the hand he closed over her shoulder. If only because it kept her from going for Jeremy's throat. "If you come within five feet of my son, I'll—"

"My son, too."

Emma shook her head. "Go home to your wife, Jeremy. I'm not interested in anything you have to say."

"Emma, I'm not going anywhere yet."

"She said get out." Kyle's voice was deadly soft.

Jeremy didn't have the good sense God gave a goose. He looked at Kyle and his lip curled. "She's good in bed, of course. Wild, actually. But you'll find she's expensive in the end. It took my parents fifty thousand to pay her off."

Emma caught Kyle's arm before his fist found Jeremy's sneering face. Jeremy smiled, satisfied. Probably thinking she was trying to protect him or some such ridiculous notion.

"And what does the silly girl do? Goes out and buys a bunch of furniture." Jeremy started to step around them toward Chandler. Kyle blocked his path.

Emma darted down the short hallway and threw open the closet door. She dug around in the box on the shelf for a moment and came back out just in time to see Kyle looming over Jeremy. She slipped between them, slapping a legal document against Jeremy's chin. "Read it," she snapped, nudging Kyle back a few inches with a warning look. "I can handle this," she murmured, then turned back to face Jeremy. "Refresh your memory, you smarmy twit. That's your signature at the end of those twelve pages. You very clearly stated you were not responsible for the child carried by one Emma Valentine."

"You took money in exchange for this document."

"That's a lie!"

"My parents said you cashed the check."

"Did they?" She shook her head, leaning back against Kyle for support. "I believe it would be more accurate to say that your parents made very generous donations to the Dooley Community Church in Dooley, Tennessee, and the Buttonwood Chapel and the Buttonwood Baby Clinic right here in scenic Buttonwood, Colorado."

Jeremy's eyes narrowed. "You wouldn't have." He waved at the baby grand. "Where did all this come from, then? Darling, you've barely got a pot to your name."

Kyle had had enough. Sure, Emma was more than capable of standing up to the jerk on her own. But she wasn't on her own; they were together. And if the jerk hadn't interrupted them, she'd realize that by now. He gently scooted Emma to the side, deftly slipped the legal document out of Jeremy's slack grasp and handed it to her. "Keep hold of that, sweetness. It might come in handy when I officially adopt Chandler."

Her eyes widened.

He smiled into her lovely eyes. Then turned to face

the jerk. Now he didn't smile at all. "Emma asked you to leave."

Jeremy opened his mouth.

Then Kyle smiled. And wrapped his fingers around the younger man's throat, squeezing just enough to make the younger man's eyes bulge in fear. He walked toward the door, making Jeremy shuffle backward. When they reached the landing of the stairs, Kyle looked deliberately down them. "It's a long way to the ground, isn't it?" he said, and felt Jeremy's nervous swallow against his palm.

He lowered his hand. "Don't come back," he suggested softly. "Or I'll tie you and your family up in court for so long that whatever means you've got will end up in the hands of very happy, very wealthy attorneys."

"Now look here. I don't know who the hell you think you are—"

"I'm Kyle Montgomery," he said softly. Waited a moment until Jeremy recognized the name. "I made it my business to know all about you and the St. James clan weeks ago. And you *will* regret it if you cause my family one more moment of pain."

"Your family?"

"That's right." He glanced back at Emma, who was sitting on the couch, cradling Chandler protectively in her arms. "My family."

"I'm not afraid of you, Montgomery."

Kyle shrugged, unimpressed. "That's your right, of course. But it's not me you should fear. It's Emma. Because she'll claw out your eyes if you come close to our son. And I'll take great pleasure in standing aside to watch. Then I'll feed you to her friends in Buttonwood. The ones who know how you treated her once you'd had your fun. Emma brings out great loyalty in people, you know. She's that kind of woman—with integrity. Then we'll make a trip to the bar association. They don't take kindly to law students who cheat on their bar exams."

Jeremy paled. "You wouldn't. I didn't cheat—"

"Who are they going to believe, Jeremy? You do have that incident on your record from your sophomore year in college. You know the one?"

Jeremy swore. "Fine. Forget it. She can keep the little brat. She always was more trouble than she was worth. Wouldn't even sleep with me until I told her I'd marry her. And then—"

Kyle shut both doors in Jeremy's face, cutting off his bitter tirade, and turned to Emma. "Now. Where were we?"

Emma rose, with Chandler still in her arms. "I'm sorry," she murmured. "I never dreamed that Jeremy would reappear and be so…unpleasant."

"That's not your fault, sweetness. I believe we were somewhere around here." He nudged her back onto the couch and sat down on the footlocker across from her. "As I was saying—"

"It was good of you to try to protect us," she interrupted. "But truly, I could have handled him."

"You did fine," he agreed. "And I know you don't need me, but I'm hoping—"

"I didn't keep the money, either," she added. "I truly

did send it off to Dooley and to the chapel, and baby clinic here."

"I don't doubt that for a second."

"And I plan to send back all this furniture, Kyle. It's just not right that I've got it all. And the piano. Oh, I love the piano, just as you knew I would. But it's much too generous. And I really don't have the space—"

Kyle sighed and cupped his hand behind her neck, covering her mouth with his. She moaned softly, her words finally ceasing. He kept right on kissing her. It was an activity he'd become addicted to.

But Chandler squawked between them and Kyle sat back on the footlocker. "Be quiet," he said to both mother and son.

Emma's mouth opened. Then slowly closed. Chandler kicked his legs happily, little gurgles and grunts coming out of his tiny bow mouth.

"I meant what I said to the jerk," Kyle said. "You are my family. You and Chandler. I didn't say I wanted to adopt him to scare off Jeremy. I said it because I want it to be so. For me. For you. For Chandler."

Emma's heart squeezed. Then Kyle took Chandler out of her arms and settled him in his crib on the other side of the cramped room. "There's just gonna be times I want your mama to myself," he said conversationally. "Now and then." He returned to the footlocker in front of the sofa and handed Emma the fat binder he'd brought in with him.

She frowned, looking down at it. He opened it for

her. Inside were small carpet samples and a rainbow of paint colors. "What is this?"

"You hate all that white in my house," he murmured. "As it happens, so do I. Add color to my house, Emma Valentine. Add color to my life."

A tear worked its way from her eye and dropped onto the book of samples.

"Remind me to look at the view," he continued, his voice dropping a notch. "To smell the flowers. Give me a reason to come home from the office an hour early. Or go in an hour late, because I'm too busy making love to my wife to beat every single employee into the parking lot. And play your beautiful music, sweetness. Because with you by my side, I can really feel it."

Emma looked into his eyes, feeling faint as that intense green gaze absorbed her.

"I'm looking for a wife, Emma Valentine," he said softly. "A real one this time."

Emma laughed softly and swiped the tears from her cheek. Kyle smiled, too. And stuck his hand in his pocket. His long fingers shook a little when he held out the diamond solitaire ring. It was as different from the glittering diamond-crusted band he'd presented that day at the Crest as a ring could be. No less beautiful. But much more suited to Emma's elegantly simple style.

He took her trembling hand and slipped it on her finger. "Let me be Chandler's father. Let me give him a houseful of brothers and sisters if that's what you want. I love you, Emma. Give me your heart. God knows you've both already got mine."

She curled her hand around his and pressed it to her, then slipped into his arms with a soft cry. "It is yours, Kyle. I love you."

He rose, pulling her with him. "Then you'll marry me?"

She nodded, blindly seeking his mouth with hers. "Yes. Anytime you say. The sooner the better."

He laughed, low and exultant and so masculine that she melted inside even more.

"We could elope," he suggested, his eyes full of love and desire. He lifted her right off her feet, and Emma wrapped her arms around his strong shoulders.

She chuckled, delighted and weak-kneed and plumb crazy about him. "Well," she said, her voice honey smooth despite the giddy bubbles dancing in her chest, "we do have the wedding photos already taken care of."

Their eyes met. "So we could head right on into the honeymoon," he finished.

Emma smiled slowly. "Oh, sugar. The way you think."

"Oh, Emma, honey," he drawled right back at her. "The way you love me."

Her lips curved. "Did I ever tell you how much I love the way you smell?" she whispered against his ear.

Kyle smiled, then shuffled them toward the couch and pulled her down over him, filling his hands with her dark glossy hair. Filling his heart with the love shining from her eyes. "I won't ever stop loving you," he said.

She went still. Then she laid her palm against his jaw

and kissed him, impossibly sweet. Impossibly desirable. "Neither will I, Kyle, my love. Neither will I."

Their lips met.

In his crib across the room, Chandler gurgled softly. When nobody rose to dote on him, he kicked his feet a few times. Then stuck his fist in his mouth and sighed with satisfaction.

* * * * *

REQUEST YOUR FREE BOOKS!

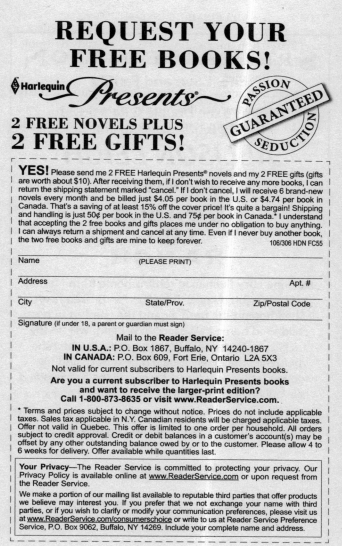

Harlequin *Presents*

2 FREE NOVELS PLUS
2 FREE GIFTS!

PASSION GUARANTEED SEDUCTION

YES! Please send me 2 FREE Harlequin Presents® novels and my 2 FREE gifts (gifts are worth about $10). After receiving them, if I don't wish to receive any more books, I can return the shipping statement marked "cancel." If I don't cancel, I will receive 6 brand-new novels every month and be billed just $4.05 per book in the U.S. or $4.74 per book in Canada. That's a saving of at least 15% off the cover price! It's quite a bargain! Shipping and handling is just 50¢ per book in the U.S. and 75¢ per book in Canada.* I understand that accepting the 2 free books and gifts places me under no obligation to buy anything. I can always return a shipment and cancel at any time. Even if I never buy another book, the two free books and gifts are mine to keep forever.

106/306 HDN FC55

Name	(PLEASE PRINT)	

Address		Apt. #

City	State/Prov.	Zip/Postal Code

Signature (if under 18, a parent or guardian must sign)

Mail to the **Reader Service:**
IN U.S.A.: P.O. Box 1867, Buffalo, NY 14240-1867
IN CANADA: P.O. Box 609, Fort Erie, Ontario L2A 5X3

Not valid for current subscribers to Harlequin Presents books.

**Are you a current subscriber to Harlequin Presents books
and want to receive the larger-print edition?
Call 1-800-873-8635 or visit www.ReaderService.com.**

* Terms and prices subject to change without notice. Prices do not include applicable taxes. Sales tax applicable in N.Y. Canadian residents will be charged applicable taxes. Offer not valid in Quebec. This offer is limited to one order per household. All orders subject to credit approval. Credit or debit balances in a customer's account(s) may be offset by any other outstanding balance owed by or to the customer. Please allow 4 to 6 weeks for delivery. Offer available while quantities last.

Your Privacy—The Reader Service is committed to protecting your privacy. Our Privacy Policy is available online at www.ReaderService.com or upon request from the Reader Service.

We make a portion of our mailing list available to reputable third parties that offer products we believe may interest you. If you prefer that we not exchange your name with third parties, or if you wish to clarify or modify your communication preferences, please visit us at www.ReaderService.com/consumerschoice or write to us at Reader Service Preference Service, P.O. Box 9062, Buffalo, NY 14269. Include your complete name and address.

SPECIAL EDITION

Life, Love and Family

Return to the Double C Ranch with
USA TODAY bestselling author

ALLISON LEIGH

RETURN TO THE

DOUBLE
·C·
RANCH

Ballerina Lucy Buchanan returns home from NYC to
heal her injured knee, as well as her broken heart.
She's hoping the fresh air and the comfort of her
childhood home in Weaver, Wyoming, will do the
trick. Lucy finds more than she expects when she
befriends the lonely little girl next door and her
widower father. *Will the widower and the ballerina find
their footing in an intimate dance of healing and love?*

**Find out in THE RANCHER'S DANCE,
available in April 2011 wherever books are sold.

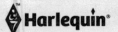

♦ Harlequin®

A *Romance* FOR EVERY MOOD™

www.eHarlequin.com

SE0411AL

See below for a sneak peek from
THE RANCHER'S DANCE,
Allison Leigh's latest Silhouette Special Edition® book,
available April 2011!

He didn't expect her to be so small.

Beckett Ventura watched the woman from the corner of his eye as he finished fastening on his tool belt. And despite her diminutive stature, she *was* a woman, curves and all.

But he hadn't come to the Lazy-B damn near the crack of dawn to be noticing anything at all about his neighbor's daughter, Lucy Buchanan.

For one thing, she wasn't even supposed to be there.

She was some fancy dancer who lived in New York and had for years.

Or so he'd heard.

He lifted the tool chest out of the truck bed and turned toward the side of the house.

Cage Buchanan, his neighbor who owned the ranch, had called him just last night, ostensibly to check on the building project—a long-planned addition to the Buchanan's two-story brick house. Beck suspected, though, that his neighbor had also wanted to let him know that his dancer-daughter was unexpectedly home for the summer.

Maybe Cage figured she needed looking after, though he hadn't said it outright. But he had mentioned that she was getting over some sort of mild knee injury.

The last thing that Beck wanted was someone to look after.

He had his hands full enough looking after his six-year-old daughter, who was so shy that she rarely managed anything above a whisper, even with her own father.

He set his jaw and angled away from his pickup. His boots crunched across the gravel, then hit the lush grass as he walked toward *her*.

The fact that she was blond was evident all along.

The fact that her eyes were as pale as the palest aquamarine, surrounded by the thickest, blackest lashes only became apparent as he neared her and finally came to a stop several feet away.

She had a faint smile on her face, which was too narrow to be considered perfect. Her hair was pinned messily up at the back of her head, some of it falling around her neck.

There was no reason for him to think she was stunning.

But she was.

Will the widower and the ballerina find their footing in an intimate dance of healing and love?

Find out in THE RANCHER'S DANCE,
available in April 2011
only from Silhouette Special Edition.

Start your Best Body today with these top 3 nutrition tips!

1. SHOP THE PERIMETER OF THE GROCERY STORE: The good stuff—fruits, veggies, lean proteins and dairy—always line the outer edges of the store. When you veer into the center aisles, you enter the temptation zone, where the unhealthy foods live.

2. WATCH PORTION SIZES: Most portion sizes in restaurants are nearly twice the size of a true serving and at home, it's easy to "clean your plate." Use these easy serving guidelines:
- Protein: the palm of your hand
- Grains or Fruit: a cup of your hand
- Veggies: the palm of two open hands

3. USE THE RAINBOW RULE FOR PRODUCE: Your produce drawers should be filled with every color of fruits and vegetables. The greater the variety, the more vitamins and other nutrients you add to your diet.

Find these and many more helpful tips in

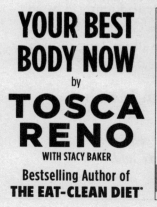

YOUR BEST BODY NOW
by
TOSCA RENO
WITH STACY BAKER

Bestselling Author of
THE EAT-CLEAN DIET®

Available wherever books are sold!

NTRSERIESFEB

Top author
Janice Kay Johnson
brings readers a riveting new romance
with
Bone Deep

Kathryn Riley is the prime suspect in
the case of her husband's disappearance
four years ago—that is, until someone tries
to make her disappear…forever. Now
handsome police chief Grant Haller must
stop suspecting Kathryn and instead begin
to protect her. But can Grant put aside the
growing feelings for Kathryn long enough
to catch the real criminal?

Find out in March.

Available wherever
books are sold.

HARLEQUIN *Presents*

USA TODAY *Bestselling Author*

Lynne Graham

is back with her most exciting trilogy yet!

SECRETLY PREGNANT CONVENIENTLY WED

Jemima, Flora and Jess aren't looking for love,
but all have babies very much in mind...and they may
just get their wish and more with the wealthiest, most
handsome and impossibly arrogant men in Europe!

Coming March 2011

JEMIMA'S SECRET

Alejandro Navarro Vasquez has long desired vengeance after
his wife, Jemima, betrayed him. When he discovers the
whereabouts of his runaway wife—and that she has a two-
year-old son—Alejandro is determined to settle the score....

FLORA'S DEFIANCE (April 2011)
JESS'S PROMISE (May 2011)

Available exclusively from Harlequin Presents.

www.eHarlequin.com

HP12975